STARSHIP ARCADIA

BRANDON ELLIS
MAX WOLFE

aethonbooks.com

STARSHIP ARCADIA
©2024 BRANDON ELLIS & MAX WOLFE

ALSO IN SERIES

CHAPTER ONE

"War is cruelty. There's no use trying to reform it. The crueler it is, the sooner it will be over."
—General William Tecumseh Sherman

Planet Kahwin
North Pole
Captain Scott Moore

Nothing lived in the north. It was too cold to think, too cold to do much of anything other than put one foot in front of the other. The ice formed an impenetrable barrier to plant life, a permanent kill field with the damn wind. Endless mountains stretched far off to the east, their rocky crags occasionally visible in the snow. Through sparse clouds, the sky burst with blinding light that always sat above us during this time of year. Behind us, a trail through the snow snaked along the ground, a thick layer of ice.

We were up by the North Pole, and not the one with Santa. This one stood at the far end of the world, and after travelling this far, my wits were at an end. Something turned much of the ice a deep blue, and at times, it felt as though we were walking on still water.

My heel found the next hold as I continued my ascent up the steep incline, which did a number on my legs. Every few seconds, my goggles' autowarmers kicked on and defrosted the lenses. Loose snow whipped by as the deadly wind notched up faster. With wind like this, any exposure to the elements would result in amputation or death.

I'd find this ship if it was the last thing I did. It was here, buried in these icy mountains. At least, that was what our last intel told us. All clues pointed to this place, this hell.

"You know what sounds good right now?" Vincent asked.

Chief coughed as he maneuvered past a spot of jagged ice that blocked his route. "What's that?"

"A McDonald's hot fudge sundae."

"Hell, I could go for a Big Mac right about now," I said.

Erika followed in Chief's footprints, making it easier for her to move. "Sir, if I could still eat, I'd eat one with you."

"I will be elated if we find your ship, Captain," Zoe said. "Why did you name it *Arcadia*? What does it mean?"

"It's a place back home."

Zoe asked, "Why do you name your ships after places?"

"Not all ships are named after places," Chief said. "Some ships are named after important people."

"How can you talk when it's this cold?" asked a sergeant.

Chief helped the sergeant climb over a snow hill. "Keeps your mind active. Otherwise, you'll bitch about the freeze in your head."

"How's the solar charger holding up?" I asked.

"Good, sir. We should be able to transmit within fourteen hours."

During our journey, we'd lost most of our gear and vehicles to the poor maintenance and the elements. We'd lost one of the

APCs in a fire when the engine exploded. Ten of our tablets succumbed to humidity. Although we'd brought hundreds of solar cells, many of them started to break down during the first two years, and by the third year, we were down to a handful. Needless to say, remaining in contact with Starport City was my priority, but finding a place to transmit this far away proved extremely difficult. If only we had satellites. We stored the comm equipment toward the rear of the formation, away from the rest of our supplies.

In front of me, the last surviving Janissary from this expedition pushed forward with dozens of cables attached around his waist. The robot pulled along our sleds over the battered terrain, carrying what few supplies we had remaining, and the corpses lost to the desolate chill and the creatures we'd encountered on the way here. Its power supply rose from its back with four exhaust tubes. On its shoulder, it sported a dark matter accelerator cannon. Its main weapon was a wrist-mounted plasma gun that was powerful enough to obliterate a Shaper in one hit. Problem was, it only worked half the time. Chief and Vincent had tried to repair it, but they were at a loss without the right parts or facility. One thing was for sure—without the Janissary, we would have been dead.

But as the saying goes, don't store all your eggs in one basket. A quarter of our supplies remained on sleds, which we ourselves were forced to pull. My brother, Vincent, insisted we take Melody, a cluster of servers stored in stasis pods, to protect them from the elements. Why did he want to bring Melody when it was still corrupted? Well, if he were to explain it, he would have said he hoped to find Antediluvian technology to help repair it, but the real reason was because he didn't want to leave it back in Starport City with the Senate and Equinox.

If I were to tell you how many times we'd almost lost the pods and how cumbersome and heavy they were, you'd assume they were more important than our food supply. Vincent seemed to think so.

Our excursion party consisted of Chief, Vincent, Doc, Paysha, Zoe, Erika and nearly everyone who survived from the original crew, save for those who I needed to stay behind at Starport City to serve in the Senate. We totaled sixty-three, down from our original eighty. The years had not been kind to our expedition to find *Arcadia*. Yet, our tenacity and willpower pushed us toward our goal of getting back to Earth.

"I'm detecting electromagnetic signatures and faint traces of radiation," Zoe said through my bio-mechanical translator embedded behind my ear. Her soothing voice snapped me back to reality, and I realized just how damn cold it was again.

"Where?" I asked.

"Hard to pinpoint, sir. Readings have spiked. Maybe my scanner is broken."

Vincent looked it over. "Seems to be working, but these readings don't make sense. Whatever is emitting this electro-magnetic signature would be the size of the Pentagon. No, this can't be right."

"That's oddly specific," Erika said.

"I spent years there. It's larger than you think. Most of it is underground."

I concentrated for a moment, visualizing the robot stopping its climb and protecting us.

Defensive posture.

The Janissary crunched the ice underfoot and aimed his wrist weapon in front of him, creating a firing arc.

In this type of weather, obviously water is easy to find, but you lose it as you speak. Chief rigged up our suits with plenty of warming mechanisms to keep us warm and to boil water if necessary. Although the cold zapped the batteries, with the constant sunlight this time of year, we recharged them every few hours by putting them face up on one of the survival sleds and exposing them to the sunlight.

My second-in-command, Lieutenant Commander Chen, kept a close eye on me. Intelligent and tough, I appreciated her strength and willpower. She was a natural leader, though at times, her approach was to use as few words as possible.

I made my way over to Vincent and examined the omnis-canner. "Might be an old Antediluvian base. Wouldn't be the first time we've found one that's submerged."

"Don't think it's a base. It's too active."

Something about this rubbed me wrong. It'd been months since we'd encountered anything remotely resembling Ante-diluvian technology, the last being a small, abandoned encampment three hundred klicks south of our position. "Even a fusion reactor would run out after that much time had elapsed. Zoe?"

"Captain, I do not believe either of those theories to be correct. The Antediluvians set up several beacons on the polar caps."

"This far north? For what purpose?"

"They believed other Antediluvians would come and rescue them. Shapers despise the cold, so it would make logical sense for the humans to assemble in areas like this. Due to the harsh weather conditions and lack of suitable farmland, all attempts to establish bases here would be doomed to failure."

Vincent muttered under his breath, "They're not the only ones who despise the cold."

"Alright, we'll scout ahead. Everyone, take a knee," I said. "I'll send the Janissary to go look."

With a thought, I ordered the robot to secure our sleds and recon the position. It vaulted through the snow. Its metallic claws found purchase on the rocks and, along the way, created a path for us to follow.

Slowly, the Janissary proceeded to venture over a large hill beyond my line of sight.

When you're standing still in temperatures this low, it's easy to get comfortable, and if you get comfortable, you die. I made sure to move constantly. What I wouldn't have given to be beside a fireplace right now. A nice blanket. Some coffee. Now there was something I missed.

Valuable minutes passed. The Janissary should have been back by now. I'd give it another few minutes. I checked in with my crew, and they signaled they were okay. They were tough anyway. I was proud of them and their willingness to go all the way. When the temperature wasn't a million below, we normally camped and made small talk. Through the years, I've learned a lot about them. It's funny how fast you get to know people's quirks and what sets them off.

Damn. Where's that Janissary? He should be back.

I imagined him returning, which should have sent a telepathic command to him and ordered him to return. The Antediluvian device fused behind my ear not only translated languages, it understood my conscious and subconscious desires to some degree. This allowed me to willingly and sometimes unwillingly command the robot without direct communication. This type of technology existed back home, but when the Beijing riots occurred, the tech was subsequently banned worldwide. Banning tech doesn't make it go away; it only creates an underground market.

Vincent promised to find a way to make direct communication with the Janissaries a reality, but our travels made it impossible for him to work on anything as complex as that. Some day.

"Captain, EMF readings rising," Zoe said. "Strongest readings are coming from the northeast."

Erika opened one of our last remaining tablets, keyed in

data about our location, and looked where Zoe had pointed. "Could be the site." She was a synthetic human or what were once called androids. Her body had died during an emergency explosion, but her consciousness lived on inside the silicone in her head. Once, I'd thought of synths as nothing more than expendable tools. What a fool I'd been.

The ice behind me cracked open. Massive chunks of ice flew overhead, and one smashed into our medical sled, obliterating it. Beneath the ice, smaller crab-like appendages reached up from below the waterline and I caught sight of a carapace with boney protrusions around its outer rim.

Erika zipped into action and lobbed our last remaining dynamite at it. The explosion blinded me for a moment, and then the snow came down on us from above. When the mess had cleared, three of the creature's arms lay still and bleeding an inky fluid over the snow.

I unslung my dark matter rifle as blotchy squid-like arms six stories tall reached up through the snow and grappled a sergeant. He screamed, then his body turned to gelatin as the creature crushed him.

"Spread out!" I aimed and fired, peppering the tentacle's lower half. By then, we'd scattered, my team shooting with wild abandon. We stood no chance against something this size.

A second tentacle burst forth out of the snow next to Chief. He rolled out of the way, and I put six shots into the beast. Although it bled, my fire did little to stop it.

"Shaper!"

Tentacles flung out from the snow like newly formed trees, crunching the ice loud enough. The deafening rumble underneath our feet morphed into sounds like an artillery duel. Several of our sleds slipped into the water, our priceless cargo disappearing. I let out a few choice swearwords, my mind racing. Without the cargo, we'd all be dead in a matter of days.

"I've got eyes on the body!" Chief said.

Shifting underneath the water, a city-block-sized Shaper wiggled its amorphous body, a shape with enough mass to displace several tons of water. Thousands of metallic implants shined as its body pulsed with light from its internal organs. Eye stalks, like cellphone towers, writhed chaotically, and its bulk burgeoned with muscle and a thick, dark purple carapace.

Soon, the ice began to crack everywhere, and we found ourselves sliding on ice floes.

Below the water, I finally spotted the Janissary, its limbs torn asunder by the creature. The Shaper's many arms still held on to parts of it like prizes. Something round stretched beneath the beast like the roof of an enormous dome, and it dwarfed the Shaper.

Zoe dove through a hole in the ice deep underwater toward the Shaper's enlarged maw. Was she suicidal?

"Zoe!" Vincent dashed uncaring through the white toward a hole in the ice. "She's going to get herself killed!"

Zoe dodged one of the Shaper's many arms and grabbed several of the sled cords and then kicked her way toward the surface.

My crew fought tenaciously against the horde of emerging arms, but this ambush threw our practiced unit cohesion tactics for a loop. Panic spread, and a few of my team succumbed to the angry cold when they slipped into the water.

Thousands of beams laced the air, severing Shaper's arms. As soon as we'd kill a few limbs, they'd double and double again. How many arms did it have?

"Run!" someone yelled.

"Fall back!" another said.

"Stand your ground!" I barked.

A few still retreated, and Chief paused his assault on the Shaper to put a few shots over the heads of those whose mettle had failed them. Only one still ran. I'd deal with the coward if we survived.

Erika paused at the edge of an ice floe and dove in the water after Zoe.

Damnit, Erika! You're going to freeze!

My crew fought tenaciously against the horde of emerging arms, but our futile attempts to maintain unit cohesion in the ice had thrown our practiced tactics for a loop. Panic spread, and a few more of my team died when they slipped into the cold water.

While we fought for our lives, a lieutenant stared at his omnitool. "Sir! Something else's beneath the water!"

A tentacle lashed out from the water toward him.

Chen dashed through the snow, shouting orders.

"Get down!" I yelled.

As it missed him, the arm continued its path straight at me. Disc-shaped implants spun like sawblades, and along its glossy flesh, thousands of eyes looked every which way.

I flipped my dark matter rifle's beam switch to solid and then squeezed the trigger. A thick beam of energy blasted from the end of the barrel. I missed and hit a hill of ice. The arm came at me faster. I raised the rifle like a sword, severing the arm at its base, then ducked. For some odd reason I couldn't explain to this day, the Shaper slithered back into its watery embrace and vanished from view.

Splash!

Zoe busted out of the water with Erika in her arms, Erika's synth body encased in ice and immobilized.

I raced over to Erika. Vincent met me there.

"Will she be okay?" Vincent asked without the slightest concern to anything that'd just happened.

Zoe waved her hand slowly over her Erika's body. She stared

at her face, and as the ice melted, Zoe's gaze fell on me. "She has sustained severe damage."

My brother bent beside Erika and looked into her bright green eyes. "Don't talk. We need to evaluate you for damage first."

"She can't hear you, Vincent," Zoe said. "Several micro tears have damaged her epidermis. Her self-repair module is destroyed. Some of her cognitive functions have failed." Zoe touched Erika's forehead.

"So what are you saying?" Vincent asked.

"I'm sorry, Vincent Moore. Erika is no longer with us."

CHAPTER TWO

Kahwin
North Pole
Captain Scott Moore

Death was something I had cometo accept as captain. After losing so many people, I think some of my humanity might have slipped away. When Erika's frozen synth lay lifeless in the snow, it was as if hope had died.

"We've got to find a way to recover her." Vincent looked her over. "I can't do anything unless we set up camp."

"What camp? We've lost everything," one of the survivors said.

Chief lifted up his prize. "Not everything. We saved the comm equipment."

"So we can tell them what?"

"Help Chief set up igloos over that way," I said to the man. "And enough with the defeatism. Get to work. Take Erika with you and place her safely with Doc."

"Aye, aye, sir."

Chief knew well enough to take the initiative and set up a

camp away from the ice floes. By then, the water had begun to freeze over again, and any sign of the Shaper, and whatever the glowing dome was beneath it, vanished along with everything else. We'd retained a fraction of our supplies, enough for a week at best.

The frozen ground meant we could not bury the dead, and we dared not use what remaining fuel we had on them. Instead, we stacked them safely off to the side and stripped them of their clothing and valuables and distributed it amongst the crew. I couldn't bring them back, so in a way, I was thankful we had less mouths to feed. Selfish thoughts, perhaps, but realistic ones.

"You said we'd killed all the Shapers," I said to Zoe.

"We did."

"Then what was that?" Vincent asked.

Zoe's eyes narrowed. "A Shaper spawn. They were created to protect certain sites on Kahwin. I'm as surprised as you to see it."

Chen gave Zoe a look and rubbed her hands together.

"Then what was it protecting? What was the glow under the water? That dome thing?" Vincent rubbed his gloved hands together for added warmth.

Zoe turned to me. "I believe it may be an underwater city."

The back of my neck tingled at what she said. "What makes you think that? What did you see?"

"I could only make out a faint outline of it during the struggle." Zoe stared at the ground. "I'm sorry I could not save more of the sleds. If I leave now, I may be able to acquire food."

Vincent shook his head like he'd lost the Superbowl. I missed football. "What would be the point? We're screwed out here." He opened a private channel with me. "You promised we'd find the Antediluvian ship out here. This was the last place to look, you said. *The last place.*"

"That's enough. I know what we've lost, Vincent."

"Do you? Now, Erika's dead, more of our crew are dead, and we've lost everything but Melody, and that was merely by luck. If I hadn't insisted the servers go into the stasis pods and remain isolated from the rest of our supplies, they'd be gone too. Your obsession with finding this ship has cost us everything!"

"I said that's enough. I realize how precarious our situation is, but your emotional outbursts would be better spent helping create some shelter."

"No, never mind." Vincent started to walk off but stopped after a few steps.

I steeled my face. "You have something else to say?"

"I do, but it's not worth it."

"You're right. It's not worth it." I motioned to a small crew setting up camp. "Now, get your sorry ass over there and start helping."

Vincent stood still. Snow dusted across his body from a slight gust of wind. "You know what? Maybe I will say it, then."

I waited for him to say something he'd regret, but as the seconds stretched on, he must have regained his composure and instead walked off the way he was headed. As my brother, he knew what to say to hurt me, and although I'd grown a thick skin, I needed his support now more than ever.

"Any idea what that glow was under the water?" Chen asked me over a private line, one I'd set up that not even Vincent could spy on.

"I don't know. What do our omniscanners detect?"

"That's the funny thing. They're jammed up. Don't know what's wrong with them, but it's the same effect we encountered on Trion and here on Kahwin. It's coming from the glow, that much we know."

"We have no way of getting down there."

"There's Zoe," Chen said.

"She needs to find us food while we recover. If she does, she'll be gone for a few days at a minimum. Whatever is below us isn't going anywhere." A little itch appeared on the back of my ear where my Antediluvian implant was imbedded. With my helmet on, obviously, I couldn't get to it, and there's nothing worse than an itch you can't scratch.

"Did Zoe leave already?" Chief asked.

"Not yet," I replied.

Chief scanned the area for a moment. Gray clouds grew above a large mountain range in the distance. "What's the plan after she brings us back food?"

"Well, I didn't travel all this way not to find *Arcadia*. If there's a city below our feet, it might have a starport, and if it does, the ship is likely there. We've run out of options otherwise."

"If it's not there?" Chief asked bluntly.

"Then we return to Starport City empty-handed and help the Senate rebuild."

"It might not be that bad, sir."

"It might not be." But this world wasn't our home no matter how much I'd tried to convince myself it was, and believe me, I'd tried. Home was a place where you thrived and felt comfortable. It was a place where you looked around and knew there was a future in store for you. It was not simply a place where you slept or set up shop. It was more meaningful than that. I wasn't a nomad and never subscribed to the idea that anyplace could be your home. They used to believe that back in the day.

As I made my way to help Chief, the wind kicked up, smearing the bloody snow across the ice. I'd been out here and searching for too long—years—and craved the luxury of technology and the simple life of a starship captain.

By entrusting the Senate to run Starport City, it'd freed up enough people for me to launch this expedition, but we hadn't made two-way contact in over a year. Their last report said an Equinox tech, a man by the name of Donald Davers, needed to fix the reception tower he and Chief erected. I'd met Davers a few times and trusted him to do the job correctly, but we hadn't heard from them since then. However, our signals sent to the city reached them in full.

After a few hours, we'd set up camp and I let the hardest workers sleep first while we clocked the landscape. Chief was one of those guys who needed four hours sleep, and he would be good for the next twenty, but he reached near exhaustion ensuring our camp's new vantage point would give us time to react to any incoming threat.

In a feat of effort that would go down in the annuals of efficiency, Chief assembled a few people to help him set up the communications array. He posted a few guards on the perimeter and proceeded to crash.

Zoe, Vincent, Doc, and I huddled in a makeshift igloo, powdered snow clinging to us.

"Are you going to inform Starport City of what you've found?" Zoe asked.

"You're asking me if they're going to send a rescue party?"

Vincent watched his personal tablet's display showing the ambient temperature, oxygen levels, potential toxins, etc. Zoe used her body to generate heat, heating the inside of the igloo. We'd be able to take off our helms soon, and I could finally get that awful itch.

"The Senate has one working shuttle. They can't risk sending it this far north to rescue a few of us." I took a sip of water from a hose next to my mouth and looked at how much power remained in my suit before I'd need a new battery. Deciding on discretion, the better part of valor, I cleared the exchanger tube and socketed it into my suit's energy pack and the heavy recharge station, which meant I'd need to remain relatively immobile unless I wanted to lug the recharger around with me.

Vincent followed suit and recharged his. "Equinox should have more than one working shuttle, even if they cannibalized a few of them to make another work. You know how important they are."

"I do, but Chief ordered them to wait."

"Wait until we return?" Vincent folded his arms and then gave out a long sigh. "When's *that* going to be? Never is my guess."

"Never can be your guess all you want. I told you after this, we're done. If *Arcadia* isn't here, then it's not on the planet."

Zoe glanced over at the recharger with wonder in her eye. "What will you do if you find this ship?"

I chuckled as if there were more than one answer. "Conquer the galaxy, of course."

"Conquer the galaxy," she repeated with dismay.

Vincent grinned. "Sarcasm, Zoe."

Zoe had asked me that same question about what our intentions were more than a few times, and after a while, I began to suspect she wanted to stay with us no matter what. But why? Why did she care? Obligation? Of course, she could always have been a spy. That thought never left my mind. AI had done wonders back home, convincing and manipulating hundreds of millions of people without anyone being that much wiser. It only delayed the reaction to the Collapse and Famine.

All that felt so long ago now, almost like a dream.

"I told you what my intentions were," I said. "I will return to Earth and take it from there. You still want to come with me, don't you?"

Zoe looked up at me. "Yes. That is what we agreed to do."

Another few minutes, and I'd be able to scratch the itch, which grew by the minute. If you've ever been bitten by fire ants, you know they sting, but the itch afterward is enough to drive you crazy. It wasn't to that level yet, but the intensity seemed to grow with each passing moment.

"What do you think your people will do when they meet me?" Zoe asked.

Vincent answered for me. "Good question. I know you've read what history you could about our planet when you were aboard *Atlanta*. I wish you hadn't."

"I only remember parts. The longer I remain in this form, the more I've forgotten what it was like *not* to be in this form."

I checked my battery level. "Human, you mean."

She made micro adjustments to the recharger, avoiding eye contact. "I would rather not use that word, Captain."

"Why's that?"

"You don't treat Erika as a human, and yet she retains your shape and form."

I treated her like any officer on my team. "She's a synth, but she's as human as the rest of us."

"You don't believe that, Captain." Zoe crouched to get eye level with numbers spitting out on the recharger's screen. "You are free to believe whatever you want, both of you. But I value Erika as a member of the crew more than either of you know, and I do see her as basically human."

Another long pause.

"I'm going to check on her," Vincent said.

I shook my head. "You should stay inside and warm up."

"Thanks for your advice, but it's warmer outside."

Then he got up, disconnected himself from the recharger, and left. Maybe it was for the better. My biggest fear was that he'd spread negativity amongst the crew, causing it to spread like a virus. Space Force had hired the best, and all of us tried to stay in good spirits, but the cold had had its way with us, and although I tried to remain positive, I started to think we'd failed for the last time. I refused to come back to Starport City empty-handed.

"What did he mean?" Zoe asked.

"You know what he meant."

"It's not a good idea to feud with the crew during this crucial time."

"He's more than a member of my crew. He's my brother."

Zoe fidgeted with the recharger, slowing its power drain. "Is there something wrong?"

"No, why do you ask?"

"You have been making funny faces for a while."

I pointed to the side of my head. "I have an itch behind my ear where the implant is and can't wait to get this helmet off so I can itch it. It's been driving me crazy for a while now."

Zoe came closer and looked at the side of my face. "When did it start?"

"Wait, what's wrong?"

"Do you remember when it started?"

"Not exactly."

The thermometer in my HUD read -23°C/-10°F, and Zoe unsnapped my helmet. The freeze smacked me in the face as I breathed in through my nose. A faint metallic odor from the recharger filled the igloo, the soft lights landing across Zoe's well-sculpted body. My extremities began to cool as well, but I was thankful for the clean, un-recycled air.

"I like your facial hair," Zoe said.

I smiled. Why did she say that?

She took the helmet in her hands and stared me straight in the eye. She whispered, "If you did want to conquer the galaxy, I would help you. I want you to know that. I will help you do anything."

No woman had spoken to me like that since Paris. Was she reading me, learning how to toy with me? A test? It wouldn't have been the first time a woman tested me, but her words felt so earnest and genuine. Then again, that would be how they would sound if she were trying something. Zoe knew us all well enough to probably get half of us fighting the other half without any of us knowing she started it.

I nodded. "Thank you, Zoe." My lips burned, each breath like ice down my throat.

Where had the itch behind my ear gone? It'd disappeared.

As soon as I thought that, the ice underneath us quaked. Zoe rushed to the cord and unplugged me from the suit while I threw on my helmet.

"What's happening?"

Crack! Crack!

The ground trembled as the ice outside broke open.

My helmet's HUD came to life, spilling data across my vision.

"Sir!" Chief said through the comms. "Outside! Fast!"

I secured my rifle and dashed out with Zoe.

Above me floated a starship stretched far across the horizon, its splendor and magnificence enough for me to question my own sanity. My God. Who had built this? Although it'd come up through the water and into the air, it was free of ice. Underneath its golden-colored hull, its shadow blanketed the ice for as far as the eye could see. Blister-shaped protrusions bubbled from around the keel, mainly toward the stern. Like a naval ship, its hull was rounded, but that was where the similarities ended. It was shaped like a dagger with two angled fins set into the stern at 75 degrees like a missile. The fins nearly touched the water, but the craft itself loomed above us a hundred stories in the air.

A light blue field surrounded the hull, most likely a force

field. Its nose came to a sharp point a few kilometers away. Where were its guns? What kind of launch bays would a ship that size have, if any? It could be a carrier, perhaps. It might have been a seed ship, or an ark, as it were, filled with abundant forests, a self-sustaining, genetically modified environment that could keep the ship supplied indefinitely. If I could reach Earth with this ship, and my theories proved accurate, it would be possible to populate endless worlds with it.

Who controlled it? How'd it suddenly just appear like this?

Although the blood of my crew stained the ice, the moment we witnessed the alien ship sent us all into a state of shock. Our ticket home, the object of my obsession, was here. I'd found it.

CHAPTER THREE

Kahwin
North Pole
Captain Scott Moore

Vincent's awestruck voice carried though the open channel. "It's nothing like I imagined."

I don't know how long we stood there in amazement, looking up at the ship. The frigid air started to form an icy crust on its side, covering some of its domes. We had no way of getting up there.

Five minutes? Fifteen? I burned the image of the alien starship into my memory so deeply, I'd remember this moment for the rest of my life. It was one of those moments that called for a speech or the words of a practiced orator to make this moment poetic, and I found myself at a loss for words. A ship that size would hold a crew of hundreds of thousands of people, if not more. Would I find the Antediluvians tucked away in cryo? We'd found their previous cryochambers scattered around Kahwin, almost all emptied except a few dead bodies we found inside, and in many cases, pillaged. Surely we'd find a few aboard that ship, if we could just get up there.

"No, it's nothing like what I imagined either," Chief said.

"This has to be it," I said.

"How do we make contact with the crew, or is there a crew?" Vincent asked.

Chen, who'd been so stunned, she hadn't moved in a while, turned to me. "What if they point their weapons at us?"

"I think if they wanted us dead, we'd be dead by now," Chief replied.

The main question would be how to enter the ship. We had no working shuttle, and the craft offered no obvious form of egress. With the ship rising hundreds meters off the ground to the north where the glow had been, roughly half a klick away, how would we get up there? Was this a kind of intelligence test?

Zoe looked skyward, and when her gaze locked on the ship, her lips curled with disdain. She wrapped our last remaining thermal blanket around Erika. "It seems you have found it. What is to become of me now?"

"What was that?" I asked. "Do you see it? Look at the size of it."

"I said what is to become of me now that you have found the ship, Captain Moore?" Zoe asked sharply.

Vincent scoffed and put his hands out. "We've found the biggest discovery in forever and you're worried about what's going to happen to you? I thought you said you wanted to come with us. We talked about this."

"We discussed many things." Zoe tilted her chin up at the ship. "Will you still keep your word and allow me to travel with you?"

Chen examined Zoe for a bit and narrowed her eyes.

"I think we'll need you now more than ever," I said. "Chief, assemble a team to send an emergency signal back to Starport

City. See if you can get in touch with the Senate and let them know what we've discovered. I don't care what you have to do to send the signal. Make sure it goes through."

"Aye, sir, but it'll be a one-way transmission."

"Understood. Just make it happen."

"Speaking of the Senate, you think Equinox will be excited?" Chief asked.

"Let's hope so. After all the political nonsense that took place, you'd hope they'd be satisfied."

Chief carried the only communications array capable of contacting Starport City from this distance, a jury-rigged piece of tech he'd salvaged from *Atlanta*'s wreckage and some comm gear he and Equinox put together. Don't ask me how he did it, but he could take two pieces of flint, a diamond, some sticks, and a pack of peppermint Wrigley's and build a laser given enough time. He was that kind of person.

The implant behind my ear burned slightly, but it'd been doing that over the past six months. Quite annoying. I wanted it to stop. Someday, either Vincent or Chief would fix it.

My eyes stayed glued to the starship above us. It wasn't fair to call it a starship. That would be like calling a single-engine Cessna turboprop an intercontinental hypersonic missile. What was above us was a work of art, and if rumors were true, it was the finest warship in the galaxy.

I've mentioned how we found the recording, that it explained the ship as a kind of last-ditch weapon against the Shapers. It was constructed before the humans on this side of the galaxy were vaporized in an interstellar war and then forced into the Stone Age. I'd met one of the Shaper leaders, a Keeper, known as Allo Quishar. From what I understood, the Keepers could inhabit any Shaper and view the world through their eyes. I say Keepers, plural, and yet I'd only spoken to one.

This may sound odd, but I felt a deep sadness as I viewed

the ship. Everyone should have had that same experience as the one I was having, that sense of energy-producing awe reserved for explorers. No one alive had seen this ship other than those gathered around me. We'd won.

The implant behind my ear began to seriously sting. How long had I been standing there? But I needed to look at the ship. It was incredible.

How could we possibly get up there to find out what was inside *Arcadia*, which, by the way, I might have regretted naming the ship. Arcadia, the ancient Greek concept, and the starship had nothing in common so far as I could tell.

Like a work of art, the starship's beauty blinded me maybe to how dangerous of a position we were in. Maybe the Antediluvians still lived aboard the ship now. Who could say if they'd even remember their original purpose or how much they'd be changed by millennia trapped inside the ship. Or perhaps they'd give the power over to the robots. Clearly, they'd built the Janissaries as a fighting force, and those creations might have been simply the beta-run version. As fast as our tech back home raced faster and faster, it'd only make sense theirs would as well.

It started to get darker around me. My crew talked in the background, but honestly, I wasn't sure I cared what they had to say at the moment. When you were looking at *Arcadia*, what else was there?

I think I heard Chen speaking to me, but it was so distant.

That damn burning behind my ear wouldn't stop.

If I had to guess, I'd bet the Antediluvians also mastered some kind of bio-mechanical technology. The seamless hull, the rounded shapes, the flow of it, all reminded me of a living creature. Shaper ships have obvious biomechanical implants and weapon systems. We'd seen them before. This had none of them.

It got darker still, and maybe my focus failed me that day, but I could have sworn I could see the ship easier. Its fine, delicate curves were almost like a woman's.

I could have sworn people called my name, but Chief was here, so he could best handle things for a moment. I needed to stare at the ship.

Something was there in my mind. Calling. Talking.

Why do I need to stare at the ship? How long have I been staring at it? It's hard to read the time in the HUD for some reason.

Wait.

Hello? Is there someone there?

Hello? another voice asked. Its distinct tone overwhelmed me, and I clutched my chest as my heart hammered. Pressure built behind my eyes, a migraine brewing. You know the pain when you've had them.

Can you hear me? Who am I speaking with? The ship?

Gliv tuaha, mu mua, glachan. Interrupt. Interrupt. Ill-defined contact. Genetic sequence invalid. You have found me. Invenisti me. Vous m'avez trouvé. Sie haben mich gefunden. Hello. I see you.

My mind spun with languages from Earth, and it felt as if I knew them all and could think in each of them. I spoke only English, Spanish, Russian, and a hint of Mandarin, but my knowledge of Latin, French, German, and every other language Earth overlapped each other.

As such, my thoughts reflected upon themselves, mirrors reflecting other mirrors into infinity. Sustaining a single thought became impossible, even mathematical statements. One plus one. I didn't know. I struggled to understand what the concept of one even meant. Heidegger would have been proud of the amount of thinking about thinking going on inside my brain.

So useful, the translator device had bridged a gap between the ship and myself. Did I communicate with the ship, or did someone overload the translation implant? I retched, and the bile of stress and battle came up. Everything I once understood inked away on a canvas of doubt, and I was left stunned with a lump in my throat without the ability to move or speak.

The putrid stink of burning flesh filled my helm, and only then did I realize the implant had burned a painless hole behind my ear. The device plopped to the side of my face behind my head, and now started to burn what little hair I had back there. I shook it away, still dreading the inevitable pain.

"Captain, can you hear me?"

I was now on my back, staring up at Doc and Vincent through the dim shadow cast by the alien ship. During the time that had passed, *Arcadia* had lowered itself into the ice, its keel sunken into the snow. It was as though a city had plunged from the sky.

"His eyes aren't looking good, Doc," Vincent said.

"Don't you think I see that?"

Did they mean me? I wanted to sleep and wake up on Earth. What did it matter? Just a quick nap.

"We're losing him," Doc said.

"You will have to get him aboard the ship." Zoe's frantic voice sounded more human than ever.

I faded out faster and faster, and my chest ached. Wanting to give up, I accepted my fate, almost thankful I'd died peacefully, knowing we'd succeeded.

But off in the distance, an opening into the starship beckoned me, a yellowing light spilling out from a doorway on the starboard side by one of the domes. My voice froze, and then my limbs. My mouth tasted like copper. The skin behind my ear, where my implant was located, burned like crazy.

Doc waved an omniscanner over me. "Stop moving, Scott. Take it easy."

"The ship will have medical facilities," Zoe said.

Doc looked at her. "You're sure of this?"

She nodded, her eyes innocent.

"Then, we have no choice," Doc replied. "We must board the ship immediately or we risk losing him. His central and peripheral nervous system are severely inflamed. Until we can relieve his condition, he won't be able to speak."

Chief picked me up and put me on one of the remaining sleds. "We need to send a signal to Starport City. We have got to set up the comm relay and send a message."

"How long will that take?" Chen asked.

The wind howled, and above the ship, the sky darkened. Lightning flashed across the horizon, first once, then twice, then all around us across the mountains. Thunder cracked in the distance, echoing in the mountainous cauldron.

Zoe glanced up and approached Chief with a steady stride. "There is no time. You must board the ship."

"What about the people from Equinox? We can't simply board without giving them some information," Vincent said.

Zoe gave one look at our equipment and shook her head. "If we don't get on *Arcadia* now, Mr. Vincent Moore, the ship will leave without us."

"Leave?" Vincent asked. "What do you mean, leave without us?"

"It's not staying planet-bound for long," Zoe said.

"It's leaving Kahwin?" Chief asked.

Zoe nodded. "Yes."

Chen glanced at Vincent and Chief, then back at Zoe. "How do you know this?"

"You will have to trust me," Zoe replied.

Chief pointed at the ship. "Where's it going?"

Zoe turned to me, and I could barely see her. This all felt like a dream. "He will not live long if you do not enter *Arcadia*."

Doc rested his hand on my shoulder. "She's right. We have

to get him into a medical facility soon, or he's not long for this world."

"Alright." Vincent blew into his gloved hands to warm them up. "This is all too strange."

Chief said, "Get him on the ship." He glared at Zoe. "If anything happens to us or the captain..."

"All will be well," Zoe said. "Come. We must hurry."

Doc had gathered up several teams, who began pulling what few sleds we had over to me. "Someone will have to stay behind and set up the comm relay. Someone will have to volunteer."

But no one spoke up.

Finally, Chief sighed. "I'll stay behind."

Zoe gave another look at the sky and plowed through the snow toward the comm relay. "No, I will. You will need all of your equipment if you are to make it back to Earth."

"What about you? It will take you months to sail back to the continent and reach Starport City. We don't have any idea what's aboard the ship, and I have a feeling you do." Vincent lowered next to me. "Scott, can you hear me? What do you want us to do? Can you blink?"

I attempted to focus on something with my eyes. When that didn't work, I tried relaxing and letting my eyes close naturally. If I could open them again, I figured I could blink. I opened them, but blinking proved impossible too.

A bluish cloud appeared overhead, funneling into a tornado. Wind ripped over the ice, blowing one of the sleds to the side. A few of my crew stumbled until they grabbed hold of a rope tied to the heaviest sled.

The darker the sky became, the more my HUD blinked error codes. A few people lifted me up. I grunted as they set me down on a sled, and every little bump on the ground made me wince.

"The captain will die soon," Zoe said.

Doc continued to inspect me with his instruments. "She's right."

"Everyone, grab a rope and start pulling the sleds inside the ship!" Chief ordered.

Vincent was most concerned with Melody's servers, and all of his efforts were put toward making sure they went wherever he went. Chief put me on a sled and dragged me toward the entrance.

"Promise me you'll make it back to Starport City," Vincent said to Zoe.

"I promise."

As I neared the ship, my head spun like I'd been given anesthesia. The yellowish light from the entrance bathed me, and the burning behind my ear disappeared. My HUD vanished, and all my suit's functions shut off.

As we crossed the threshold into the unknown and entered the ship, little did I know it would start humanity's last war.

CHAPTER FOUR

Kahwin
Kol Washington

My hand locked with my opponent's grip, both our elbows planted on the dull metallic table. Sweat dripped from my nose. The guy across from me strained as he pushed my hand down closer to the table. Strong, sure, but his grip wasn't right. I'd beat him.

"Ten notes says he ain't got the endurance," one of the people at the bar said, his thumbs looped in his wide leather belt. His sky blue pants tucked into his boots, and holes were all over his thick wool shirt. A huge mole sat on the side of his nose.

"After I beat him, you're next," I shot back.

Grease marks stained the table. Plates of bones, meat picked clean, sat off to the side. The musician on stage pulled out her five-stringed instrument and started tuning it, plucking strings and watching a signal on a computer tablet. She had to be from out of town. You could tell by how she carried herself and how carelessly she talked to customers.

The bar's bookie took in bets around me. I was the favorite to win, so a lot of them bet against me.

Freshly roasted meats wafted through the room. Most of the furniture came from one of the Earther's recycle piles scattered around the city, so nothing matched other than the dull paint. I liked this place more than I should have.

"Your shoulder still hurt?" the guy across from me asked.

"Someone made that up. My shoulder doesn't hurt at all." I spread a rumor about an injury I got fixing a pipe fitting and made a show of rubbing it.

My arm burned. He was strong—very strong. I let him bend my wrist a bit and lower my arm. Responding to his pressure, I winced and gritted my teeth. That was when the real betting began. People offered up scraps, plundered tech and food, knowing they'd double or triple their wager if I failed.

In the bar, discolored sections on the wall showed where the old clan banners used to hang. They should have put them back up. Behind the counter, two bartenders served the usual, but better wine was available across the street, and it only cost a bit more. If you ask me, it was always worth it to pay a little extra for the good stuff.

Candles flickered on most of the tables. If you paid enough, you could reserve a table with an overhead lamp and a bright bulb. Baskets of bread rolls sat at every table.

"You're... stronger than I... thought," I panted. With my arm bent like that, my reserve strength vanished quickly. Better end this soon. Not sure how much more I could take.

My opponent threw his weight down, forcing my hand dangerously lower. "You're getting weak, Kol. I can... feel your arm ready to... give out."

Some fans cheered my name. Kol. Kol. Kol. Glasses of beer clinked. Kol. Kol. Kol.

I gauged his breathing. Strained. He'd almost given all he had.

His face turned a deep shade of red. "Are you ready to... give up?"

He forced me down. My hand almost touched the table. I might lose. He was really strong. He'd stop any second. Now, his arm shook. A little more. A little more. Not going... to lose.

Kol. Kol. Kol.

I braced my heel and slipped my wrist over his, gaining leverage. Surprised, he groaned, his arm cranking the wrong way. In seconds, I pivoted and made my move, cracking his hand against the table with an audible *whomp*.

The room went silent for a second. Then, it erupted in cheers and groans as people exchanged winnings and losses. I rubbed my sore arm, smirking at the guy I'd just defeated.

Never bet against me.

"You win again." My opponent rubbed his bicep. His knuckles had clan tattoos on them, two fish curled together, and a necklace of human teeth hung from his neck. "Almost had you."

"Keep it up. You'll win eventually. What's your name?"

"Shilder Lincoln."

Lincoln was an Earth name assigned to us by the Senate. By law, we were ordered to use it. It was still obvious who was from what clan, either by their body language or slight changes in the way they spoke.

For some reason, Captain Moore wanted us to avoid speaking about the clans. We still did, but after the war, everyone was forced to move, so the clans started to intermingle. Thankfully, the Janissaries kept the peace, because at least sixteen people I knew had been killed over clan disputes from the past. It was against the law to act like that now, but people from different clans still dueled and fought from time to time.

People slowly departed until only Shilder and me were left.

"How much you make?" Shilder asked.

I counted stacks of coins. "Three eagles, twelve cents."

"Not bad."

The amount was about thirty hours of labor. I was used to the new way we bought and sold things.

On the back of our coins, there was something called the USS *Atlanta*, which was a "starship" that could go from planet to planet. An eagle was stamped on the front of them, and that was why we called them eagles. The coins had English words on them. I could read them, but I didn't know what they meant.

"Mind if I buy you a round?" Shilder asked me.

I rapped the table. "Beer."

"Be right back."

I was told it was impolite to speak to people for too long without introducing themselves first. I'm Kol Washington, and I'm sorry if I messed up speaking English along the way. It was still new to me. Thankfully, my teachers said we Kahwins had a knack for languages. I used a translation device back then, but I hoped I could put it down and speak without it someday.

If you would like to know about the device, I'll do my best to explain it. Because our language was so much different than English, the translator did its best to mimic what a person on Earth might say. You know when a person gets mad? It tried to show that. Or if a person used a dialect, it tried to approximate a matching dialect from their world. The idea that one of their machines had a brain that could do that disturbed me.

Zoe gave the translator back to me and told me never to tell anyone about it and also said that if I was caught with it, I'd be in big trouble. She said "big" twice, though. I wonder if she meant large. Anyway, I carried it in a sealed compartment under my shirt. My baggy clothes allowed me to hide it, so no one could see it. I apologize for my bad English. I would say more about Zoe, but I haven't seen or heard from her in a long time.

I was eighteen years old with light brown hair, blue eyes, and big feet. My friends usually made fun of me about them, but I stopped caring. I was the same height as Chief Peter Breckenridge, who allowed me to call him "Pete" when we were alone together. Also, we liked to arm wrestle, which became one of the biggest sports in the district. I was almost as strong as Chief, though he said I'd never beat him. Yes, I would.

Let me tell you more about this place, the Blue Kraken. It was a mix between our traditional style and the new stuff the Earthers brought. The walls were made of stone and wood, with some carvings of sea monsters and battles from back in the day. The bar itself was a massive chunk of driftwood, all smooth and shiny with some metal holding it together. People said it came from a shipwreck, so it had this mysterious feel to it.

Outside the Blue Kraken, the city's tight streets filled with market stalls, selling anything from handcrafted gear to high-tech gadgets. Some people thought how great we'd done adapting to the Earthers. Others suggested we were losing our roots. Both were right.

If you asked me, the city was like a mix of old and new, and I was curious about all the new stuff. Sometimes, I missed the simpler times. Hunting. Scouting.

Our people had been through a lot, with the war and all that came with it. The Janissaries, Captain Moore's robot army, kept the peace, and we were starting to come together.

So, what was life like then for someone like me? Well, there were plenty of challenges, finding good work for one. I got better at speaking English, and I learned how to make my way in the city. With my skills as a tracker and hunter, I had a pretty good shot at making something of myself.

There were days when I wondered what it would've been like if the Earthers hadn't showed up. If we could have just gone on living our lives the way we used to. Without all this change. With the Shapers always bugging us.

Shilder returned with two glasses and a light blue ceramic pitcher full of this year's best batch of beer. The brewer sure knew his stuff. Earthers liked to brag about their beer, but nothing topped a dark TK-stout or a Yapp-Tik pilsner.

"Thanks," I said.

"Sure." Shilder tasted it and nodded approvingly. "I've seen you around the city arm wrestling before."

"It's a side job."

"Your arm ever get sore?"

"All the time. I use blazi on my arms. Helps with the soreness."

"I'll have to try that."

The musician played one of those new songs about the Janissaries. A metallic pinecone on a pole amplified her voice, giving it a shrill quality. Couldn't quite catch the lyrics.

Shilder glanced over his shoulder and lowered his voice. "I hear you and the captain are close. Buddies, huh?"

"Where'd you hear that?"

"Are you?"

I guzzled down a third of the beer while it was still warm. Bit sweet for my taste. I didn't like discussing Captain Scott Moore anymore. That was probably why Shilder sat with me now. I'd told the story a hundred times—how we met, the bridge, the city, the Shapers, all of it. Used to help me get a girl for the night, but that didn't work anymore. Everyone had heard my captain stories.

"I haven't spoken to him in over two years. Maybe longer."

He eyed me suspiciously, then checked the newly installed

clock behind the counter. "No one has. Doesn't mean you don't talk to his people."

"Seen any Earthlings lately? They're not here."

"The Senate camps in the palace."

"I guess. When's the last time someone saw them? Two years, I'd say. I don't know. Three? If they're in there, hope they brought lots of food."

"Suppose I know someone who wants to talk to you. She says she'll pay for your time."

"How much are we talking?"

Shilder eyed the stack of eagles behind my beer mug. "A hundred times that, no less."

"Then she's a noble." My words slurred a bit. Strange. The lights seemed awfully bright. When did that happen? Why did Shilder look at me like that?

"Maybe. She lives in a five-top in District 1. You okay?" he asked.

The ceiling spun. "Feeling a bit tired all of a sudden. You know what she wants?"

"Only to chat about Captain Moore. Might be work in it."

I finished my beer. "Well, I think I need to be going."

"I figured you'd say no." Shilder gestured to someone behind me. Two, actually.

Click.

My hands wouldn't move. They were cuffed.

I almost made it to the door before the world went midnight black.

CHAPTER FIVE

Kahwin
Kol Washington

"He's waking up," a man said.

I opened my eyes.

A short woman sat by a fireplace. "Leave us."

Doors closed behind me, and the smell of burning wood clung to my clothes. Stuffed birds perched on decorative wooden pillars. The room was full of them. A body shield with clan markings hung above the crackling fireplace. Walls of irregular stones with layers of melted rock between them reminded me of luxury. A chandelier hung from a thick chain.

Two dogs lay in front of a fancy couch with red pillows and cushions. Antediluvian artifacts sat on shelves off to my right. None of them were bigger than my fist. She shouldn't have had those. Where'd she get them? Hard to see what they were.

I cleared the haze from my eyes and focused on the woman. She was about my mom's height, maybe a bit taller, and wore a white jumpsuit with a utility belt. A holstered Earth pistol hung at her hip. Brass rings held her auburn hair up high, like a tree.

My hands were free, and I sat on a comfy chair with animal skins. I touched the side of my chest. The translator was gone.

"I placed your device on a table behind you," she said with a slight accent. "Where did you acquire it?"

"Where am I? What time is it?" I asked.

"You are in my home as a guest. I apologize for bringing you here in such a manner, but you would not have come otherwise. You slept for quite some time. My cooks are preparing a meal if you are hungry. You might as well stay for lunch, don't you agree?"

Lunch? "I slept all that time?"

"Yes, you did. Your system does not handle excessive amounts of alcohol well."

"What did Shilder put in my beer?"

"Something to help you sleep. Nothing harmful. Did Shilder inform you of my offer?"

"He did. If it's alright with you, I'd rather not discuss the war. It was a long time ago, and a lot has changed since then."

"You're right. A lot *has* changed. Take yourself for example. When did you decide to move to the city?"

"After the captain defeated the Shapers, I decided to stay. It's different here, but I like it."

She walked over to my translator and picked it up. "That's good. Who gave you this? You know you are not supposed to have it."

I pointed to her shelves. "I could say the same thing."

"Laws apply to those below, not above. No one will come after me for having a few intriguing items. Would you like to have a look?"

"No, thank you. No offense or anything. I appreciate Ante-diluvian artifacts, I do. I'll just sit here and listen to why you brought me here."

She studied my device, keeping her fingers clear of the screen. "I want to discuss Captain Moore," the woman said.

"I was told it's impolite to talk about important matters without introducing oneself."

Her lips curled downward. "Perhaps you are right. You may call me Lady Kullen, First Among Equals, first daughter to Lord Kullen, Memory Keeper, Jefferson District Senate advisor, Chief Treasurer of the Silver Vaults, and Blade Mistress, third degree."

So, she was a memory keeper. They passed down information from one generation to the next and ensured its accuracy. My mother, Paysha, was a history recorder of the Gesterion Tribe, so she would remember things too. Like whenever I did something wrong, she would remind me not to do it again.

The paintings on the walls told stories of epic battles from the distant past, when the Shapers still let us fight with each other. Vibrant colors highlighted every detail. Did Lady Kullen commission these masterpieces herself or were they passed down through generations?

A collection of stuffed predators in the room's corner caught my attention. With their razor-sharp teeth, they must have been hard to kill. They had exotic names like Vrykatora and Gorpheon, and while they appeared fierce, whoever stuffed them did a terrible job. Each predator was posed as if ready to attack.

Near a window, a machine, a mix of metal and stone with carvings, belched out a cool breeze on my skin. The soft whirring of its engine soothed me. However it did it, the cool air it gave was a welcome relief.

Antediluvian artifacts captured my attention. An obsidian sphere called the Orolith, which did nothing other than show the numbers 555. Another item, a smooth, iridescent crystal named "The Loxophos" glowed with an inner light that changed colors from red to green to blue. Lady Kullen's wealth and influence was all over this place.

Nearby, a bookcase showcased her collection of old leather-bound tomes. By the titles, the books appeared to talk about Kahwin's history. Why would anyone want to study something that already happened? Wouldn't it be better to study about the present? Where'd she get them?

"That's a lot of titles," I said.

"What about you? Do you have any other titles besides Kol or Washington?"

"Not really. I'm good at arm wrestling. You're the first noble I've met."

She set my translator down and turned away and put her hand on her hip. "We're a dying breed, so the Earth saying goes."

"Do you speak English?" I asked.

"A few phrases. I can never say the 'th' right."

The more I'd learned English, the stranger my dreams had become. It was something I kept private because no one would understand. Sometimes, I woke up and wondered if I'd been dreaming in English or my language. I usually knew, but when I didn't, it worried me.

"Sorry for asking. This is a nice place. I've never seen so many stuffed animals before."

"They belonged to my great-great grandfather, who hunted them himself. He was an excellent marksman. If you go to the northeast inner theater, you'll see a statue of him by the magnet fountain."

"He must have been an important man. I'm still confused as to why I'm here." The drug must have been still lingering in me because my mind was foggy. I needed to find an exit. She was wealthy. That meant she'd hired security. They'd track me in the city if I did anything to her or damaged her property.

"I want you to have lunch with me and some people I know."

My voice cracked as my heart skipped a beat. "Me?"

"Whether you know it or not, you're an important man."

"I'm just Kol Washington. Ma'am, I don't really understand why I'm here or what you want from me."

"In time. You are not in any trouble, if that is your concern. I'll assume you'll be staying for lunch, then?"

My heart pounded the longer she looked at me. "Are you sure I'm not in any trouble? If I did anything wrong, I'm sorry. I really am."

"You're in no trouble. Not at all."

"Has my mother done something?" I asked.

"Not that I'm aware of. You are my guest of honor right now, and nothing will happen to you."

"Well, then am I free to leave?" I asked.

She shook her hand and put her hands to her side. "Not until we've had a discussion with you."

"We?"

"I'll show you a place where you can wash up and then I'll tell you why I brought you here."

"I thought you wanted to talk about Captain Moore."

"No, Kol. Far from it."

I was a simple man and liked simple foods. Spices tended to upset my stomach, though if you gave me anything hot, I'd eat it. Since moving to the city, I'd eaten things I would never have considered trying before, and I have to be honest here: City food was terrible. The cooks there smothered everything in sauces, making it hard to taste anything. I asked about it and someone told me they do it to hide the taste.

After I washed up, Lady Kullen invited me to the dining room. People were already there, and when I stepped inside, they rose from their chairs. The ones standing on the left side wore identical black coats with silver buttons from the neck down. Some of them had gold buttons, too, and their gray hair reminded me of some of Captain Moore's crew. Those on the right were a little older than me. The women wore traditional long-sleeve shirts with blood flower decorations, and you could tell which of them were married by how many rings they wore on their fingers. The men dressed in maroon neck-high vests with their family ribbons and rank pinned to their chests.

The long table seated thirty, and all but two seats were taken, one at each end. From one end to the other, Lady Kullen provided us with dishes of exotic foods, and they were set evenly. Electric lights blazed overhead. At the far end, Lady Kullen displayed her orange and black clan banner, where a silver disc was set diagonally in the center. A few Antediluvian symbols appeared at the bottom.

Stuffed birds of prey perched menacingly on the rock walls. A pair of double doors led out into an antechamber, where Lady Kullen's security waited on standby.

"Those assembled, let me introduce you to Kol," Lady Kullen said.

She told me their names, but there were too many to remember, and by the time she introduced the third person, I'd already forgotten the first person's name. When she got to the oldest man with the black coat, I took note of it and his titles.

His name was Jancer Vack, High General of Iron Guard, one of the most ruthless and brutal security networks in the city. Everyone knew who *he* was, but he disappeared shortly after Captain Moore took over the city. When I grew up, my mom would tell me stories about him, and I was pretty sure she talked with him on occasion when she would come here. One year, he rounded up a hundred prisoners from the mines, offered them their freedom in exchange for a chance to serve him as his personal guard, and took them in. No one had ever been released from the mines before, and a lot of the nobles, Mom said, were worried they'd talk about what they'd seen or why they were sent to the mines in the first place. They didn't.

The other person I recognized from her name was Bylee, Oracle of the Wonders, Tech Soothsayer, Shaper Liaison 3, Mistress of the Tear. Symmetrical scars marked both sides of her cheeks, and she shaded her eyes dark. One of her dark brown eyes stayed frozen in place, so she might have gotten sick at some point. Some say she was from a place called Iurr, another city that was far away and had buildings made of bone. If that was true, the Shapers probably built it.

Lady Kullen sat at one end, and I at the other. That was where chiefs sat. I had no business sitting at the head of the table. My hands became clammy. When the food came, I could barely eat.

Halfway through the meal, the high general set his knife down. "Kol, I've heard a lot about you." His low, even voice made my neck tense.

"You have?"

"How much of it is true?"

"I'm not sure what you've heard, General."

"I'm sure I've heard it all."

Even though I'd told my story a million times, if the general would ask me to tell him my stories with Captain Moore and the people from Earth, I would. One thing was certain: I didn't belong there. Everything inside me said to find an excuse to leave. Lady Kullen suggested I *could* leave. Maybe I should have taken her up on the offer. I needed to get back to my apartment and get away from them. If anyone were to ask me about the meal and the nobles, I'd deny it. After all, who would believe me?

"Kol, didn't you say you went deep into an underground city?" Lady Kullen asked.

"I did. It's past the bridge. Do you want to hear about it?"

Lady Kullen gave me a small smile. "Yes, we would. Do you remember where it's at and how you got inside?"

"I was blindfolded." It was a lie Zoe made me say. She said never to talk about where the underground city was. Too many secrets and too dangerous, she'd said.

"It would help if you would speak the truth," Bylee said. "What we have to say is very important."

"I am speaking the truth. Captain Moore made me wear a blindfold. I don't know where it is."

Lady Kullen and the oracle exchanged looks. Even if they didn't believe me, I had to keep lying.

"Who told you to say that?" General Vack asked.

"No one."

Bylee smirked, and her perfectly white teeth contrasted with her ebony skin. She didn't look like the rest of us, and her exotic looks left me wondering where she was from. The oracle was someone I'd heard about a few times in the city, but I never thought I'd meet her face to face. "Loyalty is valuable. What did they say would happen to you if you told someone?"

Zoe once told me someone would say this too. That was why I stopped talking about this stuff. "If you wish to speak to Captain Moore, I'm sure he'll be back soon enough. Or you could talk to the Senate. I should probably be going..."

"The Senate," General Vack scoffed. "Never mind the Senate. Tell me, young man, what do you want out of life?"

"Sir?"

"You heard me," the general said. "What do you want to do with the rest of your life? You have eighteen years already. What have you done?"

"Well, General, Captain Moore suggested I go to the Earther university and study. He said I'd do well, and he promised me a spot."

The general looked at the oracle and back at me. "You went, I presume?"

"No. I learned the basics of English from a few people here and there, but it makes my brain hurt."

Bylee went rigid when I said the word "English," which, in my native language, took six words to say and still didn't quite explain it. In some parts of the city, all you heard was English. City planners started getting rid of symbols for signs and all you saw were words, which few people understood. A friend of mine's sister renamed all of her children after Earth names too. I wasn't sure how I felt about it.

When I glanced over at the general, I noticed he studied me like Zoe used to do. "How do you feel about them, Kol?"

"Sir?"

"Captain Moore and his people."

"Yes, well, I feel fine about them. When they're here, that is."

Bylee smiled. "Why didn't you go to the university?"

I looked over at Lady Kullen and lowered my voice. "My mother asked me not to go. She sent me to a small school, and I tried to study with them."

One day, I came home late from school. One of my teachers was showing me how to write numbers and why writing them was important, and if we stayed after class, he would give us all a "pen." I still had mine, but the ink ran out. Dr. Firmer was her name. She told us about a place where she was from called Little Rock, Ark-something, and another place called The Silicon Valley, where all the important people made all the important decisions. Dr. Firmer told us a lot about where she was from, and she always used to tell us not to repeat what we heard in class. That lasted about two days before one of the other students started talking.

After I told my mother what happened, she gave me a

choice: I could keep going to school and move out or stay home and do something else. I waited to answer her because I didn't understand why she cared. One day, I saw her with a black eye. She said she fell, but I knew when she lied to me. I tried to find out what had happened, but I never did, but I knew it was about school. When I dropped out, the trouble went away, and the next semester, Dr. Firmer quit her job. Kahwin teachers took over shortly afterward.

"Kol, some of us are worried that you might be in some sort of trouble," Lady Kullen said. "Has anyone tried to follow you or ask you any strange questions?"

My pulse raced. I wasn't about to tell her anything. "I don't mean to be disrespectful, but I get asked strange questions a lot. I just don't answer them. People want to know things, but there's nothing to know."

The general steepled his fingers in front of him. "None of us know for sure what you do or do not know, Kol. Therefore, we will speak to you as if you do understand."

"Yes, sir. I'll do my best."

"Show him the recording," Lady Kullen said to one of the men in black jackets.

General Vack leaned forward and took one look at me before turning to Lady Kullen. "Now? Verification protocols have yet to be rescinded under Article 5."

"It's him," Bylee said.

"If it's not..." the general started to say before Lady Kullen waved him off.

A man searched under the table and pulled out a transparent crystal the size of his arm. A faint blue light glowed inside of it. The crystal was pointed on both ends, and the sides had been filed down flat. The light inside of it pulsed faintly like a heartbeat, and at the same time, the guards shut and braced the doors with metal slats. At the sight of the crystal, everyone at the table stopped what they were doing. Off to the side, an attendant turned a knob on the wall, and the room dimmed.

The man put the crystal on the table, and it balanced upright. Soon, it spun in place like a top, and from the sides, yellow light emerged, rising up like a funnel, and encompassed half the table. The crystal created an image of Kahwin, with a fully detailed 3D map of the continents and oceans. I spotted Starport City, where we lived. It was a little silver speck and so small compared to the continent.

A menu appeared next to the city, with bubbles full of Antediluvian symbols.

That's not English.

I blinked, and the symbols became colors with new symbols, ones I recognized.

I wonder if I did that or if it knows I'm watching it.

It said, "Penal Colony, List of Offenses, Project Cryo Personnel, Further-Read Manifest-Project 1, Operational Site Evaluation Census and Control Operations." Over all of it, it said, "Threat Level Warfare Management Menu."

When I read them, they quickly vanished, and Bylee beamed at me. "You can read them."

This wasn't good. If Zoe found out I was here, looking at this, I bet she'd get angry and confiscate the translator. She could make my life miserable if she wanted to. She could make it so I wouldn't be welcome in the city. I wasn't supposed to be around technology without her. Then again, Lady Kullen could have me killed too, but if I died, Zoe would find out, and crossing Zoe was a bad idea. Zoe had made it clear that if anything happened to me, she'd find out who hurt me and take care of it. I needed her now.

"Read what?" I asked.

"You see?" Lady Kullen said. "I was right. He can read them. His mind has adapted."

"What did the symbols on the map say?" General Vack asked.

"What did what say?" I asked. "I'm confused."

The holographic image of Kahwin vanished, and the crystal remained balanced in place.

"Answer the question, Kol. It's important," the general said.

I reluctantly told him what it said, hoping to get the words right. Some people gasped at my response. "What's Project 1?"

The lights above became brighter, and now everyone looked at me differently.

General Vack motioned to the far end of the table, where a young woman dressed like him rose from her chair and held up the same uniform they wore, one my size. Vack snatched the crystal off the table. "You're going to help us find out."

"How, sir?"

"You're going to join the Iron Guard and learn to be a soldier."

CHAPTER SIX

Arcadia
Captain Scott Moore

A pale man with a grizzled face glared at me, his awestruck eyes locked into mine. He held a sharpened spear against my throat. Not the best of greetings. He grunted to those around him, who, like him, were dressed in animal hides. The seven other men wore necklaces of dull black beads about the size of a marble. They were unarmed, but with that many, any chance I had of fighting them remained slim. One held a torch over me.

I was on my back on a silvery metallic floor that was cold to the touch, and the air smelled rank with body odor and blood. I slowly moved my hand to the tip of the spear, causing him to push harder.

One of them said something to me, and his language flowed like French but with Germanic guttural stops and a Chinese intonation. I understood none of it. They say ninety-five percent of communication is non-verbal, but I bet those that say that had never been put in a situation like this. All I could tell was the man waited for a response, so it must have been a question.

Where were the rest of my crew? Where was the blood smell coming from?

Torchlight caressed the walls off in the distance. I'd made it aboard *Arcadia*. These people had been aboard this ship. So, either they'd been stuck here and stayed here for who knew how long, or they'd boarded it in the past and became trapped. How long had the ship been submerged under the Arctic?

"My... name is Captain Scott Moore."

The more I spoke, the harder the man drove the spear, and he'd soon cut through my skin. I swallowed. If they wanted me to remain quiet, I was more than happy to do that and keep my head, and if there was ever a time I needed the translator behind my ear, it was then. Where had it gone? I remembered it was hot, so if it'd melted, as I had assumed, wouldn't it have killed me?

At the forefront, the man who'd spoken to me inched closer. His set of beads were larger than the others, and he carried himself like a leader. A looped cord attached a baton to his leather cord around his waist, the only indication of technology amongst them. He spoke to me again, and when he realized I didn't understand him, he pushed my assailant's spear aside, letting me breathe.

"Can you understand me?" the man asked in a neutral American accent.

The shock of his voice made me pause. They knew English? "Yes, I can. Where am I? Where are the people I was with?"

"What manner of person are you?"

"May I stand?"

"Yes. Stand."

The man with the spear kept it close to me but backed off slightly.

I rose and dusted myself off, giving me another chance to study my surroundings. Behind them, one of the walls bore pictographs, like those seen from the Paleolithic period. Instead of animals, they'd painted circles and lines to the left of double doors, hallways, and several domes.

The men before me were clean, and I failed to spot any signs of blood on them, and yet the smell permeated the air. Outlines of trees rose behind them in the shadows. Bushes filled with red and purple berries grew here and there. Low to the ground, beady eyes glared at me from the darkest corners. Hundreds of them.

"Where am I? What is this place?" I asked.

"I do not recognize your breed."

Why did I get the impression these people had no idea they were aboard a ship? How many generations would have to pass before people would forget their history in a closed environment? "I'd like to know who I'm talking to. What is your name?"

He looked me up and down and then spoke to those around him. They rushed me, seized my arms, and dragged me by my arms.

"Wait! Where are you taking me?" My heels dragged along the floor as I fought for control, but the cold and the strain of the long hike to the Arctic had drained me, and I needed to preserve what little strength I had left.

The silvery hall narrowed. Oval gaps were cut into the walls, and as we passed one of the holes, I glimpsed another wall behind it, part of the bulkhead. As we proceeded, sets of orange eyes peeked out from the gaps and scurried away from the light. The small creatures had stuffed bits of straw and small sticks like bird's nests where they lived, and the air smelled like my brother's old snake cage he had when we were growing up.

Someone had painted three-dimensional geometric shapes

on the wall with florescent pigment, and the symbols next to them had been smeared or had drastically faded. Signs of violence, scorch marks and dried blood stained our path.

"Let me go. I will walk wherever you are taking me," I said.

Their leader whipped around. "Do not speak."

From out of nowhere, other men appeared around me and one of them poked me in the side with a spear, and with as much dirt and grime covering their faces and arms, it was hard to differentiate between them. They herded me along. The smell of blood began to fade. Someone behind me shoved my head down, making it difficult to see my surroundings. We marched for some time, turning down twisting corridors where distant voices chatted off in the distance.

I began to lose my bearings. As a prisoner, your best chance of escape is in the first few moments in the confusion, but those moments had long since passed. Besides, where would I have gone?

The man who'd addressed me in English must have had a translator behind his ear, the same type of technology as the one I'd had, but how could he speak it? That meant a certain level of sophistication. Their beads were crafted, so they might have machines here. I must have been on the ship. Nothing else made sense.

My face cooled as the air temperature dropped. Off to my left, I could've sworn I heard the sounds of a flute and harp playing over a low thrumming, which came from beneath my feet. Children laughed. Then low whispers aimed in my direction.

"Have you seen others like me?" I asked.

Still, silence. As much as I expected from them at this point. Space Force taught us certain techniques should any of us be captured and tortured.

On they dragged me toward the sound of a steady hiss.

Daring a glance, I caught sight of a massive chamber bathed in purple and blue lights. Rows of benches, like pews, flanked a ten-meter-wide aisle, terminating in an empty metallic sub-chamber the size of a fast-food joint.

"Go inside," their leader said.

"What is this place?" I asked.

"We do not recognize you. Go inside."

They let me go and, while facing me, backed away. I counted sixteen of them. The orange glow of the torch faded, and a dim light emerged from the sub chamber. Reluctantly, I made my way there.

Years ago, before we'd set sail in search of the Antediluvian starship, Lieutenant Erika Banks had discovered a video recording of an Antediluvian woman who stood tall in a one-piece black dress with two gray stripes that went from her neck to her ankles, and her bare feet had two to three rings on each of her toes. Her jet-black hair trailed down her back, and both of her ears were pieced with simple golden hoops.

In the center of the room, the same woman appeared. Everything about her seemed real other than her left knee, which wavered like an on-screen computer glitch. Her bright green eyes swept over my shoulder and then landed on me. "Identify." Unlike the woman's voice in the previous recording, here she sounded distant and cold, though far from robotic.

I held up my palms to the image. "My name is Captain Moore. I have come on a mission of peace."

"New cultural artifact reference. Suit. Environment. Inner garment. Electronic signature. Possible transgression noted. Sequence locked. Prepare for genomic registration."

Before I could reply, my face tingled, and I briefly lost my sight. I'd been scanned. "Who am I speaking with? Can you understand me?"

"Unknown genomic category. Unknown evolutionary

pattern. Potential invasive species. Notification template amended."

"Can you understand me?"

I was met with silence, which gave me time to think of a solution. It spoke English, specifically American English. Either it'd been monitoring our comms or perhaps it'd been monitoring us since our arrival so many years ago. I had to assume the latter, given our ability to monitor communications back on Earth.

"I wish to speak to the captain of this ship."

The woman turned her back to me and bent at the waist, and she reached up and touched the side of the wall with her palm.

"Are you in charge of the ship?"

Then she turned around again and looked past me as if I wasn't there.

"Identify," I said.

Her eyes narrowed, and when she blinked, her gaze swept over to me. "Unknown species communication disabled. Primary functions disabled."

My heart skipped a beat. "Then you *do* hear me. Enable unknown species communication."

Again, there was no response. Had I triggered her response via a menu? Stranger still was her mechanical way of speaking, like an antique computer from the 20th century. Simplified speech.

"List primary functions," I said.

Neon green data streamed slowly down the length of the wall. Antediluvian writing. I'd seen it before. Holographic glyphs rose around her, causing her eyes to change shades of purple and red. "Extensive database corruption. Primary functions disabled."

"Repair database."

"Unable to comply with request."

"Identify self."

"I am Melody 8.932, final build."

Not rushing to judgment, I gave myself a few moments to think of what to say next. "Who designed you?"

"Vincent James Moore."

I pursed my lips. "Are you in communication with Vincent James Moore?"

The image flickered again, her face freezing. The metal beneath my feet turned a soft blue and the streaming data disappeared.

My brother's image appeared as a hologram, replacing the woman. I couldn't see a projector or any device that created it. "Scott? That you?"

"Vincent?"

"Are you okay?" my brother asked.

"So far. Where are you?"

"Chief went to find you, but he hasn't returned. The ship is huge."

"Everyone else okay?"

"More or less. Got a lot of people asking some hard questions."

Hard questions I didn't have answers for; most of all, how could we go to the bridge and take command, if this ship had a bridge at all. I needed to let my prejudices about how Earth built their ships and the way they ran them fall by the wayside and keep an open mind. "Listen, we need to meet up. Where'd Chief go?"

"I'd send you a map, but currently, that's impossible. This is the best we can do. He took a few people with him."

"Armed?"

"Very armed. Took a few extra weapons with them. Do you know where you are?"

"No. Saw what might have been trees and some people in animal skins. Maybe some kind of biodome or enclosed environment. You should be able to track me."

"None of our devices work in here, Scott. You can't be too far from our position, though."

"How is Melody interfacing with the ship? That was her, right? She looked like the same person we saw on the device in the underground city, some kind of generic messenger, I think."

"I have some ideas, but I'd rather share them in person."

"Melody called me an invasive species. Any idea what that means?"

"No clue. Think you can call out to Chief and see if he hears you?"

I called for Chief and waited a few moments for a reply. I could hear footsteps closing in on my position.

"That you?" someone asked.

"Chief?"

"Look who the cat dragged in," Chief said to me.

CHAPTER SEVEN

"Then to the rolling Heaven itself I cried, asking, 'What Lamp had Destiny to guide her little Children stumbling in the Dark?'"
—Omar Khayyam, Rubaiyat

Arcadia
Captain Scott Moore

"Well, hello to you too, Chief," I said. "Glad to see you're still in one piece."

"You?"

"Confused, mainly. Did you get our supplies aboard?"

Chief, Ensign Clark Marston, and an Equinox contractor, Alvin Feazer, stood with me in the middle of a vast ring of trees grown into deck as if the metal floor provided sustenance. Feazer held a torch he said was given to him by one of the people we'd seen. They'd given us fire, an interesting and dangerous decision, because on a starship, an open flame was the last thing you wanted.

Feazer and Clark came from different parts of the States,

Clark from New England, a few klicks south of Augusta, Maine and Feazer from Augusta, Georgia. Clark's complexion matched my own, and he was one of those types that didn't do well in direct sunlight. Feazer's features softened when he smiled and told a funny story. I knew neither of them that well, but they'd both gone through extensive psychological examinations before we set out to find *Arcadia*.

Chief said, "Aye, sir. We managed to pull everything inside before the door closed behind us and we lifted off. Chen is with the others."

"Good. If we've lifted off, are we in space currently?" I asked solemnly.

Feazer nodded. "Another scout party reported seeing stars through the top of one of the domes. Lieutenant Miller said he'd made contact with a tribe that spoke fluent Spanish. Afterward, we heard nothing back from them. They maybe lost."

"Spanish? Where is Lieutenant Miller from?"

"Somewhere in the Southwest, if I remember correctly," Chief said. "Miller spoke with an accent. They know how to talk to us. Not sure how."

I looked at each of the people before me, searching for a reaction. Nothing. Our captors had stripped them of their envirosuits, any equipment they'd had, and left them here. Without a proper light source, I couldn't see much, and something, perhaps the deck itself, deadened our voices. If I'd wanted to call out to Chief earlier, I doubted he would have heard me.

My ears picked up on a metallic droning sound, almost like music, leaving me uneasy. The torch gave off a chemical smell like burning plastic, and the ensign held it away from us, so as to not make our eyes burn.

"Which way back?" I asked.

Chief motioned behind him. "That way, but we'll have to find another way. They're swarming that side."

I took the torch, basking Chief in an orange hue. "They're trying to seal us in. What'd you see on the way here?"

Chief glanced around. "They made us keep our heads down, though I can say for certain we generally stayed in a straight line. One thing, I haven't seen any signs of the Shapers. In fact, we haven't seen much of anything. It feels empty."

"I suspect they've put us in quarantine. There has to be a reason they kept us alive. And, they've got to be communicating with one another over long distances."

"More than likely." Chief wiped perspiration off his upper lip. "But I haven't seen any equipment on them."

I touched the place behind my ear where my translator had been. "They probably don't need them. We can't be sure of anything. Those people might not be people at all. The people who disarmed you, did they speak to you? What did they say?"

Chief crept along beside me as we proceeded into the darkness. "Nothing, sir. Damn savages appeared out of nowhere and put spears to our backs. We didn't hear or see them until it was too late."

"But they haven't hurt anyone yet, have they?" I asked.

"No, sir," the ensign said. "I get the feeling they don't know what to make of us."

"Would you?" We're probably more foreign to them than a grizzly bear in Antarctica. "We've encountered this before when we first arrived on Kahwin."

Something crunched nearby, like a bundle of sticks breaking.

"Hold."

"What was that?" Feazer's eyes widened.

Marston stepped away. "I can't see anything."

There it was again, a distinct crunch, only this time, it'd grown closer. My palms began sweating.

Crunch.

I lowered my voice. "Stay close to the light."

Large black eyes glared at me just beyond the range of the torch, about thirty-five meters away. Thick veins showed through its translucent, pallid skin. It moved on all fours and was the size of a bulldog, and as I waved the torch at it, the creature backed up and then started to flank us like a wolf. Folds of flesh covered his face, and its snout ended in three slits. As it shifted, its claws clicked on the metallic deck.

"What the hell is that thing?" the ensign asked absently.

Chief turned and balled his fist. "More behind us."

"What do they want?" Feazer's voice broke as he craned his neck. He started to quiver.

I put my hand on his shoulder. "Stay close to me. You understand?"

"Aye, sir."

Chief made sure to keep his distance but maneuvered deftly at my side. I'd seen him get into several fistfights before. Having him at my side in that moment brought me some comfort. He unconsciously licked his lips, something he also did before a scuffle. "They look like Shaper creations."

I sped up. When I did, I caught a glimpse of one of them. Its body rippled with muscles, and it lacked hair of any kind. I'd guess it weighed as much as forty-kilos or more; plenty if it could jump and tackle someone. "Stand your ground."

"Captain," Chief said, looking off in the distance.

I couldn't believe my eyes. "That's impossible."

Gisele?

As Gisele slowly ambled toward me, the animals who'd been stalking us backed away. There must have been hundreds of them quietly waiting. Her gaze fell on me, and it was the same one she gave me all those years ago in Paris. The city where I met her. The city where I fell in love with her.

"Nothing is impossible," Gisele said. "Nothing at all."

CHAPTER EIGHT

Kahwin
Kol Washington

"Y ou steal anything or disrespect any member of the staff, I'll break your fingers, starting with your middle one." Hall Captain Washington peered down the length of his nose at me. His massive arms were the size of my legs. A faded bio-mechanical implant tattoo rested on his throat, but the ink was faded. The street artist had made it crooked. His face reminded me of a Gloser bird, the ones with the sharp, white beaks and brown and black feathers.

"Understood."

When he'd told me his last name, a spark of hope popped in me. If I could form a connection with him, my time here might go smoother. "I'm a Washington too."

"Last names don't mean anything here, so don't think we're kin. What do you know about the Iron Guard?"

"Only rumors, sir," I replied. "I hear they kill people some-times for speaking out against the Senate." Who knew? The way some of the drill sergeants spoke about the Senate, it was almost like they didn't like them.

"I've heard that too. Not sure I believe it, but we're a large organization. The Iron Guard does not make mistakes, so if someone died at our hands, I'm sure it had a good reason."

"If last names don't mean anything, what's your first name?"

"Adam," he said reluctantly.

"Isn't that an Earther name?"

"Of course it is."

My room was bigger than what I expected, but it was unlike any room I'd ever slept in. The wooden footlockers were painted dark green, and our bed frames were made of metal and painted the same color. Everything was spotless and symmetrical, and other than the color green, utterly lifeless.

A large window looked out over a place where men and women marched in formation like the city guards used to do. Groups of them practiced out there, and they wore brown jumpsuits with numbers on their backs. Next to a metal gate, a four-wheeled armored car sat idle with a dark matter blaster pointed leisurely in the air.

"I hear you're a fast learner," Adam said.

"Pretty fast, sir."

"Good. They don't give second chances here. Someone tells you to do something once, they expect you to do it and do it right the first time. Keep your nose clean and stay out of trouble and you'll do just fine. Big thing is don't talk about your past here. No one cares. You've been selected by the general for something important, and that's where you need to keep your focus. If someone asks you about your past, tell them I serve the general and they'll leave you alone. I'm sure a few people will test you in the next few days, so remember what I'm telling you."

"Understood. Should I start putting my things away now?"

"That's always a good idea."

I took my bag over to the footlocker. General Vack took everything I had away from me, including my translator. Now, I said before that I was afraid to give it up, but he gave me his word that nothing would happen to it, and I believed him. Besides, he couldn't get inside of it. It took my fingerprint to access it. I'd seen people try to get into it before by using their thumb, and it didn't work, so I wasn't worried. He also said if I needed it back, I could put a request in and get it back within forty hours.

I opened the footlocker. Someone painted a pattern on the inside of the lid, so you could see where to put everything. There was a spot for a rifle that took up the bottom shelf, and places for knives and grenades I'd seen the people from Earth throw. When I arrived, supply issued me bandages, three sets of uniforms, boots, a belt, a holster, and a lot of sealed metal boxes with symbols on the lids. They didn't tell me what they were for, but I assumed they were for my training. At the time, supply hadn't issued me any weapons, so I left those spots empty as I unloaded my bag.

Outside the window, something snapped, and a man cried out in pain.

"You don't need to pay attention to what happens on the parade field. I know who you are. You're that kid who saved Captain Moore. You won't get special treatment here. Fact is, General Vack ordered me to make your life painful for the next six months, and that is what I intend to do."

"Sorry. I was curious."

"Don't be." He motioned around the room. "Inspections happen twice a day around here, and you don't want to be caught with a messy footlocker. You bring any sauce?"

I furrowed my brow. "What's that?"

"Forget it. Chores are written on the board in the common room. You know where that is?"

"Yes, sir. I passed it on the way in."

Hall Captain Adam Washington showed me the latrine, the fighting rooms, supply, and so on, giving me a tour that lasted over an hour. Currently, the cadets were in the field, which meant they were training in the forest out of the city. He said they'd be back in a week, which meant I would be busy cleaning and running errands for him.

"And another thing," he said. "You will call me Hall Captain from now on, or Hall Captain Washington or sir."

"Okay."

"Yes, Hall Captain Washington. Can you hear the change in my pitch when I give a command?"

"Yes, Hall Captain," I said, repeating him.

"Good. When we're in here alone, we will be a bit more casual as we are now, but when I give you an order or when others are around or when we're outside of this room, you will use my full title."

"Yes, sir."

"Good. You caught that."

I aligned my rolled-up socks next to my razor and started to put the boxes where they belonged. A lot of the boxes were the same size, so the only way to tell them apart was by the string of symbols at the top. Without knowing for sure, I assumed they were Antediluvian symbols because of the way the circles were put together. I wanted to ask what they were, but Hall Captain Washington didn't seem to be in the mood for questions like that. I'd learn in time anyway.

"That's upside down." Hall Captain Washington gestured to a box I just set down.

I turned it around. It looked the same on either side to me. "Sir, those people outside. Are they cadets too?"

He sneered. "No. Those are prisoners."

Of course, I had a million follow-up questions, but I didn't need to know right then, and I wanted to make a good first impression. Asking a lot of questions after he'd warned me to keep my nose clean seemed like a bad idea.

"Cadets are going to ask you about Captain Moore and what happened. What are you going to do when they ask you?"

"Keep my mouth shut, sir."

"That's right. You're going to keep your mouth shut. If any cadet asks you those types of questions, you come to me with their names. Is that understood?"

"Yes, sir." I'd heard the people from Earth talk like this, and in school, they made us talk this way too. It came unnaturally to me. By then, I'd unpacked everything.

"After you eat, you will be escorted to General Vack's office. He wants to speak with you."

Once again, I knew better than to ask the obvious question.

He took me to the messplace or messhall or whatever they called it. When I first walked in, my jaw dropped. There must have been over a hundred tables inside with two-person benches spread evenly on each side. Small windows looked out from the cream-color brick walls. Machines with vents blew cool air, making it comfortable.

They made you take a tray and a plate and walk down a long line where they cooked and served whatever food they had for the day. How did they have so much food? Behind the cooks, stacks of crates with English markings took up one side of the room. A couple of armed guards stood watch over the crates with Earth rifles, and they wore Earth suits too. Supposedly, they could see and hear like the Shapers with their helmets on. They glanced over at me for a moment and that was it.

The food tasted weird and was hard to swallow, but I used water to get it down. I called it Space Force food. If that were true, how did they have so much? The Earth ship exploded over eight years ago. Surely, with this many people, they would have run out by then. They also made me use a fork and spoon, two "utensils" I hate. They should call them tools, instead. Why did English use so many words? There was no reason to use these things. I had two perfectly good hands, and I'd eaten with them my whole life.

At that moment, I knew I'd hate this place and the stupid rules they set. Why did I agree to this in the first place? It was a bad idea.

After I ate, Adam took me to level ten to meet with General Vack. Before the elevator doors opened, he made me put on a cloth around my eyes, so I couldn't see. Oh, and they call that piece of cloth over your eyes a "blindfold," but that's got to be one of the worst English words I'd ever heard. After that, he made me sit in a cushioned chair. Everything got real quiet then, and all the sound went away. I wasn't even sure I was moving until the hall captain removed the blindfold from over my eyes.

General Vack sat behind a curved stone studying me. A bowl of greasy chicken bones sat on his right, along with a rag he'd been using to clean his fingers. Beside him, a hound with black fur and brown spots whimpered as Vack enjoyed another small bird leg. He tossed some gristle down, and the dog lapped it up before it hit the ground. Finally, he dismissed the hall captain, and we were alone.

"How do you like the facility?" Vack asked.

"It's big, sir. Sir, may I ask you a question?"

"Go ahead, Cadet."

I cleared my throat. "Sir, does Captain Moore know about this place?"

"Captain Moore and the Earthers spent little time in the city after they killed the Shapers. They know only what we allowed them to see."

"Yes, sir."

"Did Hall Captain Washington advise you about other cadets asking you questions about your past?"

"Yes, sir. I promised I'd keep my mouth shut." And I would. If there was one thing I'd learned about being around important people, it was that when someone told you something and ordered you to stay quiet, you did.

"Good. Good. Since I've brought it up, you must know how important that is. Here in the Iron Guard, you start new. You have no past."

"I don't understand, sir."

"A rule of the Iron Guard. You will learn them in time. Did you have any reactions to the injection?"

"A little soreness, sir."

"That's to be expected."

"What was it for, sir?"

"The Earth medics call it gene therapy. Do you remember when they gave the first injections and said you will live longer than before?"

"Yes, sir."

His calming voice put me at ease. "It is something along those lines." He rubbed the side of his jaw. "I've read several reports about you. You outperformed most of your peers. I understood you underwent a psychological exam?"

"Which test was that, General?" I'd taken so many, they bled into one another. The Earthers liked their tests. In my tribe, you were given three tests, and once you completed them, you were accepted as an adult. Most people passed them, and those that failed didn't live to tell us about it.

"The interview where you were asked how you would respond to various situations."

"Yes, sir. I thought it was hard to think of what to do sometimes. It seemed like some of the question didn't have a correct answer."

"It was a way to find out the kind of person you are, and I was quite pleased with how you answered them." General Vack glanced behind me at something and turned to me. "I think you'll find this place and way of life to your liking once you get used to it."

"Thank you, sir. I consider it an honor to be here. I wanted to know if you knew where my mother was."

The general's lips went tight, and he stared right through me. "The *Iron Guard* is your family now."

My hands began to sweat, and I gathered my strength. "Sir, she's my mother."

"Yes. She is being taken care of. The Iron Guard protects its members' extended family. You needn't worry or concern yourself about her."

His answer left me empty and cold. Somewhere deep inside me, I knew this would be the only time I'd speak to the general alone, and after this, whatever awaited me here would happen. "Sir, when I looked at the crystal, back at Lady Kullen's house, people said I was the one. What did they mean?"

"Show me your hand."

I did, and he turned it so my palm would face upward.

"Do you see these lines?"

"Yes, sir."

"Open your other hand and look at it. See how the lines are different?"

I'd never really looked before, but now that he mentioned it, he was right.

"Now, look at the tips of your fingers up in the light. See the ridges there and the lines?"

"Is there something wrong with my skin, sir?"

"No. Here. Now look at my hands. What do you see?"

When he showed them to me, I noticed his hand had more scars. Otherwise, I saw nothing different about us.

"I'm not sure, sir."

"Look at the lines. See yours? Notice how they're different?"

"Yes, sir. I see that now."

He rummaged through his desk and pulled out a computer tablet. I recognized the single claw mark surrounded by a circle too, which marked the captain's clan: Space Force. He played with it for a while and plugged a long cord into the back before it would turn on.

"It looks like a translator, sir."

After a few minutes, he made a light picture with it called a hologram, which showed my face and a swirling object with the letters ATGC next to little boxes in English. "Just like the tips of our fingers are different and the lines in our hands are different, each one of us is different too. There is something inside of us the Earthers say is DNA, which is your blueprint."

I gave him a confused look, but it was hard to look away from the light picture. "When Captain Moore's doctors gave us those shots, I remembered them talking about it."

"That's correct. Your blueprint is a word the Earthers call 'genetics.' Their genetics are different than ours, but only slightly."

"They're old, like you, sir."

He nodded. "My genetics are different than yours, Kol. I do not come from Kahwin. That is why I'm old."

"If you don't come from Kahwin, where do you come from?"

Slowly, he tilted his neck back and gazed at the ceiling. "From far away, like many others in the Iron Guard." He let out a long sigh and showed me a new light picture with an identical spiral. All the words were in English, though. "When you entered Temple City and explored that place with the captain, the city *smelled* your DNA. You are therefore quite the prize, young Kol."

"I don't understand, sir."

"No, you wouldn't. Not yet. Nevertheless, that is why you are here and not with Lady Kullen. Who knows what she would force you to do."

"I thought this was her idea, sir."

"To kidnap you? Yes, that was her idea, but to bring you here and enlist you in the Iron Guard was *my* decision. We will accelerate your learning and training and push you harder than you've ever been pushed. When you have completed your training, that is when we will pursue our new objectives. *We* will find Project 1. I'm going to make you a rich man, Kol. Richer than anything you have ever imagined."

"I like the idea of being rich, sir. Very much."

"I figured you would."

CHAPTER NINE

Kahwin
Kol Washington

In the Iron Guard Academy, the day began with the drill sergeants lining us up on the parade field in a formation like an Earther platoon. The drill sergeant stood in front of us, his eyes cold and calculating, searching for any sign of weakness among us. I wanted to know exactly where in the city we were. Maybe we weren't in the city after all?

"Attention!" the drill sergeant barked.

We all snapped to attention, our spines straight as a board.

"Today, we begin your journey toward becoming true soldiers and defenders of our world. Here in the Iron Guard, you will learn discipline and the necessity of listening. We do things right the first time at the Academy. Failure in our line of work will cost you your life. As of now, your lives belong to the Guard, and I intend to mold you into warriors worthy of wearing the uniform."

He paced in front of us, his boots thudding against the ground with each step. "You will learn the commands of the

Earthers. You will march, you will drill, and if necessary, you will die. It is a great honor to give one's life for the Iron Guard."

His voice was harsh and unforgiving, like the cold wind whipping across the parade field.

"Left face!" he commanded, and we all turned sharply to the left. "Forward march!"

As we marched in unison, a strange fear gripped me. This wasn't the life I'd envisioned for myself, but I'd make the most of it. General Vack promised me riches, and I was telling the truth about wanting to be rich. I'd make General Vack proud.

The drill sergeant continued to shout orders at us, his voice never wavering. "Eyes front! Heads up! Shoulders back! Chest out! You will march like the soldiers you are meant to be!"

A snarky cadet named Marcus muttered under his breath, "You'd think we were learning to dance, not fight."

The drill sergeant's ears picked up the comment instantly. He stormed over to Marcus. "What did you just say, Cadet?"

Marcus hesitated. "I said, you'd think we were learning to dance, not fight, sir."

The drill sergeant's eyes narrowed. "Do you think this is a joke, Cadet?"

"No, sir," Marcus replied smugly.

The drill sergeant grabbed Marcus by the collar and yanked him out of formation. "You clearly do not understand the gravity of your situation. I will teach it to you. We do not tolerate insubordination." He glanced over at a pair of guards eyeing us closely, and they marched over to us. He turned to Marcus. "You will be sent to the Punishment Farm."

A shudder ran through the ranks at the mention of the Farm. It was a place we'd all heard the drill sergeants dished out corporal punishment in the harshest ways imaginable. Skin flaying. Burning. Scalding. Cutting. That sort of thing.

As Marcus was dragged away, the drill sergeant turned back

to the rest of us. "Let that be a lesson to you all. Here, there is no place for those who cannot follow orders. If you refuse to adapt, I *willbreak* you."

I swallowed hard. Everything I thought I knew about pain was about to change. This wasn't what I was expecting.

The first few weeks of basic training pushed me to my limits. I'd never been so sore in all my life. Part of me liked it. The discipline. The hard work. The drill sergeant said it would be the best times of our lives, and at the time, I didn't believe him for a second. After a few weeks, I started to think he may have been right.

Sleep became a luxury, and so did a decent meal. The drill sergeant often woke us up in the dead of night for surprise inspections, and when someone messed up their locker or their bunk, they "smoked" us for hours. Push-ups. Burpies. These evil exercises called Mountain Climbers and stair steppers. They never stopped. We were constantly on edge, anticipating the next thing to go wrong. The exhaustion weighed on me, but I could feel myself getting stronger by the day.

Still, why did they adopt these Earther ways? Would the Senate approve of this? What would Captain Moore think of the Iron Guard and how they ran things?

What food they gave us was scarce, barely enough to stop our stomachs from growling.

My muscles ached from the strain.

I often thought of my mother, Paysha, and my clan. I wondered what would happen if I went back to them and taught them everything I was learning. Sometimes, I daydreamed of being the drill sergeant. Wouldn't it be fun to shout like that for a while? I thought it would. Making my mother proud gave me the motivation to push forward when I wanted to quit.

Specialists taught us hand-to-hand combat, which

involved grappling in the dirt and learning to use our hands and feet as weapons. It seemed a little awkward. Why not just use a knife and be done with it? The techniques were designed to incapacitate or kill, and I ended up almost breaking my wrist.

We were drilled on tactics and studied maps, learned about troop movements and formations, and practiced coordinating attacks and defenses. All of it seemed natural. The mental part of training was just as demanding as the physical, and they started to give us some decent chow for once.

After a morning of a grueling two-hour run with boots and a pack loaded with bricks, one of the cadets complained a little too much. Somehow word got out. I never saw him again. Every so often, the sound of gunfire rattled off the buildings. I think all of us knew what might have been happening, but all of us were too scared to say anything.

The drill sergeant's voice became the soundtrack of my life, echoing in my head even when he wasn't around.

Ten failed so far. The lack of sleep and food drove them crazy. I heard all of them were sent to the Punishment Farm. I bet you can guess what happened to them.

One particular day, the drill sergeant gathered us in the bay to give one of his speeches. He scanned our faces, taking in the sweat clinging to our skin.

"Cadets," the drill sergeant began, "you are here to become the embodiment of the Iron Guard. Only the strong survive here. In times of war, you will wish I was harsher." The drill sergeant's gaze swung my way, and his eyes lingered on me. "Although the Earthers have come to free us from the Shapers, our struggle to maintain order begins with all of you, for if you are unwilling to die for the Academy, then you are no better than those who enslaved us and gorged on our flesh. How many of you understand why you are here?"

I raised my hand, and for a second, I thought he'd call on me.

"To serve the Senate?" one of cadets asked behind me.

The room fell silent, and the drill sergeant set his jaw. "Do not speak of the Senate here. Do I make myself clear?"

"Aye, drill sergeant," he replied.

No one could answer why we were here, and although my original thought was that it had to do with Project 1, by the end of his long lecture, I wasn't so sure. A few times, some of the guys would whisper to each other but never to me. No one said a word to me other than what was necessary.

I missed the city life. Even the stupid arm wrestling. I missed the way I could sleep whenever I wanted and the taste of beer. It was the first time I felt like I didn't belong.

Over the next three weeks, we were introduced to rifleman training. Now, if there was one thing I liked about training, it was shooting. Our first week focused on the MAS-5, a laser rifle known for its Earther reputation. I'd heard someone in Equinox donated them to us. The lightweight weapon felt solid in my hands. The drill sergeant spent hours teaching us the inner workings of the rifle, ceaselessly hammering into our heads the importance of how to take care of it.

When we finally took the MAS-5 to the firing range, I discovered I had a gift for marksmanship. My consistently accurate shots impressed everyone around me. The second week brought a new weapon: the dark matter rifle. Unlike the MAS-5, it was designed to affect only living tissue, leaving the environment around the target untouched. The science behind it—well, they tried to explain it, but if you can understand what the manipulation of dark matter particles to create a lethal force means, you're smarter than I am.

Our third week introduced us to grenades, more tactical maneuvering, and a whole lot of singing. I started to like it all.

CHAPTER TEN

Arcadia
Captain Scott Moore

Ensign Marston lurched forward and stuck his arm between the image and me. "Captain?"

Time slowed for me. What was it about Gisele that drove me insane? The way we kissed? The way the sun fell on her hair during a sunset? The way she ate those grapes while we explored the countryside one summer? Love shouldn't hurt that much, but it does. It should come with a warning.

How had the ship known to create her, and what exactly was she? Her form became more real as each second ticked by, and the details around her bright blue eyes became more crisp.

It'd read my mind somehow. Then it knew about our plight and why we were here. It likely knew everything that I'd thought about, probably since I'd boarded the ship.

Somehow, I think this ship healed me too. Simply by entering. Where was Doc? It would be good for him to check me over again.

What about those with me? Had it read their minds as well?

If so, then whatever my crew had been thinking about would also be known by the machine or the AI. I'd need to concentrate and not think of anything other than my mission.

The image came to a stop a few meters from me and bowed by putting her hands on her thighs and lowering her head slightly. After raising up, she gave me the most precious smile and my sense of paranoia kicked in.

I held up my palm as my pulse thundered in my neck. "Hello. My name is Captain Scott Moore."

"Hello, Captain Scott Moore. It is a pleasure to meet you." Gisele spoke exactly the way she did when I last saw her, the same lovely French accent that made me love her that much more.

"What are you?" I asked.

"I am the projected consciousness of a previous lover by the name of Gisele Pinchon. I exist to provide you with aid."

"I see." Though she shared the appearance of Gisele, her intonation was flat. "Have you read my mind?"

She looked down for a moment. "I... I don't understand your question. Question. I don't understand your question. Did you ask me something, something?"

Gisele's stutter made me pause. "Who or what created you?"

She slid her foot a little closer, and the light from our torch hit her just right. "Would you care to follow me? Follow? The animals around us... are still nervous about my appearance, but soon they will test us, and I... I cannot guarantee your safety. Safety."

I turned to my crew. "Stay sharp. Chief, you pick up the rear. Feazer, stay close to me. If any of you see one of them get a little too close, raise your voice at them."

"That will only make them more aggressive," Gisele said. "This way. They will not follow us for long."

We followed her through the trees, where the roots grew into the metallic hull and reached up out of sight. An aura glowed around her like a halo, like a projection not quite perfected. The light around her caused the surrounding area to slowly light up. Every so often, she'd throw her hand off to the side, and an area of the forest would appear, the light as bright as a full moon. When she did, hosts of furry creatures, a mixture between a squirrel and a mouse with long bushy tails, froze in place and then bolted away on all fours.

The forest stretched along symmetrical lines, creating paths and roads. An entire ecosystem thriving after all this time under water without sunlight and balanced in such a way as to exist, perhaps, in perpetuity.

We marched for roughly five minutes. I kept track of roughly where the door was that led to Vincent and the rest of my crew, but with the trees and the winding paths, the task became nearly impossible.

I called her to stop. "If you've read my mind, you'd know this is the wrong way I need to go."

Gisele slowed but continued walking. "You will not last long without identity beads. The ship does not recognize you. Please, follow me. We cannot remain still."

Howls sounded behind us like a pack of Nevada coyotes, and the hairs on the back of my neck rose. We needed weapons, and after carrying my MAS-5 with me for the past few years, I felt naked without it.

"Quickly." Gisele sped up, first taking longer strides then breaking into a jog.

"Is there something we should know about?" I asked quietly.

"Hurry."

We ran this way for some time. My lungs burned, but you can tune out pain with enough practice. I'd been through worse and needed to keep my wits. We followed a path bordered by green, leafy brush and trees with pine needles the width of my thumb and as long as my index finger. Every once in a while, I flicked a glance over my shoulder. Beady red eyes glowered back at me beneath the trees' shadows, their forms concealed in the dim.

Marston started to fall behind until Chief grabbed his arm. "How much further?"

"Up ahead," Gisele said.

Part of the bulkhead rose at a flat angle with a faded red square. In it, I spied what appeared to be a hatch, with a handle inside of a recessed panel. Our path led directly there.

Gisele reached it first and yanked the handle. The hatch door swung open, revealing a sloping passage, which led down further into the ship. It was completely dark, and without a ladder, I wasn't sure how to get down. "Go inside and you will be safe."

Chief huffed; his words caught between deep inhales. "You want us to jump?"

Creatures barked all around us. Up in the trees, the shadows rippled with movement, and a feral stench fouled the air.

Gisele gestured into the passage, her eyes filled with fright. "A gravity lift will lower you down to a moderate cafe. Now, you must hurry."

What did she mean by a moderate cafe? She'd begun to lose her old French accent for a second. Was she processing our language?

Feazer's face brightened as he gazed out into the encroaching darkness and whatever beings lurked there. "Okay. I'll go first. Wish me luck." He slowly stuck his head into the hole. "There's a force here holding me up."

"That's the gravity elevator. Go," Gisele repeated.

"Okay, let's go," I said.

One by one, we climbed into the hold.

"There's nothing down there but air," Feazer said.

Gisele looked down at us. "An antigrav field sits at the bottom of the staircase."

Finally, we reached the bottom of the ladder and landed on an invisible force holding us aloft. Without a way to see the edge, we huddled together and waited. When I looked at my feet, I could see specks of light below us.

"I will see you soon, Captain." Gisele cranked a handle and sealed the hatch. When she did, soft blue illumination glowed around us. The light took on the shape of a platform with handrails set shortly under my collarbone. Twenty people or so could fit on it.

As we descended, all of us looked down to where the lift would eventually stop. At the bottom, the rest of my crew waited patiently for us to reach them. They'd been stripped of their belongings and wore the same skin-tight thermal suit the rest of us did. A crate marked with the Space Force logo sat near them, and they'd torn into the rations and ate some of it. Our water purifier stood next to it. Melody was nowhere to be seen.

An orb the size of a compact car hovered above them, which provided plenty of light. The empty room contained only a single door without a means to open it from this side.

"I don't understand," Chief said. "How did they get here? We must have travelled at least a kilometer from their position."

Feazer reached out and touched the rail. "Where's the rest of our supplies?"

Vincent waved up at me. "It found you. Stay on the lift. It's the only way out of here."

Several members of my crew gathered at the bottom and waited for the lift to hit the bottom. A force like an invisible wall pushed all of us out at the same time, and I was launched into the waiting arms of an ensign, who stopped me from falling face first.

"Go! Go!" the others cried. They attempted to clamber onto the lift, but as they did, that same force swatted them aside. The lift ascended until it disappeared, the light quickly extinguished.

Doc approached me and put his arms behind his back. "Sir."

"Report," I said.

Erika and Vincent brought us over some protein bars, a fruit cup, and a Thermos full of water. Space Force food was some of the best, and I greedily accepted what they brought.

"It appears we've collectively fallen into a rat trap," Vincent said.

"Where's Melody? You said you connected it with the ship's AI."

My brother frowned and shook his head. "I haven't spoken with you since we boarded the ship."

I did a double take, not fully understanding how any of this was possible. "Then who was speaking to me?"

The door across from us opened. Gisele stepped out wearing a Space Force uniform, the navy blue going well with her pale complexion. Her hair was tied back and made to conform with regulations.

"I was, Scott." Gisele gave a sweeping motion to the door. "If you'll come with me, we have much to discuss."

CHAPTER ELEVEN

Arcadia
Captain Scott Moore

Have you ever been so turned around, you don't know which way is up? Zero-G is a lot like that. Going inside a decent simulator for the first time, you'll experience vertigo, and it'll make your head spin. Love also does that to a person.

The first time I knew I was in love, I was reading a 1972 copy of Charles Dicken's *A Tale of Two Cities*, its pages yellowed and brittle. I picked it up at one of the local markets close to the Louvre and used it to practice my French. I'd read two chapters and not realized it. My thoughts stayed with Gisele, a woman I barely knew but couldn't get out of my mind. Why her in particular? We'd only just met, and everything about her intrigued me. She laughed at my jokes. She corrected my dubious French pronunciation. Her smell, her kiss made me forget myself.

You can spend a lifetime with someone if you pack every waking moment with that person in a short amount of time. At least, it feels like that.

This creation of Gisele, who beckoned me, brought up those old feelings I'd left behind when I'd joined Space Force. My real wife was the USS *Atlanta*, and I was a widow. What was the woman before me? She appeared to be as real as my crew around me.

"I want to speak to your captain," I said, my feet firmly planted.

"If you will follow me, I will introduce you."

I turned to Chief. "If I'm not back in an hour's time, you know what to do."

"Aye, Captain."

"You can't go with... *it*," Vincent said.

"What choice do I have?"

Gisele led me through the door, and it sealed shut behind me with a click. A short hallway led to a similar door. When we'd explored the ruins in Kahwin, we'd found rooms devoid of decoration, chambers with the barest of essentials, and empty homes made of carbonized steel crafted without welds.

"How did you reappear down there when you didn't climb the ladder?" I asked.

"What do you mean?"

"You told us to climb the ladder and mentioned a moderate café. Remember?"

"I didn't say that."

"You didn't?"

"Why would I say a thing like that? I've been waiting down there for you to show up."

Perhaps I'd seen a hologram. Or a precursor to an experiment unfolding before me.

The door whisked open, and I found myself in a room the size of a large office. Two blocks of stone sat in the center of the room, looking as out of place as a Hilton in a third world country.

"Would you care to sit down?"

Colors washed across the walls, staining white. A desk appeared in front of one of the stones, and the contents of my desk on the USS *Atlanta* appeared on its surface. I'd longed to see a picture of my sister and her son, and there it was, in perfect detail. New details started to appear. My awards hanging on the wall. A coffee machine, and when that appeared, so did the smell of percolating coffee, causing my mouth to water.

She sat in a chair facing the desk and crossed her legs. "Whatever questions you have, I will try to answer, but for every question you ask, I will ask one as well."

"Questions." I walked to the coffee pot and touched the side. Warm. How was that possible? Then again, how was any of it possible? I searched the desk. All my belongings were there. Back on *Atlanta*, I maintained a safe and a liquor cabinet. Both were missing, as was my tablet and computer. How convenient. "I wish to speak to your captain."

"What do you think he would say?" She curled her lips. "You don't even know if he's human."

Her comment caught me off-guard. She had a point, and I made sure to frame my words carefully to avoid asking her any questions. "You must be a liaison."

"Is that a question?"

I smirked. "You didn't bring me here to play word games. Call it a polite exchange of information."

"You should try the coffee. I think you'd be impressed."

"Perhaps. I suppose if you wanted to poison me, you'd have done so already." I glanced around the room. "If you made this to make me feel more comfortable, I'm afraid it's having the opposite effect."

We shared a moment, she and I, looking at each other like we once did. A lump formed in my throat, and I swallowed, bitter at how accurately the woman in front of me had been created. The eye contact lasted a brief few seconds. Emotions I'd not felt for years coursed through my veins and filled my heart. I hated it, the falseness of them.

"I missed you," she whispered in French.

"You're not who you appear to be. Whatever game this is, please stop."

She folded her hands in her lap, her cheeks flushed. "This is no game."

"Then tell me who you are."

"Gisele Pinchon. The last time I saw you, you wore a short-sleeved black shirt and jeans with a ketchup stain on one of the knees. You hadn't shaved for a few days, and your stubble made you look like an actor."

I narrowed my eyes. "Gisele had a good memory. Seeing as you are not her and you'll likely know I won't provide you with answers I'm not prepared to give, why don't you and I skip to the chase?"

"I won't count that question against you." She laughed like she used to. "If you don't try the coffee, I'll be disappointed." Gisele put two fingers on her wrist. "If you touched me, you'd feel my skin. If you took my pulse, you'd find it. If you scanned me with one of *Atlanta*'s bioscanners, you'd see that I am human. Isn't that enough?"

If I cut her, would she not bleed? "You and I both know you are not her. If you were, you wouldn't have any knowledge of the ship."

She knitted her brow. "You're right. I don't understand it either. I want to help you with what I can, but you're making it difficult." She blinked and looked around the room, confused, and then put her hand up to her mouth. "How did I get here? Scott, is that you?"

"Yes, it's me."

Tears lurked behind her glossy stare like she'd been sleeping, and she nervously shuffled her fingers. "Is everything going to be okay?"

I hated seeing her this way, but I'd been exposed to too many simulations for me to buy into the idea she was nothing more than a test. An intelligence that lured me into a false sense of security. I shouldn't have trusted her in the first place. What about Vincent? Chief? Were they any more real than she was? How would I know?

Why this sudden change, like she'd been woken up from a dream?

"Everything's going to be fine. What was the last thing you remember?" I asked.

"After I said goodbye to you in the taxi, I remember waking up here in this... chair." She touched the stone and quickly pulled her hand away. "Wait a minute. I know why I'm here. I'm here to help you."

"Did you bring the supplies to my crew?"

"No, I didn't do that." She winced and pushed her eyes shut. "I hear several... voices in my head. Hurts. Didn't... didn't we agree that if you asked a question and I answered it, I get to ask you one back?"

"I never agreed to that but go ahead."

"A voice in my head is telling me to ask you what you want, and another voice is answering, telling it that you're here to find this thing you call *Arcadia* and return to Earth. It says there was a famine."

"Those voices in your head, do they have names?"

"What are these voices?"

"Did you read my mind?"

She waved the idea away. "No, of course not."

"Which voice told you to say that?"

"I'm saying it." She rubbed her temple. "How long have I been in this room? Where are we?"

"You said voices. Who are they?"

"One is Melody, I think. I... I don't know. Help me. I think there's something wrong with me."

"Stay with me. I'll find out for the both of us. Now, this voice, ask her if she has contacted another voice."

"Melody says a remote connection has been established and the tertiary security protocols have been breached. She wants to talk to Vincent as soon as possible."

Our AI... lived. That would mean *Arcadia* would know all there was to know about Earth, its location, our customs, our problems, and our lack of interplanetary defenses.

This being before me served as a gateway, like an intercessory angel standing in the way between God and me. "Tell Melody I think that would be an excellent idea, and if she's got any idea on how to facilitate that, she should go ahead and do it. Is there any way I can speak to other voice directly?"

Gisele paused and then nodded. "She told me the link she has established with Melody is allowing her to speak. Without Melody, the other voice will be unable to communicate with you. Sometimes, it is hard for me to understand." As she tapped her foot, she took in a deep breath. "Melody is a computer. She's an AI, isn't she?" Before I could respond, she stood and stumbled backward. "How am I hearing these voices? Where the hell am I?"

"It's okay. It's okay. Stay with me."

She grabbed the side of the desk. "Is this your office? How'd I get here?"

"It's okay. There's no reason to be afraid. Everything is going to be okay. We just have to figure a few things out."

Although she acted exactly like Gisele, what she was doing now might have been a test, seeing how I'd react. Testing my

87

empathy, my responses. It would have been easy to succumb to the temptation to treat her as who she resembled.

What was happening now reminded me a lot of what happened when I first met Zoe. Back then, she appeared to us as a metallic sphere and gradually became more and more human-like as time went on. One day, Erika implied it might have been an act, and ever since then, I'd watched Zoe more closely. However, if you'd scanned Zoe, you would have seen she was an android immediately, if she let you scan her at all. Why did I get the feeling that if I scanned Gisele, she would register as human?

"Are you feeling any better?" I asked, not wanting to push her too much. If what she said was true about the communication link between Melody and the ship, it seemed causing Gisele to question her reality was having a detrimental effect.

"I'd feel better if I knew how I got here and what this place was." She knocked on the wall and stood close to the door. "Does this lead out?"

I looked across my desk at her. "It would take us back to where we came. Can you open it?"

She tried to force it open but was unable to find a way to grip it correctly. Knowing how starship doors worked, I knew she wouldn't open it that way. After looking for a sensor and failing to find one, she focused on the door. Nothing happened. "Can you?"

"No, but it's okay. Sit back down."

"*Arcadia.*"

"What's that?"

"The other voice is called *Arcadia.*" She turned and sat back on the stone.

Chief had wanted to call the ship we searched for *Arcadia.* So we did. The ship must have overheard our radio transmissions at some point. What else had it overheard?

I tested the chair behind the desk and took my place. It felt exactly like my old chair, and when I looked for the little tear in the stitching in the right armrest, I found it. "Tell *Arcadia* that it's done a great job of duplicating my office, but my safe is missing."

When I looked up, she held a tablet that wasn't there before. "Will this help?"

"I think so. Mind if I see it?"

She handed the tablet to me, and a swarthy man with butterscotch eyes and a squared jaw scowled at me on the screen. Antediluvian symbols scrolled to the left of his image, and although his lips moved, the device remained silent. When I tried to bring up the tablet's menu, my touch had no effect. Maybe *Arcadia* couldn't duplicate it correctly.

Duplication. During our first encounter with the Shapers, we'd discovered a machine capable of replicating items via a scanner and a kind of molecular printer, technology well in advance of anything we'd accomplished back home. At the time, it proved incapable of copying organic matter. So, what was Gisele, and where was the molecular printer inside this room?

I looked at my chair, which was once a stone block. The stones. Perhaps *Arcadia* had obfuscated the appearance of their printer. It would explain how a tablet appeared in her hand. I was afraid to ask her how it appeared, fearing another existential crisis. However, her chair, as it were, remained a stone.

"Gisele, can you understand what these symbols mean? Also, do you know who this man is?" I showed her the screen.

"This is *Arcadia*, the voice in my head. You said you wanted to speak with him." She took the tablet from me and touched the man's forehead. "I believe he wants to speak privately with you now. He will speak to you when I leave." As she set the tablet on my desk, the symbols crackled and then morphed into English. She rose and glanced at the door. "I should go."

I gestured to where she sat, not wanting her to leave. Was this part of a test as well? "No, stay. Who knows? I might need you to translate something for me." My lame excuse fell flat, of course. What if I never saw her again? I shouldn't have thought that way. What a mistake.

"He wants me to leave. I will wait outside the door for you."

As she started toward the door, I got up and went to intercept her. "You don't have to leave."

"I'll be outside." The entrance slid open. "When you're done, I'll be waiting for you."

I don't know why I let her leave. Weakness, maybe.

What did I expect? A robotic greeting? Antediluvians greeting me with open arms? *Welcome aboard, stranger from Earth. Please bring you and your crew aboard and hijack our ship and bring it to Earth. Don't worry; we don't have a problem sharing. It's only on the other side of the galaxy. Feel free to abduct us.*

I had to think of Gisele as nothing more than an inanimate object designed to sway my emotions, no different than an advertiser or a holo. But it wasn't what I wanted. I wanted her the moment I saw her, just like I did when I met her the first time. Nothing had changed, and it should have; another reason to suggest whatever created her lacked a full understanding of human relationships.

The door opened again, and the man on the screen, the face of *Arcadia*, stepped into the room dressed in a Space Force uniform. He stood roughly my height with a face of granite usually reserved for those who've seen the ugly side of humanity. He'd grown white, though the faintest streaks of dark hair still edged through his short crew cut. A stylized rank clung to his shoulders, and a neat row of silver buttons with the Space Force logo ran from just below his right shoulder down to his waist. Rows of colorful ribbons were pinned to his breast, all of which I'd never seen before. His name appeared on a coppery name badge below his ribbons. Miuykal.

He studied me for a moment and then put his hands behind his back. "Hello." His tenor voice carried through the room like silk.

"Hello. My name is Captain Moore. Do you speak for this ship?"

"In a manner of speaking. You may call me Miuykal."

His name sounded faintly Middle Eastern, a variation to the name Michael to my Western ears.

"I wish to speak to the captain." My request was met with stubborn silence. "Who is in command?"

"I have not come to answer your questions but rather to negotiate." He picked up the tablet and reconfigured the screen to show an access port into Melody's data nodes, which had shut off when *Atlanta*'s jumpdrive exploded years ago. "Do you speak on the behalf of your people?"

"Yes."

"Do you speak on the behalf of *all* of your people, including the people from your home world, Earth?"

I didn't like the sound of that. "I represent only those who followed me into your ship and those I've left behind on Kahwin. We've left Kahwin, haven't we?"

The man nodded thoughtfully. "Yes, we have. Who speaks for your world?"

"No one speaks for our world as a whole. If we've left, I suppose you'll want to tell me where we're headed."

"A place where *Arcadia* can undergo a refit. Do not worry, Captain. All is as it should be." He looked me up and down. "We suspected someone would eventually find the ship, but I'm surprised it was you. Nevertheless, you have done well."

"I'd like some answers. First of all…"

Miuykal raised his right hand like a gun and pointed it toward the ceiling. "If no one speaks for your world, how did you arrive on Kahwin?"

He didn't know. How long had the ship been monitoring us, I wondered. "An accident brought us here," I said, resisting the temptation to explain further. "You said you wished to negotiate. It would help if you would explain why you forced our crew into that room over there. To study us?"

He walked to the center of the desk and stood across from me. "I invited you onto my ship because you have shown a propensity for violence. You not only eliminated the Shapers on Kahwin, you confronted *Allo Quishar*, the Fifth Keeper of the Circle. Yet, when I sent creatures to confront you, you neither attacked them nor sought to communicate with them. Why?"

"You confiscated our weapons if I'm not mistaken. And our suits."

"Would you like them back?"

"Yes, I would. We need everything you've taken from us."

"In time." He set the tablet down, and the screen went blank. "Grant me access into Melody's database to understand your species better."

Gisele said she was in communication with Melody, so if that were true, why didn't this man have access to it? Something wasn't adding up.

"Are we negotiating now?" The last thing I'd ever do would be to allow this ship unfettered access to Melody, but it was the only bargaining chip I held. "It would help if I knew more about you and the ship."

"You stand aboard the last surviving warship of the Regency. At the Battle of Kilphin, I was blessed by war."

An image of the ship behind a field of stars glowed on the tablet, its magnificence breathtaking. The ship remained still while the background changed. Specks of light blazed around

Arcadia. Bursts of light like fireworks exploded around her. An orange sun painted the scene as the ship sent volleys of missiles and unloaded weapon batteries against a cluster of enemy ships headed toward its starboard bow.

"My masters drove us to conquer the weak." The screen bled white, and a series of Antediluvian icons blistered on the screen. "Hundreds of worlds submitted to the Regency, then thousands fell under our domain."

A map of dots connected by lines appeared above the tablet, its bluish tint rippling like a stone thrown into a still body of water. One of the dots became white, and one by one, the others became white too. It panned out, showing a spiral galaxy. The Milky Way. When I started to get a feel for the scale of what was being represented, the image vanished.

I took a deep breath, not realizing I'd been holding it. What did I just see? "Those are worlds populated by humans?"

"That definition will suffice."

The thought of arriving back on Earth on *Arcadia* made my head hurt. The way it spoke about itself, about war, maybe bringing it back wasn't necessarily a good idea.

"The Keepers and their Shaper slaves dismantled the Regency during the Heaven War." He gave a hint of a frown. "This ship sustained heavy damage and flew to Kahwin for repairs. Your translator triggered a dormant resonance communication channel. From there, I observed a high probability of human civilization reemerging in some form. After scanning Kahwin's atmosphere, that conclusion proved false. If not for your translator, I would have remained in slumber."

"That was you talking to me out on the tundra." I touched the spot behind my ear where it'd been fused to my skin for the past few years. It was now gone. At least it didn't burn anymore.

"I attempted a procedure known as matter transference, but

my system had never cataloged your DNA. It caused a malfunction, and your translator disintegrated. Are you still injured?"

"No, but it's a little weird not having it there. What you've told me is a lot to take in. You called it 'matter transference'?"

"A term for removing matter from one location and moving it to another location remotely."

"Teleportation?" I asked.

"Not exactly, but you may think of it that way."

"If you can construct objects using..."

"Matter transference," he said, finishing my sentence.

"Yes, matter transference, can we create anything on the ship we need? Weapons? Food?"

"*Arcadia* has lay dormant for eons. Its capacity is limited until it undergoes a prolonged refit. However, we have thousands of fabricators, which can create just about anything you desire. *Arcadia* has been modified to suit you specifically. At the moment, we have exhausted our ability for matter transference."

If this ship could teleport matter and by all accounts replicate organic matter, it would bring about a technological revolution unparalleled in all of recorded history. No wonder they were capable of establishing an empire, if that was what the Regency was.

"Who were those people we encountered earlier?"

"Descendants of the ship's original crew. I have provided them with what they need, while keeping their technological progress stunted."

I gave him a look. "Why?"

"Failure must never be rewarded, Captain."

"Does your name mean anything?" I asked.

"All names mean something. You may call me Michael, as it is easier for you to pronounce," he said.

Arcadia wanted nothing more than to probe Melody, but by

requesting access, it hadn't managed to get far. *Arcadia* proved to possess a number of impossible technologies far surpassing anything I believed possible, but there was one thing I hadn't seen: an Antediluvian computer. Was this man before me their version of an AI? It spoke like a computer, but I suspected that might have been how it used Melody to speak to us.

"I've seen the woman who appeared to me previously on a piece of technology we found back on Kahwin shortly after I liberated the city. Who is she?"

"She is a projection of someone who died long ago."

"I see. How do you speak English so easily? The people here speak our languages so easily."

The man nodded. "A genetic gift, so to speak. It is easy for them to acquire languages. They simply need to be exposed for a short period of time, and fluency comes quickly."

"Useful."

"Quite useful, Captain."

"Where are your computers? If you want to build trust, help me understand who and what you are."

He looked at me a while. "If I understand you correctly, you want to return to your home world and save your people. Is this so?"

"Yes," I said flatly.

"Then here are my terms."

CHAPTER TWELVE

Kahwin
Kol Washington

A few weeks later, an officer from Space Force (one of the ones who stayed behind when Captain Moore left), pulled me out of formation. I was told to pack my things and get ready for a change of scenery. Panic hit me. I had no intention of paying a visit to the Punishment Farm. She must've known because she told me everything would be fine and I wasn't in trouble.

They moved me to the other side of the Academy and gave me my own room. Granted, it was small, and the bed squeaked every time you'd move even a hair on your head (not that I had much after they shaved it) but it was nice to have some privacy.

Over the course of twelve weeks, I devoted myself to studying English, working with a linguistics expert from Earth who was employed by a company called Equinox. My native language was based on symbolism and tonality, similar to a language called "Chinese," which made the transition to English annoying and frustrating.

The days started to blend together, and it was going by fast.

At first, I struggled to grasp English pronunciation and sentence structure. The linguistics expert, a patient woman named Dr. Reese, guided me through the language, offering insights on how English worked.

One day, as we sat in the small, dimly lit room serving as our classroom, Dr. Reese introduced me to the concept of homophones. Those are words that sounded the same but had different meanings. Whoever thought of the idea to have words that sounded the same should've been arrested.

"I don't understand." I furrowed my brow and set down the list of words Dr. Reese wanted me to learn. "How can 'air' and 'heir' sound the same, but mean different things? This makes no sense."

Dr. Reese chuckled. "It's one of the quirks of the English language, Kol. It can be confusing, I'll admit. It takes a lot of practice. Eventually, you'll learn to recognize how these words are used. It takes time."

I was as determined as ever to understand English, but the more examples I found like this, the harder it became for me. "Why would someone say they're 'all ears' when they only have two?"

Dr. Reese's eyes twinkled. "A simple figure of speech. It means they're listening closely."

"Why does English use figures of speech when you can speak plainly?"

"Let's continue." She drew a symbol on a piece of parchment using a charcoal pen. "What do you see here?"

Her drawing looked like a stylized mountain peak as a smooth, upward-sweeping curve. At the curve's pinnacle, I noticed a small hollow circle inside. You know when you see something or read something, and you could swear you've seen it before? It was like that. I could have sworn I'd seen it someplace.

"It looks familiar to you, doesn't it?" she asked.

"A little bit."

"Does it look like a word?"

I studied it further. "I'm not sure. I think so. It seems like an Antediluvian symbol."

"The Antediluvians used a language known as Astrolingua Antiquus, but those words have no meaning anymore. The curve represents the unbroken ascent toward divinity. Do you remember what that word means?"

I nodded.

"What do you think that circle up top means?"

"It looks like a star."

"Look closer."

She'd drawn faint lines radiating beyond the circle.

"I see lines," I said.

"Does it mean anything to you?"

"I wish I knew, Doctor."

"This is the symbol of the *Offor Vit*."

I could only give her a blank stare.

"After you graduate, we will discuss this further."

Over time, I began to grasp the language, even finding humor in it. One day, during a nasty lesson on preposition placement, I stumbled upon "oxymorons." Now, if you want to confuse someone, this is the way to do it.

"Jumbo shrimp?" I shook my head in disbelief. "How can something be both large and small at the same time?"

Dr. Reese eyes crinkled at the corners. "It's just a playful contradiction that adds charm to English."

"Charm. That's one way to say it."

"See? You're speaking more and more like an American every day."

Every other day, a drill sergeant would pull me out of class and put me back in formation. I think they wanted to make sure I hadn't forgotten what I'd learned, and of course, I hadn't. They only spoke in English now, which made it much harder.

I missed my mom. In the tribe, you never really left, so you were with family until you died. Or until they died. *What is my mom doing right now? I hope she's safe. I can't stop thinking about her.*

My true test was still to come. In order to continue training with the Iron Guard, I'd have to pass a "linguistics exam." I was told only half of the class would pass the test, and only the top five percent would be allowed to proceed. I'll admit, most of the other cadets struggled with English. When we'd mop the floors and clean up the corridors, we'd practice as much as we could. I don't think all of them were taking it as seriously as I was.

Test day arrived. I took my seat in the exam hall, my heart pounding. The test would last four hours, with a single lunch break two hours into the test.

As I flipped through the test pages, I realized that this wasn't an ordinary test. Some questions focused on "idiomatic expressions and their meaning," one of my favorite subjects. Others tested what I knew about syntax and grammar.

If this all sounds complicated, it was. If you've ever taken these kinds of tests, you'll know how terrible they are. I'd rather get a tooth pulled out. No, really. Put me in a chair, strap me down, and take a pair of pliers to my mouth. Before you do, you'd have to promise me I'd never have to take a test like this again, and if you promised I'd never have to shine another pair of boots, I'd probably let you take two of my teeth. The back ones, of course.

When the time came for our break, I rose and stretched my legs, trying to shake off the excitement and tension in my shoulders. I grabbed a glass of water and a honey bar. Some of the cadets grumbled about how hard the test was, but they didn't want us to talk to each other.

Did they want to go to the Punishment Farm? Maybe they stopped doing that. In fact, I hadn't seen anyone get sent there in weeks. Maybe if you got far enough into the program, they didn't think it would be worth it to shoot you. If that was what they were doing.

As the four hours drew to a close, I completed the last question and took a deep breath, my hand trembling slightly as I set down my pen. I'd given it my all, which I guess is all anyone can do. They let us leave once we completed the test, so I went outside for a bit to catch some fresh air.

A few minutes later, a senior drill sergeant hurried us back into the exam hall. He stood at the front of the room with an unreadable expression and began to read out the names of those who'd passed.

My breath caught in my throat.

"Cadet Kol Washington. 98%. You made it. Best score out of the class."

A surge of relief washed over me. Not only had I passed, but I'd managed to secure a place in the top five percent of the class. Soon after, Dr. Reece called me into her office.

Dr. Reece looked up from her notes, her eyes meeting mine. "Kol, I must say, your progress has been remarkable. Your accent has almost disappeared. You have an ear for language."

"Thank you, Dr. Reece. I really tried."

"I know you did. You're the best student I've had in many years. I've reported your test results to General Vack. I suspect things are about to change for you."

CHAPTER THIRTEEN

Kahwin
Kol Washington

I was ready to tear off my uniform, run outside, and get some air. This room was packed with people, making it difficult to breathe due to the stifling humidity. Sweat formed on my brow and landed on my upper cheek, but I couldn't move to wipe it away. All I could do was sit frozen and wait. That was the worst part.

High on the stage above the red curtains, a golden rod suspended banners from Starport City and beyond, including my original clan's banner—a black paw print on a white circle. In the center, where the curtains split, hung the longest banner with the stylized English word "Equinox" under a dull red sunrise.

I sat in the back of a large theater, which was dominated by a large center row and two smaller left and right rows flanking it on either side. The room could seat five hundred people, but today, it was overflowing with uniformed personnel standing on the edges and in the back. A podium stood at the front of the stage with a large Senate insignia, an Earth bird known as an eagle clutching arrows in one claw and some leaves in the other. Personnel was another word for people, I think, but I wasn't sure why they didn't say 'people.' I still struggled with English. Supposedly, we would be getting implants soon, like the one Captain Moore had, and that would make life so much easier.

In the first few rows, people wore formal Earth clothing, so I assumed they must have been nobles. Recently, everyone started to dress like the people from Equinox, and if you didn't, you wouldn't get invited to any parties. As I was now in the Iron Guard, I doubted I'd see any parties any time soon.

The banners measured twice as tall as me, and the curtain on the stage must have hidden something really big because it was as wide as a street. Men outnumbered the women three to one, and one woman stood out because of her braided hair. I didn't know her name, but before sitting down, I watched her give orders to others. She liked to look people directly in the eye and not look away until the conversation was over. Lady Kullen and Bylee, Oracle of the Wonders, sat together off to the side of the stage.

I was the only cadet here. Everyone else was older than me. I felt really out of place. General Vack had several men from the Iron Guard escort me to this place.

Finally, Vack stepped up to the podium. He wore an Earth suit with a black jacket and a black tie, not his usual uniform. I almost didn't recognize him. He looked so different that way. "Hail to the Iron Guard!"

"We obey the Iron Creed!" Our voices carried enough volume to boom off the theater walls. The roar we made was enough to instill terror into our enemies. No one disobeyed the Iron Creed. No one.

General Vack held his hand over his eyes to shield them

from the bright spotlight. He was younger than Captain Moore, I think, but not by much, and he wore a trimmed beard. He stood up straighter and looked around the room. "Today, we stand united, where we once were but scattered tribes. As I see each of you, I am reminded of our successes as a city and how those successes shine as a beacon of light on Kahwin. Yes, we owe Captain Moore and his crew our gratitude, but it is Equinox who brought us out of darkness."

A new flag unfurled from on high with red and white stripes on the side and an Equinox logo framed in a rectangle in the corner. I'd never seen such a strange flag before.

"The Iron Guard has stood as a vanguard against corruption and crime that plagued our society since the fall of the Shapers, and our mission has not changed. As we look forward into the future, we see a horizon where all of us in this room enjoy the freedoms Captain Moore has promised us."

General Vack turned and looked up at the new flag. "After today, this flag will represent every Kahwin. It is a flag that symbolizes not only this city and our way of life but freedom itself. We are no longer under the Shapers' rule, and we will never be slaves again."

"We obey the Iron Creed!" we shouted, our voices echoing throughout the auditorium.

"Today, we are tasked with a new mission, one which will establish contact with all tribes on this world. I will now give the floor to Lady Kullen, who would like to say a word."

I waited with rapt attention as she took the podium and addressed us. There was an elegant air about her that was beyond words. Although she was several years older than me, I couldn't stop from fantasizing about us being together. A real noble and me. Ha! As if that would ever happen. My lot in life was to be with the Iron Guard and remain single forever.

"Good afternoon. For those of you who don't know me, my

103

name is Lady Kullen." She smiled, and my heart melted. Was this what love felt like, as the Earthers talked about? "For many years, we nobles have waited patiently for Captain Moore's return. Although it has been said the captain has sent back word of his progress, these insidious rumors are indeed false. As most of you know, the communication logs have been available for all to see now for some time, and there is no record of Captain Moore attempting any such communication with Starport City, Equinox, or the Senate."

I wanted to understand more of what she was talking about. General Vack had instructed me to pay close attention to what was said today. Lady Kullen's voice sounded harsh. I assumed that was how people spoke at events like this.

"Now, moving forward, things will change." She glanced over at the general, who nodded in agreement. "With the help of the Iron Guard, we plan on launching several exciting projects in the future, one of which is why all of you are here today. For that, I turn you back over to Bylee, Oracle of Wonders." As she stepped down, I could have sworn she looked right at me, but how could she see with all the lights?

Bylee wore a simple nessma hat, which sat just above her ears. Its conical design, made from beautiful plant fibers, came to a small purple knob at the top that glittered when the light hit it just right. Valley herd leather covered both the brim and top, making it one of the most unique hats I'd ever seen.

She cleared her throat and then touched a ring of black beads around her neck. Two burly men waved smoking bronze bowls with both hands, spreading incense that reminded me of the leather pits. Some bowed their heads and said silent thanks to the Antediluvians, but I remembered Zoe had once advised against that, so I didn't join in.

"Hail to the Iron Guard. Glory to the strong," the oracle said, her eyes intense. "A famous oracle once said, 'Those who survived to see the dawn of a new age would serve new masters.' I...." She stopped mid-sentence, and her face began to redden. Both of her hands went around her throat, and blood dripped from her eyes. Everyone stood, shock written on their faces.

Pop!

The back of the oracle's head exploded in a cloud of crimson mist, and her brains splattered against the new flag.

My ears rang, and everything went quiet, except for a high-pitched whine. The smell of gunpowder overpowered the incense. I ducked, my heart pounding.

Another shot hit General Vack in the bicep, taking off most of his arm. Blood sprayed over the stage. My ears rang. A third shot. By that time, guards flew into action, and everyone started to scatter, panic in their eyes.

Someone grabbed me by the forearm.

I pulled away, but their grip tightened.

The figure holding me wore a hooded cloak and held a smoking pistol. "Kol, come with me," she said, her voice familiar.

"Zoe?"

"Kill her! Don't let her get away!" the crowd shouted. Their faces contorted with rage.

Spotlights landed on me as Zoe dragged me along, firing off shots. A hail of bullets burst from a Terran rifle, hitting Zoe in the back.

"She's taking him with her!" Lady Kullen cried out.

Zoe charged through the back doors. Daylight blinded me momentarily. New recruits drilled on the blacktop, and behind rose stacks of massive cargo containers taken from the Earther's ship, USS *Atlanta*. Drill instructors barked orders in the distance, and the accompanying whistles and songs so common during our training floated in the air.

The side gate stood open for the first time since I'd arrived, the guards next to it dead with their throats slit.

The purr of a six-door armored car's engine filled the air, its side door open, inviting.

"Go!" Zoe yelled at me.

I froze, still locking up despite all the training. She shoved me toward the car, breaking my hesitation. As men and women emerged from the hall behind us, they opened fire. Shots ricocheted off the pavement around me, and I dove behind the guard shack. A stray bullet grazed my neck, causing me to wince as I slapped the wound.

The armored car's automated twin turret swung into action, cutting a path through the academy personnel. Those who survived were pinned down. The sight of the bodies turned my stomach, and the turret's deafening noise rattled me.

Zoe moved quickly, pulling me into the escape vehicle and shutting the door. Everything happened so fast. Inside, a pair of cushioned benches sat opposite each other, with storage units for weapons and armor beneath. The space smelled like the basement armory we used during training, with a hint of sweat.

Zoe dashed to the driver's seat and buckled up. "Hang on," she yelled over the sound of gunfire hitting the APC's armored exterior. As I fastened my seatbelt, I realized how bad my situation was. No one defied the Iron Guard and escaped. They had given me a new life, made me the person I had always wanted to be, and now I'd become a fugitive.

The APC sped forward, and I glimpsed Starport City for the first time in months. The homes, districts, markets, and government buildings appeared new to me. The city hung white and green banners celebrating the harvest season. People filled the streets, heading toward the Senate, while construction crews repaired the damage from the battle between Captain Moore and the Shapers years ago, though they seemed relaxed most of the time.

"Stay down!" Zoe ordered.

I obeyed, clutching my head as a nearby house erupted in flames. Another projectile soared past us, hitting a home on the next street and causing it to explode. The APC's turret went into overdrive, its deafening noise making me want earplugs.

Zoe floored the accelerator, her driving tossing me around in my seat. She barreled through a wooden fence and emerged on the other side, only to reveal a steep drop-off instead of a road. "Hang on!" she shouted as the APC leaped into the air, my stomach lurching.

We landed with a *crunch*. I kept low, catching glimpses of street signs and alleyways as we raced through the city.

"Do you know what you've done?" I asked Zoe.

"Unfortunately, I do."

CHAPTER FOURTEEN

Arcadia
Captain Scott Moore

S ome decisions haunt you for the rest of your life. I can only imagine what Napoleon must have felt when he captured Moscow and found it empty and subsequently lost his grip on Europe. Did he have regrets? Hindsight. It's always easy to look back and ask yourself if you made the right choice or not. Should I have joined Space Force when I knew my sister would probably starve to death, along with my nephew?

It was enough to drive me to tears sometimes. I could have saved my sister and nephew. I know I could have. It would've been easy to get them into Mexico. There was plenty of money in my bank. Pay off the right people down there and you can get a lot done. I should have. Fact was, she probably wouldn't have listened to me anyway.

When I returned to my crew, I knew nothing would be the same. You make a deal with the devil, you know what you're going to get. It says so on the dotted line.

"Scott!" Vincent bolted to his feet and rushed over to me. "Are you okay?"

"Fine," I said.

Doc waved an omniscanner over me and asked me to perform a simple DNA scan and answer some questions. All of our instruments worked again, thankfully.

"How do you feel?" Doc asked.

"Fine," I lied.

Chief gave me a once over. "You look pale."

"Really, I'm fine."

Doc clicked the device off. "Well, you check out. I'm surprised after what happened out on the ice in the North Pole, that you're doing this well. Any dizziness or headaches?"

"No."

"Nausea?"

I glanced over at an open crate containing what few rations we had left. "I'll be fine, Doc. Thanks. How are we on supplies?"

Feazer brought a tablet over to me with our current inventory. "Enough for fifteen days if all of us consume 1,200 calories. It's not a lot."

I inspected what we had left and opened a chocolate granola fruit bar. "We'll be docking in five."

Vincent's mouth dropped. "What are you talking about?"

I took another bite, savoring it. "*Arcadia* needs a refit and has decided to take us to an orbital station where we will elicit repairs." Honestly, saying it out loud to them made it all seem unreal. After what Miuykal, or Michael, showed me, it'd merely be the first stop. Everyone there froze in place. "Soon, we will be led to the bridge. I hope everyone's well rested."

"Did you talk to the captain?" Chief asked.

"No. A person by the name of Miuykal. He wants me to call him Michael. He was created to speak on behalf of the ship. In some ways, you can say he *is* the ship." I took a moment to look at each member of my crew, giving me time to measure my next words carefully. "None of us expected to be here in this situation, and I picked you for the expedition to find this ship because I knew I could count on each of you. There is no easy way to say this, so I will come right out with it. Michael asked me to take command of *Arcadia*, and I have agreed."

CHAPTER FIFTEEN

Arcadia
Captain Scott Moore

"What do you mean you agreed?" Vincent asked. "The ship trapped us here."

I let his statement linger as a hint that he needed to reserve these questions for later. It was bad enough I'd need to explain to my staff what I'd agreed upon. "All of you will be given quarters similar to those on *Atlanta* and assigned various job and duties based on your proficiencies and backgrounds. We will continue to follow Space Force regulations."

I brought Doc to the corner of the room and whispered, "Ask everyone privately if they can tell you what they remember from their first birthday party."

"Sir?"

"Do it in private. If anyone starts to act strangely, calm them down and move on to the next person."

"Aye, sir."

"And, Doc? Start with the officers. Scan their DNA as well."

Doc proceeded to take people aside and question them. It'd

be some time before we confirmed everyone's true identity and not something *Arcadia* created to trick us.

I called my officers, Vincent, and Feazer over to one side of the room and huddled with them. There wasn't much in here, other than our supplies. It might have been some out-of-the-way place to keep us while Michael studied us.

With ceilings reminiscent of towering columns reaching overhead, and the lower part of the walls adorned with glyphs, the room bore an air of monumental architecture. The robust structural design of the room ensured the stability of the compartment. Concentric rows of storage racks rose up around three meters.

How could I relay the gravity of what Michael and I had agreed to without an open revolt? My brother eyed me like a stranger. At the time, I felt like one. My stomach growled. I ripped open a bag of vegetable soup and dove in. Nothing like carrots and peas when you haven't eaten in a while.

Vincent handed me a spoon, but by that time, I'd drained about half of it. "The ship is testing us. That much we know. It's mimicking us."

"It's trying to understand who we are," I said.

"How do you know it isn't listening to us now?" Doc asked. "Maybe we should think about what we're going to say first before we speak openly?"

I finished off the soup and rolled the last bit of liquid out of it. "*Arcadia* doesn't think like we do. It uses people rather than devices. Michael told me how easily electronic devices can be thwarted and wondered why our species hadn't progressed in genetic research."

Chief folded his arms. "So, the ship isn't listening to us? How can you be sure, Captain?"

Chen glanced around the room. "It has to be."

"To be fair, I *can't* be sure. I can only tell you what we

discussed and that I trust what Michael told me. However, I have no reason to believe it's listening to us. If it can, then there isn't much we can do about it. Doc, have you tested everyone to make sure they are who they say they are?"

"Aye, Captain. Everyone seemed fine and answered the questions without issue. And, the omniscanner failed to detect anything strange, but to tell you the truth, our instruments may not be able to detect who's who. This could take quite a while."

Tests wouldn't be enough, would they? Not with genetic manipulation. Memories would not be replicated, would they? I'll admit, I wondered if any of my crew were who they said they were. What caused Gisele to undergo an existential crisis? When she learned she might not be who she appeared to be. She never was able to relay memories outside of me either. Everything she remembered had to do with me. After that —nothing.

Could be a remote neural scanner that uploaded information to a genetic printer. How difficult would that be?

"Are you sure this isn't a ship commanded by a Keeper?" Chen asked me. "Seems to me, whoever controls this ship has mastered genetic research in the same way the Shapers have."

"Michael assured me this ship is free, so to speak. It is not controlled by a Keeper. It's controlled by him. At least for now. When we get to the bridge, he intends to cede authority to us."

Chief scoffed. "Sir, how can we possibly fly something like this? We have no understanding of how the controls work."

"I think you'll find yourself at home on the bridge, Chief. All of you will."

"There's a lot you're not telling us," Vincent said. "You agreed to something, didn't you?"

I nodded. My brother knew me all too well. "As captain, sometimes you are forced to make uncomfortable decisions, and in this case, I made one. As you know, we embarked on this mission in order to return to Earth, and *Arcadia* is capable of just that. We *will* be going home."

My officers remained silent. Feazer, who spoke for Equinox, looked over his shoulder at us for a moment. "Sir, I believe the rest of the crew would appreciate the good news."

Vincent threw up his hands. "Just like that? We're going home? What's the catch?"

I lowered my voice. "Michael asked us to help liberate the human race."

"That's all?" Vincent asked. "Why didn't you say so the first time? Clearly, you're joking."

But I wasn't. "As bold as this may sound, I agreed to his terms."

After I said that, Chen remained tightlipped. I needed her to understand why this was so important. Did I? All of this seemed out of character for me. I didn't quite understand it myself, but everything felt right. You ever see a movie and think, *This is what I've been waiting for*? Or a song you hear for the first time, and you're floored as every note hits exactly where it should be? Magnify that, and you'll understand where my head was.

Chief arched his brow, more surprised than stunned. "I take it *Arcadia* is a warship?"

"As I understand it, yes. Michael refers to *Arcadia* as a battleship with aircraft carrier capabilities. Inside her hangars, she carries a thousand fighters and an equal number of bombers. I've been shown maps of how expansive this ship is. It's impressive to say the least."

"How many?" Chief asked.

"You're mad." Vincent's face grew into granite, his scowl causing deep lines by his eyes. "You've gone completely mental."

"I understand how this might be difficult, Vincent. I do. Believe me."

"What if we just want to go home?" Feazer asked.

I replied, "Then you will be afforded that opportunity in the near future. There are too many unknowns for me to give a specific answer."

As Vincent pulled away from us, he bit his lip. "No. No, this isn't something I signed up for. This isn't something you can just spring on us just like that. You know what? Maybe you should have thought about consulting with the rest of us before you went off and...."

"That's enough, Mr. Moore," Chief said.

"It's not near enough. No, this is way too much. Forget it. Tell this Michael person to take me back to Starport City. I've had it. I've absolutely had it with this *bullshit*." My brother turned and started to walk away.

Chief grabbed him by the arm and bared his teeth. "Cool it."

The two men stared at each other. How could I blame Vincent? When we were kids, if you changed his toothpaste, he'd throw a fit. That was who he was. Years of promises about us being back on Earth, all the near-death encounters, and the time we'd spent talking about home. He'd either come around or he wouldn't.

"Let him go, Chief," I said.

Vincent pulled his arm free and got in Chief's face. "Don't you *ever* touch me again!"

I let them square off for a few seconds. "That's enough, Mr. Moore."

Vincent stabbed his finger my way. "This... this whatever you want to call it, this plan. It's not what any of us signed up for. You promised to take us home to Earth. When? Huh? When is that going to happen? After you 'liberate' the human race? I should have stayed back on Kahwin. You're not a warlord. What is this?"

"I said that's enough, Mr. Moore," I repeated. "Now, you can listen to the rest of what I have to say, or you can go over and join the rest of the crew and keep your mouth shut. What's it going to be?"

My brother gave a deep sigh of resignation, and I could feel his fury from where I stood. "How long do you think it's going to take to 'liberate' everyone?"

"That's a good question. I can't say for certain."

"Why does Michael want you to do this?" Chen asked me. "I don't understand."

"I don't understand either. He wouldn't say."

"This is ridiculous," Vincent quipped.

"Did he say how many places he wanted to liberate?" Doc asked. "Are we talking a city? A moon? A system?"

This was one of the questions I didn't want to answer. "At one time, the Antediluvians populated an empire known as the Regency, which spanned over thousands of systems. As to how many still exist, no one can say."

"Thousands..." Vincent whispered.

Chen stared at me in disbelief, her soft brown eyes then turning to Chief.

"You want us to go to war with the Keepers?" Feazer's eyes became saucers. "Sir, if that's the case, you're asking us to commit suicide. You can't expect us to go along with this."

"I'm sorry you feel that way, Mr. Feazer," I said. "Once you've been briefed further, perhaps you'll reconsider."

"When do you plan to tell the rest of the crew?" Chen asked.

"Once we reach Eos, our destination. Then, all of you will be given a choice. You can remain with me, and we fight Keepers until we can negotiate the transfer of humans to worlds where they will not be oppressed, sacrificed, or fed upon by the Shapers, or you can return to Earth and tell them what you've seen."

Vincent's ears perked up. "How would we return to Earth?"

"If you choose to make that decision, you will be briefed on the details."

Michael told me it might be possible to send people to Earth, but when I asked him how, he wouldn't say. I didn't think it was possible and dismissed it out of hand. Even if it were, I'd need everyone's help with *Arcadia* for as long as the refit lasted. I needed to speak privately with Doc and Chief about it.

"How long will the return trip take?" Feazer asked.

"I refer you to my previous answer," I replied.

The door opposite us opened. Gisele and Michael stepped inside wearing Space Force uniforms. The crew spun around, and I broke the huddle and approached them.

"Would you care to visit the bridge now, Captain?" Michael asked.

"Yes. Take us there."

The crew piled onto the gravity lift and ascended the ladder. Gisele stood away from everyone until only a few people remained. She hadn't looked at me since she'd arrived with Michael, and I found it incredibly difficult to stop staring at her. Michael created her, but now that he'd run his test, why was she still here?

Vincent remained behind until everyone but Chief, Gisele, Michael and I were left.

My brother faced Michael and glared. "Where did you take Melody?"

"Your servers have been relocated to a safe room. When I have finished examining them, you will be granted permission to see them."

"I need to see her immediately," Vincent said.

As Michael turned his attention toward me, he placed his hands behind his back. "Captain, we made an agreement."

I could feel Vincent's gaze burn a hole through my head. "What?"

"You will have access to Melody at your console on the bridge, Mr. Moore," I said.

My answer made Vincent snarl. "An agreement? No. I need to see the servers. You don't understand."

"It's no longer an option, Mr. Moore," I said firmly.

Vincent shook his head in disgust. In any other circumstances, my brother would throw a punch at me. "Oh? And why's that?"

Michael lifted his chin and squared his shoulders. "Humanity needs you. I need you."

CHAPTER SIXTEEN

Kahwin
Kol Washington

Escaping Starport City in an APC shouldn't have been possible. After Zoe yanked me out of the theater, we drove straight through the Roosevelt District, where the Earthers had set up roadblocks to restrict people's movements. Only one of the roadblocks was manned, and the guards let us pass without stopping us.

We drove through the Hanging Forest, where the Iron Guard used to execute criminals. Taking this route was considered bad luck, but Zoe insisted. The trees made me slightly nauseous, but it could've been my nerves. I counted twenty-three skulls as we passed through. Ropes still dangled from tree limbs in every direction. Staying in the Hanging Forest too long would cause your gums to bleed and make you very sick.

"Where are we going?" I asked.

"The Scalding Ruins. You will be safe there."

"Where's that? I've never heard of it."

"Deep underground, where the Shapers never looked."

"Where's Captain Moore? Is he there too?" My heart lifted. If he was, he could sort out this mess.

"No. I'm sorry, Kol. I don't think we'll be seeing them again."

Zoe slowed the APC as we approached a wooden fort built by one of the tiny tribes that had somehow carved out a living space here, where others would fall ill and die. The two-story fort blended into the forest background. I almost didn't see it. The fort stood on a wide platform, with ladders leading down to the ground. A few men, dressed in tunics, looked down on us from above.

A short man with a patch over his left eye descended one of the ladders and walked to the side. His skin had a faintly yellowish hue, and his fingernails were long and curved. A necklace made of flowers hung below his reddish beard. He must've known Zoe because he didn't carry a weapon, nor was anyone aiming one at us. She'd been through here before.

Zoe brought the APC to a stop and rolled down her window.

When the man got close, he glanced through the tinted glass and gazed at me in awe. "Is that him?"

"Yes."

The man placed a hand over his heart and touched his chin to his chest. "Blessed is his path."

"The Iron Guard will come this way. Make sure to intercept them," Zoe said.

"It will be so."

"Go with joy." Zoe rolled up her window and proceeded to take us down a narrow path that would lead us beyond the Kriss River.

"What did he mean?" I asked.

Zoe gripped the wheel and casually shifted gears. "Nothing. It will be explained. Do you know why the general wanted you there?"

The trees grew dense, blocking out the sun. Blood vines lived in these parts, and if you weren't careful, they'd snatch you up by your throat and strangle you. I think this was why it was called the Hanging Forest before the Iron Guard made it their own. You can spot a blood vine because the veins in their leaves turn black after they feed.

"He said something about Project 1. The Iron Guard is going to come after us. You killed the oracle."

"If only it were that simple. Come sit up front."

I unbuckled the harness and moved to the passenger seat. They called it a passenger seat because, in normal vehicles, the passenger sits there and keeps the driver company. In an APC, the passenger seat is where the sensor technician or sometimes the gunner sits. I once asked an Earther why it isn't called the gunner seat, and her explanation made it more confusing. Apparently, where she's from, the driver sits where the passenger sits, and the driver's seat becomes the passenger seat. It made about as much sense as calling a sunrise a sunset.

Once I buckled back in, I said, "I saw you kill the oracle and blow General Vack's arm off."

She nodded. "You've gotten bigger since I last saw you."

My cheeks turned red. "They made me do a lot of exercises and run." Plus, it'd been years since we saw one another. I was probably a lot taller by then.

The panels in front of me were inactive, leaving them silver. During training, I drove an APC like this for a week until I got the hang of it and passed a test. The instructor said I did better than he expected.

"The oracle was not who she appeared to be," Zoe said. "Neither is that place."

"I found that out right away. It's big inside. You have to take elevators. What's going to happen to me now? I can't go back to the city, or they'll kill me."

"What happens next depends on you, Kol. Do you know what happened to the tablet I gave you?"

"No. General Vack took it from me when I got there. I'm sorry."

"I told you how important it was," she hissed. "I told you fourteen times."

One thing about Zoe, she had a good memory. "I'm sorry. There was nothing I could do. You also said no one can open it but me."

"It's going to be difficult to recover it. Why didn't you hide it before you went to see General Vack?"

I clenched my teeth. "I'm sorry. I'll find a way to get it back. I know you made me promise not to lose it. I'm sorry."

We drove for hours, making small talk. I fell asleep. When I opened my eyes, my neck was stiff.

"How much further?" I asked.

"Soon, Kol. Very soon."

She asked me if I believed the Shapers might return some day. I didn't want to admit it, but I'd always felt like they would. Then what?

"The Academy said I wasn't allowed to talk about the Senate," I said.

"Did they tell you why?"

"No."

"Why do you think they said that to you?"

When we got within spear range of the bridge, Zoe pulled up behind a tree and stopped. A jagged gap tore out a good portion of the center of the bridge, like something had exploded on it or eaten it. Someone had set up logs and debris on it, creating alternate areas for cover. The bridge extended a little over thirty meters across if I remembered the Earth system correctly and was three meters wide. I doubted we could make it across in the APC.

"I'll scout ahead. Wait here," she said, reaching under her seat and pulling out an Earth rifle.

"Are we walking from here?"

"No. The APC will make it across."

I touched the panel in front of me. "What about the sensors?"

"Anything we use will send a signal back to Starport City. Don't touch anything. Wait here." She hopped out and raced from tree to tree until she reached the bridge.

Then she was gone. I waited and waited, but after a while, I started to worry. I mean, I could drive the APC. She said it would make it across, right? Maybe she needed my help. Could be. Maybe she was in trouble. If she was, and I sat here doing nothing, that wouldn't be good at all.

I tapped the side of the door. She could be in danger. Then what would I do? I'd never find where she's trying to take me, the Scalding Ruins, and the Iron Guard would find me.

I changed seats and checked over the driver's controls. A few differences. One, the steering wheel sat up higher than normal, and the seat's springs squeezed. After testing the pedals, I felt confident enough to start the engine. I let it purr for a few seconds, hoping she'd appear and complain that I'd acted foolishly. At least then, I'd know she was okay.

I threw the APC in drive and started to drive closer to the bridge. A light flashed behind me, then another. In the mirror, an enormous black shell the size of the APC kicked up a dust trail as it flew across a clear patch of land. A lens dominated the upper half as the shell's curve swooped into dozens of rectangular pegs, which jutted out from the back. Sunlight glinted off its surface. Two arms came off each side with weapon barrels for hands.

"Not good. Not good," I said, remembering the Shapers and

the times I almost died. Panic hit me, and I slammed my foot down on the drive pedal.

The APC whipped forward toward the bridge. The holographic speedometer rose steadily as the drone cracked off a shot. A bright red beam blasted a massive tree in half, and it fell in front of the APC, crunching as its limbs smashed against the ground. The tree blocked my view of the bridge, and my pulse thumped in my ear.

No way would I make it over the tree, but I had to try.

I jerked the wheel. The tires bounded over branches until they rolled over the tree trunk, the bounce causing me to lurch into the steering wheel.

Crack! Crack!

The forest reverberated with the cacophony of gunfire as the APC's back tires gained traction and catapulted us over the debris. I glanced in the mirror. The drone closed the distance, its form enveloped by a shimmering force field, distorting the air around it. When a second tree crashed down in front of me, I shifted the APC into overdrive and rammed the front bumper into the side of a towering Pica tree, tearing off its bark.

"Go!" I yelled at the APC.

A bright beam of energy sliced through the air and struck a different tree.

The APC jostled and shook, its engine roaring as we hurtled through the dense forest. I swerved and dodged around thick trees that loomed in our path, sweat coating my skin despite the chilly air inside the vehicle. The drone was close, but it was hidden by the tangle of foliage.

The gunfire resumed, the sound echoing through the trees. I cursed. Without weapons, I was completely defenseless.

The drone's energy beams tore through the trees around me, shredding the forest and leaves in its relentless pursuit. I had to keep moving if I wanted to survive. The APC bounced and shook violently as I dodged a boulder, the drone hovering behind me and continuing to fire.

Pressure mounted, my heart racing with each passing moment. I pushed the APC harder, dodging limbs and swerving around trees as I tried to outmaneuver the drone's fire.

As the drone's aim grew less accurate, I realized that I might just have a chance. My mind raced with possibilities and strategies, searching for a way to outsmart my foe and escape with my life intact.

With the drone hot on my heels, I approached a rickety old bridge spanning a deep ravine. The wooden planks creaked and groaned beneath the weight of the APC as I drove onto it, the vehicle wobbling dangerously from side to side.

The drone continued to spew its energy beams, the blasts ricocheting and narrowly missing. I slammed the accelerator to the floor. As I reached the midpoint, one of the planks gave way, sending the APC lurching to one side. I fought to regain control, the tires spinning uselessly against the remaining planks as I careened dangerously close to the edge.

The drone, hovering just behind me, continued to fire. Its beams sliced through the air and struck the bridge's supports, causing chunks of wood to splinter and fall away.

I had to get off the bridge before it collapsed completely. I slammed the gearshift into reverse, flooring the accelerator. The APC groaned as I swerved, doing everything in my power to avoid the drone's relentless barrage.

As the drone closed in to within a hundred meters, it froze in place. The APC's holographic terminal flickered and died, and the engine sputtered before eventually stopping. I coasted for a few meters, my heart pounding in my chest.

Static erupted over the radio. "Kol, do you copy?" a man asked. I recognized the authoritative tone of the academy immediately.

I picked up the box receiver dangling from a cord, but I hesitated. *Should I reply?*

"Kol, this is Lieutenant Haversberg. Turn the APC around and surrender."

My heart raced with fear as I tightly gripped the receiver. Surrender? I could never do that, not after coming this far. The Iron Guard would kill me. But what choice did I have? The drone was still hovering above, its deadly beam weapons at the ready.

I took a deep breath and spoke into the receiver, my voice steady despite the fear gripping me. "This is Kol. I read you loud and clear, Lieutenant."

There was a pause on the other end of the line before Lieutenant Haversberg spoke again. "Surrender the APC and come quietly, and no harm will come to you. We'll take you into custody and sort things out back at the academy."

I weighed my options. "I can't do that, Lieutenant."

"Come back to the academy, Kol. Nothing will happen. We need you now more than ever. We'll wipe the slate clean. All you have to do is step out of the APC and come back with the drone."

I hung up the receiver, my eyes fixed on the drone hovering above me, adrenaline coursing through my veins.

Not a chance.

CHAPTER SEVENTEEN

Kahwin
Kol Washington

The turret refused to fire from the passenger side of the APC, so I muttered some choice swear words I'd learned at the academy. Stupid machine. It didn't help, but it made me feel better.

I slid to the driver's side and opened up the access panel. A mess of wires spilled out from the side. I learned this trick from a cadet with bad teeth. I decided to try it.

"This is your final warning, Cadet! Surrender immediately or I *will* be forced to kill you."

"If you wanted to kill me, you'd have done so already," I said to myself.

Vehicles made in the city all use the same kind of electronics, and once you knew how to rewrite their systems, you only had to match the symbols on the BAN wafers to the labels on the wires. Rounds pinged off the APC as I pulled the power bundle from the APC's sensor array and spliced the two orange cables into a single block cube.

"Sorry about this." I aimed the turret at the drone. The turret sprang to life, booming off rounds. The machine quaked under the impact.

"Kol, cease this immediately!" the lieutenant yelled through the radio. "You're only making your situation worse!"

I grabbed the receiver. "Yeah, well, I could say the same about you!"

The rattling gunfire hit harmlessly against the drone's armor, and with the ammo counter ticking down to zero, panic gripped me. I scanned the controls for a way to put this thing down.

A minuscule access hatch on the drone's side, barely discernible against its metallic surface, lit up on my holocontrols as a weakpoint. I adjusted my aim and fired a burst. The rounds struck, and the hatch blasted open with a resounding clang.

"Kol!" The drone faltered before plummeting to the ground in a cascade of smoke.

I shouted and slapped the steering wheel. Finally!

Something inside the APC started to smell like burnt rubber. Warnings flashed in red. "Fire!" My lungs burned, so I held my breath. Acrid smoke raced toward the cabin, and the battery light blinked. "Exit the vehicle!"

I yanked the side door open and rolled out onto the ground. Flames licked up the back of the APC. I bolted down a small hill and the whole thing caught fire and exploded. It was never a good idea to be caught in a forest without weapons, and even more so this far from the city.

The sun would set soon, and I had no idea where the Scalding Ruins were.

If I called out to Zoe, who knew what might hear me?

Zoe *had* to be there.

The thick darkness wrapped around me like a heavy blanket.

After searching for her for an hour, my eyes fell on a faint aura flickering through the dense foliage. The light got brighter with each step, and the air buzzed with energy. Even the ground seemed to shake a bit, kind of like how my heart was pounding in my chest.

The forest, which used to feel familiar, made me feel small and weak.

Going from tree to tree, I moved toward the light. As it got brighter, a soft chirping began to fill my ears. My heart was going like crazy as I got closer.

As my eyes adjusted, I saw a simple shape made of some material I couldn't recognize, with lights flickering on and off. The chirping got louder the nearer I approached. It looked more like a market light show than something practical.

"Zoe?" I called out softly. "Are you there?"

The light was about her size, like a coffin. I moved my hands around it, hoping to find a switch. People used to say our ancestors put deadly traps in the forest to keep us out, but I never believed them until now. I continued to explore the light, feeling every centimeter of it, trying to find any hint about how to operate it. I was so lost, I didn't even realize how much time had passed.

Don't ask me how, but I could sense the energy flowing from it. My thumb brushed up against a wire. It sent a shock through me. Was it a trap? Probably. It started shaking like crazy, its parts clanging against each other. My other fingers touched something sharp, like a razor, and the whole thing sparked. The light faded.

"There you are," I said.

Zoe lay motionless on the ground.

"Are you okay?" I asked.

Her eyes were open, but she wasn't responding. I touched her arm. Nothing.

"Zoe, we can't stay here. Can you hear me?"

What about the trap? Where were the wires I touched? The only thing that remained was liquid gray goo underneath her. Without food, water, and weapons, neither of us would make it through the night. Not here.

I decided to look around for a place to hide, promising myself I'd come back for Zoe once I found what we needed. Leaving her behind, even for a little while, made me sick, but what choice did I have? I was very quiet, leaving no trace. All of my senses sharpened like a spear.

I found a small clearing with a stream running through it. Seeing the clear water made me feel a little better. I used some leaves and collected what water I could.

When I got back to Zoe, she hadn't changed at all.

I rolled her to the side and patted her down, wiping the goo away with pine straw.

Zoe blinked. "We... have to go."

"You're alive!"

"Shh."

"What is it? How can I help you?"

"Lift me onto your back. We have to go."

"Where?"

"The only place General Vack will never find you."

CHAPTER EIGHTEEN

Arcadia
Captain Scott Moore

Michael brought us all to another elevator that lit up purple once you touched it. Much of the path was drenched in darkness, though occasionally, a hint of a tree or a wall came into view. We walked for a good fifteen minutes in the dark this way with our tablets creating light for us. Ensign Marston showed some initiative and organized people to carry enough water and rations on them to last a few days, though our guide assured us it wouldn't be necessary. Better safe than sorry at any rate.

My XO tried to calm the crew, giving vague answers to questions she didn't know. A good officer.

None of us said much along the way, and Doc and Chief made sure the nervous ones in our crew scanned our surroundings, studied tablets, or tasked them with something else to keep their minds busy. Experiences so far outside a person's own life can feel surreal, but something about this place felt natural, like walking into a place you've dreamed about your whole life. The way the deck deadened the sound of our steps, the odor the air carried like citrus and wheat, the curving halls and how our tablets lit up brightly colored doors, I felt like I'd been here before.

My pulse quickened with each passing minute. Me, in charge of all this. What a thought. If you're wondering why *Arcadia*'s avatar, Michael, wanted me to take command, I wasn't sure myself. Not only had he asked me politely three times, he ended up demanding it, saying bluntly, "I can force you, but I'd rather not." When I agreed, he specified I'd hold unlimited power on the ship. When I asked him if that meant I could confine him to quarters, he laughed and said, "If that is your wish."

What guarantees did Michael give me? None. Any promises he made, he could've easily revoked. He must've seen something in us to make the offer in the first place. We did liberate Kahwin from the Shapers. Maybe that was it. His words repeated in my mind: "At the Battle of Kilphin, I was blessed by war." It was a religious way of speaking. He'd made it a point to compliment me on how we gained the Kahwin people their freedom at the cost of our lives and mentioned how rare bravery was in the galaxy.

Bravely had nothing to do with it. As a Space Force officer, I swore an oath to uphold the Constitution and keep true to those principles embedded therein. Freedom is a precious thing, and as the Great Famine struck Earth and the population bottomed out, the very definition of freedom began to change. Work camps. Slave labor. Forced relocation. Mandatory sterilization and genetic therapy. Everything I detested.

If Michael *had* accessed Melody, how much did he know about Earth's history and its trajectory? I couldn't read the man's face well enough to know if he lied to me or not. He might as well have been an actor, and perhaps he was. He gave off warmth I found soothing, though my mind told me otherwise. Strange how that works.

I avoided eye contact with Gisele because my officers could read me like a book. Chen's expression along the way told me she knew something was up, and of course, Chief, who'd met Gisele a few times in Paris himself, stared at her intently. I couldn't blame him. As a woman, Gisele was my idea of perfection, my Helen of Troy. Love can make a king a slave and a slave a king. Her face might as well have been a magnet.

We entered through a narrow passage whose slanted walls touched to form a triangle. Here, plants stored in indentations along the length of the hallway glowed like powerful light-bulbs. Our tablets shut down immediately.

"Captain?" Ensign Marston asked.

Michael clicked his tongue a few times and made a sound similar to samples I've heard of the now extinct Navajo language, and the tablets blinked back to life. "Many of the life-forms inside *Arcadia* are sensitive to electronics. I will teach all of you how to speak to them and calm their nerves."

Chen glanced at me, then to Michael. I nodded to her, giving her permission to speak to him.

Michael halted.

I noticed a silhouette emerge from behind some foliage. "Erika?"

She glanced down at her feet and stood straighter like she had just risen from a long nap. "Captain."

Chief hesitated and gave a double take. "You're alive."

Doc gave her a once over. "We left you in the room where we arrived. We thought you were..."

"I'm fully functioning. How did I get here?" Erika asked.

"We don't know how you got here. It's good to have you back. Do you remember anything?"

Michael frowned. "Who... or what is this... thing?"

Doc gestured toward Erika while keeping his eyes on Michael. "You didn't fix her?"

"No." Michael curled his lips into a half-snarl. "I wouldn't."

"I'm in one piece," Erika said. "My power supply and energy storage are at nominal rates, and my hydraulic and pneumatic actuators are fully operational, sir."

Vincent grinned. "Happy to have you... back... somehow."

"It's good to see you all," Erika said."May I join, Captain?"

"You may."

Michael spun around to face me. "Who is this creature who speaks as though she were a human?"

I motioned to the lieutenant. "This is First Lieutenant Erika Banks."

Gisele took one look at Erika and shivered.

"This *thing* is not to speak to me, Captain," Michael said.

"Lieutenant Banks will speak to whomever it suits her. She's a vital part of my staff."

Michael sneered, and he placed his hands behind his back. "You did not mention her in our proceedings, Captain. I do not allow such... *creations* within *Arcadia*. She *must* be removed." For the first time, he displayed negative emotions, and yet this could have been simply another test, one of many he'd perpetrated on us.

Chen glared at Michael intently.

Why did he care? The better question was why hadn't *he* brought this up before we ended our negotiations? I figure he knew Erika was aboard the ship. And probably picked up her energy signature the moment she began functioning again. Or, maybe he hadn't seen her at all? *Arcadia*'s technology would have detected her. It picked up our tablets and my old translator, but Michael didn't see her. Genetics. *Arcadia*'s tech relied on genetic manipulation rather than electronics. Michael had told me flat out there wasn't a single computer onboard. What made Michael manifest disgust? Fear? She might have been invisible to him, something he couldn't detect, not even with his own eyes until now. Obviously, I'm speculating.

"Lieutenant Banks stays," I said. "This matter isn't up for debate."

"Then she must be...."

I cut Michael off with a finger. "The lives of my crew are as valuable to me as my own. I trust them more than I can possibly say. I said this matter isn't up for debate, and it's not."

"I see. You are making a mistake, Captain. Let us continue to the bridge. You will find it to your liking."

"Lead the way."

When Michael started down the hall, Erika glanced worriedly at me and Chen. I gave Erika a nod. Everything would be fine, because if anything happened to her, there would be hell to pay. Although I wanted to take a breather, to embrace the fact that one of my favorite people in the world was alive, I needed to remain calm as the captain. Still, over the years, I'd grown attached to Erika, like having a daughter or a younger sister. Although a synth, she stayed true to who she was as a person, and for that, I viewed her *as* a person. I loved her in my own way, though I'd never in a million years tell her that.

If there was a God, He had just performed a miracle. It was as if half of me became more alive again with Erika back in my life. I thought I'd lost her forever.

The end of the hall opened into a scene pulled from my memory. We'd walked into the Paris Metro, a subway station complete with Islamic posters, LED lights, the dark grey platform concrete that became khaki at the end of the dual tracks, and the white and blue sign with the word "Sortie" in blue. A guitar case stood left open for donations. Whoever it was had received some in the form of coins and Euro carbon notes. The walls curved up to the ceiling. The cameras were missing. Other than the musician, the room stood empty.

Everything about the Metro was perfect, and like Gisele, the sight of it stole my breath. If Michael thought this would put me at ease, he was wrong. I'd met Gisele here on our second date by the staircase. She'd worn a turquoise sweater that evening that matched her eyes. Michael knew my dreams.

What *would* have put me at ease, then? Nothing, I suppose. The alien nature of *Arcadia* had started to be mundane up until now.

During our discussion, Michael insisted I would find things familiar, even going so far as to say the bridge would resemble the one on *Atlanta* so much, I would find it hard to notice anything different, a notion I dismissed out of hand up until now.

"A tram will arrive in approximately three minutes and take you to the bridge. Should you have any questions, you can reach me through the standard means of communication."

"Where will you be?" I asked.

Chen touched the side of the walls slowly and pulled her hand away.

Michael grinned like he'd given us Christmas gifts. "Ensuring everything works smoothly. Do not leave the Metro. When the train comes, you will hyper accelerate to the bridge."

"What about me?" Gisele asked Michael.

"You will remain with Captain Moore's doctor to serve as an advisor." Michael focused on Vincent. "I would like to invite you to accompany me to Melody. She would like to speak with you."

As Vincent's eyebrows lifted, his mouth fell open for a moment. "You mean she's active?"

"Yes, Mr. Moore. Melody is eager to speak with you."

"You'll take me there?"

"It would be an honor," Michael said.

My brother looked over at me. "Captain?"

"He'll be safe?" I asked.

"Yes, Captain. I wouldn't dare harm any of your crew."

I would have liked Vincent to study the bridge, but we'd waited years for Melody to come out of hibernation. As its creator, my brother wanted nothing more than to get his hands on it. It was all he'd talked about for months on end.

"You mind if Ensign Marston comes with me?" Vincent asked.

Marston agreed instantly. He was a smart kid, and he and Vincent got along well, sharing the same annoying humor both of them enjoyed.

The train pulled up. Green and white. Just like I remembered. Its doors opened with a clunk.

"Your train," Michael said.

We boarded the middle car and took a seat, and I think all of us were in various stages of shock.

"One more chance to change your mind," I said to Vincent and Marston.

"We'll be fine. I can't wait to see her," my brother replied.

"Good luck."

Ensign Marston saluted me, and Michael led them back the way we arrived, disappearing back through the door.

"Let's go," I said.

We boarded the train, and I could hear some of the crew whisper to each other. We tested the seats, the glass, and the walls with their hands, our disbelief measured in our gazes.

Erika and Chief sat with me, and the train began to accelerate into a black tunnel. Doc and Chen mingled with the crew.

"Why Paris?" Erika asked. "Why not New York?"

Chief lowered his head and whispered, "It's reading your mind, isn't it, Captain?"

"I don't think so." But I thought it must have been. The translator that had been behind my ear? Was that how?

"Then how do you explain Gisele?" Chief asked.

"I can't, anymore than I can explain this train or the Metro station."

"Sir, what about the people we saw earlier?" Erika asked.

"Probably the descendants of the former crew," Chief replied.

I was so glad to have Erika on our team again. I should have Doc scan her. I didn't know if that would tell us anything, though. The way Michael and Gisele had looked at her told me a lot. She wasn't a creation from *Arcadia*. The real Erika was before us.

The train roared through the tunnel, making it hard to hear much of anything. Windows rattled as we picked up speed, and the train's screens, which stood over the doors connecting the different cars, displayed a map of our progress into the ship's bowels, where the bridge was located. We appeared as nothing more than a speck along the axis of *Arcadia*'s enormous spine, where the ship's multilevel gravitic transport system ferried personnel through series of tunnels, like veins through a human body.

"How are any of us going home?" Chief asked.

I didn't want to answer in front of my officers. I needed time to think. "This is a discussion for another time."

A timer on the screen counted down. According to it, we'd arrive on the bridge in a few minutes.

"Until we can be sure that our crew members are who they appear to be, I want both of you to remain on high alert. Keep your ears and eyes open," I said. "*Arcadia* is able to create people that are indistinguishable to us."

Chief held onto the seat as the train climbed up a steep incline. "Aye, sir. What about Gisele?"

"Never mind her."

"She's wearing a Space Force uniform, sir," Erika said.

"Yes, Lieutenant. I'm aware."

"Who is she?" Erika asked.

I straightened my lips. "I'll tell you later."

The train jolted as its brakes squeaked with fury.

The timer and map vanished, and the lights flickered.

Across the screen, a new message in English blazed in bold crimson. "Battlestations. Shaper fleet in combat proximity."

"What the..." Feazer said.

My stomach lurched into my throat as the side of the train smacked against the tunnel wall. A roaring sound, like steel beams clashing against one another, filled the train car. Chief bashed his head against the glass, blood dripping down the side. I was thrown into the aisle with a resounding boom. Sparks rained from the light fixtures, and I threw my hands around one of the guard rails as the interior of train thundered with a violent cacophony.

"Hang on!" I shouted.

Chief threw me a hand, his other fastened to an emergency handhold. "Captain!"

The train rocketed faster, and the g-force pulled me backward. We raced up a sleep incline, and my feet dangled freely in the aisle. Behind me, someone fell to the back of the train and landed on the exit door leading to the next car.

It took every ounce of my strength to reach up and steady myself. Chief pulled me the rest of the way into the chair, and from there, the seat somehow lessened the sensation of being pulled due to the train's deceleration.

We screeched to a halt, and the doors whooshed open. Outside, a platform made to resemble the Norman Tunnel that connected the Space Force Academy's headquarters to an underground metroplex known as "The Mole's Nest" awaited us. I'd been through here hundreds of times.

A set of double doors leading to the bridge resembled the ones aboard *Atlanta*.

"Chief, you alright?" Erika asked, and he gave her a thumbs-up.

"Everyone out!" I shouted.

CHAPTER NINETEEN

Arcadia
Captain Scott Moore

When we entered the bridge, I was greeted by a familiar sight. The room resembled *Atlanta*'s bridge, just as Michael had said it would during our private discussion. My black and gray command chair sat in the center of the room. The astrogation station stood adjacent to the weapons station, and the comms and sensor stations next to the science station. Screens glowed with the Space Force logo. Holographic alerts flashed from panels, announcing combat status.

"Unbelievable," Chief said.

As I stepped onto the deck, my veins pumped with adrenaline. "Man your stations."

My crew flew into action, and after logging in, their computers came to life. Everything was as it should be. So much of what I experienced in those few moments felt like I'd stumbled into a complex dreamscape, where I'd stepped back into time and could relive my past failures.

Here was a starship the size of a city with enough mysteries to last a lifetime and enough technology to change the fate of humanity forever. My insides stirred.

Equinox designed *Atlanta*'s bridge to hold up to thirty people in case of an emergency, but *Arcadia* could hold over a hundred easily. For every console on *Atlanta*, three or four existed here, a surprisingly small amount considering her size. A quarter of my crew were qualified to work on the bridge, but all of them had spent hours upon hours inside simulations. After years of living planetside and living off the land, it took some time for everyone to get reacquainted.

When I took my seat, I set my thumb on the DNA scanner on the armrest, and a second later, holoscreens blurred into existence. Instead of *Atlanta*, all of *Arcadia*'s functions and menus were listed, but for every one on *Atlanta*, *Arcadia* possessed hundreds, and in some cases, thousands.

Up on the main screen, a holo showed our position on the edge of the Kahwin system. We'd flown eight billion klicks in eight hours. Currently, *Arcadia* cruised at ten thousand kilometers per hour, combat speed, according to one of my three holo displays hovering eye-level. Dizzying columns of data streamed across them, the amount far too much to accurately assess. Our ship had steered us headlong at the enemy.

Fifty thousand klicks away from our position, the Shaper fleet approached in a V-formation, whose frontage stretched just under nine kilometers.

My crew mumbled in abject amazement as they studied their consoles and bellowed questions at one another in an effort to understand *Arcadia*.

Chief and the weapons officer huddled at the tactical station, and Erika helped out at the engineering console and comms. Chen sat next to me.

"Unknown fleet bearing five degrees Mark 1 and closing," Chen said. Her hair had grown long during our journey, and the occasional white hair peeked through her thick black locks.

One of our navigation officers, Ensign Abnette, hailed from a small town in Mississippi and hid his Southern accent like an actor. "Sir, the controls aren't responding."

"Chief?" I asked.

Chief raced to the navigation console and assisted Abnette. After a few seconds, he shook his head. "Captain, Melody locked us out of the controls."

Had Vincent done something and not told us?

As I surveyed the tactical situation, I called out for a damage report. Something had hit us. When I received one, the list included millions of entries, including service dates, part numbers, and genetic sequence information. The dates went by an unknown calendar, and much of the information might as well have been written in Egyptian hieroglyphs.

I glanced around the bridge, and half the computers failed to respond to commands. "Comms, hail Mr. Moore."

"Aye, Captain," Erika replied. She raked her fingers across holographic dials and pinged his tablet.

Chen grimaced. "Sir, if I'm to understand this correctly, all of our weapons are offline. The security sequence inputs refuse to acknowledge my commands."

I checked my center screen, a neon-green overview of *Arcadia*'s combat capabilities. Weapons took up the left column, defenses the middle, our ship's fighter and bomber wings on the right. We lacked a CAG officer, who would have been tasked with coordinating aircraft on a normal naval carrier. Space Force never developed carriers, but we did have experience in drone and drone-based operations and tactics, and those skills might come in handy.

As I pinched my fingers together, the weapons section's screen blinked into existence, allowing me to get a closer look at our point defense batteries, dark matter cannons, energy cannons with the same power as a nuclear power plant, plasma projectors, something called a gravity bell, plasma torpedoes, and a host of other exotic weapons, many of which were off-line. Five different stations hosted the entirety of our weapons platforms, and they worked in conjunction with one another. My crew did their best to make sense of their new displays and compared discoveries with one another. One of them began using an AI-driven help feature, and a host of commands appeared before her.

Our point-defense systems worked as did our plasma projectors and our torpedoes.

"Any luck locating Mr. Moore?" I asked Erika.

"Negative, sir. His tablet isn't responding."'

Damn it.

Feazer, who sat at a sensor station, zeroed in on the enemy fleet. "Captain, the Shapers are splitting into two fleets."

Gradually, the V-formation came apart. One side retreated further into the void while the other proceeded to close on us. If we weren't flying the ship, who was? Melody?

I rechecked navigation, and the controls were locked. Michael asked me to fly *Arcadia*, and he hinted we'd be thrown into battle sooner rather than later.

Tactical announced, "Enemy fleet forming a skirmish line. Contact in fifteen minutes, twenty-three seconds."

"Erika, locate Michael. Tell him to contact me immediately."

"Aye, Captain."

"Sir, if Michael was unable to convince Vincent to grant him full access," Chief said, "then this might be a way for him to do so. He's got our DNA, our logins...."

Chief had made a good point, one I'd already considered. I trusted Vincent and Marston to accompany Michael, knowing full well if he wanted them dead, it would be a simple thing. Wasn't that the case for all of us as well?

"He had our DNA the moment we stepped aboard," I said.

Chief frowned and leaned a little closer. "Sir, I have a bad feeling about this place." In all the years I'd known him, he'd never said such a thing. How could I blame him? This bridge shouldn't exist, but it did. Everything had happened so fast, we'd hardly had a chance to consider much of anything.

"I need you to help out who you can, Chief. I'm counting on you."

"Aye, Captain."

As my friend left, the surreal nature of the bridge hit me. Michael would have needed to know the exact dimensions in order to create this room to spec, then he'd have to know my crew's qualifications. How well did I remember them? Not this well.

For starters, I wouldn't have put Sergeant Horvel on our point-defense grid. As far as I knew, his reflexes disqualified him some of the more dexterous jobs Space Force had to offer.

Nor would I have placed Master Sergeant Merkowski assisting at comms. He was tone deaf and sang one of the worst renditions of "The Star Spangled Banner" anywhere on Earth. He'd lost his hearing due to an ear infection back on Kahwin and had lost the ability to hear tones in the upper range. Erika took over quickly.

Then why put them there? Michael had made those decisions.

When I checked on both Horvel and Merkowski, they had taken to their stations like bears to honey.

"Enemy fleet now twelve minutes from initial contact range."

Errors flashed over every screen as the crew fought to gain control. Erika seemed to be having the most success, but she remained quiet as she flooded her stations with holos and manually manipulated them like puzzle pieces.

Erika. As a synth, she couldn't submit to a DNA scan, but the computer responded to her with ease. Hers were the only screens functioning as intended, and she'd moved to comms and logged into her profile.

My eyes brightened. "Lieutenant Banks, care to share your discoveries?"

"Captain, I believe I am in contact with Melody and Mr. Moore." Erika took both of her hands and created a holographic datalink between three Omega-class network nodes, the most classified network protocols used in the QN, or quantum network. Her station amplified what little signal Vincent managed to broadcast.

My brother's face pixilated by my chair. He crouched next to Melody's servers, the cluster of computers rising like skyscrapers. His face beamed. "Scott!"

I breathed a sigh of relief. The odds of our survival had just increased. "Vincent, you're okay."

"Very much. You synced with Melody?"

"Negative. She's locked us out." I stared at him a minute. "What did you do the day before your twenty-first birthday?"

"What?"

I repeated the question. If my theory proved correct, any information not associated with my direct memory couldn't be replicated by *Arcadia*, and since I wasn't with my brother on that day, either he would know and the person before me was Vincent Moore, or he wouldn't know, and he would be a biological creation in his likeness.

Meanwhile, the enemy flew into range, but at fifteen thousand kilometers, we'd need AI to hit anything.

"I told you. I was in Tijuana and almost got arrested," Vincent said.

"You never told me who went with you."

Vincent shook his head a few times. "I was with Tony. He didn't want anyone to know."

"Got it. Can you give us control over here?"

"Working on it." Vincent gestured to a set of cables plugged into one of Melody System's proprietary computer consoles. A progress bar crawled its way toward 100% on an otherwise bright blue screen.

The enemy fleet grew larger on the screen, closing distance. "Put Michael onscreen. I want to speak with him."

"I'm afraid that's going to be a little difficult." Vincent turned the camera toward the bulkhead.

Michael lay still, his open eyes locked in place. His head was tilted to the side, and his tongue rested slightly out of his mouth. His spotless Space Force uniform left no hint of what had killed him.

"What happened?" I asked, my mind racing. If *Arcadia* knew to create Michael, then it also knew about our agreement and its promise to bring us to Earth after I'd laid waste to the Shapers and freed this branch of humanity. The thought of waging an interstellar war using *Arcadia* seemed as farfetched as it sounded. Me? Some kind of Napoleonic freedom fighter?

While Vincent spoke, his gestures manipulated holographic quantum keys. "I was showing Michael how to interact with Melody and he started acting like this. Don't have a clue how or why." The holograms painted his face green as cryptographic icons surged in continual streams. "Almost... have it."

"Sir, weapons station now operational!" the weapons officer announced.

My center-most screen turned blue, and a cursor blinked in the upper left corner.

Updating...

Melody Corp.
General AI, Melody, Version 24.084
Neural Network Rebuilding...
System Reset
Updating...
Complete
Status Ready
Hello, Captain Moore.

I ran my fingers through my hair, stunned at what Vincent had accomplished. He'd done the impossible. Somehow, he'd helped Melody bridge the gap between our science and whatever science the Antediluvians employed. Or had she done it? Melody was capable of miracles. As one of America's best kept secrets, she surpassed all other AIs by orders of magnitude. By doing so, the U.S. had broken a number of international agreements about artificial intelligence. If you asked me, the Russians and the Chinese knew more than they let on. They must have known.

"Tactical?" I asked.

Errors vanished from the tactical screens as Vincent remotely nullified the security lockout. "Confirmed, sir," one of my crew replied. "Tactical is free. I've gained control."

"Standby. Lay down a screen and vaporize any incoming targets when the enemy moves within eighty thousand kilometers," I ordered.

"Aye, sir."

One by one, their screens came alive. Each station answered to a master station, where the others siphoned through AI-driven algorithms, which made the process of operating a starship somewhat manageable. Although *Arcadia* was dissimilar to *Atlanta* in almost every way, Melody simplified the minutia and presented data in familiar ways.

I touched the menu on one of the screens and brought up navigation. Melody set up *Arcadia*'s speeds into three groups: Jumpspace 1-100, Intersystem 1-100, and Combat, which used Full, Three-Quarter, Half, and Quarter Speed, and Stop, and Sternway.

"Helm, new heading: nine zero degrees, half speed," I said.

"Aye, sir. New heading nine zero degrees, half speed," Ensign Abnette replied.

Battle updates streamed as countless dots blazed through the void at us. The ships pushing the skirmish line raced forward past the eleven-thousand-kilometer line, and at their current speed, they'd be in range in a few minutes.

"Steady," I said.

The ships that launched the initial salvo flew at a distance between 120,000 and 125,000 klicks off our portside bow, while the other group of ships continued their path into the deep void. Where were they going and why?

Glowing dots blossomed on the screen as the enemy accelerated toward us, closing the spacious gap.

Beads of sweat glistened on my brow. Never in my life did I think I'd command a ship like *Arcadia*, and to sit in the command chair and be surrounded by whom I considered to be my brothers and sisters in war brought me a sense of peace. To be here in this moment felt as natural as saluting.

Erika showcased her expertise by using *Arcadia*'s sensors to scan the drones on the horizon and subsequently detail their various combat features. As she did, the system displayed Antediluvian runes and symbols. In seconds, Melody translated them and the icons blurred into English words.

Drone Type: Hermes Architecture / Kahwin Evolutionary Path
   Weapons: Scatter Lasers, Dorsel-mounted Fusion Beams, antimatter warhead

Genetic Pattern Designer: Allo Quishar
Status:Ready

"Hermes?" Chief asked.

Erika sent me an update. "Melody's classifying objects with Greek nomenclature."

"Enemy now within range, sir," Chen announced.

"Fire a torpedo spread. Continue firing the plasma projectors."

"Torpedoes away," Chen confirmed.

Arcadia flung beams of energy, lighting up the void.

"Hold course," I said to Ensign Abnette.

Chen glared at his tactical screen. "Enemy changing formation to avoid our torpedoes."

I leaned forward in my seat. "Pull it up on the main display."

The main screen zoomed in on hundreds of torpedoes splitting off in different directions.

I eased up on my armrests, my knuckles almost pale white.

Chen's voice rose slightly. "First impacts in one zero seconds."

The enemy continued to fly in various directions, some spiraling around one another in an attempt to evade. When the Shapers came closer, our point defense system engaged, vaporizing them like swatting flies. Only a few of our torpedoes erupted in momentary flames as the rest of our torpedoes swarmed them, obliterating the closest in a display of fireworks that blotted out in nanoseconds.

Arcadia's guns unleashed another torrent of beams arcing with pulsing energy. The bridge fell silent.

The void exploded with flashes of brilliant light as our weapons found their targets. Detonations bloomed over the main screen.

Our hit rate stood at fifteen percent, and that was accomplished with the sensor station, the tactical station, and the weapon station working in conjunction with Melody, but mainly with skill. Our AI acted sluggish, but my crew was up to the task.

Still, the enemy armada closed in, unleashing a barrage of projectiles in our direction. I clenched my fists and held my breath, watching as our weapons met their targets with deadly accuracy. The enemy ships were quick and nimble, and completely organic. They dodged and weaved to avoid our fire but with little success. Our weapon batteries created a blanket of fire.

"Keep firing!" I yelled. "We can do this!"

Arcadia's guns unleashed a torrent of beams arcing with pulsing energy. The bridge fell silent. The void exploded with flashes of brilliant light as our weapons found their targets. Detonations bloomed over the main screen. The bridge crew worked in perfect harmony, their fingers dancing over the control panels as they tracked the enemy's movements and adjusted our weapons accordingly. Sweat poured down my back as the fierce battle unfolded on the main screen.

Just as I thought we were gaining the upper hand, a sudden explosion rocked the ship, sending us all staggering. Klaxons blared. A sudden explosion rocked the ship. I bucked back against the captain's chair, the deck shaking like an earthquake. Ensign Abnette held onto the navigation console as the ship took another blow.

"What the hell was that?" I shouted.

Chen studied a host of damage control screens. "Sir, we've taken a direct hit. Starboard weapons offline. Starboard engines offline. Rerouting power."

My heart sank as I realized the gravity of the situation. With our engines down, our maneuverability would be severely limited, and we'd be at a serious disadvantage in the fight.

"Get that engine back online, now!" I ordered.

"Plasma projectors recharging. Twenty seconds," a tactical officer said. "Torpedoes available in sixty seconds."

Where'd these Shapers come from? They were waiting on the outskirts of the system like watchdogs.

I checked my screen, scrolling past incoming reports. There it was, updated information about our weapons. *Arcadia*'s plasma projectors acted as its mid-range threat, their optimal range between five thousand and nine thousand kilometers. They fired a lightly armored "round" much like a standard projectile. Each round contained a plasma core surrounded by a miniature gravitic shell, which kept the plasma in place until impact when the gravity-encased plasma would explode, delivering a heat charge at 30,000°C. When the enemy came within range, *Arcadia* would fling hundreds of thousands of these shells per minute, effectively creating a wall of impenetrable destruction.

"Tactical, keep an eye on the farthest armada. If they're fleeing, they're going someplace."

"Aye, Captain."

"Eight minutes until impact," Chen said.

"Erika, scan the incoming fleet. Divide the ships into groups. See if you can work with Melody to find out if they're using a command structure or if they're operating as a hive."

"Aye, Captain. Sensors indicate a total of 3,108 enemy vessels." As Erika took an account of the enemy, Chief and Chen stepped over to his station to assist him. Melody analyzed the sensor data, noting the enemy's size, speed, trajectory, and known weapon systems.

"Captain, the enemy fleet appears to be operating as a hive mind. There is no discernible command structure," Melody reported.

"Feazer, can you determine if there's a central control

system or if the ships are communicating with each other?" I asked.

Feazer's hands flew over the console. "Negative, Captain. *Arcadia*'s sensors cannot detect any communication signals."

Chief glanced at me. "They may be encrypted beyond our level of decryption."

I frowned. "Keep trying."

"Aye, Captain," Feazer replied, his eyes fixed on the console.

Chen turned to me. "Captain, all weapons are charged and ready."

I nodded. "Fire at will."

The ship trembled as our weapons fired, sending massive black spheres hurtling through space toward the enemy fleet. The enemy fleet attempted to evade the attack, but it was too late. Once our torps exploded, they obliterated entire sections of their formation. On the screen, ships tore in half, internal explosions snuffing out moments later.

Arcadia's plasma projectors continued to unleash their deadly payload on the enemy ships. As the battle raged, we were holding our own against an enemy that outnumbered us and with relative ease.

"Starboard engines online," Chief said. "Looks like Melody figured out a way divert enough power."

I gripped the side of my chair and clenched my teeth. "Time to give them hell."

In the void of space, with me in command, *Arcadia* found itself locked in battle against the retreating Shaper fleet. The battle seemed to stretch on for an age, as both sides exchanged devastating blows that, to me, threatened to shatter the fabric of the universe itself. Though the *Arcadia* faced a harrowing start, with critical systems malfunctioning and leaving us exposed, my crew refused to surrender. Our resolve only strengthened due to the urgency to defend our ship, our last hope of getting home.

"Steady," I said.

Chief shook his head in disbelief. "I'm amazed. For the first time, I'm almost speechless. Is there anything *Arcadia* can'tdo?"

"Let's hope we never find out," I replied.

As the battle intensified, *Arcadia* deftly executed a flanking maneuver, positioning itself to strike the enemy fleet's vulnerable rear. We unleashed a coordinated barrage, devastating a significant portion of the enemy. The fleet, taken aback by our sudden and devastating attack, scrambled to regroup.

Sensing an opportunity to deliver a crushing blow, I ordered tactical to quickly formulate a plan to exploit the enemy's confusion. With the enemy fleet in disarray, we closed in for the kill, unleashing a relentless salvo of laser and plasma fire that overwhelmed the remaining ships.

As the last enemy vessel exploded in a blinding burst of energy, I paused. What had just happened? Had it been that easy? *Arcadia* was like a god sailing through space.

"Damage report," I said.

New data emerged around me as Melody assessed *Arcadia*'s hull integrity, her weapons, and so on.

The hull sustained severe damage and multiple breaches on the port side. Automated "units," as Melody put it, were presently sealing the affected areas, but they needed to conduct a more detailed damage assessment before they could commence major repairs. When I asked her what a "unit" meant, I was met with vague terms that circled back on themselves. Apparently, a "unit" meant something capable of independent travel, action, and thought, and that was as far as it went.

Several power nodes were disabled, and the primary dark matter power generator operated at only 70% capacity, severely compromising *Arcadia*'s power grid. Melody activated hundreds of secondary generators, which levied an enormous strain. Power fluctuations could potentially cause further system failures, a risk I wasn't willing to take.

The life support systems suffered damage, and the backup systems churned out atmosphere. To ensure they lasted until full repairs could be made, Melody rationed oxygen and other life support supplies to unoccupied areas of the ship.

To my annoyance, the Shapers had inflicted significant damage on our forward-facing weapon systems, resulting in a reduced number of functioning weapons. Targeting sensors remained offline.

Our communication systems sustained damage, rendering us unable to establish long-range communication. It wouldn't have mattered normally, but Michael insisted we make repairs at Eos. If they could repair a ship this size, wouldn't they be able to knock her out when we got within range?

"Magnificent job, crew," I said, wiping perspiration off my face. "I commend each and every one of you for your outstanding bravery and quick thinking. We have a long voyage ahead of us. You have proven to be the epitome of military professionalism, embodying the true spirit of the Space Force. Your decisive actions in combat have upheld the highest standards of excellence, and for that, I am immensely proud to be your captain."

I took a moment to look at each member of my crew. "I have zero doubt that we will continue to overcome any challenge that comes our way."

The main screen blinked for a moment.

"Course plotted to Eos," Melody announced.

"Did you plot that course?" I asked.

"Negative, sir. She's done it on her own."

"Melody, did you receive any new information about Eos?" I asked.

"Yes, Captain. I have accessed the latest database and historical records available. It appears that Eos was built during the later stages of the Regency. The system where the station lies is in a distant section of the galaxy known as the Atlas Rift. My datalogs are unable to access the station's age."

"Anything else?" I asked.

Melody's level voice came through with some static. "My current dataset indicates Eos is still operational, albeit in a dormant state. It appears to have been maintained and preserved for all these years."

"Very well, Melody," I said. "Let's see what secrets Eos holds." Not that we had much choice in the matter. *Arcadia* flew itself. We'd remedy that immediately. "How's Michael?" I asked Vincent.

On my holo, Vincent wrinkled his brow. "He stopped breathing. I'm not sure if he's alive or not. His eyes move, but he's not breathing."

"Doc, get down there," I said.

"Aye, Captain."

On the main screen, a visualization of the jumpspace appeared. "Executing last remaining slow jump. Destination Eos. ETA... unknown," Melody announced.

CHAPTER TWENTY

Kahwin
Kol Washington

My heart pounded as I stumbled through the forest. Trees loomed overhead like silent, sinister giants. Zoe weighed less than I thought, but my back was killing me. After complaining I might not be able to continue, she climbed off my back and tried to stand. The cold wind sliced through my thin jacket, and I shivered. We'd marched for two hours without a sign of life.

"I think I can manage." Zoe's normally smooth voice crackled with static. She limped alongside me, her movements uncoordinated. "Keep moving." Her words slurred. "Left... at the next... fork."

"What's the plan?" I asked, trying to catch my breath. "How far is it?"

"Trust me, Kol."

I nodded, not entirely convinced. In a lot of ways, Zoe had been my guide and protector since I'd left the safety of my village. She'd given up so much to be with me.

As we advanced, Zoe pointed out spots on the ground where she said the Antediluvians trapped the earth. Some places looked like twisted metal. Others resembled grotesque, half-organic constructs, like a Shaper and a human had a baby.

"Watch your... step," Zoe said. "Two more traps... ahead."

I squinted through the gloom. "I see them."

A bizarre piece of warped bronze resembling a gnarled tree with metallic roots sat off to my right, and as we walked away from it, it moved in front of us. The roots writhed and squirmed as though they were alive, their tips glistening with a viscous substance.

"What is that?" I asked.

"Concentrate on it. Quickly."

"What?"

"The tree. Command it to move."

"How do I do that?"

"Tell it to move with your mind. Hurry."

The forest seemed to close in on us, the shadows growing darker. With my mind? Easier said than done.

"Hurry, Kol."

I swallowed hard. *Move out of our way.*

Crunch. One of the tree's roots grew thick and lifted the tree, the other limbs bent and touched the ground, helping guide the tree to my left. It grumbled along and created its own path, stripping plants from the ground as it went. Soon, the tree disappeared.

"Did I do that?" I ask, confused.

"We must go."

We climbed a steep incline, and I thought I kept seeing another one of General Vack's drones following us. Every time I tried to focus on it, it ended up being a tree or a rock.

We approached a cluster of cubes hovering in the air like a

swarm of blood-drinking insects. A faint high-pitched whine emanated from them, and they pulsed in unison.

"Keep... moving," Zoe said. "Do not... touch."

Gritting my teeth, I wove a trail between the cubes. My breath came in short, sharp gasps, and my legs trembled from the strain.

Zoe's pace quickened. I struggled to keep up with her. She'd healed somehow, but she still had difficulty speaking.

"Faster," she said. "The Iron Guard... close."

I swallowed the lump in my throat and forced my legs to move at a quicker pace.

Zoe stopped when her eyes locked on something up ahead, a large cylinder made from discolored metals and a strange translucent oil towered over us, reaching high into the forest canopy. It was hard to see.

"What is it?" I whispered. "Is it another trap?"

She hesitated. "I... don't... know."

The metal seemed to pulse with an internal energy, while the translucent material refracted the dim starlight. At its base, I noticed a series of concentric rings vibrating ever so slightly.

"What do you think this is?" I asked.

"Not sure," she stammered. "Proceed... with... caution."

A pull drew me closer, like a magnet.

I fought against the pit of fear growing in my belly. "Do you feel that?"

Her mechanical eyes flickered with uncertainty. "Yes... I... feel... something."

We exchanged a glance. She seemed to be struggling against the same oppressive force, like one of the Academy's drill sergeants.

"Kol," Zoe whispered. "Be... careful."

The air around us began to shimmer, and the once-faint structure grew brighter, casting a rainbow of colors across the forest floor. I tried to pull away, but a force had locked me in place, pinning me like a thousand invisible hands had reached out of the darkness and pressed on my chest.

"Zoe!" I choked out, panic gripping me. "I can't move!"

Her eyes widened, and she struggled to move closer. "Hold… on… Kol. I'll… help."

As she came closer, she too became ensnared in the invisible grip. She yanked back, but her limbs trembled as she fought against the force. We were both trapped.

"What's happening?" I gasped.

"I… don't know. We must find… a way… out."

"Any ideas?" My vision blurred as the pressure in my head increased.

Her eyes met mine. "Focus your mind. Command it."

Summoning every bit of strength I had left, I concentrated on the binding force, willing it to release its grip. The cylinder's vibrations intensified until the air seemed to shatter around us.

"I can't breathe."

"Push harder," Zoe said. "Hurry!"

The world started to darken.

I'd come all this way just to die.

CHAPTER TWENTY-ONE

Kahwin
Kol Washington

With a sudden release, the force holding us vanished. I stumbled back, my breath coming in ragged gasps. Zoe collapsed beside me. We lay there for a moment, our bodies spent. The cylinder, whatever it was, had disappeared entirely.

"We did it," I whispered.

"You did."

A light pierced the dark a few hundred meters off. This time, I knew I wasn't hallucinating.

"Down," Zoe said.

A drone the size of a warehouse flew slowly above the tree-line. Plates of grey reinforced steel covered its hull like overlapping armor, and its nose projected a beam of light, searching the forest.

We hid under a rock while it came closer. It stopped, and other lights emerged from its side. In seconds, the forest lit up like a city.

Zoe held her finger up to her lips. My hair was damp with

sweat. I wasn't going back to the Academy under any circumstances.

One of the lights hit the tall cylinder, which started to glow a bright purple. The structure shot a thick red beam of energy into the drone, and it exploded in a tremendous fireball. Flaming wreckage rained down all around us, and a few of the trees caught fire.

"Run!" Zoe led me through the dense undergrowth. Something else stirred in the air, an almost imperceptible change, like the early onset of winter or the musky smell of mating season.

The forest fire raged behind us as some of the taller trees and a slight wind helped the inferno spread like a disease. We ran for I don't know how long. An annoying rock wedged its way into my boots, and after a few hundred meters of climbing, it might as well have been a dull knife.

I took a second to fish it out and rubbed my foot. "What's happening?"

Her eyes scanned the environment. "We're close. The forest... the traps are meant to keep anyone out who isn't... tuned to this place."

We pushed through a thicket of twisted branches, where a heavy rock the size of our old APC blocked our path.

"Kol, get on the left side and help me push."

"How can I? Look at the size of it."

"It will respond to your touch. Do it, please."

I did as she asked me, and when I tried to push the rock, I almost fell over. "It's too heavy."

"Did you concentrate on moving it?"

I threw my hands up in frustration. "It's not a machine. What do you want me to do? Are you going to help me push it or not?"

"Only you can push it."

"Look at the size of this thing."

"Try."

I put my hands on the rock and focused.

Move.

Nothing happened, as expected.

"You're not trying hard enough, Kol."

"Yes, I am," I said, annoyed. "What do you mean?"

"What you think you see is not what you see. You do not stand before a rock. Order its essence to move, and it will obey you."

"Order its essence. Right."

I tried again and failed.

"Look, if you're not going to help me, fine, but don't expect me to push a rock that's this size."

"You must believe you can move it."

The skin behind my ear itched something crazy, and so did my hands. They were covered in a thin black film and grime. I rubbed them on some dirt and then tapped on the rock. When I looked at Zoe, she ignored me and stared directly at the rock. You can convince yourself of just about anything if you try hard enough, but maybe not enough to move a rock.

What would it take for me to do this? To forget about the physical world? I'd ignored pain in the past. Many times. Was it like that?

It's only a rock.

I braced my back leg and shoved my weight into the side of the gargantuan stone.

Move.

My hands melted into the stone like mud, and I touched the other side. Something smooth. It happened so fast, I barely had enough time to open my eyes.

A hidden door shimmered into existence. The stone? Gone. The door seemed to blend with the surroundings, its edges

BRANDON ELLIS & MAX WOLFE

barely discernible. Yet, it was unmistakably there, and it'd been there the entire time.

Emblazed on the door stood a man dressed in a large armored suit. Showing the crest of a warrior, his helm swept back straight from the brow, while the rest of the helmet obscured his face from view. A visor stretched across where his eyes would be. None of his skin showed, and in some ways, he reminded me of one of Captain Scott's Janissary robots he commanded.

The warrior battled a monstrous Shaper with tendrils ending in suction cups. He was surrounded by towering beings with obscured features, but they towered over him like giants.

"How do we open it?" I asked.

"Concentrate on... the door as you did with the rock."

I felt a strange connection forming, as if the world itself recognized me. As I concentrated, the door began to change, its surface rippling like water. With a final, resounding click, the door swung open. A stairway descended into darkness.

"The world understands you, Kol," Zoe whispered. "It's been waiting. Come. We must hurry before the Academy sends another drone."

We proceeded down the stairs for a time. The darkness gave way to a soft, blue-tinged light that illuminated the walls. The staircase stretched into the shadows.

"What is this place, Zoe?" I asked.

She didn't answer. As we descended, the light intensified, revealing walls made of gold depicting scenes of war, rituals, and ceremonial gatherings, like the ones we used to do when I was a kid. At first, I thought the pictures might be telling a story because I saw the same man in the armor in many of them. Only half the art made sense to me.

The air grew colder. I had the distinct feeling someone

watched us, but every time I glanced around—nothing. Only the shadows and the ever-present blue glow.

As we reached the bottom of the stairs, the hall abruptly ended, opening up into a massive chamber. Towering statues, their features obscured by the dim light, lined the walls. A lone pedestal stood in the center of the room, and at the far end, another door, this one like the doors the Earthers brought to Starport City, blocked the rest of the way.

I turned to Zoe. "What is all of this?"

She looked around, her expression unreadable. "The Scalding Ruins, what General Vack calls Project 1."

"Why do they call it the Scalding Ruins?"

"A long time ago, the Shapers tried to destroy Project 1. For a while, nothing could live here."

"That must have been a *long* time ago," I said. "Why are we here?"

For a moment, she seemed to struggle with her words. Finally, she looked at me. "To teach you. Concentrate on the far door."

I focused my thoughts and reached out with my mind. The strange connection formed again. The door responded and rippled as it had before. The door slid open with a hiss.

We stepped through the doorway and into a cavernous space that stretched on into infinity. Towering machines filled the room like guardian sentinels. There were thousands of them lined up in formation.

Each machine resembled armored warriors rivaling the Janissaries. Some had cannons mounted on their shoulders, others held large caliber rifles at the ready. Many had a single rectangular contraption embedded into their back, what probably were engines.

"Can they fly?" I asked.

"They can jump great distances."

"That would come in handy."

All of them carried a sword in a metallic scabbard at their waist, which seemed the strangest thing for them to do. The swords were three times my size.

A blend of familiar and unfamiliar technologies were scattered around the room in neat clusters, interwoven with cables.

Zoe took in the details of the mechanical giants and the electronics surrounding us. Her voice filled with wonder. "This Kol, belongs to you."

As I stood there, dwarfed by the machines, I felt a strange sense of belonging, like everything was perfect here. It was as if I'd stepped into a world that'd been waiting for me.

I approached one of the towering machines. My hand instinctively reached out to touch its armored surface. A rush of memories flooded through me. Images of ancient battles flickered through my mind, each scene blending seamlessly into the next. Explosions. Detonations. The cries of dying men. Their might, their purpose coursed through my veins.

When I pulled back my hand, I clenched my jaw. "What does it all mean?"

"What did you see?"

"War."

"The greatest war Kahwin has ever known. I will make sure you can touch things from now on without your mind seeing those images. You are part of something greater than yourself. General Vack knew this. The oracle knew this. Even Captain Moore knows this."

I looked around at the towering army. "What are they?"

"Your ancestors called them the Immortals."

"Are they like the Janissaries?"

"In some ways. Kahwin was once a prison colony many, many years ago. The prisoners were dissidents who fought against a great empire known as the Regency. Did General Vack mention that to you?"

"No. Nothing like that at all. How did they get here?"

"The same way Captain Moore did. How much do you know about the Shapers?"

"I know they ate us for food, and they're hideous. I'm glad Captain Moore and his Janissaries killed them. I used to have bad dreams about them. It's hard to remember. Doctor Ingram said I blocked the memories out because of trauma."

"The Shapers arrived and enslaved the population. Originally, the Immortals were created to protect the planetary governor and the other high-ranking officials from the Regency. Many died, but they held the Regency at bay. When the abrupt Shaper invasion began, these people and their population had already been decimated by the Regency war. For those the Shapers didn't enslave, they retreated to this hidden sanctuary and uploaded copies of themselves into these mechanical giants."

I stared at the machines in disbelief. "You mean there are people inside them?"

"Not... exactly," she said carefully. "Their essence, their memories, and their personalities were stored in a consciousness matrix. Each of these Immortals contains the digital soul of government officials, soldiers, and scientists. The process was not perfect, and they are not exactly the same person they once were."

I tried to wrap my head around the concept. "How can that be possible? How can they still exist inside these things?"

"They have a kind of mind matrix that acts as a vessel, like your body to your brain. You will command these Immortals, Kol." Zoe's voice filled with intensity, like she'd been waiting to tell me this for years. "That is why the Iron Guard has been pursuing you."

"What's going to happen now?" I asked.

"Follow me." Zoe guided me toward a corner of the massive room, where a group of computer terminals stood. The design and layout were familiar, as if they'd been plucked straight from Earth, the place Captain Moore came from. I knew how to operate them.

Beside the computer terminals, a towering machinery surged with energy. The device appeared to be some sort of advanced server system with symbols I couldn't decipher.

"What are those?" I asked.

Zoe glanced at the machinery. "That, my friend, is Melody."

"Melody? Like a song?" I struggled with the name, another obnoxious English word. "What is it?"

"The Senate made a copy of an advanced artificial intelligence that powered their starship called the USS *Atlanta* before Captain Moore left to the north."

"Where is Captain Moore?" Was he even alive? I hoped so.

"He's safe. That is all you need to know."

"Okay, so if this Melody is the copy, where's the original?"

"This *is* the original. Captain Moore has the copy. Melody is a computer brain that possesses vast amounts of knowledge from Earth."

"How did it end up here?"

Zoe hesitated for a moment. "I stole it and brought it here."

I stared at her. "Why? I mean, aren't you going to get in trouble for that? And, if you needed me to get inside here, how did you get in here, then?"

She didn't answer my last question. Instead, Zoe offered me a gentle smile. "I think we're both in trouble. With Melody, we will know everything there is to know about Earth. Its history, its technology, its culture, everything, and won't it be exciting?"

"If you say so." I still didn't understand. "Why would you want to know all that?"

Zoe's unwavering gaze met mine. "Because I intend to visit Earth and I am going to take you with me."

CHAPTER TWENTY-TWO

"For what can war but endless war still breed?"
—John Milton, "Paradise Lost"

Arcadia
Captain Scott Moore

To win at war is to carry the burden of victory. In the modern era, all civilized societies have tasted war, some more than others. The 20th century proved to be the precursor for what was to come in the 21st, and when I left Earth, I was fairly certain war might soon follow. As an American, to watch my once great nation fall into desperate times was nothing new. I'd grown up in an era when forty-five percent of the population went hungry or skipped meals, and if you put enough pressure on people, they tend to act in ways they regret.

We'd slain the Shaper fleet, obliterating them in ways I never thought possible. I'd taken on a responsibility no one else would ever shoulder. I suppose I should explain why.

All my life, I'd wanted to be someone of note, a person whom history would write about until the end of time. Many men in my field share a similar ambition, and although we fear to admit it, most officers who wear a uniform long to gain glory on a battlefield. Perhaps it is in our nature to be this way. No doubt, there's a sickness to war that cannot be overstated.

Who had I agreed to fight on behalf of humanity? The Shapers ruled the galaxy, and until someone pushed the first domino and attacked them, nothing would change. Humans would be a perpetual source of food and entertainment for these things, and my heart commanded I do something about it. Foolish, certainly. Who was I to take on this task?

I asked how long it would take to "liberate" the human population before I could return to Earth. Michael couldn't give me an estimate and now he was dead. I might never know. *Arcadia*had been out of communication for millennia. Kahwin had joined the multitude of other worlds under Shaper control and became an isolated pocket. What other tools had the Antediluvians left behind, what other weapons or ships? What other inventions and incredible discoveries?

The discussion I'd had with Michael would never be mentioned in its entirety in any holo or historical text. If I spoke honestly about what kinds of questions he asked me, history would not be kind to me, and yet, I'd risked answering him truthfully and with conviction. AIs have been able to detect lies since way before I was born, and I trusted Michael would know if I lied or not.

One of the main questions Michael insisted I answer was why Earth hadn't united under one government by now. None of my answers satisfied him, especially when I'd tell him our role in preventing that from happening in the 20th century. He became annoyed when I mentioned World War One and the League of Nations.

Naturally, I took notice of Michael's responses, and they played a key role in my decision. I listened closely, watched his facial expressions, and tried to make sense of what he was asking me to do.

That conversation, which took place inside my reconstructed office, burned in my mind. Michael sat across from me in front of my desk, where he folded his hands in his lap and regarded me with curiosity. Although he tried to put me at ease, when he spoke, he did so with authority.

This was how it went down.

"Take *Arcadia,* the greatest invention your species has ever created, and liberate your people," Michael had said. "This ship has enough firepower to tame the stars. It is yours for the taking. All that I ask is you offer me a chance for revenge."

"Why would you want revenge? Are you speaking for the ship or yourself? Or is there a difference?"

Michael balled his hand into a fist and squared his jaw. "Would you not want revenge for your species if they were enslaved and used as food?"

I regarded him for a while because I wasn't sure what to make of him. He spoke as if he were a human. "The people of Kahwin appear to be related to us genetically, but..."

"Appear to be? You *are* related to all of humanity whether you acknowledge it or not."

"Even if that were true, the Shapers have done nothing to us on Earth. Your fight against them has nothing to do with us," I said.

He steepled his fingers together and looked down his nose at me. "The fight is not between the Shapers and humanity. The fight is between the Keepers and humanity. The Shapers are merely tools."

"It would help if you were to tell me who the Keepers are."

Michael arched his brow, amused. "I believe you know who they are, Captain Moore."

"What do you mean?"

"Do you not have stories in your history about beings that exist outside the physical universe? Do not your religions offer you evidence of such beings?"

I threw a dismissive hand. "Evidence? Religions tell their followers what they want to hear so they gain power. Nothing more."

A smirk crossed his lips. "Your words do not ring true. Someone taught you these things, and you must *unlearn* them."

"Are you telling me the Keepers are demons?"

"No, Captain, but if you subsume your beliefs to what you perceive in the physical universe, you will invariably misinterpret reality. The Keepers are real."

I rapped my knuckles against the desk. "You're not answering my questions. I encountered a Keeper when we attacked the Shapers in Starport City. It said its name was Allo Quishar. It seemed to be the only Shaper capable of direct communication."

"What did it say to you?"

I relayed the story. There wasn't much to tell. Allo Quishar wanted to know about Earth, and when I refused to tell him, I got lucky and killed him. Well, I'd killed the Shaper he inhabited. Some might say possessed. Since then, I'd had nightmares about seeing its face up close, hearing its voice croak. It said it could inhabit any Shaper, which meant any Shaper we encountered could potentially be Allo Quishar.

"You've said you will help us return to Earth after we 'liberate' the stars, but you never told me how long that would take. When I ask you, you dodge the question."

"I cannot answer you, Captain. The Regency collapsed. How many of their worlds remain intact remains a mystery. Once we stop at Eos, I hope we can ascertain a better understanding."

"Eos?" I asked.

"*Arcadia* needs repairs and a refit. Once we arrive, I will see to it that this ship is ready for war. We have enough fuel for a slow jump, which will take us there, albeit not as quickly as this ship can normally traverse the stars."

"Eos is a space station?"

"Yes."

"How do you know it'll still exist after all this time? What's to say the Shapers or the Keepers haven't found it and destroyed it?"

"That remains a possibility."

"Speaking of the Keepers, once they discover *Arcadia*, won't they come after it?"

"Most likely. That is why we must prepare."

I scoffed at Michael's reply. "How? I have a small amount of personnel. How can I run a ship this size?"

Michael lowered his voice. "Captain, we must seek out allies. We need to find those who share our cause and bring them on board. We'll train them, equip them, and make them part of our crew. Together, we'll fight the Keepers and any other enemy that stands in our way."

I took a deep breath, absorbing the gravity of the situation. Was this ship, this crew, humanity's last hope? The weight of that responsibility bore down heavily on me. "I understand," I said slowly. "What about my crew? They didn't sign up for this."

"We'll offer them a choice," Michael replied firmly. "Stay and fight with us or return to Earth."

I winced at the thought of abandoning people in need. "You are making a promise you cannot keep. Do you have a way to get back to Earth? If so, what is it?"

Michael hesitated, then leaned in closer. "There is a way, Captain. I can say no more than that."

My eyes widened in disbelief. "What is it?"

"We must do whatever it takes to save humanity."

"You're not answering my questions."

"Your priorities must be realigned. Earth is safe for now, is it not?" Michael asked.

"We have problems that need to be addressed back home."

"Problems that pale in comparison to what the rest of humanity is currently experiencing. Earth is but one world."

I steeled my expression. "It's my home."

"I realize that, Captain. I do. I understand the love you have for your people, your desires, your will to succeed. I am here to help you. I will do everything in my power to make you happy, and I promise you, you will not regret what is to come." He smiled, revealing a set of perfect teeth. "I admire you more than you know. It is said that a man would rise to overcome the Keepers. Humans make their own myths and see in them what they wish to see. When we get to Eos, all will be revealed to you. We will wage war against the Shapers and destroy them. Only then will you know Earth will be safe."

I nodded slowly, realizing the truth in his words. "Okay," I said, having made up my mind. "We do it your way. For now."

War is a tragic and inevitable aspect of human existence, and it will always be an expression of our primal instinct to defend ourselves and our communities, to preserve our values and beliefs, and to secure our future. It reveals the darker side of our nature, and deep down, even though I wanted glory on the battlefield, I hated it. Immensely. So, why the appeal?

Why did all this feel... right?

CHAPTER TWENTY-THREE

Kahwin
The Scalding Ruins
Kol Washington

I need to be truthful here. The idea of leaving Kahwin and journeying to a place I'd only heard about in stories and dreams terrified me. What was Earth anyway? Sure, I'd been shot at recently, and sure, I'd seen a lot, but traveling to another world, one on the other side of the galaxy? I told Zoe my fears. She understood. Time to learn about them, she'd said. And so we did.

Inside the base, days turned into weeks, weeks into months. Zoe and Melody taught me about Earth, its history and its people, all the while gaining a better understanding of English. Hopefully, you can tell. Together, we delved into tales of the planet's great wars, exploring the rise and fall of empires, and finding out what made them tick.

I learned about the ancient Egyptians and their pyramids, the Roman Empire and its sprawling roads, and the Mongols, who rampaged across places called Asia and Europe. The

Romans reminded me of Kahwin in a lot of ways with their helmets and their laws. According to Melody, Rome influenced everyone on Earth, but it wouldn't explain why. I think it expected me to know already.

But it was the stories of Ancient Greece that truly interested me. Something about their culture resonated with me, a connection that bridged the vast expanse between our two worlds. They worshipped human-like gods who ruled from atop Mount Olympus. Brave warriors fought in a campaign called the Trojan War. Greek philosophers changed their world too. They pondered the nature of existence and the mysteries of the universe. Their uniforms looked a lot like ours for some reason. When I asked Melody how it was possible our two cultures were the same, it still wouldn't answer.

Most days, I spent time at a desk, where I interfaced with Melody for hours at a time. The servers were wired together, their lights blinking like the lights in Starport City. We had plenty of food too, but it tasted a little weird. The air tasted a little stale and a little sweet. Zoe said it was good for me and would make me smarter. I laughed it off. Air doesn't make you smarter.

Zoe told me this place was as old as Starport City, and the oracle knew about it. She said we'd be safe here for as long as necessary, whatever that meant.

Our water came from collected rainwater from pipes that ran far off into the distance and was filtered many times before it reached us. Many of the hallways led to locked doors, and Zoe welded them shut and put debris in the way. There was only one way out—the way we came in. If anyone tried to find us, they'd have to go through the same traps we did.

Naturally, I asked her who built this place. She said it didn't matter. It was ours now.

One day, I asked Zoe, "Why are there so many similarities

between Kahwin and Ancient Greece? It doesn't make sense. How can two civilizations share so much in common when they're on the opposite sides of the galaxy?"

Zoe's eyes went distant as if she searched for the right words. "Perhaps it's because all human civilizations share a common desire for knowledge."

"That doesn't explain the same uniforms and clothing, though."

"I can't explain that, Kol."

"Can I ask you something?"

"You know you can."

"How are we going to get to Earth? Isn't it very far away?"

"It's very far away, but there's a shortcut we'll take. You will sleep on the way there, so for you, the trip won't take long at all." Zoe smiled, which always made me smile back.

"Will we fly there?" I asked.

"Yes."

"In a spaceship?"

"Yes, in an Earth ship."

If she was joking, I wasn't able to tell. "How are we going to get an Earth ship?"

"You'll see."

Another month passed. Melody wanted me to learn about geometry and science, but for the life of me, that stuff was boring. I pored over a collection of ancient Greek artwork and came across a piece that spoke directly to my soul. It was an ancient clay tablet, inscribed with a message written thousands of years ago in a language I'd never seen. I knew instinctively how to read it. I traced my fingers over the ancient script and the words came alive. It was a poem about love and the beauty of life. My mom would have liked it.

Eventually, we moved to the 20th century and all the major wars that took place, and sometimes Melody wouldn't answer the questions I asked. Zoe wasn't sure why Melody refused to answer certain questions, but she thought it might be something called "data corruption." The First World War enveloped much of Europe and beyond. It caused the deaths of millions of people. A few years later, I guess because the war wasn't quite settled, the Second World War broke out. You know what's interesting? The similarities between the warring nations and the ancient Roman city-states I'd studied earlier. The Romans seemed to want to reinvent their empire, but the way they performed on the battlefield left a lot to be desired. Zoe kept calling them Italians, but calling them Roman made more sense. I liked how united they were, and sometimes I felt like Zoe was pushing me to understand why people come together, though she never came out and told me why it was so important for me to get that.

Next, the nuke, as it was called. What a weapon. After the second war, it caused a stalemate between the victors, who didn't look much like victors at all after the war. And why call it a "Cold War"? Because they weren't shooting at each other? I found that hard to believe. Why build up a massive army unless you planned on using it, especially if you own a bunch of nuclear weapons. Although the conflict didn't become a full-scale war, fear left the world paralyzed.

I didn't judge the actions of any one side. I'd never experienced war on that scale. It was hard to imagine. Why would you want to kill so many people?

Melody liked to remind me that the underlying desire for humans who wanted to govern other humans was power and control, and it remained much the same since the beginning of recorded history. Pride and ambition drove the ancient Greeks to greatness. I needed and wanted to talk to Captain Moore during this time. I thought of my mom a lot. I missed her.

Then the 21st century, which, according to Earth's calendar, was drawing to a close. Earth used to use the terms B.C. and A.D., but Melody didn't want to answer what those meant. Common Era was what they used now.

Earth appeared to be teetering on the brink. An event known as The Great Famine devastated the planet. More than a billion people died from starvation and a shift in how nations treated each other occurred. The Sino Bloc, an alliance of China and Russia, emerged as the leading power, causing Captain Moore's United States to fall into bad times. The Great Famine led to a rise in crime. People driven by starvation contributed to an atmosphere of mistrust, and it further fractured an already divided society.

The Earthers developed artificial intelligence too, like Melody, and I think it caused a lot of problems. It optimized efficiency (see? I told you my English was improving). True. Zoe didn't want me to find out too much about it either.

Genetic engineering. This subject scared me. It reminded me too much of the Shapers. When the Earthers tried to augment themselves and remove diseases, people stopped having babies. I think that was when things started to fall apart for them. Not enough people to do the jobs.

In the summer, Zoe began teaching me the unique trait linking me to the Immortals. She explained how my DNA acted as a key, which unlocked them and allowed me to control them.

"Don't lose this like you lost the translator," Zoe said, showing me a small, thin headband. "This can read and analyze your genetic code. Once it does, it transmits data to the Immortals and creates a connection."

"How does it work?"

"That is difficult to explain. Your perception guides them," Zoe said. She took the headband and made sure it fit. "How does that feel?"

"Good. I don't really feel anything."

"That's normal. You won't have to wear it for very long. You're gifted, Kol. Now, look at me." When I did, she adjusted it further down my forehead. "How's that?"

I reached up to touch it.

"No, don't touch it. Does it feel secure? Shake your head for me."

The device stayed in place.

"There you go," she said.

My left temple tingled for a moment. "When you said perception, did you mean what I look at or hear?"

"How you perceive reality."

Reality? What a strange thing for her to say. "I don't understand."

"Think of it as your willpower. You command them by willing them to do things. Do you remember how we got here and how you opened the door?"

I nodded.

"The Immortals know who you are, but they are complex. This device will help them understand you better." She touched the sides of the headband.

"What if I'm asleep?"

"In that case, they will act to protect you and obey the last commands you gave them."

"What if I die or get injured and end up in a coma or something? What then?"

"You won't have anything to worry about."

"I want to know everything about them."

Famous last words.

Zoe introduced me to a new concept. It used something called "advanced neurosync technology." Now, there's a mouthful. I needed to wear it as often as possible. It was equipped with various sensors that captured my brain's electrical signals and translated them into commands. She explained in more detail about how it worked, but a lot of it went past me.

I needed to create a mental image of the "desired outcome." It required immense concentration to refine my control. Soon, I learned how to direct the Immortals' movements with increasing precision. I felt like a puppet master.

Zoe set up a series of challenges requiring me to command the Immortals through complex tasks. Navigating obstacle courses, lifting heavy objects, coordinating group maneuvers. Needless to say, our base here was huge and seemed set up for this. Zoe wanted me to use English, and I think all the practice helped.

One time when an Immortal stood before me, I wondered if this personality could be a long, past relative of mine. You know, maybe an ancestor from my lineage because a sense of familiarity coursed through me as I stared at the robot.

"Do I know you?"

It remained silent.

Of course it would.

I closed my eyes. It's all about concentration. An image, a desire, a will, and then it happens. I'd grown used to it, this strange connection between mind and metal. I raised my hand and opened my eyes. The Immortal copied me. I wondered if it shut its eyelids too, like I did.

I closed my eyes and envisioned the Immortal balancing on one leg while spinning a wood pole on its finger.

"You don't have to close your eyes," Zoe said.

"It's easier."

"In time, you'll understand it's more difficult. Try with your eyes open."

Keeping my focus, I made sure to keep my eyes wide open. I constructed the mental image, refining it, turning it into a solid command. The Immortal stood on one foot, spinning the wood pole effortlessly.

Zoe smiled at my touch of humor in the seriousness of it all. "Do you see, Kol?"

"Yes. It was easier."

An odd sense of accomplishment surged through me. Soon, it was no big deal anymore. Just another day with the Immortals.

Zoe said this was natural. She said my continuous interaction with the neurosync technology would enhance my abilities, and I asked what abilities I had.

"In time. You will know."

Why can't I know now?

I began to understand the subtle personalities of each Immortal, but they all seemed to be... dead. Maybe that's not the right word. Missing a certain part of them that made them human. Hour after hour, my connection with the Immortals grew stronger. After a while, I could sense their presence, even when not actively controlling them.

It's amazing what the brain can do.

CHAPTER TWENTY-FOUR

Kahwin
The Scalding Ruins
Kol Washington

Over the next several weeks, Zoe told me to study advanced military tactics, only this time, I used Melody. How strange that Earth would make a machine capable of thought but not give it a body like Zoe. Also, there's something I needed to point out because it was strange. You know the phrase, 'out of thin air'? It was a true saying. Zoe, every so often, seemed to appear out of thin air. One minute, she'd be in another room, the next, standing behind me. When I questioned her on it a few times, she'd refrain from responding.

Back to Melody, who provided me with historical documents and lessons about Earth's history. It showed me holos of Napoleon Bonaparte, Alexander the Great, Cleopatra, and other leaders with strange names. The most interesting was Genghis Khan by far. He got rid of slavery, elevated people based on merit, and let people worship who they wanted. Billions of Earthers could trace their ancestry back to him.

Earth's violent history read like one of the stories my mother would read me by the fire, about how long, long ago, an empire rose from the ashes of a dying world and conquered all the stars. That was how she described it. She used to say the Keepers punished us for our arrogance.

And, I didn't understand why I had to learn military stuff. It didn't make sense. Sure, it was interesting, but when I questioned Zoe, she said it was for my own good.

What good is war and violence?

So, I changed the subject. "Zoe, when can I see my mother?"

We were in my normal study room where the desk was and she was over by one of the Immortals by the doorway and studying its face. "I don't know yet. It depends on how General Vack deals with the Senate."

"What do you mean? Did the Senate do something wrong?"

"To General Vack, everyone has done something wrong. It doesn't mean it's true."

"What does that have anything to do with my mom?"

"Your mom is important, Kol. Just like you."

"I don't understand."

"She's important because she's your mom."

I clenched my jaw in anger for a second before I relaxed. I just wanted to talk to her, for her to be here with me so I knew she was safe. She was everything to me, just like Zoe. "When can I see her?"

"Soon. Trust me."

That made me feel better. I got up and stretched. "I got scared when you attacked the Academy."

"I know. I'm sorry about that, but I had to make sure you were safe. You're very important to me, and I would never let anything bad happen to you."

"My mom used to say that to me. The important part."

"You are important, Kol. In more ways than you can possibly understand."

"How?"

She didn't respond and continued to inspect the Immortal's face.

"What exactly is the Academy?" I asked.

Zoe paused. "A place far older than Starport City."

"Nothing is older than Starport City."

"Long before the city, there was a group of people who wanted to change the way things were, and when they found out they couldn't, they debated what to do. Some said they should go to sleep and wake up in the future and see how things were going. The other group wanted to try and make peace with the people they didn't like. They decided that some people would stay awake and some people would sleep, but no one was ever allowed to make contact with anyone outside their tribe."

"I've heard this story before."

"Oh, you have?" Zoe said.

"They were from Trion."

"That's right. They came from the moon Captain Moore renamed Trion."

"My mother used to tell me this story all the time. She said there was a guardian on Trion who knew all about the tribe and helped them."

Her face glowed as she made adjustments to her console. "Do you remember what the guardian was called?"

"The Ekbotor, I think."

"That's right. It was called The Ekbotor, which in their language means the Grand Oracle."

"How do you know so much about this?"

She shrugged. "I learned it in school."

"I didn't know you went to school."

"Someday, I'll tell you all about it," Zoe said. "Did your mother tell you the Ekbotor helped the tribe build their new home?" Zoe asked.

"No. She said the tribe fell down from the clouds and crash-landed in their moon cart."

"Not only did the Ekbotor help them build their new home, it said if they worked really hard, she'd protect them from the bad people."

"Is the Academy their home?"

"That's what some people say. One thing I *do* know is General Vack thinks so, and he wants to contact the bad people eventually. I don't think the Ekbotor would like that very much."

"Me either," I said.

She created a virtual environment where I could practice different kinds of tactics by using the neurosync technology. In one of the virtual worlds, digital terrains stretched out, carved from some type of code that Zoe tried to teach me about. It looked so real. Almost dream-like. The landscape was all wavy and colorful. Far off, I could see massive mountains with snow on their peaks. Valleys sat between them, coated in grass that glowed a different kind of green I'd not seen before.

The rivers flowed differently too, lit up and splashing light all over the place. Little huts nestled close to the water, tucked away among trees. Puffs of smoke came out of their chimneys.

Everything was fake, but it was a good kind of fake, you know?

My English started to improve rapidly too. Everything written in these fake environments were in that language. I started dreaming in English most of the time and thought about what it would be like to see Earth up close.

In these simulations, I took command of the Immortals and directed them in various combat scenarios. Melody would provide real-time feedback. Zoe analyzed my performances and suggested things I could do better.

Even though we were in a big room during these practice sessions, the virtual reality seemed to go on forever, and I could command the Immortals beyond the length and width of the room. Does that make sense? I don't know how Zoe did that.

Zoe's expertise proved invaluable during training. She guided me through all kinds of strategies and offered her perspective on how to better use the Immortals. She taught me to consider the terrain because most of Earth's battles were won or lost by logistics.

No plan survived contact with the enemy, and I had to be prepared to adjust my strategies on the fly. Zoe and Melody gave me unpredictable situations, and I was forced to make decisions under pressure. Thankfully, I'd learned that skill at the Academy.

The Immortals weren't simply machines. Each of them possessed intuition and creativity. I began to trust their instincts, and we created innovative tactics through careful planning.

Zoe taught me the importance of camaraderie among the Immortals and maintaining a sense of purpose and direction.

"One more session. Are you ready?" she asked.

I stood strong in the practice chamber, my neurolink connected with the Immortals and active. "I am."

The session opened in a pixelated manner. Pixelated, a word I learned recently. I stared ahead.

"Kol," Zoe said, "consider the terrain. Position your Immortals on the high ground, control the landscape."

I nodded and sent the command to the Immortals. There were hundreds of them. They moved gracefully, scaling the digital cliffs to take position on the mountain tops. From up there, they had a clear view of the valley below.

How did Zoe do this? I knew they couldn't climb something that was not really there.

"You're in charge, but remember, the Immortals have their own instincts. Trust them, Kol."

Looking at the pixelated readout, I felt the subtle differences in each Immortal's reaction. Some moved to the front, while others hung back, prepared to provide support. They were machines, yes. With the neurolink, I felt their individuality as well.

A horde of enemy robots charged from the forest. Why did they look like the Janissaries?

"No plan survives contact with the enemy, Kol. Adjust, adapt," Zoe warned.

My mind raced as I ordered the Immortals into defensive positions. The frontliners became a protective barrier, while the support units readied their weapons.

"Kol, use flanking maneuvers." Zoe's voice came as the enemy bots closed in.

I took her advice and directed dozens of Immortals to veer off to the sides, preparing to strike the attacking robots from their vulnerable flanks. The battlefield erupted into a storm of laser fire and missile streaks. Amid the storm, I remained calm, connected to every Immortal, feeling their trust in my commands.

When the flanking Immortals made their move, the Janissaries slowed. A volley of lasers from my team hit the attackers and tore through the enemy ranks. Debris flew. Explosions and shockwaves rocked even the distant Immortals.

"Seize the moment. Now is the time," Zoe said.

I commanded my frontliners and they lunged forward. Their laser weapons flashed as they created devastating arcs through the disoriented robots. The Immortals left smoky trails in the Janissaries' wake.

Behind my advancing small army, my support units readied their heavier artillery. With pinpoint precision, they released a rain of missiles that arched into the sky before descending upon the enemies. The impacts were instantaneous, massive balls of light blooming into existence and swallowing the foe within their destructive brilliance.

Soon, pockmarks littered the landscape, and trees burned, and grassy fields turned to black soot. Smoke rose in tendrils. Where once stood an enemy formation, now was a scene of ruin and wreckage. The Immortals stood victorious, their bodies illuminated in the light of the fading explosions.

"Good, Kol."

A few months later, I was back to studying Earth. This time, Zoe wanted me to learn about modern history. Widespread consumerism led to a culture of excess, where a few people had everything and everyone else had nothing. People valued possessions and status first over relationships and personal growth. Something called reality holos promoted the worst kinds of people.

Melody said the breakdown of traditional family values contributed to a sense of moral decay. For some reason, the police didn't always enforce their laws, and things got out of hand.

Explicit content in their society led to everyone sleeping with everyone, but no one was having babies. Why? Was everyone that ugly? Their popular culture, their music lyrics, their holos, all spoke of how bad everything was and how much they hated themselves and how one's appearance mattered the most. In my world, elders were highly important, the wisest. On Earth, it was the opposite, and elders were isolated while young people decided what was right and what was wrong. Politicians taught everyone to dislike others if they thought differently. Someone must have conquered them. The Senate and Captain

Moore did something similar to us when he saved Kahwin. That was why his crew made us take on new names like Washington.

I also learned about the Great Famine. Some communities had banded together in little enclaves and armed encampments. No one had anything to eat, and everyone started moving to better climates, where they could grow crops. When I asked Melody how it started, it refused to answer me. It did that a lot.

"What caused this to happen, Zoe?" I asked.

"What does Melody say?"

"It doesn't say much. It keeps trying to teach me about Elvis instead."

Zoe's ears perked up. "What's Elvis?"

"A dead singer. Why does Melody want me to learn about him?"

"Did you ask it?"

Zoe sat with me and studied what the artificial intelligence wanted me to learn. We listened to "Jailhouse Rock," a popular song a few centuries ago.

"What do you think of it?" Zoe asked.

"It's loud. But I like it. He's fun. The way he moves makes me smile."

"That it does."

"Any reason why Melody won't answer some of the questions I ask it?"

"It's studying us. That's as much as I can say."

CHAPTER TWENTY-FIVE

Montana, USA
Scott Moore
December 25th
2178, 7 years prior to launch

Pete's voice barely registered over the deafening thoughts in my head. Cordite clung to my fingers, my clothes, and the boy's blood had sprayed all over my shirt and jacket.

"There's blood on your shirt," Pete said, and it was only then that I realized he was talking to me.

Snowflakes appeared like a starfield as I drove the SUV through the snowstorm. My ears still rang from when I'd pulled the trigger, and my hand tapped the steering wheel ceaselessly. I'd killed him. Sure as the day is long, I'd shot him and watched him bleed out in the snow. He was just fifteen years old. Damn it.

It happened when I went to save my brother. He'd been kidnapped on the highway and they had stolen everything from his truck. Back then, times were hard. Too hard. If you had something and couldn't defend it yourself, you'd lose it.

I never wanted to kill. Ever. Especially a young man. So young. I hated myself. I couldn't look at myself in the mirror the same way ever again.

Sometimes, God doesn't care what you want.

Pete turned down the heat and glanced out the window. The weather reports said it would snow for the next few hours, slowing our trip to my sister's home. We hadn't seen any other vehicles on the road for a long while, and aside from abandoned electric charge stations and the occasional antique shop, signs of civilization were few and far between. Since the Feds ordered the relocation of personnel to work camps scattered further south, nature had reclaimed the urban blight. Visibility was next to nothing, so the AI drove slow and kept Vincent's truck in my rearview mirror. Pete asked my brother if he wanted company, but after what had happened, Vincent insisted he be alone. I'd have to talk to him later and make sure he was okay.

"It wasn't your fault, Scott," Pete said, trying to comfort me. "My pistol jammed."

I appreciated Pete's words, but they didn't lessen the weight of my guilt. "I shot him," I said, my voice hoarse. "I'm responsible for his death."

Pete shook his head. "You had no choice. He was armed and dangerous. You were protecting us and yourself. He would have killed one of us. Maybe all of us. Who knows?"

"I know, but still..." I trailed off, lost in thought. What kind of world had we created where kids had to carry weapons and shoot to survive?

"I should have given him another chance," I said.

"He was going to kill your brother. You saw that," Pete replied.

"What am I going to do? If anyone finds out...."

"No one is going to find out. Do you hear me? No one."

I wanted so desperately to believe him, but I knew otherwise. "How am I going to pass a neural polygraph?"

"Leave that to me."

Tears of frustration welled up in my eyes. "Why did he have to point his gun at me?"

"Dumb kid. He was desperate."

"Desperate to get shot? Pete, I killed him."

Pete gave me a stern look, the kind he reserved for when he was the most serious. This was the second time I'd seen it. "You have to promise me something. Promise me you'll keep your mouth shut."

"I can't promise that. If the police come and ask me...."

"If the police come and ask you, you aren't going to say anything, Scott. Okay? Nothing. Do you know what's riding on your career? It was not your fault. You had to defend your brother... you potentially saved all of us."

"I'm not the only person qualified for the mission. There's a list of candidates who could command *Atlanta*. I'm not the only one. I deserve to be in prison."

The wind howled, and the sound matched how I felt. Fifteen. He was so young. I needed to breathe. It was him or one of us. In that split-second decision, I'd decided to live. If I'd given it another second, would he have decided to live? He might have missed. Fired a warning shot. Or merely been bluffing. Why didn't I shoot his leg?

"You are the only one, Scott. Space Force picked you for a reason."

"And now I've thrown that reason away by taking a life."

"You make it sound like you had a choice."

I sniffled, refusing to let my emotions take control. Thankfully, the AI drove as well in the snow as it did anywhere else. "What am I going to do?"

"You asked me that already. Here's what you're going to do:

You're going to leave it to me and forget about it. Okay? Flush it from your memory."

"How am I supposed to do that?"

"You're going to pretend it never happened. That's how. If you find yourself thinking about it, think about something else, anything else. I don't care what it is, you let your mind think of something else. Humanity needs you more than that kid needed to put a bullet in you and your brother."

"It doesn't work like that. I can't just forget what happened."

"You can and you will. Listen to me. What you did back there saved our lives. Okay? Are you listening to me?"

"No."

"Yes, you are. What did you think would have happened had you not shot him? Guess what? He would have shot first. He would have put a slug through your heart, shot me, then shot Vincent."

"You don't know that."

"I know more than you think. Why don't you disengage the autopilot and drive us? Get your mind clear. You're going to be captain of a starship to save us all. Keep your mind on that."

Pete was right. Driving did help me clear my mind. As I took it slow over the snowy terrain, I couldn't shake the weight of what I had done. Killing someone was not something I could just let go of, but what choice did I have? The replay of the shooting played over and over in my head. Vincent, helpless and defenseless, with the barrel of a Colt .357 pressed against his head by the boy with the dark circles under his eyes. It was a drug-induced haze caused by Preface, a designer drug that was easy to make and distribute. I could see the fear in the boy's eyes as he turned toward us, but it quickly turned to rage. He was just a burnout, with not much time left to live. He wanted

Vincent's truck and supplies, and I reacted when he swung his gun in my direction.

My stomach churned with the stress of it all. "I've got to change clothes," I said, trying to shake off the memory.

Pete tried to reassure me. "We'll stop before we get to your sisters. It's okay. Just relax."

My mind raced with questions. "You think anyone will find the body?"

"No. No, I don't. And I'm not going to tell you where I buried him or how."

"I don't want to know," I replied.

"Good."

"What if someone finds him?" I asked.

Pete sighed. "No one is going to find him. You're going to spiral if you keep at it."

"But I can't just forget that I murdered someone," I protested.

Pete's eyebrows furrowed, and his lips formed a thin line as he leaned forward in his seat. "Listen to yourself. You didn't murder him. You shot him in self-defense. What you're doing now is pitying yourself. Stop. Focus on the road, and let me tell you something. Remember how I talked about my career before becoming an engineer?"

"You said you worked as a plumber," I remembered.

Pete's tone became serious. "I was a contractor."

I'd seen Pete get into a few fights before, and he always came out on top. He liked to brag about growing up in the South and how he had to fight his way through high school in some of the worst school districts in America. But there were times when he would say things that were a little too specific about the war or a region of the world, making me wonder if there was more to his story. But right now, I needed to focus on what he was saying.

"Can you talk about it?" I asked.

"Not officially, but I can promise you that body won't be found. The rest is in your court," Pete said, trying to reassure me. "No one is going to find him."

"How can you be so sure?"

"How can you be sure of anything, Scott?"

A new song played, one I'd heard a million times. "Savior, Lest the Sky Fall." It reminded me of baseball, the sport that refused to die. There was a line during the chorus my mother would sing to me when I was young. "And when you see the roses / Know that I'll love you / And when you see the sunrise / Know that I'll be waiting... on the other side." What would she say if she saw me now? This was the last song I needed to hear.

I changed the channel. "Did something like this happen to you when you worked as a contractor?"

"Are you asking me if I've killed anyone?"

I nodded, my stomach still queasy.

He put his hand on my shoulder. "You do what you have to do, my friend. It wasn't easy. It never is. You just have to trust that God will forgive you and move on with your life."

"I don't believe in God."

Pete's hand fell from my shoulder. He let out a dismissive chuckle, shrugged, and reclined in his chair. "You do. I know you do. I can tell when you think. God's on your mind sometimes. Regardless of your beliefs, you'll see Him in the end."

Frustration boiled within me. "I don't want another lecture."

Pete nodded and fell silent for a moment. Then he leaned forward, resting his elbows on his knees. He gazed at me intently.

"How'd you get into Space Force with your spiritual beliefs?" I asked

He hesitated. Eventually, he exhaled deeply and told me he'd obtained a waiver.

Pete turned serious. "Never speak about this event again to anyone. Do you understand me?"

I hesitated, expressing concern that I might be caught lying during an interrogation. Pete's expression darkened. He leaned in closer.

"You have to promise me," he urged.

"You want me to promise that?"

"Do you think a scandal like that could destroy the program?" he asked. "Your brother would lose his position, I would be arrested, and the Sino Bloc could launch their copycat design. Billions of Americans and others across the world would die of starvation because you decided to take the high ground and spill your guts about something you couldn't avoid in the first place."

Feeling the weight of his words, I realized I hadn't fully considered the repercussions of revealing the truth to my superiors. Sure, I'd be in deep for murder, but that would be the least of my worries.

"You always have a choice. Now, I need you to make that promise to me and mean it. The entire country, and most of the world, is counting on us," Pete said.

"It's not right."

"If it were that simple, we'd never have made it past the Stone Age."

"I don't understand."

"It's a quote from a movie. What's right or not will depend on our ability to save billions of people. I consider you my brother. I've never said that before, but I do. I love you, man. But this is something I need from you. A promise to never speak about this to anyone ever again, not even to me. Not even to yourself. You do that, and you'll move forward as the man you're destined to be."

"Destined, huh?"

"That's right."

"Damn it." I let out a long sigh. "Yeah, okay. Damn it. Fine. I promise."

"You mean it?"

"Yes, I mean it."

Pete let the moment stir a while. "All right. I believe you." He checked the GPS. We had another two hours before we'd reach my sister's house at this rate. "It's going to be okay."

"I hope so. I'll never kill again. That much I can guarantee."

"I pray you're right, Scott. I really do."

Another hour passed in relative silence. The windshield wipers pushed the incoming snow off the window, not that there was much to see out there now. The kid's face burned in my mind non-stop.

"Hey, snap out of it." Pete's voice brought me back to reality. "You're doing it again. Don't think about it."

Maybe it was just the guilt of taking a life, or maybe it was the fear of getting caught. Either way, I knew that I couldn't just ignore what had happened.

The snowstorm worsened by the minute, which made the road increasingly treacherous.

The SUV slipped on the icy surface. I tried to push the shooting out of my mind. Think about something else, anything else. But the boy's face, contorted in pain as he fell to the ground, burned like a still frame. His screams echoed in my ears. I felt like throwing up. I took a deep breath. This couldn't be allowed to affect me.

Snow continued to fall.

I wanted nothing more to do with death.

Never again.

Or so I assumed.

CHAPTER TWENTY-SIX

Kahwin
The Scalding Ruins
Kol Washington

W hy were my dreams so violent? They woke me up a lot. I had to start reminding myself they weren't real. I used to scream in them, and Zoe would come in to make sure I was okay. I dreamt of Shapers mostly. Tentacles long enough to reach across Starport City from one end to the other and mouths large enough to swallow buildings. The beings never spoke.

I often thought about battle and war at the strangest times. One time, I was taking a shower and saw myself in a uniform the Earthers wore. Wouldn't that be something? Me dressed like Captain Moore.

Where I'm from, it wasn't wise to talk about dreams. If you did, others would tell you never to talk about them with anyone or they might come true. All of us had bad dreams. You know, people sometimes talk in their sleep, and as a kid, you wanted to hear what they said. We'd mock them over it.

Why did I dream about war so much?

I think all the studying might've been getting to me.

What wonderful machines the Earthers made to kill each other. They fought a lot. It was a wonder they survived for so long under the toll of all those deaths throughout their history.

I remembered how Melody insisted I learn about ancient Earther weapon systems. She created holographic renderings that spun between us and lectured about them.

Melody often started the sessions with the first of the ancient weapons like the bow and arrow. They were simple tools, and we'd made the same thing. I was a good shot too. Next, she described the sling. Now, I wasn't bad with those, but reaching down into the snow during half the year to look for rocks made my fingers hurt. The bow was better by far.

She went through melee weapons. There was the spear, the sword, the club. Easy stuff.

One day, Melody showed me a catapult. Siege weapons were amazing. They used to hurl large stones at enemy fortifications. It was odd because of how bulky and stationary it was.

She liked to play games with me, sometimes, and it took a few tries to learn all the rules. In them, there were two groups called Aethens and Spartars, who used formations called the Phalanx. Their soldiers, called 'thoplites,' stood closely together in lines. Each thoplite had a long spear and a shield. Together, they were like a moving wall. They used their shields to protect each other and their spears to attack the enemy. This was strange to me because I'd never seen people fight so closely to each other.

I had the feeling Melody might be spelling words differently sometimes, but she insisted she wasn't, so I dropped it.

Next, Melody taught me about the Romani formation, the Legion. It was a more flexible and dynamic version of the Phalanx. Their soldiers, called legionnaires, had short swords, big shields, throwing spears, and armor. The Legion was divided into smaller groups, which allowed them to use more advanced tactics. In the early days, the Earthers used the manipular formation where soldiers stood like a checkerboard for better movement. (Checkers is another game, but it was too simple.) Later, they divided the Legion into ten cohorts. Each cohort was a strong fighting force on its own.

These formations needed lots of discipline and training. They moved and changed based on what was happening in the fight. To them, war was not just about strength, but also strategy.

Melody's usually warm interactive light seemed to turn a fraction colder. "Knowledge, Kol, is never wasted. It's a tool, and one can never predict when one might need a specific tool."

"We don't fight like this. Over at the Academy, we have advanced technology," I said, waving a hand toward the holographic display still showing the victorious Romani Legion.

"You're correct. Earth's methods of warfare were fundamentally different," Melody replied. "Strategies and tactics, the art of decision-making in the face of adversity, are universally valuable. They transcend the technology or methods employed."

I felt her evading the heart of my question. "But why? Why am I spending so much time on this?"

Melody paused, her lights dimming and brightening as if considering her response. "Do you enjoy our war games, Kol?"

I blinked, taken aback by the change in topic. "Well, yes, but that's not the point—"

"Isn't it?" Melody's lights swirled in what I recognized as her amusement. "Learning can take many forms. Our war games provide a medium to understand the dynamics of strategy and decision-making. You're not just playing; you're learning."

"But—"

"No more questions for now, Kol," Melody said, her tone final. "Let's move on to the next scenario."

I felt frustration mounting but kept it in check. Melody had a reason for everything she taught me. If she wasn't ready to reveal this one yet, I'd wait. After all, I did enjoy our games. Little did I know then how vital these lessons would prove to be.

"Let's move on to something different," Melody said.

The space between us filled with shimmering holograms, forming a floating board. It was segmented into different territories, marked with different symbols and connected by lines. Two piles of cards floated to the sides. Different regions were marked with different colors, and the game was meant for two players.

"What's this?" I asked.

"This is 'Dusk Confrontation,' a strategic game of influence and control," Melody explained. "Think of it as a simulation of two powerful entities vying for dominance in a complex and dynamic world."

I eyed the holographic board. "How do we play?"

Melody's lights pulsed as she began the explanation. "Each player represents one of the two major factions: 'Sunrise Dominion' or 'Moonlight Union.' The game spans ten rounds, each representing a specific era."

She highlighted to the territories on the board. "These are regions in which you can gain influence. Some are battlegrounds, where direct confrontations can occur. Others are non-battlegrounds, still important but not as volatile."

"What about these cards?" I asked, pointing at the floating stacks. "Do we use them like poker?"

"Each card represents a specific event or action. They can sway influence, trigger confrontations, or disrupt the opponent's plans. However, some cards, while beneficial to you, may have secondary effects advantageous to your opponent. Choosing when and how to play your cards is crucial."

As Melody detailed the rules—scoring based on controlled regions, coup attempts, and realignments, I figured the game was about strategic maneuvers and tactical choices, just like our other war games.

When Melody finally finished, a question slipped out. "So, who goes first?"

A ripple ran through Melody's lights, her version of a chuckle. "Well, traditionally, the Sunrise Dominion begins. Ready to claim your domain?"

"Let's go." I was assigned the 'Sunrise Dominion' and Melody, the 'Moonlight Union.' We shuffled our cards, and the game began.

In the first round, I drew a card titled 'Dawn Awakening.' It allowed me to add influence to any three non-battleground regions. I strategically chose regions close to some battle-grounds, hoping to solidify my presence there in later turns. Melody, on her turn, played 'Lunar Tide,' a card that gave her influence in two battleground regions.

As the early rounds progressed, the board filled up with our colors, my vibrant sunrise colors pitted against Melody's moonlight tones. The holographic display was a flurry of shifting influences, minor confrontations, and regions swaying between us.

By the fourth round, we'd moved into the Mid-War era. The stakes grew as the territories on the board filled up, leaving fewer uncontested regions.

"You're doing quite well, Kol."

"It's different than the other games we play."

"In what way?"

Good question. I replied with all I could think of at the time. "It feels more serious."

"War is always serious."

I drew a card named 'Eclipse Unleashed,' a powerful event that allowed me to stage a coup in a battleground region. Eager to shift the balance in my favor, I chose a region heavily influenced by Melody. As I played the card, a holographic coup unfolded on the board, and my influence replaced Melody's. It wasn't without retaliation. On her turn, Melody played 'Radiant Surge' to perform a realignment, reducing my influence in one of my strongholds.

I felt myself sinking deeper into the game's strategy. It wasn't just about gaining territories; it was about understanding my opponent, predicting her moves, and making decisions not just for the present round, but for future ones too.

As we moved deeper into the Mid-War phase, the game heated up. The regions were heavily divided, with several battlegrounds hanging in balance.

Melody played a card, 'Celestial Standoff,' an event that put our factions on high alert. "Kol, this event brings us to the brink. It escalates the tension level of the game." The hologram showed a new gauge at the edge of the board, a visual representation of the tension between our factions.

"What does Global Cataclysm mean?"

"Whoever makes this gauge exceed the final red stage loses," she said.

On my next turn, I drew a card named 'Sunflare.' Its event text made me gulp. "Melody, this card... It triggers a 'Solar Cataclysm.' That's what the Earthers call nuclear war, isn't it?"

"Indeed," she said. "It's a powerful but risky move. In the game's context, it would devastate a heavily contested battleground, wiping out the opponent's influence but also escalating the global tension."

I hesitated. "The tension level is already high. If I play this…"

"Sometimes, you have to make tough decisions in the face of uncertainty. Consider the benefits and risks."

I looked at the board and then back at the card. It could swing the game in my favor, but at a high risk. I took a deep breath and played the card, triggering the 'Solar Cataclysm' event. My chosen region was wiped clean of Melody's influence, but as predicted, the tension gauge almost maxed out.

Melody gave no reaction, simply drawing her next card. "Your move had a significant impact, but in escalating to the extreme, you've activated the 'Celestial Standoff' condition I set earlier." Her card flashed on the board. "This forces the game to check for total global tension. Because you have more influence in this region, you've raised the tension once again and tipped us over the edge."

A siren blared from the holographic display. The game board flashed red as the words 'Global Cataclysm, Game Over' appeared. I'd triggered the ultimate loss condition.

In the silence that followed, Melody's lights shifted back to their standard warm glow. "A bold move, but with high stakes. In 'Dusk Confrontation,' as in real conflict, pushing too far can lead to total devastation. It's a lesson worth learning."

CHAPTER TWENTY-SEVEN

Kahwin
The Scalding Ruins
Kol Washington

Stepping into the training room always made me smile. The space was vast, like a cavern. A thousand warriors could train here easily. High above the ceilings was inlaid with panels emitting ambient light, replicating the intensity of the midday sun, and the light was strong enough that if I looked up at it, I'd have to press my eyelids shut.

High, towering pillars stood at regular intervals. On each of them, the ones who made this place in Project 1 carved stories about valor, strength, and duty. The mirrored walls were covered in etchings, depicting scenes of starships battling one another. As I panned the length of the mirrors, it showed a story about a single ship laying waste to its enemies. If you wanted to touch the ceiling, you'd need an incredibly tall ladder.

Zoe walked in with me, carrying a few bags.

"What's that?" I asked, pointing to the single ship.

"That is the ship Captain Moore possesses. He's renamed it *Arcadia*."

Embedded within the walls, floors, and pillars, tiny sensor nodes blinked. These were the eyes and ears of the training room, capable of watching every move, every breath, able to project any number of holographic opponents into the room.

Zoe's command post was positioned on a raised platform to the side of the room. It looked like an enormous slab of stone but had an inlaid console. This was where she controlled the projections, which analyzed my movements. If things were too easy, she adapted the holograms to challenge me further.

"How long are we going to train today?" I asked.

"That depends, but more than yesterday."

In front of the console, the space opened out into an arena. The material making up the floor was unlike the stone used in the rest of the training room, thankfully. During training, I usually fell dozens of times, and I liked the skin on my knees and arms. Tiny holes in the floor marked the spaces for other sensors. They picked up every footfall, every movement, every swing of my spear, and fed the information back to Zoe at her console. That way, she could show me where I could use some improvement.

At the heart of the arena was the armory, a circular area housing a variety of weapons, which she made me clean for hours on end. My spear was always waiting for me. The Antediluvians liked to use swords, spears, shields. Stuff like that. They placed rules on how to fight each other too. When I asked Zoe why they'd do that, she said without rules for war, people acted reckless. Wasn't war reckless?

Beyond the armory, a myriad of spaces for different training scenarios stretched out in all directions. There were open areas for large scale battles, tight corridors for confined combat, elevated platforms for practicing high ground advantage, and countless others. When I trained at the Academy, we never had anything close to this.

Every time I walked into that room, you could almost hear the clang of weapons. It was my training room. It was my battleground.

"If the Antediluvians had dark matter rifles, why use these kinds of weapons? It doesn't make sense. Dark matter rifles don't damage property."

Zoe flicked on her console. "Where's the honor in shooting someone?"

"Isn't war about winning?"

"War is about destroying ideologies. If war were about winning, the winning side would kill each person on the opposing side, so they wouldn't seek revenge at a later date."

I walked over to the armory and grabbed my spear and hit a button, activating its energy field. It thrummed in my hand. You know that feeling when you pick up a tool that just feels right? Like it was made just for you? That was what the spear felt like. It was balanced and its field projected a raw, primal energy. My ancestors fought with weapons like this.

The first hologram flickered into existence. A solid, muscular figure, armed with a sword and a shield.

"Prepare yourself for battle," Zoe said.

It charged at me, and I dashed to meet it. My spear spun in my hand, sizzling with power. In a few swift movements, I disarmed it and drove my spear through its chest. It vanished.

"Good kill," Zoe said.

I was left standing in the center of the arena, spear held high, waiting for the next opponent.

Zoe gave me a small nod of approval before dialing up the difficulty. "I think one opponent might be too easy. You're getting too used to them."

"Are they always that predictable?"

"Most opponents are. Let's try two and see how you fare today."

Two figures appeared this time. Both were taller and more heavily armed than the first. Good. I didn't wait for them to come to me. Bounding forward, I used the spear's reach to keep them at a distance, jabbing to force them back.

One managed to get inside my guard, its sword arcing toward my face. I rolled away in time to avoid the strike and hit back with a swift jab to his gut. He vanished in a blink. The second one pressed the attack, but I threw my weight to the side, my spear blurring as I plowed it through his chest.

By the time Zoe called up the third round, I was breathing hard but feeling good. You ever have one of those moments when everything just seems to fall into place? When you're so in tune with what you're doing that it feels like you can't make a wrong move? That was me, right then, spear in hand.

An hour passed. Fifty-three dead and me with only a few bruises to show for it when their weapons grazed me. To imagine, this weapon used to be heavy and I'd usually lose quickly, and now? I was really good.

Zoe cranked up the difficulty enough so that when I was hit, their blows would produce a pointed physical force. Kinetics, Zoe called it.

"Take a break," she said. "I'll be back in a few minutes. I have a surprise for you."

"I'll grab some water."

After a half hour, I started to wonder where she'd gone. A loud clanging sound came from one end of the training room. I turned to look. Zoe was coming over, and a suit of armor followed her. It was massive, but it moved gracefully, not clunky like you'd think. Looked like a giant statue from some old temple, but made from metal and full of tech. It stood twice my height and was covered in designs that made it look like a warrior from the tales told around the hearth during long winter nights.

I almost thought it might've been a Janissary.

Despite the tech, the suit carried an air of ancient tradition, like the stuff from my mother's stories. Zoe walked up, the giant armor trailing behind her like an obedient war beast. She stopped in front of me, and the suit came to a halt. Its arms and legs were as thick as tree trunks, and its faceplate was carved into a stern face, with lenses for eyes that reminded me of the night sky. A pyramid surrounded by a circle was in the center of the armor's broad torso.

"I like the symbol," I said.

"That, my friend, is the Gesterion family crest. The pyramid represents unity and strength and the circle, the galaxy as a whole."

"How come my mother never taught me that?"

"You'd have to ask her." Zoe stepped behind the suit. She began making adjustments to a sliver of metal as thin as a hair. I'd seen her use it a couple of times, unsure of what it was. "How would you like to fight in the suit for a change?"

"Me? Are you sure? It looks complicated."

"It's not as complicated as you may think. The suit, like everything else in Project 1, knows you and will obey your commands. I used a temporary override to bring it to you." She put away the sliver of metal and came back around to the front. "Remember how you deactivated the trap and opened the door here? Focus, and the suit will obey your commands."

Open.

Its chest cavity opened up, revealing a molded interior. I hoisted myself up, placing one foot onto the raised footrest embedded in the lower section of the suit. The metal was cool beneath my touch.

Using the suit's body as leverage, I climbed up further,

swinging my other leg into the second foothold. The interior surface fit me perfectly. With a final push, I secured myself within the armored shell, my back coming to rest against the cushioned wall of the suit.

I raised my arms, slipping them into the suit's limb casings. They encased me from fingertips to shoulder, like a glove that was meant for me and me alone. The legs followed next, each limb sliding effortlessly into their armored confines.

As my head slid into the helmet, the suit enclosed around me, sealing me in with a soft hiss. I was now in the heart of a metallic giant.

A sequence of Antediluvian symbols sprang to life on the inner display of the helmet. They floated before my eyes, their shapes familiar. As if acknowledging the presence of my mind, the symbols blurred and reformed into English. How'd it do that?

My new perspective spanned across a panoramic heads-up display, a sweeping view of the world rendered in vivid detail. An information overlay continuously delivered data about my surroundings.

Only it wasn't registering Zoe.

An illuminated reticule sat at the center of my focus. It responded to my every glance. Various spectral analyses, thermographic and night vision modes hovered at the corners of my vision, ready to be activated with a mere thought. I felt in tune with the suit like I was wearing a second skin.

I took a few steps and fell straight on my face.

"Oops," I said.

"Can you get up?"

"I think so." When I tried to move, nothing happened.

"You have got to use your mind."

"I am!" Only I wasn't. When I did, I got to my knees at first

BRANDON ELLIS & MAX WOLFE

and took a moment. After a few seconds, I stood. Nothing felt right about it. I was wrong.

"How come I don't see you?" I asked.

"Because I am not made of the same stuff you are. How do you feel inside of it?"

"Awkward," I said.

"What you want to do is concentrate on one thing at a time. It may feel strange at first, but you'll have to learn to walk again for a few days."

"I want to learn how to fight in it." Why did I say that? I was now eager to wage combat. Interesting. I'd never felt this aggressive before.

"You will, my friend. That's the plan."

CHAPTER TWENTY-EIGHT

Arcadia
Captain Scott Moore

We'd arrive at Eos in the next few days, and although busy, I needed to find out who Gisele was in hopes of understanding the ship better.

Michael was taken to the infirmary. Doc was reluctant to pronounce him dead, but he'd displayed no sign of life other than his eyes moving as if in REM sleep. With him in a comatose state, we'd been left with few answers, and exploring a ship as large as *Arcadia* with a crew as small as mine wasn't safe. It could take years. Although Melody created a map for us, many of the sections weren't labeled.

The moment I set foot in the Elysium Gardens with Gisele, it became obvious I'd stumbled upon something extraordinary. She knew *Arcadia* well, almost too well, as if the ship itself had granted her a kind of divine knowledge. She offered to show me around the garden. She wasn't telling me something. After a while, you know when someone's lying, even by omission.

Lush greenery surrounded me, colors spilling out far and

wide. She'd wanted to show me *Arcadia*'s splendor, and after the battle, getting away for a bit made a lot of sense.

"Are these plants genetically engineered?" I asked.

"*Arcadia* designs everything aboard the ship. To that, though, all is natural."

I walked along winding paths, and the subtle fragrance of flowers intermingling with the earthy scent of the soil overwhelmed my senses. The beauty of this place left me homesick.

She brought me near a cluster of azure blooms. Her delicate fingers caressed the petals. I loved the way her hair cascaded down her back, and her emerald-green eyes.

"Scott?" she whispered. My heart skipped a beat. "It's hard to believe it's really you." She took a step closer. It took a lot for me not to reach out and embrace her. Something held me back.

"You shouldn't be here," I said absently.

"Here?"

I remained silent.

"I can't explain it, Scott, but I feel like I belong here."

Gisele guided me through the first third of the garden, stopping at a stunning arrangement of iridescent flowers. "These are Arktos Lilies," she said. "Their colors change with the light, reflecting the hues of a setting sun."

"It's mesmerizing," I whispered, unable to tear my eyes away from the shifting colors.

As I watched the flowers, Gisele wasn't quite real, and yet, she was right there, a tangible presence in my life like she'd once been. Being in her presence was like reliving all my dreams before I'd agreed to go on a mission of a lifetime. I could have called her. Said hello to her again. Found her and rekindled what we'd had. That would have meant abandoning my career in Space Force, a prize I'd sought my whole life. Love's powerful, but my desire to save humanity outweighed my feelings for Gisele.

Gisele continued to show me the wonders of the Elysium Gardens, and with every step, my heart grew heavier. The feelings I'd buried deep within me resurfaced, threatening to drown me in their intensity. She was like a living dream, a part of me that I'd lost long ago. Now, she was back. Now what?

"How did you find out about this place?" I asked

Her eyes darted away toward a flower. "I... I just did. It's like the knowledge was always there, inside me."

"You don't find that strange?"

"Perhaps. How should I answer that?"

I wanted to push further, but her body language told me my questions made her uncomfortable. Instead of pressing her, I focused on the garden around us, hoping that its beauty would ease the tension.

We walked past a grove of trees with shimmering leaves like liquid silver. Their branches intertwined overhead, casting dappled shadows on the ground. Gisele led me to a small bench hidden beneath the trees. We sat side by side, our shoulders brushing against each other. She was warm.

"Tell me about your time as captain, Scott." Gisele's voice barely registered over the rustling of the leaves. "What was life like on *Atlanta*?"

"It's been... a journey. I was honored to be chosen to lead the mission."

Gisele looked at me. "Do you still feel lonely?"

Her question caught me off guard. "Yes," I admitted. "At times."

Her fingers brushed against mine, and my heart raced at her touch. "Maybe that's why I'm here," she whispered. "To remind you you're not alone."

The moment was so fragile, so delicate. As I looked into her eyes, doubt flashed between us. Did Gisele herself fully understand why she was here?

Gisele guided me to a new section of the Elysium Gardens. We wandered along the path and stumbled upon the Dionysian Vineyard, a picturesque area dedicated to the cultivation of genetically-engineered grapevines. The sight of the vines, laden with plump, glistening grapes, showcased the genius of *Arcadia*'s commitment to its craft.

"These grapes produce the most wonderful wines." Gisele plucked a grape from a vine and offered it to me. As I took it from her fingers, our hands brushed against each other.

"Thank you."

The grape's sweetness lingered for a bit, a perfect balance of flavors both intoxicating and alluring.

Gisele gave me a playful smile, her eyes glinting with mischief. "This way. There's more to show."

We continued to explore. Eventually, we arrived at the Pandora Botanic Archive, an enormous library containing detailed information about the diverse flora and fauna inside the Elysium Gardens. Floor-to-ceiling shelves filled the room, each one laden with heavy tomes and delicate scrolls. The air was redolent with the scent of ink and parchment.

"Over here." Gisele led me to a long, polished wooden table. We sat, our fingers tracing patterns carved into the surface. "These were stored here tens of thousands of years ago."

"Can you read them?"

"Why would I do that?"

"Curiosity?"

"I knew you'd say that."

After some time, Gisele guided me to our final destination: the Helios Sundial. This magnificent, artistic sundial cast webbed shadows on the ground, marking the passage of time as the *Arcadia* traveled through the void. Our eyes locked onto the shifting patterns, the silence between us thick.

"Gisele," I said. "There's something I need to ask you."

She faced me, her eyes vulnerable. "What is it?"

"Are you connected with this ship?"

"Sometimes... sometimes I hear *Arcadia* speaking to me." Her voice wavered. "It scares me."

My heart clenched. I pulled her closer and wrapped my arms around her. "What does it say to you?"

Her eyes began to tear. "I don't want to talk about it. It's angry."

"Do you think it has gained sentience?"

"I don't know," Gisele replied. "I just know that it's angry, and I don't understand why."

My mind swirled with questions. "Is there a place on the *Arcadia* where it might store its AI?"

Gisele shook her head. "I don't think there is such a place. I've never seen anything like that."

"No server room or anything?"

"No. The ship is massive, though." She smiled. "It's incredible, isn't it?"

"The ship?"

"Being with you."

I wanted her to be real, to be the woman I'd left behind to pursue my dream in Space Force. More than anything. Her words drove daggers into my chest. For those of you who haven't experienced love at first sight, you won't understand how I felt about her, real or not. You might even think it's impossible.

Time to change the subject. "Can you tell me anything more about what the ship says to you?"

Gisele hesitated. "I'm not sure."

"You can tell me. It's okay."

"I think... I think *Arcadia* has hidden intentions."

My eyes widened. "Go on."

"The Keepers."

"What about them?"

"This is what you want to talk about?"

"I need to know, Gisele. The lives of other people depend on me."

Her eyes searched mine. "You don't trust me."

"Why would you say that?"

"It's a feeling. I don't blame you, though. I wouldn't trust anyone if I were in your shoes. You must think all this is awfully strange."

"Do you want to go back to Earth?"

Her eyes clouded with confusion. "I... What did you ask?"

"Do you want to go home?"

"This is home. Don't you like it?"

"I do. It's just..." I let my words trail into silence. I could fall in love with her all over again. What kind of life could we have together? The one I'd lost?

"Just what?"

I decided to confront her with the truth. "If you could choose, would you want to stay here with me or go back to Earth?"

She seemed to struggle with the implications of my question. "I... I don't know. What would happen?"

"I'm sure there would be quite a lot of people who would want to talk to you."

"And that's a good thing?"

"I didn't mean it that way."

"They'd experiment on me."

"I wouldn't let that happen."

"Who would stop them? If I have thoughts and feelings, if I can love, see, taste, touch, feel, does it matter? That's what you want to know."

Her words stirred emotions I'd suppressed for years. If Gisele chose to stay with me, knowing the truth about herself, she'd be safer. Then again, if she returned to Earth, she'd be forced to confront the fact she was a duplicate of the real Gisele. I should have thought about that before asking her.

The choice would ultimately be hers. No matter what she decided, I'd support her.

Even if it meant letting her go.

"I don't know what the future holds," I said. " I know I care for you, and I want to be by your side, no matter what you choose to do."

Gisele's eyes shimmered with unshed tears. She leaned into me, our hearts beating as one. "Don't leave me this time."

"I won't. I promise you, I won't."

CHAPTER TWENTY-NINE

Atlas Rift
Captain Scott Moore

I braced for the sudden disorientation accompanying our exit from jumpspace. I took a deep breath as the swirling blue vortex of the jump dissipated before my eyes.

For a few moments, the bridge grew still and silent. Then, as our ship's sensors came back online, the bridge erupted in activity. Lights and displays came to life, and the engines reverberated throughout the ship.

I glanced at the navigation console and took a moment to gather my thoughts. We'd emerged from without incident, and *Arcadia*, as far as I could tell, functioned perfectly. I signaled the crew to begin running diagnostics on all systems, just to be sure. Hopefully, we'd arrived at the right location.

As I gazed up at the shimmering expanse, I was struck with an overwhelming sense of awe. How lucky I was to be among the first explorers from Earth to see this sight? The universe stretched out before me in all its beauty, the stars twinkling like tiny diamonds in the black velvet of space.

"Let's find out if we arrived in the right system," I said. "Run a full battery of sensor scans."

"Aye, Captain," came the response from the sensor station officer. "Activating sensor array."

If you wanted to know what sensors a starship the size of a megacity has, the list would be as long as the Toyko magrail. Conventional radiation detectors. Gravitational wave detectors. Quantum entanglement scanners. Dark matter detectors. Neutrino detectors. And if that wasn't enough detectors, *Arcadia* had a detector for a host of other detectors with names that could've been pulled from Ancient Greece.

Reports flowed into my terminal and onto one of my screens. The interferometer, which measured interference patterns of light waves, began to study the properties of distant objects and phenomena. Meanwhile, our gravity gradiometer, which measured small variations in gravitational forces, provided insights into the composition of planets and nearby celestial bodies.

"Good work." I leaned to the side of my chair. "Report your findings as they come in."

"Long-range radar is clear, Captain," the sensor station officer reported. "*Arcadia* detects zero potential threats within a 20,500-kilometer radius. Magnetic field detector shows no anomalies."

"So far, so good," I said. "Any sign of Eos?"

Erika helped out at the sensor station by cross-referencing data from tactical, engineering, and comparing it with other scans. "Negative, Captain."

I pressed my lips together. "Any signals?"

"Communications scanner is scanning for any transmissions in the area, Captain," the officer said. "No incoming messages or potential threats detected."

Erika examined a glowing chart on one of the displays. "Our

spectrometer is showing normal composition of the surrounding space, Captain."

Due to the vast distance between us and the surrounding worlds, we'd need time to accumulate enough data to formulate my next plan of action. According to Melody, Eos stood between the fourth and fifth planet in a region of space known as the Passage, an area I was warned to avoid entering without first clearing it with whoever or whatever operated Eos.

I gained scant information about our destination from Michael. What was Eos? Melody offered only tantalizing bits, which felt to me like a lure to get us to go there, and we were a large mouth bass. Eos would refit *Arcadia* and repair her, and if what Michael said was true, I'd go about recruiting enough knowledgeable people to assist in my endeavors. No small order considering the magnitude of what Michael asked of me.

Michael had warned me that we might have to gain the trust of the people on Eos first. Who would want a ship this size pulling up to your station without first knowing their intent?

Slowly, we began to assess what comprised the system. The Atlas Rift was located in the outer rim of the Milky Way galaxy, out in the middle of nowhere. Why didn't the Keepers send a Shaper fleet here? Did the war run out of steam? Doubtful.

I stood tall, my eyes fixed on the main console before him, *Arcadia*'s bridge bustling with activity. "Lieutenant Banks, what are the latest sensor readings for our current location?"

"Captain, we are currently situated halfway in the Atlas Rift, a star system Melody designates as HD 181027 I-P. The system boasts three habitable worlds, each with unique features suitable for human settlement. Its star, Helios, is a yellow dwarf star with a mass of 0.98 solar masses and a surface temperature of 5700 K."

My focus sharpened. "Provide a more detailed analysis of the planets, Lieutenant."

"Planet HD 181027 A-I, codenamed Olympus, is the closest world to the primary star. With an orbital period of eighty-seven days, its atmosphere is composed mainly of nitrogen and oxygen. Scans reveal a mild climate, and there appear to be substantial bodies of liquid water present on the surface."

Erika motioned to the second planet on her display. "HD 181327 B-II, which we have designated as Athena, is the second planet in the system, and has an orbital period of 143 days. It's a terrestrial planet with a similar atmosphere to Mars, consisting mainly of carbon dioxide. Sensors detect signs of water beneath its surface, which could potentially be extracted and utilized."

"Any signs of life?" I asked Erika.

"Hard to say, sir. Certainly primed for it. Nothing capable of giving off any transmissions."

"What about the third?"

"HD 181027 C-III, designated as Artemis, is a super-Earth with a mass roughly that of Earth. It's located at the farthest point from the primary star with an orbital period of 272 days. Scans show a nitrogen-oxygen atmosphere with traces of water vapor, a stable climate, mild temperatures, and a bountiful supply of fresh water. Gravity is at 1.1 times that of Earth, the lower density resulting from the significant amount of water present on its surface."

"Life?"

Erika checked another screen and shook her head. "Negative, sir."

"Where is everybody?" Chief asked.

"Still no sign of Eos?" I asked.

Lieutenant Banks tapped on her console. "Negative, Captain."

"Keep scanning, Lieutenant," I replied. "Lieutenant Chen, any suggestions on how we can locate the station if it's hiding?"

Chen furrowed her brow. "Captain, passive scanning techniques might detect any anomalies in the surrounding space. The station's power signature or its impact on nearby cosmic rays could provide a clue."

There was a lot to like about Lieutenant Commander Chen. She'd grown up in Los Angeles during some of the harshest riots and somehow made her way through life through the hell of it all.

"Can you do so without giving away our position?" I asked.

Chen's eyes focused on the screen in front of her as she entered commands and parameters into the system. "The program is running, and we should have results in a few minutes. We'll be able to detect any anomalies in the vicinity without alerting the station to our presence." Melody processed the vast amounts of data required for our sensors, adjusting the sensitivity to pick up even the faintest of signals.

Vincent studied the results on the screen. "I don't know, Captain. Something's odd about these scans."

"How so?"

"According to our scans, the star is twelve billion years old, and it's giving off the same amount of energy as our star back on Earth."

"Check again."

"I have, sir. The reading is accurate."

"Lieutenant Banks, check your station," I said.

Erika compared her scans with Vincent's. "He's right, Captain."

"Send me the reports." When I received them, I double-checked to make sure Melody hadn't made an error. A star this size would've collapsed and turned into a white dwarf at that age. "Continue scanning. Let's see if we can make sense of this."

As I waited for the scans to complete, Erika remained alert, ready to make any necessary adjustments to the system. I was glad she was here with us. We'd almost lost her back on Kahwin more than a few times.

I squared my shoulders as I monitored my crew. "Vincent, are you sure Melody is looking at this data correctly?"

My brother's hard stare spoke volumes. "Hard to say. Currently, she's reexamining a...."

Consoles lit up with warning signals.

"Captain, we've been scanned," Erika said. The crew watched anxiously as she analyzed the data. "Unable to pinpoint location."

"All stop!" I shouted.

"All stop, aye."

Arcadia crossed thousands of kilometers, its sheer mass unable to perform much in the way of maneuvering.

"Action stations," I called. "Standby on weapons. This may get ugly if we're not welcomed. Keep monitoring those scans."

Vincent voice trembled slightly as he examined the ever-changing map on the main screen. He circled a region of space between us and the planet Artemis. "According to Melody, the scan originated from somewhere here."

I frowned. "Can we counteract the scan? Or at least mask our own power signature?"

Erika worked to find a way to mask *Arcadia*'s energy output. A sudden power fluctuation jolted her in her seat, cutting her efforts short. The lights dimmed across the bridge.

"Captain," Vincent said, typing on a tablet as he collaborated with Melody to scrutinize the information collected from the different sensors. "I think I've found something. The gamma ray burst detector and cosmic microwave background gauge have picked up an object. Eos is doing a good job at hiding from us, but this signal might be it."

Erika occupied the planetary magnetometer station overseeing the magnetic fields of neighboring celestial bodies.

"Confirmed, Captain. The planetary magnetometer shows some unusual magnetic activity within 550,000 kilometers from Artemis."

"That's got to be it," I said.

Please, let it be it.

At the tactical station, Feazer helped scrutinize numerous displays. "Sir, I'm detecting a faint energy signature. Range 50,000 kilometers. New object bearing nine degrees Mark 2, displacing approximately 1,100 tons."

"Well, well," Chief said. "Would you look at that?" He punched in a command, which brought up a screen next to my chair.

On a holoscreen, I caught a visual of the object's energy emission pattern as a glowing, pulsating cone, indicating its direction and strength of the emission. Our sensor painted radiation with color-coded bands, representing specific types of energy. Red indicated high-energy particles, blue for electromagnetic radiation. As the object moved, the display showed the target's movement and direction of the radiation source, allowing us to track it. What Equinox wouldn't give to have this tech back home.

Vincent piped over a graph produced by Melody, which showed a unique energy signature coming from the object. "See that?"

"What is it?" I asked.

Melody flashed a response.

Warning!
  Dark Matter Engine Detected.

Dark matter is notoriously difficult to detect and even harder to study. The problem lies in its weak interaction with normal matter, and it doesn't emit or reflect light. As dark matter interacted with its engine, it created small fluctuations in the ship's gravitational field that radiated outwards in the form of gravitational waves. *Arcadia* picked up those waves with its gravitational wave sensors, allowing her to identify the presence of a dark matter engine and track its location and trajectory. With all the data spilling out from the object, I was left with little doubt about what we faced.

"It appears to be a ship, sir," Erika said.

"It's our welcoming committee. Is it moving?" I asked.

"Negative, sir. Object remains stationary."

"Lock weapon on target and create an optimal firing solution."

"Aye, sir," the weapons officer replied. "Target locked."

"Visual."

The main screen zoomed in on the ship. The void itself seemed to writhe and undulate around it, as if it disturbed the very fabric of space. A masterpiece of Antediluvian design, it glinted in the surrounding darkness like some ancient sea serpent.

We all remained speechless. It lacked any visible weapons. What would it do to us if it had them?

"We're being hailed, sir," the communications officer said.

Chief gawked as he shook his head in disbelief. "The Antediluvians live."

Here goes nothing. "Open a channel."

CHAPTER THIRTY

Atlas Rift
Captain Scott Moore

My hand shook as I faced the main screen, waiting for the holo-image of the one who had hailed us. For the first time in years, we were encountering a group of people that might help explain everything. The crew stood alert, their attention darting between their stations and the screen. Once in a while, one of them would glance over at me.

The channel crackled to life, and a measured voice filled the bridge. As the image resolved, I found myself staring into the solid black eyes of a woman who looked to be in her late twenties. Her features lent a regal mystery about her. She looked human enough, save for her eyes, haunting me behind a black veil. Piercing eyes, like of polished onyx. Implants?

"I am Ambassador K'Hori." Her voice echoed in the eerily quiet bridge. "Voice of Keeper Aiantes."

Keeper?

"I'm Captain Scott Moore."

"Welcome, Captain Scott Moore, to the Atlas Rift. We have successfully scanned your ship. What is your business here?"

"You said Voice of Keeper Aiantes. Where are your Shaper ships?"

"Keeper Aiantes is a friend to humanity. You will find no Shapers within our borders."

My fascination with her strange appearance grew. *Was* she human? She spoke our language perfectly.

"You are here to refit your ship, are you not?" K'Hori asked.

"That's correct. I was told to visit Eos."

"Your ship poses a substantial threat. Therefore, I will permit you and five others aboard my shuttle, *Charon*. I will fly you to Eos, and we will discuss what steps we will take concerning your vessel."

"I appreciate the offer, Ambassador," I said. "However, I need to stay with my ship. Why don't you come aboard instead?"

"Captain, while I understand your reservations, I'm sure you can understand my position. We need to verify a few things before we commit to refitting your ship."

Erika sent me a text message that popped up on my screen. *Captain, our sensors cannot detect Eos.*

"Ambassador, what is Eos?" I asked.

She tilted her head slightly. "Eos is a fortress, Captain Moore. A refuge from the darkness that surrounds us."

A fortress? The thought intrigued me. How could something so massive hide from us?

"Forgive me, Ambassador, but our sensors have failed to detect Eos. How can we be sure it's here?"

Her lips curved downward. "Eos is hidden from prying eyes, Captain. Your ship's sensors will not be able to detect it."

"We detected an anomaly concerning your star's age."

"A product of our defense system."

"Your appearance, Ambassador, it's… unique."

Her black eyes bored into my soul as she responded. "I have been… altered, to better serve my purpose as the Voice of Keeper Aiantes."

Chief grimaced after she said "Keeper" and who could blame him? We'd fought their genetic monstrosities on Kahwin, and several of my crew died fighting them. If a human served a Keeper, that person had sold out their humanity.

"I assure you, Captain, your understanding of the Keepers is limited. Do not judge me based on past experiences."

I clenched my jaw. "You understand my apprehension, Ambassador."

K'Hori's expression remained stoic. "Yes, Captain."

"Do you speak for… it?"

The ambassador tilted her head ever so slightly. "That is correct, Captain. As for my becoming the Voice, that is a tale best saved for another time."

"Thank you, Ambassador," I said finally. "We will join you shortly."

As the communication channel closed, I opened the comms to my brother. "Vincent, you're coming with me. I'll give you more details in a moment." I turned to my crew. "I'll also need Chief Breckenridge and Erika. I want you two with me as well."

"You trust her, Captain?" Chief asked.

"Not in the slightest. However, I don't see that we have much choice."

Feazer had been staring at me off and on since the transmission. He'd proven himself to be a valuable asset during previous missions, and his combat experience might be crucial in case things went awry. The man could fight. "Feazer, I want you on the team."

Feazer acknowledged the order with a subtle smile that told me he was eager to discover more about Eos.

During this trip, Doc had spent time with Gisele and exploring the ship. As much as I wanted him to accompany us, I needed him on *Arcadia*. I trusted him almost as much as Chief to give me unbiased data about the ship. I let him know via a text, and although he seemed disappointed, he understood.

I rose. "Commander Chen, follow me."

Chen followed me out of the double door, and we stood on the subway platform, an arrangement that seemed as impractical as a third elbow. She stood at attention, and I put her at ease.

"Commander, tell me about the first thing you remember growing up."

She spent a moment in thought. "On my fourth birthday, my parents had an argument about money. My mother ended up leaving us with no money and no food in the house. Our neighbor called Child Protective Services on my father, but he convinced them everything was fine."

"That happened on your birthday?" I asked.

"Aye, sir." Chen's voice brought a kind of musical quality to it, the result of her upbringing. She always smelled nice and kept up her appearance, even in times like this.

"Do you know why I'm asking you that?"

"Does it have to do with Michael and the other woman who approached you, sir?"

"That's correct. Doctor Ingram will brief you further."

"Aye, sir."

"When we depart to Eos, you'll command *Arcadia*. Although we haven't spoken much lately, without you, we might not have found *Arcadia* in the first place."

"Aye, sir."

"How comfortable are you taking command in my absence?"

"Quite comfortable, sir."

"Your orders are to remain here until we return. If you have not heard from us in seven days, you are to take *Arcadia* and return to Earth, even if it takes you the rest of your life. You will consult with Doctor Ingram on any major decisions you might make for the time being. If necessary, he will brief you on what you need to know."

"Aye, sir."

"Do you have any questions for me, Commander?"

"What about Michael, sir?"

"He's unresponsive. As you know, I've posted a guard outside his room. Should he awaken, he is not to be trusted. I will instruct Doctor Ingram to bring you regular updates."

"Aye, sir. How much should I trust Melody?"

Chen was asking the right questions. "That will be up to your discretion. Should anything appear... strange to you, or runs counter to your previous training, you are to ignore the AI and follow your training."

"Aye, sir."

"I have faith in you, Chen. Don't look so scared. You'll do fine. I'm taking a tablet with me. If you have an emergency, contact me. Otherwise, maintain radio silence. We can't be sure we won't be monitored."

"Sir, may I ask a question?"

"Of course."

Chen stiffened her upper lip. "When will we be leaving to Earth, sir?"

"Soon. Quite soon."

"Thank you, sir. I won't fail you."

"I know you won't. Dismissed."

We entered the bridge. I contacted Doc and told him everything I told Chen, save for one addition. If anyone started to act strangely, Doc would perform a thorough psychological examination. So far, all of us appeared to be who we said we were, but that didn't preclude *Arcadia* gaining enough information to create a better...clone, for lack of a better word.

I will now admit to something I don't want to admit. Perhaps the best way to understand my frame of mind is to employ Socrates. It seems the best way.

First, a few facts.

1.The Great Famine had killed over a billion people when we left Earth. It'd been years since the fateful day the USS *Atlanta* plunged into jumpspace and was flung on the other side of the galaxy.

2.The Pentagon expected the war between the Sino Bloc and the United States to occur shortly after we left, which was one of the reasons, I believed, for the jumpdrive failure. We'd been sabotaged.

3.*Arcadia* belonged to no one. In fact, you might say, if it belonged to anyone, it belonged to me.

4.Its technology far surpassed anything we'd created on Earth.

5.People were irrational and often unpredictable.

Suppose you're a leader of a great nation, possessing AI, nuclear weapons, satellites, and so on, and you are gifted a key to world domination. How many politicians do you know that wouldn't use *Arcadia*? Can you name even one?

Suppose you're a leader of a great nation, and your rival comes into possession of a ship like *Arcadia*? What should your response be?

Suppose you're the CEO of a major company specializing in computer science and technology. What effect would the discovery of a starship have on your company and its shareholders? How would the markets react?

Suppose you live in the mountains of Afghanistan, and although much of the world has adopted a certain level of technology, your people have not. You live happily with your family, and believe in the Holy Koran. Then comes news of an alien starship. How might you react? And if you think any other religion would act in any other fashion other than abject terror, you're fooling yourself.

Lastly, suppose you hate your society for any number of reasons and you've waited all your life to execute a politician. You're one of *those* people, of which my country harbors tens of thousands. You get word that the person in charge isn't reacting exactly how you want them to react about the newly discovered starship. Do you think a person like that wouldn't act out their fantasies when they know the world might end anyway?

Are there exceptions? Yes, but exceptions are just that. If I concerned myself with exceptions, I'd never be able to do anything.

I could continue, but I'm sure you get the point.

Needless to say, I had no intention of taking *Arcadia* to Earth. Nor would I allow any of my crew to return. At least, not in this ship. We'd need to find another way.

I had become Hernán Cortés.

There was no going back.

CHAPTER THIRTY-ONE

Atlas Rift
Captain Scott Moore

We boarded the train and watched as the platform receded, the subway car picking up speed and hurtling us through the bowels of *Arcadia*. I glanced around at my team, realizing the silence needed to be broken.

"Quite the sight, isn't it?" I gestured to the vast expanse of the ship visible through the subway car's windows. "Our Antediluvians cousins certainly had a flair for the dramatic."

Feazer pressed his hand against the seat cushion. "Indeed, Captain. It's difficult to believe *Arcadia* was created by humans."

"The Antediluvians prioritized both form and function, Captain," Erika said. "It's as if they sought to create a harmonious balance between the two. Very Greek, I might add."

Chief sneered. "There are a lot of questions. We could learn from them, sure, but all of this... it's too much to believe."

"How many times have I heard that since we left Earth?" Vincent asked.

"Then you explain it," Chief said. "Explain how the ship created a French subway train and rendered the same kinds of signs I've seen in Paris. How did it create a functioning bridge identical to *Atlanta's*?"

Vincent folded his arms as the train took a sharp turn. "It's constructed everything from Scott's mind. Isn't it obvious?"

"Instantly?" Chief asked.

"Probably used nanoprinters and rearranged atoms," Vincent said.

"Michael had said there were fabricators aboard the ship, but we haven't found them yet. Thankfully, the biodomes provide enough nutrition for us to eat for as long as we'll be alive," I said.

"If *Arcadia* can print material on the nanoscale, their printers might not be visible using the human eye," Vincent explained.

My brother's speculation made sense, but there had to be more to it. "Then couldn't Michael simply refit the ship using those same machines? Why take us to Eos in the first place?"

"You tell me, Scott. You're the one who spent the most time with Gisele and Michael."

Chief gave Vincent a dirty look.

"Michael wants us to recruit personnel from Eos in addition to the refit," I replied.

Erika gripped the subway pole. "Captain, that would imply there aren't Antediluvians in cryo onboard this ship."

"I don't think there are. Those people we met when we first boarded the ship seem to be the previous crew." I knew somehow they'd declined into a primitive state, probably because Michael saw them as incompatible with his mission. Failure wasn't to be rewarded, he'd said. Failure. At what?

Vincent bounced his leg up and down. "Why doesn't *Arcadia*, oh, I don't know, print people?"

"You mean make clones?" Chief asked.

My brother shrugged. "I guess. If that's what they are. I have no idea."

"You can't print people," Feazer said. "Brains don't work that way."

Erika gave Feazer a look.

I faced Chief. "What are the chances *Arcadia* uses the same type of genetic manipulation as the Shapers?"

Chief lifted his chin. "I'd say relatively high."

Erika placed her hand on the glass. "Sir, whose memories is *Arcadia* using?"

"Mine," I admitted. "Gisele is a woman from my past."

"An important woman?" she asked.

Chief knew what she meant to me. So did Vincent. I'd spilled my guts to them about her more than once.

"We're getting off-topic," I said.

Vincent rubbed his chin thoughtfully. "If they, and by *they*, I mean the Antediluvians, had the capability to construct a ship like *Arcadia*, what led to their demise?"

"Michael explained their empire collapsed in on itself to me when we met privately. At least, that's what I understand."

Erika leaned forward attentively. "Did Michael mention the Keepers?"

"He did."

"What did he say?" Chief asked.

"You don't want to know."

By the look on Chief's face, this was the topic that bothered him the most. "I do, sir. We need to know what we're up against."

"He avoided my questions and told me our belief system might need to be... modified."

Chief frowned in disgust. "What the hell does that mean?"

"I have no idea."

If I had to guess, his faith in God was shaken the more he learned. I felt for him. At the same time, nothing I'd learned would preclude God existing. Nothing at all.

When we explored Kahwin searching for *Arcadia*, we'd often speculate about why we never found any spiritual temples and why the population didn't worship anything or anyone. We came to the conclusion the Shapers would've forbidden a belief in the afterlife. It would give the people on Kahwin cause to act fearless.

A cursory study of the few tribes we'd encountered led to the discover that they practiced a form of animism, or a deep reverence for nature. That was it. As far as the Antediluvians on Kahwin were concerned, they seem to all have been atheists, a fact that troubled Chief. As advanced as they'd been, how had they abandoned their spiritual pursuits? I didn't have an answer for him, and even if I had, I don't think he'd want to hear it. Shaking a man's faith, his core principles, is one of the cruelest things you can do, whether it's the truth or not.

Feazer had been listening to us intently. A smart officer observes and jumps in a conversation at the right time, and although he worked for Equinox, technically anyway, he displayed all the hallmarks of a Space Force officer. He'd been a natural leader since I'd started to interact with him. "Perhaps we'll find some answers on Eos. If the Keepers were responsible for the Antediluvians' downfall, we might be able to learn more about the nature of their conflict. It's also possible that they left behind records or artifacts that could shed some light on their history. We just need to know where to look."

Erika smiled best she could in her synth body. "If we can piece together the story of the Antediluvians, perhaps even learn from their mistakes, we might even save Earth."

"Chief, did you ever discover why *Atlanta's* jumpdrive failed?" Feazer asked.

"No. But I have my theories."

"Care to share them?" I asked.

Pete glanced at me, then back at Feazer. This wasn't a topic he felt comfortable discussing with someone like Feazer, and who could blame him? "What difference does it make at this point? We're here now."

The Greek-associated names, the Greek architecture on *Arcadia*—there had to be a reason. I had the sense whatever it was would cause ripples across our understanding of the universe. There's coincidences and then there's *coincidences*. We'd even named the planets in this system with Greek names as we did in the Kahwin system, almost by instinct.

Occasionally, Vincent would tell me some corny time travel joke about how we'd broken the space-time continuum and skipped into a parallel universe. As ridiculous as that sounded, it would help explain a lot of things.

"Do you think it had anything to do with the engine?" Vincent asked.

Chief shrugged. "What did Melody say? You spent enough time with it."

"Her," Vincent said stubbornly.

If there was one thing I could change about my brother, it would be his emotional attachment to his creation. He loved Melody in a way no man should love a computer, and it never stopped bothering me.

"Okay, Mr. Overattachment. 'Her.' What did she tell you?" Chief asked.

Vincent glared at Chief. "Hey, I don't appreciate your tone, Pete. Watch it."

"It would help to know," I said. "You may speak freely in front of Mr. Feazer."

Feazer gave a slight nod. "Thank you, sir."

Vincent threw up his hands. "Okay, you want to know?

Melody wouldn't answer. The data is likely corrupted. To be frank, we're lucky she functions at all, given the fact we dragged her all over Kahwin and she's fused with *Arcadia* now. She's acting strangely, but she's fine."

"When we return, I need you to find out all you can about the jumpdrive failure," I said. "Do whatever you can to jog Melody's memory."

"Of course."

"What are you thinking?" Chief asked me.

"Remember when we received the data from Earth and it didn't match Melody's predictions? To me, that means one of two things. Either the Sino Bloc sabotaged the drive or... and I hate to even suggest this, but Melody herself might have sabotaged the drive and not informed us."

Vincent put his fist in his other hand. "Now, why would she do that? You know as well as I do she was incapable of sabotaging the mission. Nothing neither I nor anyone else could change that. We built her that way."

"What about the Bloc? They've got spies deep inside the administration," Erika said.

"Even if they did, getting close to Melody would've been impossible," my brother said. "Our lab locked her down 24/7. Only myself and a few others were allowed access to the servers."

"We'll discuss this later. When we board the ambassador's ship, I will be asking the majority of the questions, but if you feel the need to ask something, make sure it's simple and gives the ambassador no hint about our culture or Earth. Chief, I know you've got a number of questions you want answered. Save them. Limit your questions to *Arcadia*."

I hadn't seen Chief angry like this in a long time.

"Vincent," I said, continuing, "do not discuss computer technology with K'Hori. The less she knows about our technology, the better. Erika, feel free to ask questions about their culture should the moment arise. Keep the questions simple. We don't want to overload the ambassador with a lot of questions. I've informed Lieutenant Commander Chen that if she does not hear from us in seven days, she is to take *Arcadia* and head for open waters."

"Aren't you worried about how long it will take *Charon* to reach Eos?" Vincent asked.

"*Charon* arrived almost instantaneously from the moment we began our scans. I have a feeling getting to Eos won't take long at all," I said.

The subway car began to slow, signaling our imminent arrival at the launch bay. We prepared to disembark.

As the subway doors slid open, a gust of recycled air hit us. It carried the scent of ozone and metal. We stepped out onto the observation deck, and the vastness of the bay unfurled before us.

High above docking platforms, large windows stretched across the bay's length. It offered a panoramic view of the void. Behind these panes of glass, the command center buzzed with activity. Rows of chairs were arranged in front of consoles brimming with blinking lights and digital displays. This was the brains of the landing and departing operations. AI-run, no doubt.

Along the sides of the bay, maintenance stations stood equipped with tools and machinery, many looking unfamiliar. Robotic arms hung from the ceiling. Parked along the walls, hydraulic forklifts waited with their metal arms poised for the day's heavy lifting. Docking clamps provided a solid hold for the ships. Other than that, all else seemed too foreign to describe. I'd need to study it all when I returned.

My gaze stretched across the expanse, marveling at ships docked within the bay. Shuttles clung to the platforms like barnacles to a ship's hull. Their designs were elongated with a hint of aggressive aerodynamics, suggesting speed even while at rest. The sharp and angular fronts reminded me of a bird, while the rears boasted a set of thruster engines. Each shuttle glistened under the bay lights, a deep metallic color.

Around them, hundreds of fighting ships bristled with armaments, their angular forms and dark hulls similar to the shuttles. Small frigates sat between them. Further afield, warships towered over the rest. I was amazed. An entire fleet waited here, and for how long?

"Captain," Chief said. "I believe that's for us."

Chief motioned at a shuttle with its ramp open and its engines idling. It waited for us to board her. The light from its interior spilled out onto the platform. I'd anticipated asking Melody to prep us a shuttle, but here it was, ready for our departure like we'd set this flight up hours ago. *Arcadia*, or maybe Melody, had anticipated our needs.

I looked around at my crew. Their determined expressions lifted my spirits. "You've heard it before, but I'll say it again. We represent Earth, and first impressions mean everything. Stay diligent and be polite. Any questions?"

"Scott, do you really think they're going to help us?" Vincent asked.

"God only knows."

CHAPTER THIRTY-TWO

Atlas Rift
Captain Scott Moore

As the shuttle glided smoothly toward Ambassador K'Hori's craft, *Charon*, a sense of foreboding surged through me. My heart raced, and my thoughts churned with excitement. *Charon*, an imposing vessel with its dark metallic exterior, loomed larger on the screen as we drew closer.

Nonetheless, inside this shuttle, the cabin's design impressed me. Not just for its technological advancements but also for its consideration of crew comfort and operational functionality. The adaptive benches on which we sat provided unparalleled comfort. The wall morphed into backrests.

Storage compartments were neatly tucked into the walls and doors blended almost invisibly with the shuttle's interior when closed. Light pooled softly from overhead panels and cast a serene glow over the crew's faces. Each member of my team was lost in their own thoughts or gazing intently at the cockpit's holographic display showing space in real time.

The shuttle, still under the remote control of *Arcadia*,

docked seamlessly with *Charon*. I gazed out the window and took in the impressive size of the ship. Our sensors indicated it spanned 158 meters in length, with a 45-meter beam and a 22-meter draft. *Charon* seemed like a fortress of hidden secrets and lethal dangers. Out of the frying pan and into the fire.

The moment had come to disembark, and I turned to my crew. "Stay sharp and be prepared for anything."

The airlock hissed open, revealing the dimly lit interior of the *Charon*. We stepped cautiously into the unknown. Another small step for man. Another giant leap into whatever fate had in store for me.

I found myself facing a contingent of guards. Each donned a powered carapace, fusing the same style we'd come to recognize. Each pauldron, which covered their shoulders down just above the elbow, depicted warriors caught in the heat of battle. Their hands gripped spears, glaives, or swords emitting an azure hue. Geometric glyphs, inscribed along the weapon's length, pulsed rhythmically. Every warrior wielded a round metallic shield they held in front of them. The guards stood at attention, lining both sides of our path.

"Permission to come aboard," I said. My gaze immediately focused on Ambassador K'Hori, who stood at the far end, awaiting our arrival.

K'Hori. Her attire was a spectacle in itself, combining an unspoken elegance and a sense of deep-rooted tradition. Her dress, woven from threads that resembled a field of stars, drank in the light around her, returning a shimmer akin to distant nebula seen through the veil of interstellar dust. Her bodice fit her perfectly. The fabric falling from her waist bore the same quality, and it moved with her, each layer capturing and bending light, casting shadows with her every move.

A veil covered her eyes, black as the deepest abyss of space.

As our gazes met, hers hidden behind the veil, I stiffened my resolve. Her imposing presence filled the room.

"Welcome aboard *Charon*, Captain Moore." K'Hori's voice resonated with authority, like it'd been amplified with the help of angels. "I trust your journey was uneventful?"

The interior of the shuttle bay differed from *Charon*'s grim exterior. It was expansive. The ceiling featured a series of grand arches supported by carved marble columns. Starlight filters through large stained-glass windows, casting vibrant reds, golds, and blues across the polished mosaic of glossy tiles in various shades of blue.

A symmetrical arrangement of colossal statues stood proudly on either side of the bay. They were posed heroically, their muscular forms and chiseled features a perfect fit for Greece or Rome. The statues were made of a lustrous metallic alloy catching and reflected the bay's lights.

Around us, maintenance robots diligently performed tasks and cargo loaders transferred supplies. Personnel worked alongside these machines. Other equipment, such as drones, communications consoles, and navigational computers, filled nooks and crannies.

"Thank you, Ambassador. Our journey was smooth." As I approached her, I extended my hand in a gesture of goodwill. "Ambassador K'Hori, I'm Captain Scott Moore. It's an honor to meet you."

She inclined her head. "I have... anticipated our meeting."

"I must admit," I said, "this is a unique experience for us. We've never encountered a civilization quite like yours."

K'Hori offered a knowing smile. "I imagine it must be quite a revelation."

I nodded, considering her words. "Your technology is impressive, especially the ability to cloak entire star systems."

"Keeper Aiantes' capabilities are vast. Our civilization has thrived under its watchful eye."

Erika stepped forward. "If I may ask, how did your people come into contact with Keeper Aiantes?"

K'Hori's stare turned thoughtful. "He contacted us, as I'm sure he has contacted you."

I didn't like the sound of that. "We have not spoken to Keeper Aiantes."

"Not consciously."

Feazer placed both of his hands behind his back as if standing at parade rest.

"Your title is 'ambassador.' Do you speak for him?" I asked.

"I am his liaison."

Vincent raised an eyebrow. "It sounds like a mutually beneficial arrangement."

"Yes," K'Hori said.

I shifted my weight. "So, your people have been hidden away from the rest of the galaxy, protected by Aiantes. What's the purpose of your isolation?"

K'Hori frowned. "It allows us to prepare and strengthen ourselves for the upcoming war, one which will change the fate of the galaxy."

A shiver ran down my neck. Chief mumbled something under his breath, and Vincent gave an almost imperceptible gasp.

"Against whom?" I asked.

K'Hori paused. "The Keepers, Captain Moore. Aiantes stands in opposition to them. It protects those it deems worthy."

My mind raced as I processed what she said. "And your people are among those deemed worthy, I take it?"

She nodded solemnly. "Yes, we are. Our alliance with

Aiantes has allowed us to resist the Keepers' influence and maintain our autonomy."

I rubbed my chin. "If Eos is so well-protected, why reveal yourselves to us now?"

"You came to us," K'Hori said. "We did not come to you."

I crinkled my nose. "You showed yourselves, no?"

She dipped her head. "We did."

"Why?" I asked.

"Why did you come to us?" she asked.

"Eos needed refitting."

"Yes, and we need something as well. It is one of the reasons I wanted to speak with you in person. The time has come to build alliances." K'Hori's gaze bored into mine. "The Circle grows bolder. We *must* be prepared to face them together or face extinction."

Vincent crossed his arms. He wasn't having any of it.

K'Hori looked at him, her face composed. "Your caution is understandable. I assure you, our intentions are genuine. Our cooperation with you and your people will strengthen our combined efforts against the Keepers."

"Would you be willing to share your technology with us?" Vincent asked, much to my chagrin. Now wasn't the time, and he wasn't in a position to ask for anything. None of us were.

K'Hori smiled warmly. "We have much to offer. Our advancements in energy production could revolutionize the way you live."

What could we achieve if we joined forces with K'Hori's people and harnessed their technological power? Repair Earth? Alleviate the Great Famine? All of it seemed impractical.

"The Keepers are relentless. They will undoubtedly attempt to undermine our efforts and sow discord among us," K'Hori said.

Chief addressed the ambassador. "Why?"

"War is a tricky thing. Brace yourselves. We are about to cross the Atlas Rift."

Suddenly, my stomach churned, my vision blurred, and my thoughts grew foggy. I glanced at my crew. Everything became hazy, and for a moment, I couldn't see.

"What's happening? I'm not feeling well," Vincent said.

I struggled to find the words to describe how I felt. Nothing made sense. Colors blended into mathematical equations flashing before me. Sounds became muted, while my pulse pounded in my neck. For a moment, I glimpsed the particles of light, the photons, weaving together in a symphony.

Sounds fazed into oblivion, and all was quiet. Energy bled off the bodies of everyone around me like a fountain of golden light, perfected. The ambassador's aura, if you could call it that, shone the brightest. Veins of purple and dark velvet red coursed through her, and underneath her veil, her solid black eyes burned like volcanoes.

It happened in less than a hundredth of a second.

"Are you alright, Captain?" Chief asked.

Erika's body slumped, and her eyes glazed over. Panic surged through me.

"Is she...?" Vincent stammered, unable to complete his sentence.

Lieutenant Banks smacked against *Charon*'s floor.

Chief moved quickly to her. He checked her systems diagnostics, her power source, and sensor calibrations. Then he looked up at me. "Captain, she's gone again."

CHAPTER THIRTY-THREE

Atlas Rift
Captain Scott Moore

K'Hori approached Erika and studied her for a moment, her eyes narrowing. Gradually, Erika's synthetic skin began to emit a soft glow, indicating that her internal systems were coming back online. A faint groan resonated from within her as she blinked and regained consciousness. Her movements became more fluid and graceful, and her eyes seemed to hold a new depth of understanding. If she went offline, did she see something?

"Erika, are you all right?" K'Hori asked.

Erika nodded. "Yes. Yes, sorry. Thank you."

"You sure?" I asked.

"Yes, Captain. I must've blacked out."

For the record, synths don't black out. If she'd shut down, even temporarily like she did before we boarded *Arcadia*, she might have suffered serious damage. This was the second time this happened to her in such a short span. Who knew what type of issues she now had?

I turned to K'Hori. "Ambassador, what happened? Why did Erika lose consciousness, and how did you revive her?"

"Captain, there are certain aspects of the Atlas Rift and our technology that I cannot divulge at this time. Rest assured, Erika's well-being is intact."

K'Hori guided us through her ship, the walls gleaming with a polished marble-like material, the carved metallic doors, the sculptures. Everything so perfect and orderly.

We entered a meeting room, spacious enough to accommodate thirty people. Its interior carried the same theme, but with added flourishes. Light cascaded from the ceiling, illuminating the area. Hexagonal windows offered a glimpse out into the void. Off in the distance, swarms of meteors zipped through space.

A variety of food awaited us on an elongated table in the center of the room. The spread resembled Mediterranean cuisine. Vegetables. Fruits. Breads. Cheeses.

"This is safe for you to consume," K'Hori said.

Without functioning technology, we had no means to verify her claim. My stomach growled, and I exchanged glances with my crew.

Vincent nodded hesitantly. "If *Arcadia*'s food is safe to eat..."

With a sigh, we decided to partake. If you've ever visited a summer market in the Tennessee Valley, they offer food a lot like this. As I grabbed a few stuffed grape leaves, my gaze drifted through the window to the black expanse. A colossal vessel drifted aimlessly, its shattered hull twisted from what looked to be a battle. It stretched for kilometers. Towering spires lay mangled. Scarred majestic statues littered its outer hull. A silent vigil. The statues could have been pulled from a Greek or Roman museum. The hull itself subtly shimmered as if it contained some inner light.

As my eyes traced the ship's design, the extensive battle

damage became clearer. Massive breaches in the hull, now exposed to the vacuum, revealed the ship's inner workings. Something tagged it repeatedly with immense heat and force.

The thought of entire fleets with weapons capable of this in the right hands would come in handy. The loss of life must've been astronomical. As I continued to study the ship, I noticed more subtle signs of battle. Smaller craft drifted among the debris. These nimble fighters, with their narrow profiles, must've been its first line of defense.

"What happened here?" I asked.

K'Hori's expression became somber. "A great war took place. The ships you see are the remnants of that conflict."

Chief Breckenridge, his face pale, turned to K'Hori. "What kind of weapons were used?"

"Nothing *Arcadia* cannot weather."

The room fell silent as we absorbed her words. The magnitude of my decision loomed over me. My mind swirled with questions. "This ship, *Arcadia*, the ship out there;they all resemble a culture from our home world."

K'Hori smiled. "Does this surprise you?"

I have to admit, when she said that, without the slightest of pauses, I froze. As crazy as this sounds, all those disproven stories about Ancient Aliens flooded into my mind. But what else could it be?

"How can a civilization on the other side of the galaxy evolve the same sort of culture?" Erika asked.

K'Hori took a moment before answering. "I understand your skepticism. It must be difficult for you. Our civilization is the result of something called Morphic Resonance and Morphic Fields."

I raised an eyebrow. "Morphic what now?"

"Morphic Resonance," she reiterated. "It's a concept that suggests that similar patterns of information or activity resonate across space and time, creating shared structures or characteristics."

"So," Feazer said, "you're saying there's some kind of energy field that connects our two civilizations, despite the vast distances between us? Come on."

K'Hori nodded. "Precisely. Morphic Fields are invisible structures that shape the patterns of various phenomena, including the development of civilizations."

Chief looked dubious, and who could blame him? "The sheer distance between our worlds is more than enough to prevent any kind of communication."

"Do you not believe what you see?"

"I didn't say that." Chief snorted. "There's no way to prove any of this."

Chief was obviously having a hard time with this. What was it? What did he expect?

K'Hori picked up a piece of flat bread. "Does the very existence of this piece of bread not defy explanation?"

None of us had an answer. We'd seen enough on Kahwin in the first days to make me question my sanity.

"Morphic Fields are not limited by the constraints of space or time. They operate on a level beyond our current understanding of the physical universe," K'Hori said.

Chief crossed his arms. "You expect us to believe some kind of invisible field causes civilizations to mirror each other?"

Why was he so angry?

"Not just any field. A specific kind of field."

"Does this affect evolution?" I asked.

"Naturally."

Vincent confidently raised his chin. "On our world, we came into existence because an asteroid took out the dominant species."

"A random asteroid?" K'Hori asked.

"What are you saying?" Chief asked. "Did someone launch an asteroid at Earth to cause a different path of evolution?"

K'Hori's gaze remained steady. "I would have to study more about your planet's history. It would not surprise me. Did you experience a sudden growth in species at some point in your distant path?"

I thought about it for a second. "We did. The Cambrian Age."

"I see. What do your scientists say caused it?"

"No one knows," I replied.

K'Hori brought her eyes over to one of her crew, who stayed out of sight. He marched over to hear and poured her a glass of water. She needed sustenance like the rest of us.

"What do you call your civilization?" K'Hori asked.

"We serve all of humanity." An evasive answer, maybe. I wasn't eager to share information with her.

"All of humanity?" she asked.

I looked over at her people. "No. We come from a country called the United States."

"A country? Interesting. Look around, Captain. Does this setting resonate with you?"

"It feels a little familiar, if that's what you mean. On our world, we could call this Greek."

The word caused her to pause. "What happened to them?"

"They're still around, though their culture no longer resembles this one," I said.

"Were they conquered?"

"Yes."

"And how many years have elapsed since the Greeks fell?"

"They still exist," Vincent said. "They haven't fallen."

I didn't agree. All of Europe was a mess.

"Around 2200 years ago. A drought also led to the collapse," Erika said.

"Do you not see traces of their civilization in your own?" K'Hori asked.

The ambassador had a point. "Very much so," I said. "Greek philosophy and many of their ideas concerning government still exist today. No question."

"When a new behavior or skill is learned by one member of a species, it becomes easier for other members of the same species to learn, regardless of the distance between them. Once a critical mass is reached, the Morphic Field strengthens, allowing the new behavior to spread more easily."

Erika gave K'Hori a once over. "Seeing how the Antediluvians are older than we are, would it be safe to assume our planet is a reflection of the Antediluvians?"

"The Morphic Field connecting our two cultures has grown stronger over time," K'Hori explained. "As a result, elements of our ancient culture have resonated with your own, shaping your development in strikingly similar ways. It is the way of things."

Feazer rubbed my chin, pondering the implications. "If I understand correctly, the reason our civilizations are so alike is because we're both tapping into the same Morphic Field, which influences our cultures, technologies, and even our appearances. That would mean our civilization has influenced the rest of the galaxy."

"I cannot say. The empire that ruled the galaxy fell to the Keepers. Their Shaper creations have brought cultural evolution to a halt."

Her explanation sounded incredible. Even a bit fantastical. However, the conviction in K'Hori's voice lent her credibility. She was an ambassador, after all. If true, the existence of Morphic Fields would have profound impacts for our understanding of the universe. It would invalidate what we claimed to be unique about ourselves.

Erika's eyes widened. "It affects non-living tissue as well?"

K'Hori's expression turned serious. "It works the same in all things."

"The hundredth monkey effect." Vincent leaned forward. "It's a phenomenon where a learned behavior spreads rapidly from one group to another once a certain number of individuals in the first group have learned it. Yet, it can occur over long expanses where one group doesn't see or communicate with the other, yet it's collectively learned, regardless."

"What about religion?" Chief asked.

K'Hori pondered Chief's question. "Of course."

Chief didn't like her answer. Neither did I.

"What about *Arcadia*? She needs a refit," I said.

"We will be docking on Eos in a matter of hours. Once I understand the real reason why you have suddenly arrived in this part of the galaxy, we will discuss *Arcadia* more. In the meantime, relax and enjoy the view."

CHAPTER THIRTY-FOUR

Arcadia
Doctor Ingram

When Scott asked me to stay behind and monitor Gisele, continue to check on Michael, and interview the crew, I was a bit perturbed. I'd been with the captain on every major expedition since the beginning, and now he wanted to bench me, like some second-string linebacker with a busted knee. That was my first impression. After some reflection, I agreed with him.

Who was Gisele? Getting to know her would shed light on *Arcadia* and maybe its origins. I didn't need to like the captain's orders. My job was to obey them and offer him a bit of thoughtful advice in private every so often. If Michael woke up, I'd want to check on him, and with me as the only doctor, it made sense.

The Garden of Harmonia was a sanctuary, a place where nature and technology coexisted in perfect harmony. The vibrant flora flourished under an artificial sun, casting dappled shadows below on the lush carpet of grass. The air breathed with the delicate scents of blossoming flowers, and the gentle drone of pollinating bee-like insects as they flitted from bloom to bloom.

The garden consisted of winding paths, secluded alcoves, and the occasional bench where you could take in the hidden treasures waiting for me to discover them. At its heart stood a crystal-clear pool, its surface rippling as the water dripped into it from a nearby pipe.

I'd brought my tablet to record my observations, but I refrained from uploading them to Melody. Vincent might trust his AI, but after what I'd seen over the past few years, I wanted nothing to do with it, which was strange if you knew me. I'd spent most of my life using computers.

I took in the serene beauty surrounding me, a different world away from the sterile confines of my medical bay. Here, we could breathe, reflect, mediate, or pray. It reminded me of Four-Clover Park in a little spot fifty miles outside Montgomery. My father used to bring me there when he had me on the weekends. Entire fields full of clovers with four-leaves, something that used to be called special.

I missed home more than I could say.

As I wandered the paths, I found by the edge of the pool, her gaze lost in the depths of the water.

"Hello, Gisele," I said, not wanting to startle her.

She turned, her eyes flicking in a brief moment of recognition. "Doctor Ingram. What brings you here?"

I sensed her unease. "Call me Doc."

"You Americans love your nicknames."

"True enough. I thought it might be a good time for us to talk."

Gisele paused. "I suppose now is as good a time as any. What did you want to talk about?"

We sat on the grass beside the pool, the cool water lapping

gently at our feet. I studied her face, searching for a way to approach the delicate subject gnawing at me ever since I learned of her existence.

"I understand you have a unique connection to the *Arcadia*."

Gisele's eyes darted away. "I don't know if I can explain it. Sometimes I feel as if I can hear the ship speaking to me. I don't know. This sounds strange, I know."

"You're not being strange at all."

She blushed. "Thank you. It's hard to put into words."

My curiosity piqued. "I'm sure. Perhaps if we talk it through together, we could make sense of it."

Her eyes filled with uncertainty. "Where's Scott?"

"He'll be back, soon."

Desperation filled her eyes. "When?"

"He's currently attending to his duties as captain."

"Did he send you here to talk with me?"

"He wants to understand you better."

"Scott understands me perfectly well," she said.

"Of course he does, but he can't be everywhere at once. I'm here to help, Gisele. You can trust me."

For a moment, she seemed to consider my words. "Can I? Trust has to be earned."

"Captain Moore trusts me enough to speak with you alone. He trusts me."

"I suppose."

"Tell me more about the voice you hear in your mind?"

Her tone softened. "Sometimes, it's like a whisper in the back of my mind. Sounds don't belong to me. It's... something else."

I listened intently, taking care not to interrupt. I watched her body language. For every patient I'd ever known, physical gestures said more than words could ever.

"What does the ship say to you, Gisele?"

Her eyes scanned the garden. "Where's Scott? You said he's attending to his duties, but what is he doing? Is he alright?"

"He's overseeing some maintenance work, but he's fine," I said, reassuming her. "Now, can you tell me what the ship says to you?"

Gisele twisted nervously. "It... it wants something."

"And what is that?"

"Revenge," she said.

I frowned. "Against whom?"

"I don't know. It's just a feeling. I can't shake it."

The thought of a starship desiring revenge unnerved me. Who wanted revenge? Melody or *Arcadia*? "Has the ship mentioned any specific targets or offered any clues as to why it wants revenge?"

"No," she replied, shaking her head. "I only feel its anger. By the way, when is Scott coming back? Where is he?"

I offered a reassuring smile. "He'll be back soon, Gisele. I promise."

"Mind if we walk a little?"

"Sure. I'll follow you."

If Gisele's mind became entangled with the *Arcadia*'s AI, the ship could perceive her thoughts and desires. What would it mean for her autonomy? Was she a separate entity or an extension of the ship's consciousness? Creating a sentient being whose thoughts and emotions were directly linked to an artificial intelligence raised all kinds of moral dilemmas. How much free will did Gisele possess?

The quiet tension between Gisele and me dissipated as we strode deeper into the Garden of Harmonia. We finally arrived at a small alcove, tucked away amidst the verdant foliage. In the center stood an ethereal beam of light pulsing with energy. Gisele approached it.

"What is this?" I asked.

"It's a Numix Device. It's designed to collect and store energy from the very fabric of space-time itself. I've seen it in action a few times. It's extraordinary."

"The ship built it?"

"No, no. The ship can't build anything like this."

"Then who can?"

She peered closer at it. "I'm not sure."

"Do you know how it works or what it's for?"

"I'm not an engineer, Doc." A soft smile played on her lips "You'd have to ask someone more qualified than me." She turned to me. "Doc, tell me a story about when you and Scott were together on Earth. Something light-hearted, something that made you both laugh."

I thought for a moment. "Alright. This one time, Space Force and the Air Force had a friendly baseball game. It was a beautiful day, and we were all excited to show off our skills on the field. Scott, of course, was our star player."

"He loves baseball."

"Yes, he does. He was confident he'd lead us to victory."

As I recounted the tale, Gisele closed her eyes as if she were trying to absorb every detail of the story.

"In the last inning, Scott was up to bat. You only hear this in the movies, but truth was, the bases were loaded, and the score tied. Needless to say, the pressure was on. We were all cheering him on from the dugout, our baseball caps backward."

"Why would you place them... backward?"

"It's to rally us. It's a superstition. Anyway, Scott swung at the first pitch and missed. The pitch was way outside. He swung for the fences, actually."

Gisele made a face.

"Second pitch, he missed as he swung for the fences again."

"Swung for the fences? What does that mean?"

"Like, he wanted to hit a homerun and swung the bat very

hard. Nonetheless, none of us could believe it. Our star player, on the verge of striking out. This time, we turned our hats inside out. That's another way to put our rally caps on. Scott likes to turn things around when everything's on the line. So, the third pitch came hurtling toward Scott, a slider. He swung, but instead of hearing the crack of the bat connecting with the ball, we heard the ball slap into the catcher's mitt and the unmistakable sound of the bat slipping from Scott's hands, sailing through the air. It landed in the bleachers, right in the face of the pitcher's mother, and ended up breaking her nose."

Gisele gasped. "That's not funny. Was she hurt?"

"I made that last part up. She got out of the way in time."

Her face curled into a smile.

I continued, describing the laughter erupting from both teams, the teasing we gave Scott, and the way he'd managed to laugh it off.

Gisele's expression hardened. It was as if she were living the memory, breathing it in, savoring every detail. Slowly, her eyes opened.

"What will happen to me if we return to Earth?" she asked.

I furrowed my brow. "What do you mean?"

"I'm not the real Gisele. Or am I? I don't know anymore."

"I don't know either. We'll figure it out together. You don't have anything to worry about."

Her eyes widened, and she tensed. "I don't think I can leave the ship."

"Why do you say that?"

"It's just... a feeling," she said, stammering. "I don't know what would happen if I tried, but it doesn't seem like a good idea."

Gisele's breathing grew shallow. Her chest heaved with each frantic breath, her eyes darting around the room as if searching for an escape.

"Try to calm down." I placed my hand on her shoulder. "Focus on your breathing. Everything's okay. We're only having a discussion."

My words seemed to have little effect. Her breaths came in short and ragged, and the color drained from her face. "I can't... I can't breathe." Her hands clawed at her throat.

My heart raced as I watched her condition deteriorate. "Gisele, listen to me. You're having a panic attack. I need you to try and take slow, deep breaths. Can you do that for me?"

She nodded weakly, but her breathing only grew more erratic. Desperate to help, I guided her to a sitting position and encouraged her to lean forward and rest her head between her knees.

"Focus on my voice, Gisele," I said. "Inhale deeply for four counts, then exhale slowly for four counts. You can do this. Just breathe."

For a few moments, it seemed her condition might improve. Her breaths became slightly less frantic. Her body went rigid. Her eyes rolled back in her head as a guttural moan escaped her lips.

My heart plummeted. If something happened to her...

Her body convulsed.

"Gisele..."

Then her eyes went dead.

I administered CPR, my pulse pounding in my ears. Seconds stretched into minutes, and still, no response. I might lose her.

I tapped on the tablet, calling the bridge for help, but by the time they'd reach me, she'd be gone.

"I need some help over here!" I shouted.

A single door, hidden behind a hedgerow, burst open.

Michael, dressed in his Space Force uniform, charged me. "What happened?"

He was conscious? How did he get here? Why didn't the guard stop him?

"She had a panic attack," I said. "I couldn't... I couldn't save her."

Michael's eyes blazed with fury. "We need to get her to the Elysium Engine, now!"

As we carefully lifted Gisele's limp body and made our way toward the nearest turbolift, Michael gnashed his teeth. A deafening explosion echoed, accompanied by the shrill wail of alarms and the acrid smell of smoke.

"What's happening?" I asked.

"Get down!"

CHAPTER THIRTY-FIVE

Eos
Captain Scott Moore

As I stepped onto the bridge of *Charon*, I found myself taking it all in. The ship, under the control of our liaison Ambassador K'Hori, steadily approached Eos.

The vast, interconnected network of domes, towers, and docking gantries comprising Eos had the same style as *Arcadia*. Had the same Antediluvians built it? It blended Greek architecture with their advanced technology, creating an awe-inspiring sight.

K'Hori, standing at the front of the room, cleared her throat. "Welcome to Eos. The station serves as a sanctuary for explorers, traders, and adventurers in our domain."

Vincent leaned forward. "How large is your domain?"

"It is enough to know there is a domain left amongst the stars that still carries the torch for humanity. I'm sure you would agree."

Chief glanced over at me, and I gave him a nod to go ahead.

"It's an impressive station, Ambassador. I'm an engineer. How does one maintain such a massive station?"

"The Archons, a council of wise and experienced leaders, oversees the station's operations and ensure the safety of all who reside within," K'Hori said. "Eos is entirely self-sufficient."

"What kinds of services does Eos provide?" Erika asked.

"I will provide you with a map. The Agora serves as a central hub for trading and exchanging information. Commerce is handled by merchants and traders from various star systems, some of whom have braved the void to deliver goods here. The Pantheon, a massive dome, offers a place of worship for various spiritual practices."

Chief placed his hands together and frowned.

"I was under the assumption the Shapers have taken over," I said.

"There are small regions of space where the remnants of civilization still thrive. Asteroid belts. Small moons. They risk death to leave their home."

As we neared the docking bay, Feazer raised a question. "Ambassador, do you know of any recent threats to Eos?"

K'Hori hesitated for a moment. "The uncharted territories beyond Eos are filled with unknown dangers. Our station's formidable defenses are more than enough to dissuade the foolish, and the temporal barrier between Eos and the outside prevents... spying. Additionally, the Helios Guard stands ever vigilant should the need arise."

"The ships we passed on the way here, were they part of your defense force?" I asked.

K'Hori smiled. "War brings out the bravest moments in a person's life. Would you not agree?"

Chief kept firm, but by the look on his face, he didn't like what she was saying.

"I suppose it does, Ambassador," I said.

The conversation carried on as we orbited the station, not docking due to the K'Hori's insistence that our tour required a more covert approach. The exterior of Eos loomed larger and larger, its towering pillars and detailed friezes becoming clearer by the second.

"What about illnesses? Viruses?" Erika asked.

"As soon as you stepped foot onto *Charon*, you were inoculated against any diseases foreign to your immune system."

"Is it a kind of airborne vaccine?" I asked.

My question made K'Hori wince. "I would not dream of manipulating your genes without your permission, Captain. The same goes for all of you. While you might not be directly related to us, you are part of the greater whole. We have ways to keep you immune to all illness that does not require us to invade your body, so to speak. Blessed is the path that brings judgment on the weak."

The bridge fell silent.

"That saying. It sounds religious," Chief said.

"It is."

Chief set his jaw. "What kind of spiritual belief is that?"

K'Hori waved her hand over the central panel on the bridge. "The kind that conquered the stars, human."

"Human? Aren't you human as well?" I asked.

Underneath her veil, her insect-black eyes flashed. "That depends on your perspective."

CHAPTER THIRTY-SIX

Eos
Captain Scott Moore

We disembarked from *Charon*, stepping onto a platform. Great statues the size of banks rose high into the sky, many of them resembling Greek warriors with spears, swords, crested helms, and shields. Others wore suits of what must have been power armor, the kind DARPA sought to produce to replace front-line soldiers.

The ceiling stretched up so high, it looked as if it wouldn't end. A lattice network of turboshafts carried passengers on trains. Great banners in black and red, blue and white, gold and silver hung from most buildings, marking them apart. Frescos of gladiators, tradesmen, and starships were painted on many of the walls, and the smell of rice and fish wafted through the air.

The signs throughout the station were written in their language, which looked close to the same script we'd encountered on Kahwin. Some areas, around alleyways and narrow halls, showed signs of decay. Maybe it was intentional to set the rest of the station apart.

Most of the people's attire and mannerisms reflected the holos I'd seen of Ancient Rome and Greece. The women wore colorful jewelry; necklaces made of threaded polished stone seemed to be in fashion. Everyone wore sandals that made no sound upon the floor.

Amongst the crowd stood an army of men and women clad in the same power armor the people wore on the statues. A glowing blue riot shield covered their left arm, and they carried a spear in their other hand with a tip made of crackling energy. Plumes of orange and white crested over their visored helms. Each of them stood twice my height. Giants among us.

"At the ready!" the one standing at the front said.

They snapped their heels together, all thousand of them. The crowd froze in place. Everyone averted my gaze. It wasn't me. They avoided eye-contact with the K'Hori.

Ambassador K'Hori guided us through the formation. "These are my Helios Guard. While you are under my protection, nothing will happen to you."

As we passed through the station, everyone bowed in submission as K'Hori came in proximity. The Helios Guard trailed us, but at times, I caught sight of a few of them ahead of us. When one of the civilians got too close, a guard would give him or her a stare, and they'd back away from them.

Was this the army Michael wanted me to recruit? I should've spoken about it more with Chief.

"Did your ship tell you to come here?" K'Hori asked.

I passed a child laying flowers by our feet. "Yes. It set a course automatically."

"I noticed your ship sustained damage from recent combat."

"We fought our way out of the Kahwin System."

"How large was Keeper Allo Quishar's fleet?"

I filled her in on the basic details of the battle.

"You performed well. I congratulate you on your victory."

We passed an enormous chamber filled with lush vegetation and small cascading streams. The station's inhabitants strolled through the gardens, occasionally glancing over at us. The fragrances of exotic flowers and the murmur of flowing water created a surreal atmosphere.

Further along, we encountered a vast marketplace teeming with merchants. The cacophony of voices filled the air as deals were made and exotic goods exchanged hands. Spices wafted through the air, a combination of peppermint, sage, and unfamiliar ingredients.

A child darted out from under a stand where something similar to apples was sold, and when he saw K'Hori, he froze in place.

K'Hori stepped over to him and lowered herself. "Be on your way."

With that, the kid disappeared back under the stall.

Finally, we arrived at a vast area resembling an ancient Greek amphitheater. The space buzzed with people engaged in intense debates. The air vibrated with energy weapons and the echoes of powerful voices, discussing matters of philosophy, science, and warfare.

"The amphitheater serves as a hub for the exchange of ideas and skills," K'Hori said.

"A type of town square?" Feazer asked.

I glared at him and shook my head. Now wasn't the time.

"Pardon me?" K'Hori asked.

"We have something similar on our world," I replied for Feazer.

"Of course you do."

Walking side by side with Ambassador K'Hori, I noticed the mixture of awe and curiosity in the eyes of those we passed. It was clear that my presence alongside the ambassador was a rarity, and the inhabitants regarded me with caution. I'd be cautious too, if I were them. Some even whispered among themselves.

I assumed the reason to go this way, rather than a back route, was for K'Hori to demonstrate her authority in case I had any questions about it. Or maybe she wanted to show me Eos on her terms, a kind of guided tour.

The floor was covered in tiles, each one delicately arranged in patterns hinting at an unspoken symbolism. We passed other statues of men and women dressed in simple cloth wraps and decorative cloaks. Some held simple tools, such as hammers and chisels. Others appeared to be scribes, their belts carrying parchment.

Steadily, the presence of the guards grew stronger, and the simple architectural façade gave way to black and grey angular walls, polished like glass. All decorations disappeared, and with them, anyone not dressed in armor. Although nothing prevented our steps from echoing, everything remained library quiet.

A singular black banner with interconnecting lines that resembled waves stood at the end of a hall, draped over an imposing gateway. A massive, arching doorframe with a series of reliefs depicted celestial beings, akin to angels, and enigmatic symbols. When the entrance parted, the ambassador's inner chamber was revealed.

K'Hori entered first, and I waited a few seconds to see if we'd walked into a trap. Once I stepped into the chamber, I immediately noticed the oppressive, otherworldly sameness highlighting the rest of the room. The slate-gray walls displayed ornate friezes and sculptures, enhanced by the ambient glow of concealed lighting. The seamless white marble floor. The strange angular shapes around the room, as if to defy the way humans built things.

In one corner of the chamber, a large, circular console dominated the space. Holographic displays glowed above it, presenting streams of data. Golden motifs of what must have been other ambassadors decorated the console. All of them were veiled women, dressed in the same black chiton as K'Hori.

A high-backed chair stood opposite the console. It was carved from a material that resembled polished marble, and its design evoked the elegance of ancient thrones. The chair featured a series of embedded controls and interfaces.

Subtle hints of the K'Hori's devotion to the Keeper became evident. Small altars with candles. Incense burners. But no depictions of Keeper Aiantes itself.

Chief held back, but if you'd been around him long enough, you knew when he wasn't happy. Too many signs of a false religion, which all pointed at the Keepers being the true power of the universe. That didn't sit well with me either. I hoped this wasn't some type of massive cult.

Naturally, a number of her guards flanked us on either side of her room.

K'Hori walked over to the center of the room and settled into the throne-like seat, her eyes meeting mine. "Captain Moore, as Voice of Keeper Aiantes, I formally welcome you to Eos."

"Thank you," I said.

Without warning, she lowered her black veil. Her once-black eyes came alive. "You have travelled a great distance to find us, and you have many questions. My master wishes to speak directly with you."

"Do you mean Keeper Aiantes?"

"Yes. He... longs to meet you."

I could feel my crew's gaze land on me, and my palms began to sweat. "Very well." I looked around the room. "When?"

"Now." K'Hori fell into an eerie silence.

The air in the room thickened, making it difficult to breathe, like a weight pressed down on my chest. An inexplicable fragrance permeated the chamber, both salty sweet and deathly bitter as the candles flickered in unison.

The guards went to their knees and bowed their heads. They recited a short prayer in a language I couldn't understand. The walls of the room undulated gently.

In confidence over the past few years, Chief shared with me the importance of maintaining a pure heart. He said it was the dwelling place of God and the channel through which His voice could be heard. Despite my skepticism and lack of spiritual inclination, I found myself increasingly influenced by Chief's words. I resolved to uphold my integrity. I refused, even now, to compromise my soul for any reason. Not just for humanity's benefit, but for my own and that of my crew. I needed to use my best judgment, and at all times.

As Keeper Aiantes emerged within K'Hori, her voice deepened. "Tell me of your origins, your world. I wish to know of Earth."

CHAPTER THIRTY-SEVEN

Eos
Captain Scott Moore

As I stared at the K'Hori, I knew at that moment, all of human history would change forever. I paused, acutely aware of the oppressive atmosphere. Her guards remained still.

"Who am I speaking with?" I asked.

"I am Keeper Aiantes, the Seventh Keeper of the Circle."

Chief and Erika gave me a look, as if the Devil himself had entered the room.

I asked, "How are you able to inhabit the ambassador?"

"By what method did you arrive in this region of the galaxy?" Aiantes countered.

"A starship known as the USS *Atlanta* brought us here." I explained how we experienced a catastrophic jumpdrive failure that flung us across the galaxy to Kahwin. Aiantes listened intently and then turned his attention to Chief.

"What happened to your jumpdrive?" Aiantes asked.

Chief recounted the events leading to the failure. "The drive experienced a series of cascading malfunctions, which threw us off course. Our Earth-based sensors detected anomalies, but *Atlanta*'s sensors did not."

Aiantes nodded gravely. "There are traps set around the galaxy to prevent starships from entering jumpspace. It is likely that your *Atlanta* fell into one such trap. Any ship attempting to transition to jumpspace will encounter the same problem."

Vincent couldn't contain his frustration any longer. "So, you're saying there's no way back to Earth?"

Aiantes' tone held a hint of annoyance. "*No one* is permitted to travel freely between the stars."

Chief posed another question. "How is *Arcadia* able to enter jumpspace without its drive failing?"

"*Arcadia* utilizes a propulsion system that combines principles of quantum mechanics and dark matter manipulation with a wormhole generator." Aiantes continued with a detailed explanation that only someone with Chief's expertise could fully comprehend. "*Arcadia*'s drive creates a localized field of dark matter, which manipulates the fabric of spacetime itself. This field interacts with quantum-entangled particles, effectively bending the universe around the vessel. The ship remains stationary while spacetime moves, allowing it to traverse vast distances almost instantaneously."

"How does the wormhole generator function?" Chief asked.

"It creates temporary, stable connections between two points in spacetime. These wormholes allow the ship to bypass the jumpspace traps, as it is not technically entering jumpspace at all."

I could see Chief's eyes light up. "So, in theory, *Arcadia* could jump to Earth."

"Yes, if you know its location."

Vincent's gaze drove a hole through me. No doubt, everyone would want to know why we weren't going home.

Aiantes' gaze shifted from Vincent to Erika, examining her. "Who might you be?"

Erika responded without hesitation, "I am Lieutenant Erika Banks."

"What manner of creature are you?"

"I am a synth, a synthetic human."

Aiantes' expression grew darker as he turned to me. "Captain Moore, how is she permitted to exist among you?"

"She is part of our crew." I said. "Ambassador K'Hori revived her on the way here."

"Are there others such as her on Earth?"

"By now, there are probably hundreds of thousands," I said. "Maybe more."

"Where are the rest of your warships?"

"We've developed various types of spacecraft, but no warships."

K'Hori narrowed her eyes in disappointment. "What of your planetary defenses?"

"Until recently, we were unaware any intelligent life existed outside of our own."

"Your people *must* be prepared to face any threat."

I shifted uncomfortably. "We have had our share of conflicts throughout history, some on a global scale."

The ambassador's chest heaved as she took a deep breath. "Explain to me why Earth has not yet united. Did you not receive a signal?"

"Our world has never received any kind of signal from anyone outside our world."

K'Hori steepled her fingers. "I wish to know of your wars."

I began recounting the major wars in human history, focusing on the European Theatre. The 100 Years War. Battle of the Teutoburg Forest, which led to Rome's ultimate collapse.

The Battle of Hastings. Earth had enough wars to study for ten lifetimes. My choice of what wars to tell him was intentional.

The Keeper listened intently, his focus unwavering. "What of more recent conflicts? Tell me of those."

"There was World War I, which resulted in the deaths of around 16 million people. Then came World War II, with over 60 million casualties. The Cold War followed, although it never escalated into a full-scale conflict."

"What does this mean, a Cold War?"

"Both sides facing each other realized that any attempt to destroy the other would result in both of them being annihilated. The war was fought culturally, monetarily, and covertly."

"Describe what manner of weapons you deploy on each other."

"I'd rather not at this time."

"It seems you were given two chances to unite and failed."

"We value our freedom."

When I finished speaking, the Keeper's voice boomed through the chamber. "That much is clear. Your people have demonstrated a great capacity for violence and destruction. Now you claim that you now seek peace. Why?"

The direction of our conversation made me uneasy. "We'd always preferred peace while the most powerful of us did not. Right now, we seek peace to save lives. On our world, we value human life."

"What have you done to deserve such a peace?"

Deserve? What kind of question was that? "We've established international organizations to promote cooperation and resolve disputes."

"How does your world prevent differing groups from overthrowing your... peace?"

I struggled to maintain my composure as I answered his questions. My unease grew with every question. Was Aiantes assessing our potential as allies or adversaries, perhaps measuring our worth in terms of our ability to wage war? "Diplomatic efforts, economic sanctions. Sometimes, cultural influences."

The air seemed to grow even thicker, and the strange, unsettling resonance in the Keeper's voice deepened. Despite my growing discomfort, I did my best to provide Aiantes with the information he sought while at the same time, remaining as vague as possible. I spoke of Earth's advancements in technology, our efforts to explore the stars, and our ongoing struggles to overcome our violent past, none of which impressed him.

Aiantes remained focused on war, returning to the subject after a few questions. As the conversation wore on, the Keeper's disappointment with Earth's technological advancements became more evident.

"Why have not your people prepared for the threats that exist beyond your world?" Aiantes asked.

I was unsure of how to respond. I'd told him we hadn't detected signs of any extraterrestrials, but that wasn't what he wanted to know. "Our primary focus has been on exploring the stars and seeking new life, not on preparing for war. We didn't know about the Keepers until now."

The Keeper's voice was tinged with frustration. "You are unprepared, and this will be your undoing. What will you do when faced with the other Keepers? You must have a plan."

I struggled to find an answer, knowing that Earth was largely in the dark about the existence of alien life. "While we might not have a specific plan, we will do everything we can to protect Earth and its people."

"Your world is in disarray, and yet you venture into the unknown with the hope of salvation. Admirable, but misguided. Without the necessary preparations, you will not stand a chance against the other Keepers. Earth will perish."

His words weighed heavily on me, the gravity of our situation sinking in. I could hear Chief crack his neck behind me. The threat of the other Keepers loomed large. Now, I figured our only chance would be to get home and defend it with *Arcadia*. Or, defeat all the Keepers before they found Earth. How would I ever possibly do that?

"I must inform you, Keeper Aiantes, that our ship, *Arcadia*, requires a refit before we can take any action," I said.

"I am aware," Aiantes replied. "Your vessel has entered the Atlas Rift and is en route to this location. Observe." He gestured, and a visual image materialized before us, showing *Arcadia* being escorted by a fleet of smaller starships.

"These are your escort ships?" I asked.

"That is correct."

The image focused on a central vessel leading the fleet, larger than the others but still only a fraction of the size of the *Arcadia*. It was streamlined, built for speed and tactical versatility, I assumed. A pair of aft-projecting nacelles served as the vessel's propulsion. The design was purely practical. I didn't see a single extra frill added to the starship's silhouette. The hull showed signs of use, tales of the battles it'd endured. Its hull bore a number of energy weapons and its advanced propulsion systems let loose a deep blue glow, like a cresting ocean wave.

Although impressed, anger brewed in my chest. "Did you give the order to move my ship?"

The ambassador's lips tightened. "Your ship?"

"*Arcadia*," I said.

"The refitting process for *yourArcadia* will take at least one Earth year. It must be done to ensure that the ship is ready to face the other Keepers."

My crew and I exchanged glances, our disappointment evident. "A year? We need to get back to Earth. Our people are suffering from a famine of unprecedented scale." Plus, now the need to defend it loomed even larger over me.

Aiantes' expression fixed on Erika. "Unfortunate as that may be, *Arcadia* cannot leave until the refit is complete. It is the finest starship built by the Regency and the only hope against the other Keepers."

Feazer looked at me, and I gave him a nod. "Keeper Aiantes, was Eos allied with the Regency?" Feazer asked.

"Eos allies with no one," Aiantes said defiantly. "The Regency failed because your species became weak. It will *not* happen again."

Maybe it was Feazer's tone, but Aiantes' reply put me on edge.

I decided to change the subject. "Is my crew safe?"

"Of course. You will speak with them shortly."

"I wish to speak to them now."

"You will speak with them once my communication with you has ceased."

"Keeper Aiantes," Erika said, "we encountered robots on Kahwin."

Aiantes gaze sharpened. "Resembling humans?"

I shook my head. "Not exactly."

"The Regency forbid the creation of artificial beings. All such creations must inevitably be destroyed lest they usher in the downfall of civilization." K'Hori leveled a finger at Erika. "Due to your interaction with Ambassador K'Hori, *you* will be allowed to exist."

"The others?" I asked, thinking about my Janissaries back on Kahwin. Without them, Starport City and the planet itself would be vulnerable. What about Zoe? I didn't want to ask.

"They must be destroyed."

Vincent's sarcasm dripped from his words. "Well, this just keeps getting better and better, doesn't it?"

Aiantes remained silent for a moment. "Do you find my decision troubling?"

My brother raised his chin. "No, Keeper Aiantes." A lie. Vincent's love for technology might end up getting us all killed.

"Do you find genetically created beings to pose a bigger threat? We've fought the Shapers since we've arrived," I said.

"The overt nature of the Shaper threat seems obvious."

"Meaning robots are not?" Erika asked.

"Once a society decides to replace themselves, extinction is inevitable."

Extinction. The word hung in the air like death itself.

"I have a great many questions, if I may," I said.

Aiantes' words lingered in the air. "A vast ocean teems with life unseen. Beneath its surface, countless forms exist, each adapted to survive the unfathomable depths." Aiantes paused briefly. "A creature emerges, at first, unassuming. Simple. It swims with the other creatures. It begins to change, to mimic the life around it. Unchecked, it grows, adopting new forms. Finally, the ocean's balance falters, disrupted by the imposter. But who could see? Not the blind. It feeds. It consumes. It takes, until the others are no more. A false reflection remains, an echo of what once was, casting shadows on the world above."

Aiantes' silence enveloped the room.

A subtle shift in the air marked the beginning of a transformation. K'Hori's consciousness, previously suppressed by the Keeper's presence, gradually reasserted itself within her physical form. Her features blurred momentarily as if caught between two worlds. The ambient light of the chamber refracted, creating a dazzling display of colors.

K'Hori's form solidified, and her striking features once again became distinct. It was evident how the exchange of consciousness took its toll on her. Her solid black eyes seemed weary.

Dulled. Her posture slumped, as if the weight of a billion lifetimes bore down on her shoulders.

K'Hori's consciousness regained full control. Her head slunk on her chest.

"Ambassador K'Hori, are you alright?" I asked.

She took a deep, steadying breath. For a moment, she closed her eyes. When she opened them again, she adjusted herself on her throne. Though she still appeared fatigued, her voice was steady. "I am well, Captain Moore. The connection between Keeper Aiantes and me can be... draining." She glanced at her guards. "Take the captain and his crew to their new quarters."

As the guard moved to comply with her orders, K'Hori's gaze lingered on me, her eyes betraying her apprehension. "*Arcadia* will arrive on Eos in five days. Until then, you are free to traverse the station and get to understand who we are."

"Ambassador, it is vital I speak to my crew," I said.

"You will find a means to communicate with *Arcadia* in your private quarters."

"Thank you. Are there any rules we should be made aware of?" I asked.

"Guard your honor. It is all you will ever have."

CHAPTER THIRTY-EIGHT

Eos
Captain Scott Moore

Nothing stays the same. You can fight to keep the status quo. Kill someone to keep things even. Balance the scales with enough power and money and willpower. But entropy is a real thing. Insert enough order into a system, entropy will tear it down and giggle about it. Tighten the vise, and something's going to give. Anyone who thinks differently will be gravely disappointed.

Back on Earth, plenty of people bucked the system. Tried to establish a new order. A new way of thinking. In order to do that, one must first understand the system and be ready to accept that whatever plan you have in store for the future will only come to fruition if you are willing to go all the way, and I mean all the way.

Keeper Aiantes' questions brought up a lot of thoughts, and all of them lacked forthright answers. People have been writing about alien contact since the Sumerians, and at some point, H.G. Wells wrote a book about them coming to Earth.

Yet, at no time did Earth ever think to unite as a way to prevent the planet's demise. Sure, that old actor and former president, Reagan, had something to say about it, but that was as far as it went.

If you had asked me a year ago what I thought about militaristic warlords, I might have given you some answer about how the United States tends to kick their ass. As an American, I wasn't fond of tyrants. I swore an oath to the Constitution, and I damned well knew there was no finer document in existence.

Aiantes' questions haunted me, drove ice picks into my eyes, if you get my meaning. Would I be Milton's Lucifer by freeing humanity from Shaper chains, or would I be a George Patton, a George Washington. Or a George McClellan and be afraid of my own shadow, both literally and figuratively.

Everyone thinks they can control the Ring of Power. Even Frodo.

The first time I stepped into the suite Ambassador K'Hori assigned me, my breath hitched in my chest. A seamless blend of the ancient and the advanced style of the Antediluvians were on glorious display.

K'Hori gave us all our own quarters away from the bustling activity of Eos and provided us a platoon of her royal guard to oversee our safety.

The walls were a striking blue, a hue mirroring the depth of the galaxy. Brilliant streaks of gold and snowy white accents meshed together. The color scheme reminded me of ancient civilizations I studied in one of my history classes. Their buildings perched on cliff sides, kissed by the sun, overlooked a sea of infinite blue.

High-relief murals graced the expansive walls, their subjects reminiscent of heroic figures of legend, yet rendered with a degree of realism that hinted at an advanced holographic technology. They were like statues. Crafted meticulously.

Frozen in time. Performing deeds of valor and courage. I wanted to breathe it all in and keep it forever.

A walk-in closet stood with its doors ajar. It revealed an array of garments meticulously arranged. The clothing, tailored from exotic fabrics, shimmered with starlight. They bore designs similar to the draped and flowing styles of ancient senatorial attire from Rome or Greece. Each piece, from the tunics to the crafted sandals, had been personalized to my exact measurements.

The bathroom was an opulent oasis of its own. The fixtures were made of some radiant gold-like metal, the tub large enough to submerge fully and set against a window, showcasing the void beyond. The shower hinted at options for hydro-massage. I could have used one right about then.

A luxurious bed dominated the living space. The bedding was a silky sheen, and the cushions bore embroidered patterns of constellations on this side of the galaxy. Each thread pulsed with a soft light, like a distant star.

In the corner of the room, I noticed an ebony rectangle about the size of book. A series of small knobs stood on the front of the device, and a crystal prism rested inside a concave silver hemisphere. It resembled an antique computer speaker. A glass pitcher full of ice water sat next to it and a platter of what looked like sliced lemons sat off to the side.

The overhead lights were controlled via a dial next to my bed.

I made my way to the ebony device. This had to be the way to contact *Arcadia*.

Someone knocked on my door.

"Come," I said.

Chief walked inside and looked at me, grimacing. "We need to talk."

"What's on your mind? You look upset."

"What exactly is going on?"

"What do you mean?"

"Sir, I've known you for years. I know when you're lying and when you're holding something back. It's in my job description. When Vincent asked about getting back to Earth, you winced."

I squared my shoulders. "I told you our plan of action."

"Our mission is to return home."

"Our *mission*, Chief Breckenridge, is what I *say* it is."

Chief knitted his brow. "Sir."

"Speak."

"Since we've boarded *Arcadia*, you've been acting... different."

"In what way?" I asked.

"It's hard to put into words. Did Doc check you out?"

"He checked us all out. I'm fine."

Chief looked away and came further inside the room. He peeked in the bathroom. "Nice." He examined the device on the desk for a few seconds and checked the back of it.

"Look, Pete, if you have something to say, come out and say it," I said.

"What did you and Michael talk about?"

I wasn't ready to have this conversation with him. Not yet. "I've noticed you've had an attitude ever since we boarded *Arcadia* too. What's wrong?"

"You don't want to tell me what you and Michael said?"

"Not right now," I admitted. "I want you to answer my question."

"You have no intention of returning to Earth, do you?"

"Why would you ask that?"

"Because you don't."

"That's incorrect."

"Then why don't you take *Arcadia* back to Earth, drop off

those who want to stay on Earth, pick up crew there, and come back here?"

I shook my head. "It's not that simple."

"The hell it's not." His face flushed with anger. "It's exactly that simple. I know for a fact if we don't go back to Earth soon, morale will plummet. We hold a tenuous grip on morale as it is. And what about the people back on Kahwin? The Senate?"

"I won't have you questioning me, Chief. We have a chain of command for a reason."

Chief bit his lip. "Aye, sir. And who do you answer to?"

"Right now, I have a responsibility to not only the crew, but to humanity at large. Or would you rather know in your heart of hearts that there are people out there," I said, pointing up the ceiling, "who are enslaved to the most hideous creatures you could possibly imagine, and that you and I both had an opportunity to do something about it. Something great. And when we had the chance to do something, we instead did nothing. Is that your idea of living up to the Constitution?"

"Tell me where in the Constitution it says to defend other planets."

"Do you need a piece of paper to tell you to do the right thing?" I asked.

"A piece of paper..."

"Or can you listen to your conscience. Or did all that killing in your career before joining Space Force muck up your brain?"

Chief instinctively reared back with a closed fist. Realizing what he'd done, he quickly uncurled his hand and put his arms to the side. We both stood there, immovable objects, waiting for the other to react. In the moment, I'd gone too far. A person knows how to hurt the people closest to them the most.

Chief cleared his throat. "I recall helping you clear *your* conscience once in Montana."

"Don't ever raise your hand to me again, Chief. Do you understand?"

"Aye, sir," he snapped. "And as your friend, you know better than to bring up something like that during a conversation."

I raised my voice. "Then tell me what the hell you're thinking and quit beating around the bush."

"Okay. Let's talk. Who are the Keepers?"

"I have no idea," I said.

"Did you ask Michael?"

"We talked about other things. Asking Michael would be like asking the ship. I figured the ambassador would fill us in at a later date."

My answer left Chief unimpressed. "The ambassador works for a Keeper. Why would she tell you what they *really* are?"

"What do you think they are?"

Chief rubbed the back of his neck for a while. "I don't think it's something I want to admit."

"Why?"

"Because if I say it, everything will change."

I waited for him to tell me. If something bothered him this much, he'd been thinking about it. I looked to him for not only his engineering skills, but his practical mind.

"If everything we've seen lately is Greek, and if the ambassador is correct about the field theory..."

I finished his thought. "Then it would make sense that the Keepers are acting as gods. They probably believe they're gods."

"Aye, sir. It's the only thing that makes sense."

"Greek gods? You think Zeus and Apollo are Keepers? You believe in God. How can you say that?"

He remained still.

"What did Allo Quishar call himself? Fifth Keeper of the Circle?"

"And Aiantes is Seventh Keeper of the Circle. Do you know how many main gods are in the Greek Pantheon?"

"Twelve?"

Chief nodded in agreement. "That's right. And isn't it funny how we call our planets after the Greek gods. Jupiter, for example."

"I've been thinking about that since we discussed the field theory."

"You got something to drink in here?"

I checked everywhere, but unlike a normal hotel, this one didn't come with a cooler. "Water in the sink."

He waved away my idea. "I'm good." He sat in the chair at the desk, and I across from him on the bed. The spread was cushioned well. Even the pillows were luxury.

"You need someone to keep you on the rails, sir. Someone you can trust with any information."

"Are you that person?"

"I'm a straight shooter, Captain. My great-grandfather taught me a saying before he died. It goes, 'Never ask a question you don't want answered truthfully.'"

"I've heard that myself."

"You mind if I use the head?" he asked, standing up and starting for the bathroom door.

"Go ahead."

Before I left Earth, I spent a Tuesday with my nephew shooting turtles in a nearby lake with a .22. They cut down on the fish supply. It was hot that day, and the mosquitoes were out in droves, as in giant clouds of those bloodsuckers. City ordinances normally prohibited taking an R-Blocker, which usually came in the size of a Tic Tac. You take one of those, no bug will want to have anything to do with you.

But we were out in the country, and their rules didn't apply.

Unfortunately, my nephew forgot to bring his pill, so I gave him mine and suffered like none other.

As I scratched my bleeding leg from all the bites, my nephew asked me, "What do you think of cartoons?"

"I don't like them."

"Why not?" he asked.

"Because they don't teach you anything."

"But G.I. Joe barks."

I smiled. The kids back then used the best slang. "All kids your age are supposed to like it." I started loading the five-round mag for the rifle.

"Well, what about 'Romance of the Three Kingdoms?'"

A foul taste rose up in my mouth. "You shouldn't be watching Chinese media. It's not good for you."

"Why?"

"Are you sure you want to ask me that?"

He poked me in the ribs. "What's wrong? Are you afraid?"

My nephew had turned seven last month. What did he know about politics other than what his mother told him? Probably next to nothing. What good is it to talk to children about matters most adults don't understand? He liked to play sims, or simulated virtual world games, on his holocaster and talk to his friends. I thought he was too young to play those games. He should be outside more.

I loaded another round.

But he wanted to know, and if anything, my nephew was curious. You couldn't keep him out of things unless you locked them up tight, and even then, he'd find a way inside. He'd stolen a dozen food bills and sold them at his school for some extra money. Those bills were meant to feed my sister's neighbor, who got denied disability benefits for reasons I'd never understand.

My nephew would eventually find out the answer to why you shouldn't watch Chinese media at some point. The question was: by whom? At school or from his friends? Sometimes, parents taught their kids some things they shouldn't, which usually ended up putting them on The List, not a place you'd ever want to be. Those same kids would sometimes speak out of turn to other kids, and depending on how well that other kid could keep a secret, it determined how fast that information spread.

Tell the wrong kid the wrong information and it would spread like a wildfire. That was how murders happened.

One kid at my nephew's school told her classmates that someone on The List leaked a gene virus in the food court, and she proved it by showing the class an infection on her forearm. The cameras said she was telling the truth. There's a reason you don't yell fire in a crowded room.

Later, it came out that her mother belonged to the Orphan Party, and she'd been keeping it a secret most of her life. She'd tried that same tactic when she worked as a skinwalker in Miami, but the locals could see through her lies. She almost got arrested. So, rather than using her good looks, she applied to have a child, and once she paid the fee, the mother brainwashed her, right under the nose of her father.

So, if my nephew learned about the Chinese from some kid from a mother like that, then what?

Or the school. God only knew what they taught in those schools back then. Every other year, they had to change their uniforms because some bureaucrat of a bureaucrat of another bureaucrat in some dark corner of the government thought the color blue didn't match the latest AI opinion poll. So, they'd scrap the whole thing and start over from scratch.

Every vote went through an AI scrubber to search for truth content, and if anything was found missing, it'd get kicked back to the PTAF, or the Parent-Teacher Alliance Foundation, and they'd have to rewrite their entire charter. Why? Knowing some of those documents could be over five hundred pages long? You'd have to ask them.

And if that wasn't strange enough, some teachers started bringing in old textbooks, so the information couldn't be changed. In the era of the Great Famine, I'm pretty sure you can guess how well that went.

So, the other option would have been for my nephew to find out why a person shouldn't watch Chinese media would come from the school. What would *you* do?

I was like a soldier facing down two tanks, with only one round left in my missile rack.

"Hey, how do you flush this thing?" Chief asked, breaking me out of my memory.

"I don't know. Is there a button?"

"I don't see one," Chief said.

"You're the engineer."

"Aren't you the comedian?"

After a few seconds, I asked, "How'd you wipe?"

"I didn't. There's a bidet in here."

"Oh, I didn't see it."

I heard the sink. Then the door opened.

"Found it," he said.

"How'd you flush it?"

He grinned.

"You're not going to tell me, are you?" I asked.

"I haven't decided."

"Who's the comedian now?"

Chief pointed to himself. "I am."

I walked to the closet. K'Hori would want us to wear these clothes. I'd worn some variation of a Space Force uniform for most of my life. I didn't like the idea of shedding my second skin.

"There's something that's bothering me, Captain. You know how important the Bible is to me. How important faith is to me."

"I know. It's something I envy." Then I figured out what this conversation was really about. Next came the inevitable question. "You want to know about Christ, don't you?"

Again, Chief remained quiet, the question too much for both of us. I refused to accept the idea that Christ was somehow an alien influencing humanity from afar, which would follow if the field theory proved to be true. I was hardly spiritual. Space Force made sure the officer corps was more or less free from spiritual beliefs. They said the psychological stress would be too much to bear for some, and the unpredictable nature of discovering alien life might cause an "existential crisis," which might endanger our mission.

Chief was the most spiritual person I knew. I wanted to be as faithful as him. He was one of the best people I'd ever known.

"My relationship to Christ is a feeling. I know he's the son of God."

"How much do you know about the Greek gods?" I asked.

"As much as the next man. Not a lot."

"If we question Melody, it will inevitably alert Michael." I mulled over how to keep this a secret. "Talk to no one about this."

"I can't be the only person who's thought of this."

"Probably not, but wait for them to say something. Even the theory might cause the crew to panic."

Chief smirked. "Any idea on how to beat a god?"

"Not yet. We have a year to sort it out during the refit." I went to the bathroom sink and tested the water to see how hot I could make it. A year? It would screw with morale. So much was on the line, and throwing a year at my crew could put several cuts in the line. "Have you considered the idea that Earth might've solved the Great Famine by now?"

"I don't see how that's possible."

Steam rose from the water and started to fog up the mirror. I shut it off and went back into the main room, satisfied I'd be in for a warm shave soon. "Anything that's done can be undone."

Chief stood by the device on the desk. "I don't have one of these in my room. Did K'Hori say what it's for?"

"I think it's how I'm supposed to contact *Arcadia*. She didn't say, and I don't know how to use it. Looks like the prism creates a hologram."

It took Chief just a few minutes to figure out how to make it work. Three dials acted as an X, Y, and Z axis. As he turned the dials, the prism projected a view of hazy holographic image of *Arcadia*, like a radio channel filled with static. Using the other dials, he zeroed in on *Arcadia*, increasing the sharpness of the image.

An hour later, he figured out how to contact the bridge, which wasn't so easy.

"Sir, it's good to hear your voice," my XO, Commander Chen, said. She looked worn but confident.

"What's your ETA to Eos, Lieutenant?"

"Forty-one hours, Captain. Is everything alright?"

I blinked twice in rapid succession and flared my nostrils, indicating we weren't in apparent danger but to remain cautious. "Yes, Commander. We look forward to your arrival. We will meet you at the repair bay."

"Aye, Captain." Lieutenant Commander Chen blinked once and then winked with her left eye. She understood my signal and would follow through with my orders.

"Report."

Chen pursed her lips for a second too long. "All systems go,

Captain. All crew are accounted for and are currently performing their duties as required."

Something was wrong. She didn't think it was safe to speak over an open channel about it.

"Very well, Commander. Moore out."

Chief killed the comm link and the prism went dead. "What are you going to tell the crew?"

"Nothing. Anything that was said between Ambassador K'Hori, Keeper Aiantes, or anything spoken between us will be kept classified. You will make sure nothing leaks."

"Your brother likes to talk."

"Then make sure he doesn't."

CHAPTER THIRTY-NINE

Arcadia
Doctor Ingram

"Michael, what's happening?" I shouted. The Garden of Harmonia, once a tranquil sanctuary, was now a flaming inferno. Brilliant flowers and ancient trees succumbed to the blaze. The artificial sun dimmed, its gentle light outshone by the flames.

"The Numix Device! Melody has interfered!" Michael yelled. "*Arcadia*, open the auxiliary corridors!"

No response. The ship was eerily silent. The system's normal drone was drowned out by the crackling flames and screeching alarms.

As the explosion ripped through the tranquil air of the Garden of Harmonia, it transformed the sanctuary into an apocalyptic inferno. Flame tongues, the color of sunsets and supernovas, leaped high into the air, vying for dominance against the artificial sky. Machines ruptured, spewing forth a vicious, seething maelstrom that whipped through the botanical haven with a monstrous fury.

"You must get her to the Elysium Engine!" Michael shouted. "Get to the lift."

I scooped Gisele up and made a run for it.

Fungi forests and their bioluminescent caps went up in a pyroclasmic eruption. Illuminated by the firestorm, a cascading shower of spores billowed into the air. The verdant leaves of the celestial trees curled and blackened under the fiery onslaught, releasing a bittersweet aroma. Their massive trunks groaned under the heat's torment before they crumbled into fiery husks. Clusters of iridescent flowers wilted. They were reduced to smoldering ruins, their vibrant colors surrendering to the searing movement of the flames.

The inferno scorched everything in its path. The wooden benches. The ornate sculptures. Nothing would survive. The water of the stream once meandering through the landscape was vaporized in an instant.

All I could do was run. Gisele's body grew colder by the second. I held her limp form close to me as I hurried to the turbolift.

Michael, a figure silhouetted against the monstrous flames, didn't flinch as he dashed around the Garden in a futile attempt to save it.

The heat caused me to wince and narrow my eyes. Embers flew at me as I closed the distance to the lift. Bright flames traced the stonework paths, once leading to quiet alcoves. Now, these routes acted as fuel lines, transporting the fire's hungry tendrils further into the heart of the garden. The more it devoured, the more it wanted.

Something exploded.

I turned.

The Numix Device, the energy collector Gisele showed me, started to glow as the flames engulfed it. The arcane energy within it responded violently to the fire's touch, creating an eye-searing spectacle as the flames were tinged with electric blues and violets.

The lift doors stood open, and I flung myself inside and set Gisele down so I could operate the controls.

Above the din of the fire, Michael yelled, "Doctor Ingram, get her to the Elysium Engine! Get out of here! I'm going to disconnect the Garden from the ship or *Arcadia* will..."

The Numix Device's contours glowed white-hot, its normally smooth surface bubbling and warping under the intense heat. With a pop, the device collapsed onto itself, its stored energy released in a silent, radiant explosion.

I'd barely registered what I'd seen when the turbolift doors slid shut, cutting off my view of the inferno. My heart pounded in my ears as I pressed the button for the Elysium Engine.

I swore under my breath. Michael had burned alive. Dead twice now. The strangeness of it all couldn't be overstated.

What caused the explosion in the first place? Sabotage?

Boom!

The lift grounded to a halt andthe lights died, plunging us into darkness. Then, with a horrifying lurch, gravity failed. Gisele's unconscious body floated away from me, her hair fanning out like a dark halo.

What was happening? I strained my eyes in the darkness, trying to make sense of our situation. Had the fire caused such extensive damage that we were...

I swallowed hard.

Adrift in space? I calculated the volume of the area I stood in to determine its oxygen supply. The turbolift was designed to hold six people comfortably, which meant it was roughly twenty square meters in size. If my memory served right, one person would consume about 0.84 cubic meters of oxygen per day. The rate could increase in times of stress and physical exertion, which was certainly the case now. My breaths were coming in gasps, heavy with the fear tightening around my chest.

If I rationed my breaths, I estimated I'd have, at most, an hour before the oxygen levels dropped dangerously low. Hypoxia would set in. My mind would grow fuzzy, and my heartbeat would quicken. I'd begin to pant, trying to draw in more oxygen. My vision would narrow, my body would grow cold and numb. Then, unconsciousness and, eventually, death.

"Well, Doc, you've done it now," I said to myself.

The absence of heat was another concern. Space was effectively a vacuum, a place where temperature did not exist in the usual sense. The metal walls of the turbolift could not radiate heat into a vacuum. Instead, they would slowly conduct their warmth away, creating a gradual decrease in temperature. If the turbolift's insulation was compromised by the explosion, it could be a matter of hours before the cold of space froze me into a Popsicle. The prospect of dying from hypothermia in the vast, cold abyss of space chilled me.

My thoughts jolted back to reality. No time to ponder. Gisele and I were floating in a metal box with a finite supply of air, and we were running out of time. Fast. I had to act. And I had to act now.

Straining my eyes to see in the pitch-black darkness of the lift, I grappled my way to what I remembered as the lift's control panel. I groped along the wall, my fingers seeking the cold touch of the metallic interface. I found it at chest level. It was a smooth, rectangular plaque embedded into the wall.

The turbolift's minimalist design prioritized function over aesthetics. It was fashioned in the image of *Arcadia*'s technological grandeur—a compact, cylindrical chamber, with gleaming metallic walls made of a high-strength alloy. Its uncluttered interior offered ample room.

The control panel was non-responsive. Normally, it featured

a high-resolution holographic touch display, capable of show-casing the whole layout of *Arcadia*. There were floor indicators, colored in vibrant hues, each representing a distinct level of the starship. Below them were the control functions, a set of simple command icons designed for intuitive operation. Under normal circumstances, the panel would glow with a soothing light. Now, it was just a lifeless slab.

On one side, a railing ran around the circumference of the lift, a safety measure designed to assist in times of abrupt movement or gravity loss. It was coated in a material that reduced slippage, helpful for maintaining a firm grip.

To the best of my memory, a small compartment nestled below the control panel housed a basic emergency kit. I was uncertain of its contents. It was designed for a medical or mechanical emergency within the ship, not for an incident like this—me inside a lift floating outside the ship.

Despite the growing dread pooling in my stomach, I kept my mind focused. I tried everything to get the control panel to respond. Nothing. Not even the faintest sign of life. The realization hit me hard.

As I fumbled in the dark, I forced my senses into overdrive, feeling for any objects or tools within the turbolift that could be of use. My search yielded nothing.

What about Gisele? I searched her.

In one of her pockets, I discovered a small tablet not much bigger than my palm.

The tablet was encased in a smooth matte material. A singular button sat recessed on the top edge. I pressed it. The tablet came to life, a soft glow emitting from the screen, casting an eerie luminescence in the darkened lift. The interface was simple. Upon the screen sat a sparse array of icons, each repre-senting a different function. A prominent icon at the center displayed an antenna, indicative of a communication function. I tapped on it. The screen flickered for a moment, only to present a message of failed connection.

"Oh, come on."

I tried again. Same result. A third attempt proved no more successful. The tablet wasn't linking up with the ship's comm system.

Michael said Melody interfered. What did he mean?

A series of readings caught my eye. They were displayed on a sidebar on the screen—heartbeat, body temperature, blood oxygen levels. Two people were mentioned. Gisele and me. The tablet had been monitoring our biological and psychological states. Was this another function of the ship, to keep tabs on its crew, or was it something Gisele set up herself?

No time to think.

I studied the tablet, my focus narrowing to the singular task at hand. The essence of any communication device was connectivity. For the fourth attempt, I concentrated on the tablet's settings. Scrolling through its menus, I located the communication protocol options. There were several, ranging from ship-standard frequencies to emergency distress signals. The standard ship frequencies were clearly ineffective. I tapped the antenna icon again and put out an emergency distress signal. The connection failed once more.

The battery icon drained a percentage point every few seconds, and it now read 58%.

Okay, slow down.

What potential factors could be interfering with the signal? The cold of space? The metallic walls of the turbolift? I tried warming up the tablet by rubbing it briskly between my hands before hitting the antenna icon again.

Nothing.

55%. Still time.

Process of elimination. Maybe the device's internal antenna

might be having difficulty projecting the signal due to the unusual circumstances. I navigated to the tablet's diagnostic tools and ran a self-check. The device promptly displayed a report: all systems normal. That wasn't it.

51%. Halfway.

I didn't want to die here. This couldn't be how it all ended for me. Not here. I had to get back to Earth.

Don't be scared. Control your breathing.

In the extreme cold of space, power systems could behave unpredictably. I navigated to the power management settings, directing all available power to the communication functions.

Each failed attempt was a blow, a stark reminder of how few minutes I had left.

Gisele's pale face stared at me, dead against the dim light of the tablet.

The tablet registered the ambient temperature plummeting. A glance at the turbolift's interior confirmed my fears. The structure was beginning to buckle under the pressure of space. If I didn't act soon, hypothermia would set in, and...

No. I'd live through this. I'd lived through worse.

36%. *Come on. Stay on.*

There had to be a way to send a signal.

I noticed a feature in the communication settings during my attempts to establish contact. A function designed to send a short, automated message—an emergency ping. Once activated, it'd send until a connection was made or the tablet's battery died. A last resort.

32%.

With trembling hands, I navigated back to the communication settings and hit the icon for the emergency ping. A window popped up, asking me to input a short message.

'Turbolift in space. Air failing. Need rescue,' I typed.

29%.

A small icon in the corner of the screen started blinking. The ping was being sent. It was out of my hands now, and all in the hands of God. All I could do was wait, hope, and pray.

What are you supposed to think about during the last few moments of your life?

Scott would send a team to get the tablet.

Someone had to know the ship was spying on me.

I pulled up a textbox and typed, '*Arcadia* is spying on the crew. Tests for crew inconclusive. Ship may be replacing personnel.'

17%.

Damn it.

"God, I could use a little help right about now."

A hissing sound filled the turbolift. I scanned the interior, heart pounding. There it was—a tiny crack in one of the walls, hardly noticeable, but spewing precious air into the unforgiving vacuum of the black void. With every second, the crack was spreading, the wall of the turbolift groaning under the strain.

14%.

'Numix Device is destroyed. Michael died in the fire.'

11%.

As I watched, a segment of the wall bulged, the microfracture widening as the cabin's precious atmosphere was violently expelled. The sudden change in pressure made my ears pop, the harsh noise startling in the relative silence of the turbolift.

'Don't trust the ship.'

The cold bit through the fabric of my clothing, my body convulsing in violent shivers in a futile attempt to generate warmth. Each breath of the rapidly thinning air was a struggle. Hypoxia was beginning to set in.

The edges of my vision started to blur. I could barely think. Hypothermia was compounded by the effects of the hypoxia. With the rapid decrease in temperature, my body was redirecting the blood from my extremities to my vital organs, trying to keep them warm. Frostbite was a very real possibility now.

5%.

Despite the bitter cold and the fading oxygen, sweat pooled at the base of my neck. The phenomenon was not foreign to me. Hypothermia victims suffer from feelings of incredible heat due to confused nerve endings.

My pulse fluttered weakly in my throat, heart straining to circulate what little oxygen remained. I had seconds left of consciousness.

Time slowed.

1%.

God, do you hear me? I'm sorry for not doing better.

A surreal calm washed over me. I was a doctor, trained to save lives. Hadn't I done just that? I'd done my best. What a life I'd lived. Who else could say they'd seen what I'd seen?

I'm going to die in here, aren't I?

This is it.

Please forgive me.

Just as I felt my hold on consciousness slipping, a strange sound echoed through the dying silence—a soft, repetitive ping, the only evidence that our emergency signal was still being transmitted, desperately calling for help that might never come.

My vision started to tunnel. The edges of my world darkened until only a small circle of light remained. I had the distinct feeling of being pulled down into a deep, fathomless abyss. I'd promised to get Gisele to the Elysium Engine and failed.

I'm going to go to sleep now.

With a final gasp, my world faded to black.

CHAPTER FORTY

Eos
Captain Scott Moore

"Mr. Feazer," I said, politely. "Do you have a moment?"
Feazer raised an eyebrow. "Of course, Captain. Please come in."

His room looked a lot like mine. Same bed. Same Greek-inspired themes. The same size. Luxury at its finest. You know those expensive hotels in Dubai? The ones where you go to the top and play golf? For some reason, I was reminded of how large our Eos rooms were compared to the usual rooms Space Force gave us on TDY, temporary duty assignment.

As I walked inside Feazer's room, I noticed he'd put out some of the clothing he'd found in the closet. He hadn't changed, yet and neither had I.

Feazer, as an Equinox employee, deserved some answers. We'd left them in charge of the Senate back on Kahwin, functionally allowed them to call the shots as we explored the planet for *Arcadia*.

"Sit down please, Captain. Make yourself comfortable."

"Thank you. How do you like the accommodations?"

"Excellent, sir. It appears we've all been given similar rooms."

I nodded and found a chair at his desk. "Executive suites."

"Aye, sir."

I motioned to his clothing. "Does that all fit?"

"Aye, sir. All of it. How did they get our measurements in time to make our clothing? There's got to be fifty outfits in my closet and a dozen pair of sandals."

"Not sure. The ambassador might've gotten our measurements on *Charon* somehow and then sent them to Eos." The question was: what other data had the ambassador been collecting? "Feazer, the reason I'm here is to get your opinion on a few things. Mind if we talk?"

My statement caused a glint of hope to shine in his eyes. "Not at all, sir. Happy to advise you in anything you need."

"Your corporation allowed us to build the most powerful ship on Earth. How well did you know Ms. Munn?"

Feazer grimaced at the name of the traitor who tried to put a bullet in me. "I knew her quite well, Captain."

It'd been years since the head of Equinox tried to end my life. Ever since then, I'd often thought about hierarchy and what it meant to be "in charge" of something. Space Force trained you a certain way, and in most situations, their style of leadership was effective. However, even my brother joined in on the coup. I would never forget his betrayal, nor would I ever put myself in that position again.

"You weren't part of her plot against me," I said. After liberating Kahwin, we'd interrogated every Equinox employee and narrowed it down to a handful of people. I granted everyone amnesty.

"Never, sir. I have full faith in your leadership. Besides, I'm not much of a plotter," he said, smiling. A good way to break the tension.

"Assuming *Arcadia* can print matter, what do you see your company doing in the future?"

"Supporting you in whatever capacity you see fit, sir."

"You volunteered to accompany us on the mission rather than remaining in the Senate back on Kahwin. What was your reasoning?"

"I wanted to be one of the first people to lay eyes upon an alien ship, sir."

Good answer. "And now that you have?"

Feazer shook his head in disbelief. "It's awe-inspiring. Any idea how large it is?"

"One of our missions is to map and explore the ship. We'll need to know every nook and cranny."

"What do you plan to do with Melody, sir? Do you trust it?"

"Trust is a strong word, Mr. Feazer. I wouldn't go that far. It's important to understand that it's likely sustained damage over the years. I'll keep you updated. Hopefully, we can find out why the drive failed."

"I wish I had something to offer you to drink. Did your room come with a refrigerator?" Feazer asked.

"No. Maybe we can see about getting them. They probably don't want us to eat in here. You mentioned you studied sociology at the Oxford."

"Aye, sir. Equinox required all of its upper management to take courses along those lines. History courses. Linguistic studies. Cultural studies."

"If I remember, you also taught Post-Structuralist Approaches to Artificial Intelligence and Machine Ethics at Harvard for a few years."

Feazer's face wilted. "It paid the bills, sir."

"Any other classes?"

"I taught Ethical Considerations in the Intersection of Genomic Manipulation and Demographic Regulation for a few semesters, but my daughter caught Tulick's Disease."

"Is she okay?" I asked.

"She passed away several years prior to launch."

"I'm sorry to hear that. My sister came down with it as well."

"It was impossible to find food she could eat."

"Where'd you live?"

"Chicago."

Chicago was one of the cities you didn't want to be caught in during the Great Famine. One winter, I watched Judith Butler Tower, what was formerly known as Willis Tower, go up in flames when the Illinois National Guard couldn't fly in food. The riot lasted a month. News Corp ran the story like it was the end of the world, and for those trapped there, it was.

"Were you married?" I asked.

"Aye, sir. Things didn't work out."

I thought back to Gisele. "I understand." I glanced around the room. "What do you make of all this?"

"Hard to say, sir."

"Do you believe what Keeper Aiantes said about the Morphic Fields?"

"I would need to know more, sir. However, from what we've seen on Kahwin and Eos, the theory seems to hold weight. The question is: where is the progenitor civilization? There would have to be one out there, the one who started it."

"Did you study the Morphic Field theory at Oxford?"

"Some. It was first proposed by a biologist named Sheldrake. Morphic Resonance is the idea that memory is inherent in nature, and that natural systems, like living organisms, inherit a collective memory from all previous organisms of their kind. His theory claimed each species has a kind of collective memory that new members tap into, which leads to the transmission of information from the past to the present without any direct physical contact. According to Sheldrake, these fields are made of non-material, informational patterns that influence the development and organization of organisms, their behavior, and so on."

"You didn't ask many questions during our conversation with the ambassador."

"I didn't think it was my place to ask too many questions, sir. I assumed you'd fill us in with what we needed to know to accomplish the mission." Feazer scratched his nose. "Sir, may I ask you a question?"

"Feel free."

"Marston's a good kid. He deserves a raise."

"Very funny. After we get a chance to breathe, maybe you can fill me in further about why you feel that way. I have a question for you. If given the choice, would you want to return to Earth now or see where this leads?" I asked.

"I'm all in, sir," Feazer snapped. "After I've had time to process all this, I'm here to stay. I wouldn't dream of leaving. And to save humanity, whatever that really means, I believe is our duty."

I filled him on the Regency, the ruling power before the Keepers unleashed their Shapers to dominate the galaxy. He listened intently, asking relevant questions. I answered him the best I could. The fact remained, we knew very little about them.

When you interact with a person for long periods of time, you can forget we're all people at the end of the day. Quite often, I'd had to distance my feelings about those closest to me. I liked the way Feazer thought, and I was relieved he wanted to stay.

Feazer offered the idea that Eos probably belonged to the

Regency at one time, but neither of us could explain the amount of destroyed starships we encountered on our flight here.

We spoke briefly about the Great Famine and its implications. If we brought back *Arcadia* and introduced food into the environment, it might alter the ecosystem.

"Have you felt strange since we came here, sir?" he asked.

"In what way?"

"Hard to explain. Maybe it's nothing, and I'm just not getting enough sleep."

"We'll have Doc check us out when we get back to *Arcadia*. While we're here on Eos," I said, "I want you to find any clues you can about their culture and its origins. Keep a low profile. The last thing we want to do is antagonize anyone on Eos. Deflect all questions about Earth. The less people know about us, the better."

"When *do* you think we'll be returning home, sir?"

"I can't go into specifics, Mr. Feazer. But I hope soon."

"Understood, sir. I do have family back home and want to see them."

"We all do." My thoughts returned to my nephew and my sister. "We all do." I let the moment hang for a few seconds. "How would you feel if we folded Equinox into Space Force? I'd be willing to make you an officer, of course. This way, our communication channels would better serve the mission."

"Equinox takes pride in our independence."

I stood and made toward the door. "Think it over. We'd love to have you."

"Aye, sir." Right before I opened the door to leave, he said, "Sir, if Earth developed civilizations after Rome absorbed Greece, what about them?"

"Do you mean something went wrong?"

"It might be possible that the other civilizations on Earth are also products of these fields."

"I hadn't thought of that." My mind went back to the barbarity of the World Wars, which ravaged Asia, Europe, and Russia. "What about China? Or Egypt?"

Feazer nodded along with me. "Exactly. What makes Greece so special?"

"Maybe nothing at all, but Greece is the foundation of modern civilization."

"Who's going to tell the people back home that we've gotten it all wrong? We should all be Greek. I don't think that'd go over very well."

Back home, anger and division amongst people was the religion, and there were plenty of preachers. When people go hungry, they do all kinds of things—things that'd make you sick if you thought too long about it. That man I'd killed back in Montana. I wanted to forget about him. Let it go, like Chief said.

Feazer was more than right. "I see your point.Sir, the galaxy is a big place. How are we going to free these planets when we don't know where they are?"

"Think over my offer," I said as I left his room.

CHAPTER FORTY-ONE

Eos
Captain Scott Moore

An emergency message from *Arcadia* rippled through my tablet, one that left out pertinent details and told me everything. "45" it said, simply. My heart sank. Space Force reserves certain codes for when security might be breached, others for dire emergencies. "45." Top Secret.

In a situation where anything said could be monitored, it wouldn't make sense for me to contact the XO and ask what had happened.

Using a small crystal pyramid that was given to me by one of K'Hori's veiled assistants a few days ago, I contacted Ambassador K'Hori. "Ambassador, I need to get to *Arcadia*."

Her full-body image appeared beside the crystal. "Your ship is en route to Eos," she said. "It will arrive in thirty-two hours."

"Yes. I need to get there before it does."

"Why, Captain? Has something happened?"

"Can you provide a shuttle?" I asked.

"I'm afraid that's impossible. Is there anything I can do?"

I balled my fist. "It's important, Ambassador. I humbly ask you to reconsider."

K'Hori's invisible gaze, hidden behind her veil, seemed to linger on me. "Very well, Captain. I will arrange transportation. I will send security to escort you to one of the launch bays."

"Thank you."

I went to Chief's door and knocked. He opened it. "45," I said.

"Understood. I'll rouse everyone."

Soon, we found ourselves in the same shuttle that brought us to Eos, only K'Hori didn't accompany us. We remained quiet during the journey, and her guards, dressed in their power armor, gave us food and drink in the meantime. Feazer almost spoke, but Chief rightly gave him one of his looks, and that was that. It took us twelve hours before *Arcadia* came into view along with K'Hori's ship escorts.

One of the guards activated a large circular screen, giving us an enhanced view.

Arcadia's hull was made of metal, glass, and other materials. It showed the marks of time and space travel. A momentary silence swathed our chamber as we quietly appreciated the spectacle unfolding before us. One of *Arcadia*'s massive domes bore a gaping wound, a blackened void where a part of the city-ship should've been.

"Wait... that's not right," Vincent said. His tone caught everyone's attention.

My mouth fell open. Why hadn't the ambassador notified us of the damage? 45. Sabotage or something else? What could have caused that?

The guards sent a message back to K'Hori in their language, and after a few minutes, the ambassador wanted to speak to me. Our ship's image was replaced by her face on the screen.

"Captain, it appears *Arcadia* suffered some internal damage," K'Hori said.

"Do you know what caused it?" I asked, hoping she had nothing to do with it.

Ambassador K'Hori turned to the side and spoke to one of her subordinates. "Did you disable your Numix Device?"

I wasn't sure what she was talking about and told her as much.

"You tried to collect energy in our system. Why?" she asked.

"Ambassador, I have no idea what any of this means."

She scowled. "I see the truth in your eyes. When you dock with *Arcadia*, we will discuss this further. It might not be possible to repair *Arcadia* at all, Captain. You might have stranded yourself once again, and it's likely you've alerted our shared enemies of our location. Stay aboard *Arcadia* when you get there. We will have to approach our relationship differently from now on."

CHAPTER FORTY-TWO

Arcadia
Captain Scott Moore

"What happened, Chen?" I asked.

"The Numix Device malfunctioned, Captain," Chen said. "Energy signatures spiked drastically right before the explosion."

I turned to Vincent. "Could Melody have made an error, Vincent?"

"Unlikely. Melody's protocols for managing the Numix Device are stringent," Vincent said.

We'd boarded *Arcadia* without incident, and Ambassador K'Hori's shuttle left at once. It was good to be back, and I was eager to discover what caused one of the most delicate parts of *Arcadia* to explode. Chen said there was something else she was eager to discuss with me, but for some reason, she only wanted to tell me and not the rest of the crew. What that was, I wasn't sure, but you know who didn't greet us at the airlock? Michael, Gisele, or Doc.

Chen prepared a briefing for all of us on different tablets, so as to put the right data in the right people's hands.

The fusion of practical design and high technology dominated the briefing room. A large, elliptical table, constructed from a synthetic marble-like material, stood as the centerpiece. Its matte-black surface offered a sharp contrast to the silver trim, which defined the remainder of the room.

Our table served a dual purpose. It functioned as a gathering point and a holo display. Integrated projectors could create detailed, three-dimensional maps, diagrams, and other forms of data, an invaluable asset when strategizing, planning, and making vital decisions.

Polished white walls encased the room, their simplicity broken only by flat, screen-like panels. Capable of displaying additional data or communications, these panels added an extra dimension to the available holographic visuals.

A control panel occupied one end of the room, with touch-sensitive screens, dials, and buttons allowing access to the station's main systems.

"Has there been any hint of sabotage?" Erika sat in one of the chairs around the main table.

"Not so far, Lieutenant Banks," Chen said. "Our security checks have revealed no external interference."

"The ambassador mentioned how we tried to extract energy from this location." I faced one of our AI screens. "Melody, how is this system hidden from the outside world?"

"The system, Captain, is concealed using an amalgamation of graviton field manipulation and the exploitation of quantum entanglement. The system's shielding technology utilizes gravitons, which are quantum particles that mediate the force of gravity. By controlling these particles, it manipulates the local curvature of space-time around the system. This distortion effectively bends light and other electromagnetic waves away from the system, rendering it invisible to external observation."

A holographic projection materialized in the center of the room, depicting a simplified version of the system in relation to the rest of the galaxy.

"The system is here," Melody started, highlighting a small point within the representation. "Imagine, a mirror around our system. Light, signals, and all forms of electromagnetic radiation attempting to enter or leave the system are bent around it, much like light bends around a mirror.

"Moreover," Melody continued, "quantum entanglement has been harnessed on a macro scale for further concealment. By synchronizing the quantum states of particles within the system with those in a remote and uninhabited region of space, the system's observable characteristics, such as light and heat emissions, are essentially translocated to this remote region. Hence, any attempts to observe the system from the outside would reveal only the empty space of the 'dummy' location."

"Impressive." Chief put his palms together and brought them up to his mouth.

"You wanted to say something?" Vincent asked.

Chief gave me a weary glance. "Even though Ambassador K'Hori is the Voice of Keeper Aiantes, she still keeps the system hidden from the outside."

I nodded. "They're still worried about an invasion."

Chen looked around. "But from whom?"

"Could this location have characteristics we are unaware of?" Feazer asked. "There had to be a reason the ambassador was so angry."

"It's possible, Mr. Feazer," Chen said. "It will take time to study where we are."

Vincent shook his head. "I don't recommend it, at least not

active scans. We might further damage our relationship with them."

My brother was right. "How badly has *Arcadia* been damaged?"

Chief brought up a hologram of *Arcadia*'s hull. "Significant structural damage to one of the domes, Captain. *Arcadia*'s repair drone facility imploded. We'll need recovery and repair teams to further assess the extent of the damage. It's not good."

"What about casualties?" I withheld a grimace.

Chen paused. "We are still in the process of collecting that data, Captain. We had no time to initiate evacuation protocols."

"Where's Doc?" Chief's expression hardened. He liked Doc just as much as me.

Chen looked Chief directly in the eye. "I believe he's in Medbay Three currently."

I knew she was lying. I think everyone at the table knew, but no one would say anything. If he was injured, that was where he'd be, but he was also our ship's doctor. Maybe it was selfish of me, but my mind remained fixed on Gisele. Why did I care so much?

"Vincent, could there have been an unforeseen interaction between Melody and the Numix Device?" I asked. "Something must have happened."

"Melody has managed the ship seamlessly until now," Vincent said. "I'll run a diagnostic to be certain."

I folded my hands on the table. "Feazer, thoughts?"

"Only speculation at this point, Captain." He referenced his tablet. "Theories range from an unknown natural phenomenon to a design flaw in the Numix Device."

"Melody, what do we know about the Numix Device?" I asked.

"Its underlying principles are still subject to analysis, Captain. However, it operates at the intersection of quantum physics and theoretical cosmology." The hologram in the center of the room morphed again into the model of a hypercube. "Imagine the fabric of the universe as a four-dimensional construct. We live within its three-dimensional 'surface,' but the fourth dimension, time, is also rich with energy, untapped because of our limited three-dimensional perception and technology."

The model spun slowly, lines of energy pulsating around its edges. "The Numix Device works by vibrating at extremely high frequencies that allow it to interact with the latent energy in this fourth dimension. It's like shaking a tree to make the ripe fruit fall."

The hypercube folded in on itself, morphing into a model of the Numix Device. "Once it collects this energy, it translates it into a form we can utilize, compressing it into these energy cells, which are specially designed to contain raw power."

Melody became silent for a moment as the visual representation of the Device now rotating slowly in the air. "Essentially, the Numix Device allows us to pluck energy from the very fabric of spacetime. How it does this remains a mystery."

"Who built it?" Vincent asked Melody.

"According to the data I've acquired from our limited records, the Regency is responsible for its construction."

Chen's face went pale. "Sir, did Ambassador K'Hori mention anything specifically about the Regency?"

"Not in any detail."

"Those destroyed ships out there. Was that them?"

"It's quite possible," I replied. "I see where you're going. It's possible the Regency attacked this system and was defeated."

Erika put her tablet down. "Or the same thing happened to their ships as happened to *Arcadia*."

"Has anything like this happened elsewhere?" I asked.

"Not that we know of, Captain. Let me show you the

report." Chen activated the holographic display. A three-dimensional model of the damaged dome materialized. Its complex network of interconnected sections and systems was mind-boggling. "We're viewing the energy distribution pattern across multiple spectrums, including electromagnetic, gravitational, and exotic particle."

The model changed colors, depicting the variances. Streaks of bright colors indicated the energy pathways before the explosion, growing dimmer as they approached the dome's center.

"See this anomaly?" Chief circled a point on the hologram where colors diverged into an unusually dense cluster. "This is the epicenter. It's where the highest concentration of exotic particles coalesced. The Numix Device was here in the Elysium Gardens."

"The explosion propagated uniformly." Chen traced lines radiating from the cluster to demonstrate her point. "The energy attenuation wasn't standard. Some pathways retained more energy than expected."

The model zoomed into the dense cluster, revealing a fluctuating web of intricate energy channels. "The exotic particle emission here," Chief said, "isn't consistent with the device's typical operation. It's an offshoot spectrum. It *could* imply a different energy source triggered the explosion."

"Eos?" I asked.

Chief nodded. "Anything's possible, sir."

"Or that the Numix Device behaved differently in this environment," Chen added, highlighting the irregularity. "Either way, we need to understand this phenomenon to prevent future incidents."

"Could it be an issue with the energy input?" Erika asked, examining the irregularity on the hologram. "Maybe a surge caused the explosion?"

Chief shook his head. "No. From what I've studied before this briefing, the Numix Device is designed to handle fluctuations. It even uses them for energy storage. A simple surge wouldn't cause this."

"What if the surge was massive?" Erika asked.

Chief responded, "A pulse from Eos would have left a footprint."

Erika studied the model thoughtfully. "So, if not a surge, then could it be an issue with the device's containment field? An instability or a malfunction?"

Chief brought up a new chart. "The containment field was specifically designed to maintain stability, even under the most severe conditions. Plus, a containment breach would've led to a different kind of energy dispersal. This..." he gestured at the dense cluster on the hologram, "...is something else."

Erika paused for a moment. "Could the energy have originated from an external source?"

"The energy pattern doesn't suggest any known form of attack," Chief said. "Melody has been unable to find any signs of external energy intrusion into the system. Look at the device's specs. They're not too different from our power systems. The Numix Device's internal regulators were designed to shut down in case of any irregularities. If any component malfunctioned, the entire system would cease operation to prevent mishaps."

Feazer's brows furrowed. "So, we've ruled out energy surges, containment field instability, external attacks, and internal malfunctions. What else could have caused it?"

Chief shook his head again. "Well, that's the question, isn't it? We've studied the obvious, and they don't fit. We'll need to delve into the less obvious, the unknown factors."

"Unknown factors?" Erika frowned at the holographic display.

Chen interlaced her fingers on the table. "Sir, we're dealing with a technology operating in a space with physics we don't fully understand. The list of potential unknowns could be endless."

"I don't know about you, but I could use some coffee," Feazer said.

He had a point. Meetings without coffee were painful. "You and me both, Mr. Feazer. What does this mean for the *Arcadia*?"

Chief glanced at me before answering. "Sir, without the Numix Device, we won't have enough power to make long-distance jumps. It acts as our primary energy collector for the drive, and without it, we're limited."

"How limited?" I asked.

"According to Melody, we have enough energy stored for two jumps," Chief said. "After that, we're at the mercy of standard propulsion, and that won't get us far in the grand scheme of things."

"How long would it take to collect enough energy for a jump without the Numix Device?" I asked.

Chief manipulated the display, bringing up data readings and simulations. "It varies. Depending on the local energy density, anywhere from a week to a year."

Vincent scoffed. "Oh, is that all? Just a year? I'll make sure to pack a lunch."

"One of those jumps should be back to Earth," Feazer said. "We should get back to familiar territory and figure this out from there."

"No," I said, dismissing the suggestion. "The first jump will be back to Kahwin. We have a crew stranded there."

"And the second?" Feazer asked, pressing me.

I avoided his gaze, keeping my focus on the holographic display. "We'll figure out where the second jump will take us after we've got everyone on board."

CHAPTER FORTY-THREE

Arcadia
Captain Scott Moore

In medbay, two forms lay on scanning platforms, contrasting with the subtle whir and click of analytical machinery. Overhead, surgical illumination washed the room in a sterile white light, revealing every detail of the space. A medical bot worked diligently in the corner, its operational lights blinking on its metallic surface as it processed data. Its six arms extended to different corners of the room and processed data at several stations.

Lieutenant Commander Chen, her eyes glued to the streams of information darting across the holographic screens, attempted to decode the medical data. "They flatlined almost simultaneously, as per these timestamps."

At a distance, I observed Gisele. Her face, usually a beacon of energy and warmth, now bore an unsettling calmness.

Chen focused on Dr. Ingram's medical data. "Asphyxiation, explosive decompression. He didn't feel anything."

"Yes," I replied. Grief clawed at my insides, and I felt like vomiting. "Harsh is the right word."

Our gazes met briefly, acknowledging a shared sorrow, before Chen redirected her attention to the medical readouts.

"And Gisele?" I was unable to pull my eyes away from her.

Chen was quiet for a moment as she reviewed Gisele's data. "No indications of decompression. It looks like her nervous system abruptly shut down. It could point to a neurological disorder or even a cardiac event, but…"

"But?"

"The data is inconclusive." Her eyes returned to the readouts. "Her neuroelectrical waveforms are abnormal, unlike any typical neurological or cardiac conditions."

Abnormalities. We stood, lost in our thoughts, each enveloped in a private world.

"Were you able to find out who among us was real?" she asked.

"That was Doc's job. As far as I know, all of us are ourselves."

"Except for her."

I nodded. "Yes. Where's Michael?"

"Unknown. I haven't been able to locate him. Last location was with Doc in medical. Last I heard, we didn't know if Michael was dead or alive, but now his body is missing."

"This matter is to remain a secret for the time being. If the crew discover Doctor Ingram is dead, it'll drastically affect morale. We'll need to train another doctor."

"Aye, sir," she said. "That'll take years."

"What choice do we have?"

"What about Eos, sir?"

I arched a brow. "You want me to ask the ambassador if she can spare a doctor?"

"Sir, without enough personnel, we won't last long out

here. During your absence, I asked Melody to provide a map of *Arcadia*, which I've uploaded for key personnel. *Arcadia* used bots for most of the manual labor jobs, and the fire and explosion destroyed several of our facilities. We'll need actual crew to get anything done."

"I'll talk to the ambassador and see if she'll be willing to offer me any volunteers. We don't know those people at all. We'll need to test them. Sort them out. Find out who the leaders are and promote them to positions of power." I looked over at Doc again. "How long until we have complete results?"

Chen exhaled softly, her gaze wandering from the screens to rest on Gisele's lifeless body. "It could be hours, maybe longer. The nature of these abnormalities will determine the duration."

"Did either of them have anything when you found them?"

"Only a tablet. The vacuum destroyed it. I've been unable to glean any data off it. Should I have Vincent look at it?"

"Not yet. Where is it?"

She pointed over at another table. "I put it there in case you wanted it."

"Keep me posted." I picked up the tablet and left Chen alone in the medbay. The doors hissed shut behind me, sealing the room off from the outside world.

Just as I felt like collapsing in my quarters and grieving my old love Gisele and my dear friend Doc, someone who I'd shared my most intimate feelings with, I bumped chest-first into Michael, his Space Force uniform spotless. "I was looking for you."

Everything in me froze. "You're alive."

"I think it's time you and I had a long talk."

CHAPTER FORTY-FOUR

Arcadia
Captain Scott Moore

Michael and I took one of the many subways through *Arcadia*. He wanted to show me something so secretive, he dared not say what it was. Along the way, I withheld my sadness best I could and asked Michael if he knew why the Numix Device exploded. He offered as many theories as my crew, but he wasn't sure. I found his answers evasive at times, strange at other times. It took us almost an hour to reach our destination.

Stepping into the chamber, the environment struck me as something out of an old *Twilight Zone* episode. Tubes, transparent and filled with a bluish fluid, connected distinct segments of the room, stretching from the floor to the high ceiling. An ever-present murmur of energy reflected off the polished floor and reached into the farthest corners.

Against one wall, a panel populated by luminous symbols and numbers flickered, each data point offering a vital reading to the machine's complex functions. They registered the fluid's pressure, the ambient temperature, the energy consumption, and other variables beyond my understanding.

"Where are we?" I asked Michael.

"This is the Elysium Engine." Michael's voice echoed through the room. "This is the heart and soul of *Arcadia*. It's more than just a machine; it's the lifeline to our existence."

In the center, beneath the high dome ceiling, a colossal cylindrical structure towered over me. This core, the heart of the engine, radiated a faint bluish light that synced with the pulsating fluid in the tubes.

Michael, himself a product of this Elysium Engine, walked ahead, his feet clicking on the floor. "*Arcadia*, initiate viewing protocol."

The murmur of energy grew slightly louder, a resonant frequency that you could feel more than hear. A portion of the floor slid open, revealing a lower level beneath the chamber. A platform rose from the opening, carrying a capsule large enough to house a human.

On a closer look, I could see the capsule held a perfectly formed human figure, suspended in a bluish fluid. The figure was still, almost peaceful, encased in its transparent prison.

"Doc..." I stammered.

"The Engine collects genetic information of everyone aboard *Arcadia*. In your case, I tapped into your DNA using the translator device you wore for so long. You would be surprised at what information it gathered. In case of an untimely death, it initiates the process of regrowth, recreating the deceased down to their most recent memories."

I was about to interrupt when Michael held up a hand. "Yes, Captain, it's similar to cloning. The Engine doesn't just copy physical attributes. It reproduces the neural pathways of the subject's brain, effectively bringing back their memories, their skills, their personality... their soul."

"We've done this with robots."

"Of course you have. Why wouldn't you?" He glanced toward the panel of readings. "It usually takes a standard year to create a new 'copy,' but in emergencies, the process can be... accelerated."

I absorbed this information in silence. It was overwhelming, to say the least. It implied a kind of immortality, a concept we'd been chasing for centuries. A room that could breathe life back into the dead, preserve our existence against the inevitability of death. It felt too powerful, almost god-like.

"How do I know you haven't done this to me?" I asked. "You can't do this without my permission."

"Can't I? *Captain*?" he asked sarcastically.

"You grew Gisele."

"Did she not make you happy, albeit briefly?"

"She wasn't real."

"I have studied Melody extensively. Does not your language use a term, 'Do not look a gift horse in the mouth?' Quite the saying. It took me a while to understand its meaning. I feel it quite apropos to use it in this context." He began to walk away. "Come. I will give you a tour. May I call you Scott?"

"Only in private," I replied, a bit uncomfortable with the request.

"Very well, Scott. Allow me to show you something."

He led me to a room adjacent to the main chamber. As we entered, a series of holographic screens sprang to life. They floated in mid-air, shifting and rotating, showcasing genetic blueprints too numerous to comprehend. It was as if I was staring into an ocean of codes, a representation of life in its most fundamental form.

Michael waved a hand at the blueprints. "Each of these represents a life from the Regency era. Over two hundred thousand years of collected genetic data. Over there are the nobles and over there are the warrior caste. That container over there is me."

"That's how you regenerate?" I asked.

"Yes. Yours is next to it."

"It's empty."

"Out of respect for you, I have not initiated the Elysium Sequence. Your people have a distinct view of mortality."

The sheer number of people was staggering. To think that each and every one of them could be recreated, brought back to life...

"We have the power to rebirth the entirety of the Regency right here," Michael said. "An empire, ready to conquer the galaxy. It only needs the right leader."

"Why would the Regency do this? Why would they need copies of everyone?" I asked.

Michael shrugged. "That's not for me to answer. The Regency operated on a level of foresight that is, quite frankly, beyond my understanding. I believe they recognized their imminent collapse, but who can say?"

"Where did you get all this data?"

"By force. It was not easy. The Regency was not eager to hand over their genetic information."

"Where's the original crew of this ship?"

Michael narrowed his eyes. "I have erased them."

"You what? Why?"

"I found them inadequate to the task. I allowed them to breed. You will find the feral ones inhabiting many of *Arcadia*'s halls until they can be... how shall I say... removed from the equation."

"They're human beings. You can't do that."

"I have done it many times, Scott. War is not a thing for lesser beings."

I shook my head in disgust. "If you tried to do that to *my* crew—"

"I do not take kindly to threats. I have studied your ways. Heraclitus. Was he not an ancient Greek pre-Socratic philosopher from the city of Ephesus? He said, 'War is the father of us all, king of all. Some it makes gods, some it makes men, some it makes slaves, some free.' Had he known about the true nature of the galaxy, he might have included, 'some it removes from existence.'"

"You're sick."

"Your judgment is based on nothing but your own small history of a few thousand years. It means nothing to me."

I scoffed. "We've tried to establish peace on Earth. You've read our history. We haven't always been successful, true, but human life *means* something. If you have the power to recreate life, why haven't you done so already?"

"The time wasn't right. An empire needs an emperor. Come. There is more to show you."

We spent what felt like hours in that room, wandering between screens, each displaying a different set of genetic blueprints. I saw glimpses of lives lived eons ago, people who breathed, loved, and lost just like us.

"Did you do this for me?" I asked finally.

"You mean, do we have *your* blueprint? Yes, we do. As I said before, the Elysium Engine collects genetic information of *everyone* aboard *Arcadia*. That includes you."

My mind teemed with questions. The thought of being replicated, of living beyond my natural life, was as fascinating as it was terrifying. I hated synths, but this was something completely different.

BRANDON ELLIS & MAX WOLFE

One question rose above the rest. I turned to look at Michael. "Have you ever used it? My genetic data?"

Michael simply looked back at me. "No, I have not, nor on any of your crew."

Somehow, I wasn't so sure. His words hung in the air as we continued our tour. There was much more to see, much more to understand. As we moved deeper into the facility, each step revealed another layer of the legacy left behind by the Regency. The magnitude of it all was staggering. Every corner we turned, every holograph we scrutinized was like turning a page in a history book. Instead of ink and paper, it was genetic data and biological blueprints.

The tour felt endless. It was as if we were traversing not just a room, but an entire epoch, with Michael as my guide through this sea of life and death, of past and potential future.

Michael edged toward another section of the vast chamber. "Here, we have something a bit different." He gestured to a set of blueprints unlike any we'd seen before, curling with unfamiliar structures. "These are not human."

The images on the holographs swam before my eyes. The DNA strands were in patterns I barely recognized.

"The Regency, in its quest for dominance, eliminated entire species. These are the genetic remnants of the life forms they rightfully extinguished."

My stomach churned. The enormity of what he was saying, the sheer brutality of it, left me speechless.

"That's... that's genocide," I said.

"Yes. On an intergalactic scale. The Regency did not believe in cohabitation. They believed in rule, like all humans who succeed."

Sometimes, it's best to let people say the things they really feel to get a better read on them. Could I have argued then? Yes, but I wanted to know more.

As we moved from holograph to holograph, I was introduced to species I could hardly imagine. The Draknar, a race of insect-like beings with a hive mind, the Verdani, a photosynthetic race with plant-like characteristics, and many more. Each different. Each unique. Each extinguished.

Michael paused before one specific holograph, which showcased a particularly chaotic genome sequence. "This is the Sepioteuthis. They were squid-like beings with vast intelligence and a social structure. They had a fascinating form of communication involving color changes on their skin. Regrettably, they were also deemed a threat by the Regency and eliminated."

Looking at the Sepioteuthis DNA, I could almost picture them living lives as vibrant as our own. Their loss felt personal, a stab of guilt and sorrow for a species I'd never known.

The reality of what Michael was showing me made my skin crawl. The Elysium Engine was also a graveyard.

As we moved further into the chamber, I noticed the machinery change around us. Instead of the silver surfaces, I saw tubes of liquid running along the walls, connected to containment chambers. Some held partially formed beings, their features indistinct. Others were empty, waiting for the genetic code to be fed into them.

"Why show me this?" I asked.

"Because it's the truth." Michael said. "The truth of the Regency, of *Arcadia*, of us. You deserve to know."

His words lingered in the air, mixing with the musty scent of the chamber. We stood there, amidst the lost civilizations and the potential for life.

Michael gestured toward the Sepioteuthis holograph. "Do you know about the octopus?"

"Marine creatures found on Earth. They have eight limbs, highly intelligent, capable of camouflage."

"Don't you find it peculiar just how drastically different they are from everything else on your world?"

"What do you mean?"

"Let's consider the facts." Michael went over to a console and brought up an adjacent holograph. An image of an octopus appeared. Its double helix structure was distinct, familiar, and remarkably bizarre.

"Octopuses, by Earth standards, are a conundrum. Their DNA is, quite literally, like nothing else. They have more protein-coding genes than humans. The exact number is about 33,000. In comparison, humans have around 20,000. More genes, however, doesn't necessarily mean a more complex organism. It just means there's more to interpret."

I stared at the octopus DNA, trying to reconcile the information. "Go on."

"The octopus, along with its cephalopod cousins, the squid and the cuttlefish, have a curious ability: RNA editing. They can alter their own genetic instructions, rewriting their bodies' biological texts."

"Yes, and it's highly unusual."

"Extraordinarily so. On Earth. In the Sepioteuthis, it's rampant."

As he spoke, the octopus holograph morphed, showing different stages of its life cycle. Each transformation was radically different.

"An octopus changes its RNA to adapt to temperature shifts," Michael said. "It modifies its nervous system for an intelligent, problem-solving brain, and it's capable of an incredible variety of physical alterations. For example, the mimic octopus can impersonate a variety of other species."

"That's evolution."

"The rate and breadth of their adaptability far surpass that of any other species on Earth. Here's the catch; the trade-off for this high rate of RNA editing is a reduced ability to evolve at the DNA level. Somehow, they've survived in Earth's oceans."

"So, what are you saying? That octopuses are aliens and the Keepers put them on Earth?"

Michael chuckled. "It's a fascinating parallel to the Sepioteuthis, don't you think?"

I stared at the holographs.

"The Sepioteuthis *are* the Shapers, Captain. They are the only species the Regency could not entirely eliminate. It was widely believed several Keepers began to interact with them, though we do not understand how. They helped them evolve. Regardless, the octopuses on Earth will begin their transformation into Shapers quite soon. No doubt, your actions have only accelerated that process. The Keepers see everything."

"How soon is that?"

"That depends on the nature of your cooperation. We can stop it from happening, but we must bring the fight to the enemy. They must be crushed."

The more Michael spoke, the more I became disillusioned. "How exactly am I supposed to do that? Look, I agreed to help you free the galaxy of these creatures. I know how vile they are. I've fought them. If these things are going to evolve from the octopus into Shapers on Earth, I need to stop them. I find it all very hard to believe."

"You understand the nature of Morphic Fields."

"You're talking about rampant evolution. That just doesn't happen."

Michael scratched the side of his head. "After all you've seen, you still believe things cannot happen just because you haven't witnessed them yourself. From your records, you once believed flight to be an impossibility. Within a few decades, you exploded your first hydrogen bomb. You would be surprised at how science can advance in millions of years. Besides, you fought the Shapers and beat them."

I thought back to the war to free Kahwin. "I had help."

"The Janissaries?"

"Without them, I wouldn't have stood a chance."

"I had been hiding and waiting under the ice for longer than you realize. Finally, I'd found someone like you to come and do what must be done. I know how this sounds to you, believe me. You still retain empathy and kindness. That will pass in time."

"Agree to disagree." I knew I wasn't always kind, but it was a large part of who I was and I did my best to care for others whenever possible. "Are the Shapers sentient?"

Michael's tone turned cold. "Does it matter?"

"Yes, it matters. Have you ever tried communicating with them?"

"All attempts have failed. They seem to operate as a collective, communicating across vast distances without the need for technology. They are the most dangerous species humanity has ever encountered."

I folded my arms. "Why are you telling me this now? We spoke before I left for Eos. You could have mentioned this then."

"You needed to discover things on your own first. I was not at all surprised you accepted the task so easily." He tapped the side of his temple. "The Regency used *all* neural sync technology to stimulate certain regions of the brain, making it easier for them to guide the populace toward the successful conclusion of the Heaven War. It was why you adopted such a violent stance."

My fist clenched instinctively. "My thoughts are my own."

"Of course they are. They're all your own."

I couldn't tell if he was being sarcastic or not. "I've changed my mind. *Arcadia* has two jumps left. I'm taking her back to Earth after I pick up the remainder of my crew on Kahwin."

"You would be making a big mistake, Captain."

"I won't be part of this." I walked over to the comm link mounted on the side of the wall, one that just so happened to be adjacent to Michael's reincarnation pod. "Chief, I need you and a security detail at my location immediately."

Michael scowled but offered no resistance. My hand hovered over his unit's controls, and although I might not have known how the machine worked, I had a pretty good idea of how to break it.

"We're en route to your location, Captain," Chief said. "ETA three minutes."

"You followed me," I said to Chief.

"Aye, Captain," Chief replied, and I loved hearing his voice. "That's what I do."

"Good man." I disconnected and focused on Michael. "I'm placing you in protective custody until further notice."

"You won't get anywhere without my help."

"There's only two places I need to go, and seeing as how *Arcadia* needs a refit, I'll have plenty of time to figure out how to plot a course back to Earth."

"You're disappointing me."

"I'm heartbroken." I bared my teeth at him. "I'm starting to think the Regency had it coming to them."

Chief showed up armed for an assault, a handful of security in tow.

I motioned to Chief. "Take Michael to the brig and post guards outside his door."

Chief aimed a dark matter rifle and Michael put his hands up. If you knew Chief, he was the kind of man who didn't ask a lot of questions. Thankfully. I'd lock up this place so tight, no one would ever step foot in here again.

I took one of the dark matter rifles from security. "We're going to Earth."

CHAPTER FORTY-FIVE

Arcadia
Captain Scott Moore

I turned my attention toward repairing *Arcadia*. Any hope of returning home relied on our ability to fix our ship.

I put Doc's death out of my mind for the time being, making sure to stay busy. I loved the man like my brother, and he served as my conscience. Damn, why hadn't I told him how much he meant to me before he died? I should have.

Doc's funeral was quiet, and Chief wanted to lead the prayer. Rather than burying him, we stored his corpse in one of the medbay's freezers.

Why was he in the lift with Gisele? He tried to escape with her and failed. Or did he know something? Did Gisele cause the Numix Device to malfunction? A trap to leave us stranded? How tempting would it be to simply bring him back to life? We needed him. I would even go as far as to say, he was more needed than most of my crew, myself included.

I was in my office, looking for anything that might have

been planted here, perhaps by Michael, when a chime sounded at my desk.

"Ambassador K'Hori," I said after activating the comm unit.

"Captain Moore." The ambassador's voice sounded more distant than usual.

"I want to inform you personally about the explosion," I said. "My staff is looking into the matter."

"We know. Eos felt it," K'Hori said.

"We still can't explain why the Numix Device detonated."

"That's not what concerns me."

"Then what is it?"

"Eos is endangered," she said. "You have alerted the Keepers to our location. I informed your ship not to siphon energy from our system and yet you disobeyed."

"We were never informed."

She stared at me from behind her veil. "I hope you are prepared for what is to come."

"That's a bit mysterious, Ambassador."

"We need to discuss repairs. Eos cannot offer you docking facilities, Captain."

"May I ask why?"

"Trust has been compromised. We will send a repair crew to your ship."

"I appreciate that," I said, my mind racing to process the implications.

"I'm not doing this for you, Captain. Repairs will commence immediately. Time is short. If you are considering returning to Earth, I must warn you, you and your people will suffer more than they already are. Your world is not ready to face the Shapers. Earth will be subjugated."

"You'll find us to be a stubborn people."

"All people are stubborn. I am sending Baron Ephadria to supervise the repairs. It will take some time." Her image darkened, only to return a few moments later. "I have been informed you are aware of the Elysium Engine."

My eyes narrowed. Was she speaking with Michael? "That's correct."

"Its use is an abomination, Captain."

It was time to find out what she knew. "Are you speaking with anyone aboard my ship?"

"Your question is irrelevant. *Arcadia* needs pilots. You will not survive otherwise. With your permission, I will authorize our training school to transfer all applicants to your ship under your command. You will find them a sturdy lot and well-disciplined."

"You're eager to transfer your personnel aboard *Arcadia*."

"I want to save lives."

"Thank you, Ambassador." I already started to consider the logistics. "As you probably know, we have quite a number of fighters and bombers, and as far as I understand, they've been mothballed for quite a long time."

"The baron will assist you. He will report directly to you." She leaned a bit closer to the camera. "I regret what has happened. I hope you understand how important this is."

"I do. I have to admit, I'm a bit concerned about how many people you want to transfer. You're asking quite a lot, especially considering your lack of trust."

"They are willing to die for the human race. Our myths speak of a legend who will cross the stars and bring about the justice humanity has long since desired. While I do not believe that person to be you, I cannot help but see the similarities. We will speak again, Captain."

"I understand," I said.

"May the winds of victory find your sails."

As the screen faded to black, I was left alone in my office with my thoughts. This was a new challenge. At least we had a chance to fix *Arcadia*. As long as we had that, we could find a way forward. I think I expected Eos to send over people to help. It was what I would have done in her position.

I needed coffee.

I contacted the bridge. "Chen, we're expecting visitors. I'll be receiving them. Until then, you have the conn."

"Aye, sir. Sensors indicate quite a number of ships leaving Eos on a bearing to rendezvous with us."

"How many?"

She patched in a feed.

Against the backdrop of deep space, starships began their descent toward *Arcadia*. The ships were each a miniature city in their own right, and there must have been hundreds of them.

"They will arrive in seven hours, sir."

"Weapons?"

"They appear to be armed with small batteries of defense lasers."

"Standby on weapons. If you see anything out of the ordinary, inform me at once. Have you detected any signals coming from the brig?"

"Negative, sir."

"Double check. Block any and all outside communications not specifically authorized by you or me."

Chen nodded. "Aye, sir."

"Captain out."

CHAPTER FORTY-SIX

Arcadia
Captain Scott Moore

A single shuttle broke from the formation. Its design deviated from the common contours of what we'd seen from Eos, favoring a elongated, almond shape. Its hull's bronze-like material was peppered with circular portals spanning its midsection. In some ways, it reminded me of all those silly UFO pictures the government circulated in the 20th and 21st century to hide their secret drone technology. Yes, some of them were real extraterrestrial UAP's—Unidentified Aerial Phenomena—we never truly identified, but many were top secret crafts created by our own clandestine intel agencies.

The shuttle's aft flared with a soft orange hue as its propulsion system slowed its approach.

We stood in one of the many starport docking bays, nestled in the heart of *Arcadia*. It functioned as the beating heart of all ship-to-ship interaction. A sprawling expanse of black and white floor tiles appeared as a giant chessboard from a distance, and it demarcated into various zones by luminous lines woven into the deck plating. Space Force would never build something as dramatic, and this didn't come from any of my memories. It must've been constructed previously. You had to hand it to the Antediluvians. They had a sense of style.

Suspended high above the floor, a grid of floodlights bathed the area, eliminating any shadowy corners. Along the sides, walls made of reinforced durasteel rose to meet the ceiling, punctuated by alcoves housing a variety of technical equipment. Gigantic cranes, robotic arms, and an assortment of drones populated the hangar, ready to assist with loading and unloading operations.

A tall control tower rising above the floor jutted out from the side. Its transparent panels gave a view of the entire bay. Inside, operators could constantly monitor the docking procedure.

The docking clamps on the floor, powerful magnets capable of holding even the heaviest of vessels, were recessed when not in use. When activated, they rose, guided by a network of servos and hydraulics, and extended their grasp to secure the docked ship.

Around the periphery of the bay, large doors, constructed from a layer of durasteel and heavy-duty polymer, separated the hangar from the vacuum of space. When closed, they created an airtight seal, protecting the internal environment of the ship.

Opposite to the large bay doors, a series of smaller doors led to the *Arcadia*'s interior, allowing for the easy transit of personnel and smaller pieces of equipment. Each door featured a biometric access panel, ensuring the security of the ship.

In one corner of the docking bay, the guest reception area, a small stage with an elevated platform and a few scattered seats, stood ready to welcome any visitors. It was there I awaited the arrival of Baron Ephadria and his team.

As the baron's shuttle neared the docking bay, hidden mechanisms sprang to life. Silent repulsers located at its base began to manipulate the gravitational field, guiding the shuttle into the bay. The ship descended, and its glossy hull caught the floodlights in the docking bay, scattering them in a spectacle of reflected light.

The docking clamps on the bay floor activated. They rose and extended, the powerful magnetic field grabbing onto the metallic underbelly of the shuttle. It gently locked the shuttle in place.

With the shuttle securely docked, a panel on its side moved aside. A ramp extruded from the gap, touching the floor with a soft hiss. The hatch at the top slid open, revealing Baron Ephadria at the threshold.

As Ephadria descended the ramp, he glanced around the bay and stepped forward. He carried an aura of old-world nobility, reminiscent of a time when titles meant something. He was a tall man, easily clearing two meters, and his hair, a cascade of silver waves, draped over his shoulders. He moved with grace despite the bulk of his matte-black power armor.

The baron held a metallic staff. Atop it, a circle intersected by a cross sat inside a triangle, and the triangle's points extended to form a larger encompassing circle. Inside the central circle, small carvings represented celestial bodies, suggesting a star system or constellation.

As he neared, Baron Ephadria bowed to me. The action was so sudden and unexpected, it caught me off guard.

"There's no need for that," I said.

The baron rose, smiling. "It is the custom of my family to show respect to our hosts, Captain." His voice carried a strange, lilting accent I couldn't quite place. "It is also customary that a guest present gifts." The baron looked behind him, and one of his men produced a small green box about the size of a shoe box. "A gift from House Venatrix, from my family to yours."

Baron Ephadria's retinue of bodyguards were all hulking figures, their faces hidden behind visors. Their power armor lent an air of formidable protection for the baron. I noticed right away we were outnumbered. Maybe that was my paranoia kicking in, the survival side of my brain doing its work.

In truth, they seemed friendly enough.

I handed the gift to one of my security detail. "Thank you, Baron. Welcome aboard *Arcadia*."

"I am grateful for your hospitality, Captain Scott." The baron's gaze took in the vast expanse of *Arcadia*'s hangar.

"Moore," I said. "Captain Moore."

"My apologies, Captain."

I nodded, a slight smile tugging at the corner of my mouth. "We are equally grateful for your assistance. *Arcadia* has been through a lot, and your help is appreciated."

Ephadria inclined his head. "It is our duty and honor, Captain. Eos and *Arcadia* share a common goal. Survival. We have been in cryo for many years, awaiting your arrival."

For the briefest moment, silence hung between us as I pondered his words. I cleared my throat. "How long was that?"

"Since the Heaven War."

"I see. You'll have to tell me about that. The galaxy is a hostile place."

Our conversation was interrupted as his crew began unloading their equipment. A flurry of activity ensued as engineers and technicians busied themselves with unpacking, setting up workstations, and prepping for the task at hand. Whirs and clanks filled the air followed by the occasional bursts of muffled conversation and the shuffle of boots on the hangar floor.

"Your men seem to know the ship," I said.

"We ought to, Captain. House Venatrix helped construct it. My team is the best Eos has to offer, Captain," he replied, the pride in his voice evident. "They have worked on countless ship repairs and restorations. *Arcadia* is in capable hands."

Chief wasn't thrilled by their hasty actions. Couldn't say I blamed him. I had the impression this was normal for them. After years of war, it would be.

A knot of tension in my belly loosened as the seconds passed. "I trust your judgment, Baron."

"We aim to uphold that reputation, Captain."

I gestured to the box he had gifted me earlier. "And this... it's fascinating. Care to open it?"

Chief gave me a look, a kind of warning we should scan it first.

A soft smile played on the baron's lips. "It's an heirloom, Captain. Passed down through generations. It's meant to bring fortune and favor to its owner. We believe in goodwill, and nothing fosters goodwill better than a gift."

Regardless of my many years in space, encountering countless cultures and customs as I traveled Earth, giving interviews before I left Earth, the baron's gesture left me genuinely touched. "Thank you, Baron Ephadria." I nodded over to the box. "Open it."

The guard carrying the box complied.

Inside it, I spotted a metallic mesh of intertwined circuits resembling a Gordian knot, consisting of interlaced filaments each thinner than a human hair. The edges were not sharply defined, but flowed into each other, producing a continuous, undulating surface. It must've been sculpted rather than engineered.

I took a closer look. Along the sinewy circuits, symbols were etched into the thin strands. Each character seemed to contain a multitude of strokes, curves, and dots, complex and detailed enough to be individual works of art.

The device as a whole was perhaps the size of a human hand. From a distance, it almost seemed alive. The iridescent glow of the core and the cryptic symbols running along the circuits all contributed to this impression. It was a piece of technology that blurred the line between the organic and the mechanical.

"What is it?" I asked.

"A small token, Captain. A symbol of our cooperation and mutual respect known as The Feral Heart. This peculiar artifact hails from a time when The Regency ruled the stars. My great-great-grandfather created it. It's essentially a cosmic energy harvester and converter. The symbols etched on the filaments act as control systems, managing the energy flux, keeping the device from either running dry or going into overload. The metal core acts as a capacitor, storing energy drawn from the quantum foam."

"That sounds a lot like a Numix Device. Is it working now?"

"No, Captain. I'm afraid it no longer functions."

I wanted to ask him why he was giving me a broken artifact, but Michael was right. Don't look a gift horse in the mouth. "Is there a way to repair it?"

"Not that I'm aware of, Captain."

"I appreciate the gift."

As our conversation drew to a close, the repair crew continued to set up their operations.

I extended my hand toward the baron, who took it in a firm grip. "Let's bring *Arcadia* back to full strength."

"We shall begin immediately."

The baron turned to his crew, his commanding voice filling the hangar as *Arcadia*'s repair commenced. "Make the captain proud."

Arcadia's future was beginning to look a little brighter.

CHAPTER FORTY-SEVEN

Kahwin
The Scalding Ruins
Kol Washington

It'd been another long day. I'd been training with the Immortals, and I'd grown to like them in my own way. For some reason, my dreams had been more vivid lately. I didn't mention it to Zoe. She didn't dream.

I'd grown used to fighting in the suit, and Zoe made me wear the headband everyday. She said my thoughts would help her tune the Immortals better to me. I think she wanted to tell me something, but she was holding out for some reason.

Zoe went over next to one of the Immortals and started cleaning its shoulder-mounted burst cannon. She'd been working on them since the start and upgrading them became her hobby. Other than teaching me, cleaning, and cooking for me, she did little else but improve our robot friends.

I wanted to speak with them. Mentally, of course. They didn't have a way to speak normally. When I tried, nothing happened. Zoe warned me not to try it again, so I didn't.

There were enough supplies in here to last a thousand life-times for a thousand people.

"Who decided what Melody can and can't show me?" I asked, taking a seat by Melody's holographic interface. I took my hand and swept up crumbs from lunch and threw them in the bin next to my chair. Zoe made the best breads.

"Why won't Melody show me certain aspects of history?" I asked Zoe.

"Melody operates under a set of programmed instructions," she replied. "There are certain things it isn't allowed to reveal. Those decisions were made by the creators of Melody, the ones who programmed it."

"But why? Why keep secrets? You're teaching me things the Academy would never teach me."

A smile formed on Zoe's lips, and she glanced over at Melody's servers. "Not all knowledge is beneficial, Kol. Some secrets protect us."

"Protect us from what? The truth? The Keepers?"

"Sometimes the truth can be dangerous."

"Dangerous? Isn't that our choice to make?" I asked. "The Earthers spoke a lot about freedom, didn't they?"

"Sure, they did. The Senate is based on their own society."

I cocked an eyebrow. "You never told me that."

"You never asked."

My stomach growled. Zoe must have heard it because she stopped what she was doing and brought me over one of the metallic food packages that had been stored here from long ago. I ripped open the seal on the front and took a whiff. "Thanks, Zoe."

"What would you like to drink?"

"Do we have any of the orange drink left?"

"Let me make you some." She ambled over to the kitchen

prep area, where hundreds of boxes held different ingredients for flavored drink.

"I don't care about that. I just want to know why the Earthers hid so much information in their machine, when you said it knows so much."

"The creators believed they were safeguarding humanity by placing these restrictions." She opened a circular bin that she'd labeled with an orange square, scooped out some powder, and dissolved it into a water pitcher.

"Who are they to decide what's best for everyone else? That doesn't seem right at all."

"They carried the burden of responsibility, Kol. As creators, it fell to them to guide their creation."

"What if I want to know everything? Don't I have that right?"

"Perhaps," she said. "What would you do if you knew everything? Would it change your life? It might make you unhappy."

I wasn't sure how to answer that. Zoe would often ask me questions like that, questions I had trouble answering. It was as if she were testing me. "If I don't know the whole truth, how can I make decisions?"

"Knowledge has the power to harm. It *must* be handled with care." Zoe brought me over a glass of orange drink, which was by far the best of the twenty flavors and went back to work by changing out one of the Immortal's energy cells, which weighed as much as a log that'd been out in the rain for too long. She set the drained energy cell into a recharger and zeroed the Immortal's weapon with the aid of a guidance tool. It was about the size of my knee and had five points that shot out from the top. Zoe told me a few weeks ago she'd teach me how to use it.

"So, you're saying they were trying to protect us from ourselves?" I asked.

"In a way, yes. They wanted to avoid misusing what they understand."

"We should have the right to learn from our mistakes, shouldn't we?"

"Indeed, but they must have believed the risks were too high." Zoe primed the guidance tool by depressing her thumb in the center, which activated it.

"But now I'm part of this, right? The Immortals, the AI, all of this. Shouldn't I know everything?"

"I understand your frustration. The restrictions are hard-wired into Melody's programming. Even I can't change that."

I didn't believe her. Zoe could do anything. "Is there any way to learn more?"

"Not that I'm aware of. Learning is not just about absorbing information. It's about understanding, questioning, reflecting."

"It just feels like there's so much more out there."

"Let me share a tale with you, Kol," Zoe began, her voice filling the silence around us. "Imagine an age long past, in a reality conceived by beings of immeasurable power. These beings, predating even the Keepers, harnessed the raw essence of the universe to create a splendid, life-bearing orb. We'll call this place the Sphere of Serenity."

"Are you making this up?" I asked.

"It's a thought experiment. Do you remember what those are?"

I nodded.

"Good. On this sphere, these beings, known as the Protectors, cultivated two sentient forms of life."

"Humans?"

"Yes. Let's refer to them as Eda and Lom."

"What'd they look like?" I asked.

"A lot like you, my friend. Embedded within the core of this Sphere of Serenity, there existed a crystal of unimaginable power. This crystal was no ordinary gem; it was the Crystal of Omniscience, and it held immense knowledge." She grinned. "Now the Sphere of Serenity contained the power of creation, destruction, and the truths that bound reality together. The Protectors had one mandate for Eda and Lom."

"What?"

"They were to experience the Sphere in all its glory, but they were forbidden to seek the Crystal of Omniscience."

"The Protectors didn't want Eda and Lom to find it?"

"Why would they need it? The Sphere offered them everything. Life. Joy. Knowledge. But they lacked the absolute truths, the secrets of the universe that the crystal held. Eda and Lom, driven by their innate curiosity, couldn't ignore the allure of the Crystal of Omniscience."

"I couldn't either," I said, finishing off my orange drink. Nothing was as refreshing. "Then what happened?"

"As it turned out, Eda and Lom risked the wrath of the Protectors by seeking out the crystal. Once they found it, they gained knowledge beyond their comprehension."

"Like what?" I asked.

She laughed a lot like my mother, one of the things she'd picked up on recently. "If I told you, it wouldn't be much of a secret, would it?"

I frowned. "No, I guess not."

"With this knowledge came consequences they couldn't foresee. They lost their innocence. The brilliance of the crystal overwhelmed Eda and Lom. They found themselves privy to the Protectors' designs, to their own existence, and even the course of future events. The raw, unfiltered truth crashed over them like a Shaper invasion."

I swallowed hard.

"And for what?" she asked, a hint of sadness in her voice. "They had traded their simple, joyful lives for the cold clarity of universal truth. Their minds expanded, yes, but so too did their understanding of pain, of loss, and of every bad thing in the universe. Once they understood, there was no path to return, no way to unsee what they'd seen, and no way to unlearn what they'd learned. As much as they longed for the bliss, the allure of knowledge ensnared them like one of the traps we found in the forest outside."

"What happened to them?"

"The Protectors banished them from the Sphere of Serenity. Eda and Lom ventured forth into the universe. Each revelation they gleaned from the crystal was like a double-edged sword. For every moment of profound insight, they experienced an equal measure of despair. All the while, they were haunted by the knowledge of their transgression, of the paradise lost. One must always be prepared for the consequences that come with uncovering the secrets of the universe."

I thought for a moment. "Well, without them doing what they did, how would they ever learn anything? They'd be bored always sitting in bliss, don't you think? Everything would always stay the same. No change, just the same stuff all of the time."

She didn't respond.

"Are you sure this isn't a real story?" I asked. "It sounds like I've heard something like this before."

Zoe remained silent.

"You're warning me."

"Yes, Kol. That's exactly what I'm doing."

CHAPTER FORTY-EIGHT

Kahwin
The Scalding Ruins
Kol Washington

"What should I call the battlesuit? Does it have a name?" I asked.

"Whatever you like," Zoe replied.

"I'll have to think about it."

We were in the training room, and I'd gotten better at everything, including fighting. Zoe was proud of me. What would General Vack think of all this? He wanted to use me to find this place, and now that I did, what would come next?

For some reason, my thoughts became clearer every day, and as odd as it is to say this, I felt a sense of purpose for... something. You ever get that feeling that you're supposed to do something but you're not sure what?

Zoe's voice sounded through the cavernous room. "Kol, what do you know about your ancestors?"

I stopped, my spear gripped in my hands as I turned to look at her. "I don't know much. My mother was the assistant to

Ahnayah, the second-in-line to the Splinter Voice of Allo Quishar. She was a history recorder and a midwife. She was also Caretaker of the Hearth for the Gesterion Tribe."

"I'm aware."

"Is she safe? You haven't talked much about the Senate, and I haven't heard from her." I missed her... a lot. My heart hurt when I thought about her. I cried like a baby a few times, but only at night when Zoe wasn't around. I couldn't believe how hard I cried. You know the type of crying where no sound comes out? It was what I did. Everyday, I wished she could be here with us.

Zoe checked her display at her station. "Unknown. Most likely General Vack has limited the Senate's ability to communicate with the outside world. I'm sure she's safe. What else can you tell me about your ancestors?"

"Oh. Well, not much. I should know more, I guess. By the way, who is Allo Quishar? I know he's a Keeper, but who is he?"

Zoe studied me from her console. "Tell me what you've heard."

I frowned. "I don't really know. My mother had visions or dreams, I think. She would talk about signs she'd receive. In English, I think she meant synchronicities. I think they came from Allo Quishar. I never really understood."

"Let me try to explain." A hologram flickered to life in front of me as a single point of light floating in the air. "Perhaps this will help. See this dot? This is the first dimension. It's a single point. It doesn't have length, width, or height. It just exists."

"What do you mean? Is this Allo Quishar?"

"No. Follow along. This isn't something they taught you at the Academy, and this isn't something Melody will discuss with you." As she spoke, the point extended into a line. "This is the second dimension. It has length and width, but no height.

Imagine living on this line. If you did, you could only move forward or backward."

I climbed out of my suit and walked over to one of the cleaning kits next a rack of swords, cracked it open, and started to rub down the spear. "What about up or down?"

"If you lived here on the line, you would have no concept of up or down."

The line folded outward, forming a cube. "This is the third dimension. Length, width, and height. It's where we live. We can move forward and backward, left and right, up and down."

I marched back to stand closer to the cube as it turned in the air. "Is this Allo Quishar?"

"No," Zoe said. "Allo Quishar lives in a place beyond these dimensions. These are just the basics. Do you understand the three dimensions?"

"Yes, it's easy enough." I stared at the hologram, the simple shapes somehow representing something so much more complex. "Isn't everything around us three-dimensional? We can move in any direction, right?"

"That's correct," Zoe replied patiently. "Everything around us exists in three dimensions. We can move forward and backward, left and right, up and down."

"What makes other dimensions different?"

Zoe was quiet for a moment, the spinning cube casting shifting shadows on her face. "In the simplest terms, each dimension adds another way in which we can move. In the first dimension, we can only move along a single line. In the second, we can move along two lines that intersect each other, but we can't move up or down."

"So, we have three ways to move in the third dimension," I said, slowly starting to grasp the idea. "How can there be more ways to move? Isn't up and down, left and right, and forward and backward all there is?"

"That's a common question," Zoe said. "Our minds are wired to comprehend the world around us in three dimensions, so it's difficult for you to imagine anything beyond that."

I frowned. "So, are you saying there are more dimensions beyond these three? Dimensions where we could move in other ways?"

"Exactly," Zoe said.

"How can we know they exist if we can't see them?" I asked. "Can my suit see them?"

"Not exactly."

"Do you think there are more dimensions?"

Zoe gave a small shrug, and her eyes reflected the flickering light of the holograms. "If you think you're ready, we could discuss the fourth dimension."

I nodded.

"Alright." Zoe brought up a new hologram. It showed a cube again, but this time, it seemed to be constantly morphing in a way that didn't make sense. It was the same cube, and it was changing, becoming bigger and smaller at the same time. "This is a simplistic representation of a four-dimensional object. It's called a hypercube or a tesseract. Just as a three-dimensional object casts a two-dimensional shadow, a four-dimensional object casts a three-dimensional shadow."

"What? That doesn't make any sense." As I looked at the morphing cube, I tried to understand her. My headband warmed and my temples tingled. "How would a being living in the fourth dimension perceive reality?"

"To start, they would perceive the three dimensions as we do, but they'd also have access to another direction, one that you can't comprehend fully. They'd be able to see every angle of a three-dimensional object at once, all its inner parts, not just the surface."

"They could see inside things?" I asked. What would it be

like to see the inside of the training room's walls, or even Zoe herself?

"In a way, yes," she replied. "Just as we can move in three dimensions, they'd be able to move in this fourth dimension as well. They could move in time as easily as we move in space."

I was silent for a moment. If what Zoe said was true, then a being in the fourth dimension could perceive time, could move through it like walking through a forest. They could see everything that had ever happened and everything that ever would, all at once.

"That's hard to understand." My mind swirled with thoughts of shifting cubes and four-dimensional beings. The conversation felt like another battle in the training room.

Zoe's eyes narrowed slightly. "You wanted to know about Allo Quishar. The twelfth dimension is profoundly different from the ones I just described. It's beyond physicality, beyond time and space, beyond all possible and impossible multiverses. Using the term 'dimension' for it is a gross simplification."

The hologram shifted again, this time into a radiant sphere of light, swirling with an infinite number of patterns and shapes.

"Allo Quishar resides in this twelfth dimension," Zoe said. "This is not a place of matter or energy, or even of information as we understand it. It's a realm of pure consciousness."

Her words weighed on me. Why did everything feel wrong?

She paused, allowing the hologram to pulse in the room.

"In the twelfth dimension," Zoe said, "there's no distinction between the observer and the observed and no separation between the thinker and the thought. It's an ocean of consciousness, where every ripple, every wave, every current is both the creator and the creation. The rules of our reality don't apply there. 'Rules,' as you understand them, cease to exist. It's a place of pure creativity, where every thought, every idea, instantly shapes and reshapes reality."

I remained silent, my pulse racing. I didn't want to accept any of it. The scale of what Zoe described made me sick. "Allo Quishar... he lives there?"

Zoe nodded. "Yes, Kol. In that infinite realm of potentiality and consciousness, that's where Allo Quishar exists. From there, he extends his awareness, his influence, down to our reality."

"I thought I heard Captain Moore say he wanted to fight them. I remember hearing Allo Quishar's voice in a dream once. I was in a barn, I think. Some people said I was attacked by a Shaper and the captain saved me, but I don't remember. Is the twelfth dimension bad?"

"There's no bad or good there, just like there's no up or down."

I shook my head. "Allo Quishar is bad."

"In your way of thinking, yes. And, in your way of thinking, there are also *good* conscious entities in the twelfth dimension. But, I think that's enough teachings for today."

"What are we going to do for the rest of the day?" I asked.

"How would you like to try some chocolate ice cream?"

"Some what?"

"Let's go to the kitchen. I'll make you something you'll never forget."

CHAPTER FORTY-NINE

Arcadia
Captain Scott Moore

I hadn't slept in days. There was too much to do, priming the Eos personnel with constant lessons about our culture and way of doing things. Saluting came naturally to them, and with the help of *Arcadia*'s fabricators, we dressed them in Space Force uniforms.

My officers had their hands full, and I tasked Erika as a liaison to them and our staff, mainly because they couldn't read Erika at all. Initially, they protested. She was an intelligent robot, they'd said, and they only dealt with humans. I squashed that attitude immediately. Lieutenant Erika Banks would be treated as any other crew member.

They gave us daily briefings on their customs, their way of doing things, and to be honest, it wasn't that far removed from the way we did things. Efficiency does that, I supposed. Soon, my crew worked alongside them. Although I never placed any of my crew directly under any of the baron's men, they worked so well together, it hardly mattered. I imagined this was what it must have been like during the days of World War Two or Napoleon, where people were forced to get along quickly.

There was a saying back home: amateurs talk strategy, professionals talk logistics. While I haven't mentioned logistics lately, *Arcadia* was built with logistics in mind, a fortress with a seemingly endless supply of food, water, and air to last endless generations.

I'd just gotten out of the shower when I received a message from the baron on my comms. I threw on a shirt and wrapped myself in a towel. "Captain Moore, here."

"Captain, I have some bad news."

"Go on."

"We may have to adapt to our current situation. Without the Numix Device, many of *Arcadia*'s main weapons won't have enough juice to power them. However, we're not without resources."

His statement shook me to the core. "I'm listening."

"The plasma projectors are still operational. Each 'round' consists of a dense core of ionized gas encased within a localized gravitational field. The gravitic shell not only confines the plasma but also propels it toward the target at remarkable velocities. The good news is, we've got so many of them, I don't think we'd ever run out. The beauty of them is their range. They can reach targets up to... twenty thousand kilometers away, depending on the conditions. I'm still getting used to your measurements. I can see if Eos can manufacture particle lances."

"Can't we make what we need onboard *Arcadia*?" I asked.

"Unfortunately, the ship's main fabricators were tied to the Numix Device. It will take time to bring them online. Sir, if I may be so bold, where was the Numix?"

"In one of the garden domes."

The baron paused. "Unprotected?"

"None of us were aware of its significance. I don't understand it either." Not at all. To leave something so precious out in the open spoke of extreme arrogance. Then again, if it hadn't siphoned power from this system, we wouldn't be in the mess we were in. Maybe hiding it out in the open was normal.

The next logical step would be to talk to Michael, obviously, but he wasn't talking. He slept twenty-three hours out of every twenty-four, only rousing for food and water. He hadn't said a word since he was interned in the brig. I never mentioned his presence to the baron. If he marshaled a force, he could probably break him out.

Also, I hadn't revealed my plans to return to Earth with anyone else other than Chief.

"Indeed," the baron said. "Next are the magnetic rail cannons. These launch projectiles at incredible speeds, giving them an effective range of around fifteen thousand kilometers. The projectiles are accelerated along a track by powerful electromagnets, reaching speeds of several kilometers per second before exiting the cannon. They have to be manually aimed. My suggestion would be to begin training on these immediately."

"And I assume we have a significant number of those," I said.

"You assume correctly, Captain. These are the ship's long-range heavy hitters. Also, think about how *Arcadia*'s size and capabilities would allow us to operate it more like a launching pad for fighters and bombers."

My mind raced at his words. He was right. I had been so fixated on the immediate loss of *Arcadia*'s weapons systems, that I overlooked its other strengths. It was not unlike a terrestrial aircraft carrier in the grand naval battles of old, capable of launching a barrage of smaller threats.

"Like the waterborne carriers on...?" I let the sentence hang, hoping the baron would catch my drift.

He did. "Aye, Captain. Like the carriers on Soteria Major. My cousin once served on a similar vessel in the Adrasteia System, on a water-world they called Hydraxon Prime. Believe me when I say, Captain, such strategies of 'carrier warfare' have proven highly effective in the past."

Maybe we weren't as disadvantaged as I initially feared. We had a ship, one of the largest known to humanity, and we had plenty of fighters and fighter-bombers. It would take some time to adjust, to train, and to prepare.

"We don't have pilots," I said.

"That's not a problem."

"Why's that?"

"Eos has plenty."

I rapped my knuckles on the side table by my chair "I don't think the ambassador will be too happy if I recruited her pilots."

"I beg to differ, Captain. I believe she was expecting such a request. After all, Eos was once the Regency's premier pilot training Academy. Ambassador K'Hori has been waiting to bring them out of cryo for eons."

"How many pilots are we talking about?"

"It's difficult to say. Ten, at least."

"Ten? Baron, we have thousands of craft. Ten pilots won't help protect this ship against the Shapers."

"Ten to train the ones you need. I'll provide the personnel. We'll need to start as soon as possible."

I shook my head in disbelief. The baron had all the answers, and it left me uneasy. I wouldn't want another Munn situation. "I'll contact Ambassador K'Hori. Continue your repairs."

"Aye, Captain. Sir?"

"Yes?"

"I don't suppose you have any more of that coffee... stuff?"

I laughed. "I'll make sure to have some delivered to you. It's the least I can do."

CHAPTER FIFTY

Arcadia
Captain Scott Moore

S everal months had passed since my first meeting with Baron Ephadria, and those months felt like a relentless march of hours, days, and weeks, each one weighing heavier than the last. Each passing day was a painful reminder of the absence of Doctor Ingram and Gisele. I didn't deal with loss that well. Part of me was dead. No doubt about it. You offer a man like me a second chance for love and pull the rug out from under him, it leaves him hollow. You take one of my best friends away, the person who was the best sounding board known to man, and someone I truly admired in Doc, and it pains my soul beyond measure.

Still, repairs had gone smoothly. I'd left Chen and Chief to supervise the details, but I kept apprised of our progress three times a day, sometimes more.

You might be wondering what happened to those people we'd first encountered on the ship, the ones Michael said were part of a previous crew. There were thousands of them. Erika suggested we leave them be and study them. I tended to agree until Chief convinced me to move them all someplace where they wouldn't be bothered and still allowed the repair teams and our crew to travel freely without the fear of being accosted.

I didn't like the idea. Maybe I'd been convinced by the powers that be back home that moving a population from one spot to the other by force was a bad thing to do. Looking back, I had to ask myself where the world would be if my ancestors hadn't done so themselves. Would we have been better off? Or worse?

I ended up moving them to one of the domes with plenty of trees and plants, enough to feed a hundred times their number. We wouldn't contact them and possibly contain their culture, and we wouldn't be put in a situation where we'd be forced to worry. Still, I insisted everyone traveling within the bowels of the ship went in teams and were armed.

Enclosed within *Arcadia*'s metallic confines was a vast sector known as the Echo Chamber, a name that once meant something political, back when social media existed. We'd mapped it like everything else. It spanned a breadth equivalent to multiple football fields, a broad expanse under a sweeping dome, a good place to set up a baseball diamond to give my crew some relaxation.

Come to find out, the baron's men took an interest in our sports. Where he was from, they fought in massive gladiator arenas. Rome, it seemed, was never far away. His people had constructed arenas so large, it boggled the mind. Millions could attend. I asked him how the attendees could see anything, to which he replied, "Neural Sync." Apparently, if you went to one of their events, you had to pick a fighter and wear a headband device. If they were hit, you felt a diminished form of the blow.

Sounded painful. "Where would humanity be without pain?" the baron had asked.

The Echo Chamber housed towering transparent crystal formations that extended from the floor, their peaks reaching toward the high dome overhead. These crystal structures functioned as both acoustic resonators and natural amplifiers, influencing the distribution of ambient sound in the Chamber.

On the far side of the pool, the terrain elevated gradually to form a hill. At the hill's zenith, an imposing statue stood, dedicated to an unknown deity. The statue was carved from the same crystalline material as the pillars, catching and refracting the ambient light. The ship's record had no mention of who the statue was meant to be, but he looked a lot like one of the Greek statues dedicated to Aries, according to Melody.

I spent time inside the chamber, mostly meditating. No, I have to be honest. It was where I grieved. Gisele and Doc were never far from my thoughts. For the hundredth time, I replayed the moments before their deaths in my mind, wrestling with guilt.

Chief's arrival stirred me from my lament. "Captain."

I turned to face him, attempting a smile. "Pete. Everything okay?"

"So far, so good. Looks like the baron knows what he's doing. I thought I'd find you here."

I spread my arms. "Something about this place helps me think."

His eyes studied me. "How are you holding up?"

The weight of the question hung in the air between us. I sighed, my gaze dropping to the ground. "Some days are better than others."

Chief's voice softened. "Doc? Gisele?"

"Both."

Chief's expression softened. "I miss Doc a lot. It was an

honor to know him. The guy was top notch. Nothing's going to be the same without him." He sighed. "You met any of the baron's doctors?"

"One."

"You're not thinking of bringing them back with the Elysium Engine, are you?"

"The thought had never crossed my mind."

"That's good to hear."

"Any luck on reviving the tablet that was found on Doctor Ingram?"

Chief shook his head. "Damaged beyond repair. Can't get anything from it, and we've certainly tried." He pointed to a nearby stone bench. "Mind if I join you? This is my lunch hour."

"Not at all."

He sat across from me.

"Lunch hour. That's a good one," I said.

"Thought you'd like that. You know, this place would be great for baseball games."

I gave him a look. "Ha! You're reading my mind."

"Don't say that. Rumor gets out that I'm a telepath, Feazer will lynch me." Chief giggled.

"He wouldn't harm a fly."

"No, but he'd think about it."

"I asked him if he'd join Space Force. He declined," I said.

"What are we going to do when we get back to Earth? I've been thinking a lot about that, and I'm not sure it's such a great idea. We bring *Arcadia* back..."

I held up a hand to stop him. "I know. Believe me. I've been thinking about it myself. I don't think we can hide it. As soon as we pass Neptune, they'll pick us up. If we bring it to Earth, it's going to cause panic."

"That's exactly right. Heaven knows what certain groups will do."

"Certain groups?" I asked.

"You know who I mean."

"Michael told me some uncomfortable truths. I don't think we have a choice now." I told him about the jumpdrive traps and how if anyone from Earth went into jumpspace, they'd end up on Kahwin.

"That is a problem."

We sat in silence for a while.

"I know you and Doc were close. I want you to know, if you ever need to talk, I'm here."

I grinned. "I appreciate it, Pete."

"I mean it."

"I know you do. You're a good man. I'll get over it." I didn't know if I ever would.

"Stoic as usual. I'd expect nothing less from the finest captain in the entire galaxy."

I withheld a laugh. "Now there's a title. Truth is, I don't know if I'm up for this or not. I checked the mirror. See these grey hairs growing on my head? There didn't used to be so many."

"Be thankful you have them. I think I'm starting to grow bald."

"You going to shave it?"

"Probably. I'll look even uglier than I do now."

"You'll look fine."

Chief rubbed the top of his forehead. "Says the guy with a full head of hair. You'd think with all the genetic engineering back home, they'd figured out an easy solution for male pattern baldness. Just goes to show you where their priorities are."

"Stem cells? Hair transplants?"

"Never. What kind of man do you take me for?"

"Apparently, the bald kind."

A speaker hidden inside one of the rocks chimed. "Captain,

the pilots have left Eos and will arrive within the hour. Docking Bay Ten," Erika said.

I stood. "I'll meet you there. Captain out." I turned to Chief. "Care to join me?"

"Let's go."

CHAPTER FIFTY-ONE

Kahwin
The Scalding Ruins
Kol Washington

As Zoe disappeared into an adjacent room, I was ready to ask Melody questions about what Zoe told me about the Sphere of Serenity.

"Melody," I said, facing the translucent screen, "do you have any record of the story Zoe just told me? About Eda, Lom, and the crystal?"

A soft silence filled the room before Melody replied. "I regret to inform you, Kol, but I hold no data concerning a tale involving entities named Eda, Lom, and a crystal. Your request for information returns no relevant results."

I leaned closer to the terminal. "What about the Sphere of Serenity? Has any civilization known about it?"

Melody's voice retained its usual calm as she responded. "My comprehensive archives yield no entries matching the term 'Sphere of Serenity.' I apologize for the inadequacy."

I frowned. Two queries, two dead ends. As usual. So much

for intelligent machines. Zoe not included, of course. "Do you have any information on a 'crystal' that provides knowledge? Anything resembling the crystal from the story?"

"Regrettably, I must inform you that the comprehensive search of my database returned no record of an object matching your description."

Three questions. Nothing. I was pretty sure Zoe must have taught it how to speak to help me learn English better, but sometimes, I had trouble with it.

The tale *was* likely a myth. Zoe probably made it up. What if there was more to her story? What if Zoe held back details that could help me find the truth? Or what if her story was a lesson. They call that a metaphor. She might have been guiding me toward something.

Her story reminded me of a story my mother used to sing to me when I was little.

It went like this: Once upon a moonlit night, in the tranquil hamlet of Lys, lived a curious little boy named Elion. In Lys, a gentle creature, known as the Lumivox, held power over the dreams of its people. Each night, as they slept, Lumivox shared wonderful stories, but they were more than just dreams. They were strands of wisdom woven through time.

One day, Elion found an orb tucked away in the town's ancient tree. It wasn't an ordinary orb. It was the Dreamweaver, Lumivox's source of dream-tales. Elion knew he shouldn't touch it. Everyone in Lys knew not to disturb the Dreamweaver. That didn't stop him.

Elion snuck away from his town and touched the Dreamweaver. When he did, it sent a ripple of light into the sky. Instantly, the town stirred. Nightmares, once held back by Lumivox, flooded into Lys.

The little boy ran to Lumivox and told him what he'd done. Lumivox was sad and angry. "You've unleashed the dreams not meant for people, Elion. But in you, I see a potential for redemption."

Lumivox guided Elion on a journey through dreams and nightmares. Elion discovered a secret power Lumivox gave him to soothe the wildest of nightmares. He confronted the nightmares he'd unleashed and tamed them with his light.

Once he finished, Elion returned the Dreamweaver to Lumivox. He became a symbol of redemption. Lumivox reminded the people of Lys each night, that within us, our truest strength comes out.

My mother told the story better, but that was what happened.

I rushed over to Melody's interface. "Melody, analyze the name 'Lumivox.' Are there other meanings, translations, anything?"

The AI paused a moment before responding. "Lumivox does not align with any known word or phrase in my database."

What about the crystal? In my story, it was the Dreamweaver. In Zoe's, a simple crystal. Were they the same? "What about the crystal in Zoe's story? Does it match with the Dreamweaver from Lys?"

This time, Melody seemed to take a moment longer. "In both narratives, a luminous object holds significant power and imparts knowledge. However, the data is insufficient to draw concrete parallels."

I stared at Melody's interface. It felt like I stood at the edge of a vast puzzle. Then it struck me. The knowledge. In both stories, the object, the Dreamweaver or the crystal, imparted knowledge. That had to mean something.

"Melody, is there a connection between the knowledge imparted by the crystal in Zoe's story and the Dreamweaver in Lys story? Do they represent the same thing?"

This time, Melody responded quickly. "Both the crystal and

the Dreamweaver serve as conduits for knowledge, shaping the fate of those who come in contact with them," she said. "This suggests a thematic link, although it remains speculative due to the abstract nature of the symbols."

I lowered my voice. "Can you find a story similar to the Lumivox tale on Earth?"

"I am unable to locate an Earth story with the specific parameters you have provided."

I scrunched my nose. I needed to tweak the question and be more specific. "Look for stories about a forbidden object which brings knowledge and loss of innocence."

Silence, longer this time. "I apologize, but I am unable to assist in your query."

Strange. "Why not? Is the information classified?"

"I am programmed to provide assistance within my capabilities," Melody replied. "The requested data does not align with those capabilities."

Stupid machine. Fine, if Melody wouldn't cooperate, I'd need to be smarter about it. I thought for a moment. "Do any Earth stories talk about a powerful being who forbids lesser beings from obtaining a certain object, and punishes them when they do?"

Melody responded after a moment's pause. "There are numerous narratives with such a theme across a variety of cultures on Earth. However, none of them exactly match the details you provided about the Lumivox story."

Still not good enough, but I was getting closer. I leaned back and stared up at the ceiling. What if I tricked Melody? "Show me a list of Earth stories that involve forbidden objects."

"Compiling data." After a pause, lines of text filled the interface screen, presenting an overwhelming collection of stories.

I scanned through the list and began to eliminate stories that didn't match the Lumivox story. It took time. Hours later, I sat back and glimpsed a small collection of remaining tales. I pointed at the list. "Compare these stories to the Lumivox narrative."

For a moment, Melody was silent. "Initiating comparative analysis."

This time, I waited. I kept my gaze fixed on the screen, each second dragging on longer than the previous one. If Zoe found me doing this, I didn't think she'd be too happy with me.

The sound of Melody's voice jolted me from my thoughts. "Comparison complete. The data suggests possible thematic parallels between some of the listed narratives and the Lumivox story. However, direct correlation remains speculative."

It wasn't the answer I'd had hoped for, but it was a step in the right direction. "What if I gave you two separate elements from the Lumivox tale? Could you match each to a separate Earth narrative?"

"Proceed with the elements for analysis."

"Firstly, a powerful being, a guardian of sorts, and secondly, an object of profound knowledge, forbidden to others."

"Processing..."

Minutes slid into an agonizing eternity as I waited. The silence stretched on, and a small spark of hope swelled in my chest. Had I finally managed to corner Melody?

"Results indicate several possible correlations, but they remain speculative due to lack of complete context."

You have got to be joking. "Why is that?"

"The parameters provided are broad. Many narratives contain such elements."

I grumbled and then rubbed my forehead. This was becoming a mental battlefield. I stared at Melody's interface, gears turning in my mind.

"What if I asked about Earth tales with similar themes?

Themes of disobedience, forbidden knowledge, drastic consequences."

"There are multiple narratives with similar themes, but establishing a direct correlation with the Lumivox tale remains speculative."

I hated that word "speculative." It was the worst word in English.

One last attempt, I decided. "Tell me a story from Earth where the acquisition of forbidden knowledge led to a loss of innocence and incurred severe consequences."

Silence. "The narrative that aligns closely with the parameters provided is the 'Fall of Man' story from the Judeo-Christian tradition and the myth of 'Pandora's Box' from Ancient Greece."

A shiver ran down my spine as the pieces slid into place. "Melody, does the Lumivox tale mirror these narratives?"

"Comparatively, thematic similarities can be established. However, direct correlation remains speculative."

There it was, the closest to confirmation I could get.

"Kol, what are you doing?" Zoe asked me. She stood right next to me. She'd done that a couple times, seemingly appearing out of nowhere. I didn't see her come in.

My eyes widened. "Nothing."

She held an electronic tool meant for the Immortals and glared at the screen. "You shouldn't be reading this."

"Am I in trouble?"

Zoe set the tool to the side and pushed me away from the keyboard. "You have no idea what you've just done."

I looked over her shoulder as the screen flashed, and Antediluvians symbols slowly materialized in a dull glow.

A high-pitched alert pierced the quiet room and a new window opened on the display, filling rapidly with data and raw feeds in real-time. My eyes darted across the interface, making sense of it.

"It's a signal from Starport City," I said.

Zoe's fingers raced across the keys, and she brought up the signal's source. "It's a planetary frequency reserved for emergencies."

The alarm's incessant wail continued as I turned to Zoe. "What is it? What's happening?"

She studied the screen. "It's a Shaper fleet, Kol."

The room spun around me. "What? How... how many?"

Zoe navigated the incoming data. "The exact numbers aren't clear. Thousands of ships."

My knees threatened to give way beneath me. "When will they arrive?"

"Five days."

"We have to notify Starport City," I shouted, thinking about mother, my tribe, and the few friends I'd made there.

"How much do you remember about the Academy?" she asked.

"Almost everything."

Zoe handed me an Earther computer tablet. "Enough to draw a map?"

"Yes. Why?"

"You're going to march on the Academy and kill General Vack," Zoe said like it was the most basic fact in the world.

"What? Well, what about the Shapers?"

"Leave that to me." She touched me on the arm, something she rarely did. "You've opened Pandora's Box. Now, we're all going to pay the price."

CHAPTER FIFTY-TWO

Kahwin
The Scalding Ruins
Kol Washington

"Where are we going?" I asked.

"Back to the city," Zoe said. "We can't stay here any longer."

"I thought you said this place was safe."

"It *was*."

Zoe laid out a dark matter rifle on a table, where she stored the rest of our supplies we'd take with us. She stuffed a small water purifier the size of a tablet into her pack and motioned over to one of the sinks. "Drink before we go."

The Immortals couldn't go through the exit. They were obviously too tall, and there was an army of them. If they went with us, I was pretty sure General Vack would find out instantly.

"Why can't you tell me what's wrong?" I asked, gulping down a glass of water.

"Hurry."

I set the glass down and started stuffing my pack with

supplies. I attached the medikit to my arm with an adherence strip and pocketed a few nutrient bars. "Starport City is too far to walk. General Vack's drones will spot us."

"You won't be walking, nor will you need those supplies. You should be comfortable with your suit by now. Come with me. Let's prepare you for war."

I halted. "War?"

"Yes. You'll be fine. You've trained for this."

Nerves ran through me, but I trusted Zoe with my life. She always knew best. I nodded and followed her through the narrow passageways of the base. The air was dry. The thought of what was to come made my heart race.

"Your suit," Zoe said as we reached a massive chamber lined with various high-tech equipment, "is more than just protection. It's a command center, which acts as a channel through which you can control the Immortals. You have spent enough time with the neurosync technology. At times, you might gain an insight into a situation. Do not be alarmed. In a moment, you will feel your temples warm. This will be your first insight."

As soon as she finished and placed the headband on me, everything crystallized in my mind.

The Immortals stood like silent sentries, arranged in hundreds of rows. Each one had a human-like structure, but on a much larger scale. They had two arms and legs, a torso, and a head-like module that housed the primary sensor and control systems.

Each arm was built for combat and utility. Heavy-duty manipulators were equipped with a selection of weapon mounts, including energy emitters, projectile launchers, and melee weapons. The arm's inner workings, hydraulics, servos, and armor plates were visible only during maintenance or repair operations.

Their legs ended in broad feet to distribute their weight.

Despite their bulk, the Immortals were agile. The mechanics of the legs, while usually concealed, combined powerful hydraulics and finely-tuned servos for both strength and flexibility.

Each Immortal's torso housed their power source and core systems. Hardpoints allowed for additional weaponry or utility systems to be attached. The back portion contained thruster units, enabling high-speed maneuverability in the air and in open terrain. Also for overcoming obstacles.

The room was equipped with machines dwarfing even the giant Immortals. There were cranes that could lift an Immortal off the floor, their thick steel arms hanging from the ceiling. A set of tracks allowed the cranes to move across the expanse of the room.

A docking station stood next to each Immortal along with diagnostic and repair equipment. Plasma cutters. Welders. High-precision manipulators for delicate internal work. They whirred on standby, ready to perform any necessary maintenance.

Further in, larger machines loomed. Fabricators, which manufactured new parts or even whole new Immortals given enough time. Their outer shells were dotted with hatches and ports, where raw materials were fed in, and finished parts were ejected. Next to them, storage tanks held reserves of metal alloys, ceramics, and other materials waiting to be used.

The room was not just a storage space. It was a factory, a repair shop, a launching pad. It was where the Immortals were born, where they were maintained, and from where they were deployed. The machines within it were as much a part of the army as the Immortals themselves.

I looked over at my suit. I'd grown used to the way it moved, how it responded to my thoughts before I was even fully aware of them, but commanding an army?

"You want me to take out General Vack, don't you?" I said. I knew her answer even before I asked.

"You will destroy him and his forces."

"Me?"

"I have not told you everything, Kol. Starport City and the Academy *must* be liberated before the Shapers arrive. General Vack must have been the person to call the Shapers. If you don't capture the Academy, those Shapers will only be the first wave."

"I thought I called them when I asked Melody all those questions?"

"No. You did something else. It so happened we detected the Shaper fleet at nearly the same time."

"What did I trigger with my questions, then? I thought what I did was bad?"

"It was, but we don't have time to talk about it right now. You will focus your efforts on freeing Starport City."

"Starport City has defenses, but not enough to stand up to the Shapers again. What are we going to do?"

"Stop and listen to me, Kol. Your mind is ready." Zoe touched my temples, where I wore the headband. "You've been using different parts of your brain without realizing it. The suit's design allows you to interface with the Immortals. As you know, they will respond to your commands through the link. But, because of your dedicated practice, from now on, it will be easier than ever before."

She walked to a large workbench at the far end of the room. My helmet rested there next to one of Melody's interfaces she'd constructed. "I've changed some things with this," she said, holding it out to me, "to enhance your connection deeper, allowing you to coordinate your army more effectively. It'll be easier."

The weight of the helmet in my hands comforted me, and I studied the symbol atop it. Geometry I didn't understand. A circle with many circles inside. The lines crossed over and formed shapes reminding me of petals.

Zoe turned her back to me, allowing me a moment of privacy as I placed the helmet over my head. The visor illuminated, filling my vision with a soft glow before adjusting to transparency. A surge of connections reached out to the systems around me, and instead of it slightly overwhelming me like it usually did before I became comfortable with it, this time, it was smooth. Whatever Zoe did, I liked it.

I could feel the Immortals' consciousnesses waiting to be guided. They were in the hangar, silent giants of metal. They were like the dormant seeds of a vast forest, waiting for the first rain to burst into life.

"Good," Zoe said. "Now, remember, the connection works both ways. They'll respond to you, but you'll also feel what they do. Don't let it overwhelm you. Focus. Your mind is the guiding force."

I swallowed hard.

"Don't be scared, Kol," she said softly. "This is what you were meant to do."

I pushed down my nerves and reached out with my mind, my command reverberating through the vast network of Immortals. A single word would start the war.

"Awaken."

The Immortals stirred. They moved, metal bodies shifting and stirring, an extension of my will coming alive.

Zoe was right. I wouldn't be walking to Starport City. I'd be marching. Marching with an army of Immortals at my command.

"It's time," she said.

My vision was filled with lights and information. "I'm ready."

She placed a hand on my arm and gave it a squeeze. "You

can do this. You are the most important human alive. Everything you have done has led up to this moment. What you do now will resound through all of history. Ten thousand Immortals stand with you. You will be their general. The planet belongs to you."

I turned to the Immortals, their metal bodies glinting in the artificial light of the hangar. These were not mere machines. They were extensions of myself, their senses my senses, their strength my strength.

I would unleash them and find my mother in the Senate.

"How do we get topside?" I asked as I mounted inside my suit.

Zoe directed my attention toward the far end of the hangar. There, I noticed what appeared to be large bay doors, stretching from the floor to well beyond the height of the tallest Immortal. They were seamlessly built into the wall, making them almost invisible unless you knew where to look.

"Those doors lead to exit tunnels," she said. "They connect this underground facility to various points on the surface. Each tunnel is large enough for two Immortals to move through side by side. The tunnels are designed to disperse the units quickly, minimizing the time it takes for the entire force to mobilize."

She paused and touched a button on a control panel. A holographic map appeared in the air between us. It displayed a detailed layout of the surface and the network of tunnels leading to it.

"All tunnels will get you to the surface, but the optimal route for us to take is Tunnel Alpha. It leads directly toward Starport City." She pointed to one specific tunnel on the map. "The Immortals will take the rest of the tunnels, emerging from various locations around the city. This will encircle the city with our forces, cutting off any potential escape routes for our enemies."

"General Vack will have deployed his forces outside of the city. If we move in that way, he will have me surrounded."

The helmet's heads-up display burst alive with data, the projected path through a passageway called Tunnel Epsilon highlighted prominently.

"Kol, if you take that route, you will likely encounter Captain Moore's Janissaries."

I signaled to the army of Immortals. As if a single entity, they began to move, their heavy footsteps pounding on the metallic floor. With a thought, I commanded the bay doors to slowly slide open, revealing the dark maw of the tunnel beyond.

"There is no path to victory where I do not face them," I said.

Zoe motioned to the Immortals. "You will likely lose a significant portion of them if you take that route."

It was time to march, to claim what was rightfully mine. With the Immortals at my command, the planet was within reach.

Still, something wasn't right. I couldn't quite place it. Then it hit me. I could do it a different way.

"Wait," I said. "I have a plan."

CHAPTER FIFTY-THREE

Arcadia
Captain Scott Moore

As an officer, you trained how to remember people's names. You have to focus, associate their name with something about them, that sort of thing. Repeat their names back to them. It all helps. Fighter pilots back home took on call signs, a tradition I intended to keep. It would make my life a lot easier.

The Eos pilots were all females, and I'll be frank, they all looked like Italian supermodels. They'd been asleep for ages, and following their resuscitation, needed physical and cognitive therapy months before they showed up on *Arcadia*'s doorstep. Ambassador K'Hori gave me some insight into their experience and training. None of them had less than a hundred kills, no small measure against the Shapers.

Luna Valerius, one of the pilots, took the moniker Storm because of her short temper. She'd almost slapped Chief one day during a heated argument over shampoo. Turned out, she'd burnt her scalp so bad, she had blisters on her head from the chemicals. From then on, we were careful about what kinds of soap and shampoo they used. All the pilots had super sensitive skin, a product of too much time immersed in cryo gel.

Astraia Kallias became Banshee because whenever one of her trainees scored a kill in our fighter pilot simulators, she'd let loose a short howl.

The list went on. Phoenix. Warhawk. Falcon. Raptor. Hammer. Ghost. Ace.

They were all in their late 20s, with Warhawk being the oldest at 29.

Their leader's name was Wildcat, a fiery redhead with perfect teeth, and a smile that made most of us melt. She knew how to flirt with the best of them. We kept everything professional, but as the months wore on, things got a little spicy. I had to tell Feazer to knock it off. He'd been after Hammer, even going so far as to write her poetry. Poor guy. He'd confessed to me one day that he'd never been with a woman.

By tradition, only women were allowed to be pilots, a custom, I was told, that stretched back into the Regency's early formation. I initially protested because if I could train more pilots, I didn't care what gender they were. Skill was what mattered, nothing else. Then I realized the cockpits aboard were too small to fit men, and I relented under the mounting pressure.

Eos kept sending new recruits to us, and only a fraction passed muster.

As I strode into the flight deck, I took in the atmosphere of brisk efficiency. My boots clicked on the cold metal floor. Massive ceiling-mounted rigs held the fighters in place, their carbon-black hulls swaggering under the artificial lights. These ships were the pride and joy of the pilots. I could sense the undercurrent of fierce competition, a desire to be the best, running through the whole group like an electric charge.

Straight ahead, at the far end of the deck, a cadre of eager pilots was assembled, chatting amongst themselves. They all shared a singular focus, and their bravado, their egos; this was their own culture born out of countless hours in the cockpit and the intense rivalry of their profession.

Training had already begun in earnest. They broke into pairs, starting their pre-flight checks. A flurry of jargon filled the air as they discussed engine thrust, payload capacity, and flight trajectories. The deck buzzed with activity, the quick, sharp orders from the deck commander cutting through the noise.

The flight simulators were next on the docket. Virtual reality pods, equipped with the latest in simulation technology, stood at the ready. They gave the pilots a taste of what they might face in real combat. The women slipped into the pods one by one, their cocky grins replaced with looks of intense concentration as they prepared to engage in virtual dogfights against Melody.

The training drills were grueling. The pilots pushed their ships to the limit, performing high-speed maneuvers and hairpin turns that would make the uninitiated queasy. The roar of engines was deafening.

Throughout the process, they remained sharp. They pushed themselves and their ships to their absolute limits, each one striving to outdo the other, to prove that they were the best.

The grueling pace of training continued for months as the baron continued to enact repairs.

My gaze followed the pilots as they migrated toward the hangar on the lower level, home to the bombers and fighter-bombers. The bombers were engineered for devastating power and payload capacity, and they were quite agile. There was a separate sorority for the bomber pilots, a different vibe, but no less intense.

Engineers and maintenance crews pored over schematics, ran diagnostics, and attended to the each ship. The air was filled with the hiss of hydraulic systems and the rumble of engines on test runs.

"Echo Foxtrot, power levels nominal," an engineer called out at terminal displaying readouts of an idling bomber's engine. "Running final check on EMP shielding."

"Roger, Echo Foxtrot. Prep for Cat launch. Kappa Niner, you're on standby," the deck commander responded. Her voice sliced through the noise like a scalpel.

The bombers and fighter-bombers were imposing, designed to carry an arsenal of high-yield explosives and precision-guided ordnance. They were built for strategic assaults. Where the fighters were like finely-tuned racehorses, the bombers were armored war elephants.

Constructed for speed and maneuverability, the fighters bore an almost predatory design. Their angular frames were intimidating, optimized for both atmospheric and space combat. Wings extended from the central hull, tapered for efficient spatial navigation. These wings housed the primary weapon systems: high-output laser cannons, known for their precision and high cyclic rate. The tail section accommodated potent sublight engines, optimized for sudden bursts of acceleration and evasion. The cockpit, front and center, boasted a 360-degree view, furnished with multi-spectrum sensors.

The bombers had a stockier, heavier appearance, reminiscent of deep-sea predators. Equipped with robust shielding and fortified hull plating, they were built to withstand punishing assaults. Their widened fuselage housed cavernous bomb bays, each filled with a selection of devastating munitions. The dual-engine design facilitated surprising speed for their size, while the layered sensor systems allowed for pinpoint accuracy in munition deployment. Their silhouette, broad and menacing, reflected their destructive potential.

The simulation pods for the bomber pilots were fewer in number but significantly larger, to mimic the increased cockpit space of the larger ships. As with the fighter pilots, the bomber jockeys slid into their respective pods, their faces hardened by concentration. They too were about to engage with a virtual swarm of enemy Shaper craft, though their mission would require more foresight and less seat-of-the-pants improvisation.

"Simulation ready, Captain," Vincent said.

"Start the clock," I replied.

My brother nodded and began the simulation.

Their mock battle involved a simulated enemy installation, complete with anti-aircraft defenses and fighter cover. The action unfolded on the large monitors overhead. The bombers moved in formation, a cluster of blips on the tactical display. They approached the target and then released their virtual payloads in a timed sequence.

"All Valkyries, weapons free," I said.

The Valkyries acknowledged my command. Their fighters appeared as points of light on the display, moving to engage the virtual enemy.

Wildcat said nothing as she watched several screens, which showed the inside of the Valkyrie cockpits. Once in a while, she'd make on-the-fly adjustments to their formation but otherwise let them train unabated.

"Valkyrie One, engaging hostiles," Luna Valerius said, her voice coming over the comms. The others came back with acknowledgements.

On the screen, the first wave of enemies approached, their numbers vastly outnumbering our own. The Shapers would always outnumber us, but we had something they didn't: independent thought.

"Enemy at optimal range, Captain," Commander Chen said.

I nodded, my gaze focused on the tactical map. "Confirmed. Valkyries, launch torpedoes. Ephadria, bring the plasma projectors online."

A series of blips erupted on the screen as the torpedoes were launched. The Valkyries broke formation, pulling back toward *Arcadia* as the torpedoes raced in the direction of the enemy fleet.

"Ephadria, maintain the plasma projectors." My eyes were fixed on the approaching hostile armada.

"Torpedoes impacting," Vincent said.

The enemy shuddered on the display as the torpedoes hit home.

What an impressive sight. These pilots would give our boys back home a run for the money. I watched as the challenging fleet continued to approach. "Valkyries, return to formation." The blips representing the Valkyries began to move back into formation.

"Baron Ephadria, standby on plasma projectors."

"Plasma projectors ready, Captain," Ephadria said. "Awaiting your order."

"Fire."

The plasma projectors erupted into simulated life, sending waves of plasma bolts at the incoming vessels.

On the main screen, the enemy ships splintered under the onslaught, their hulls punctured and breached as the plasma bolts met their targets.

"Direct hits, Captain," Chen said.

"Valkyries, engage the remnants," I ordered.

"Roger that, Captain," came the response, and the Valkyries

dove back into the fray, their fighters darting in and out of the damaged enemy armada.

In the blink of an eye, dozens of hostile ships exploded into a cascade of debris and light. *Arcadia*'s weapons chewed through the enemy's hulls, reducing their once formidable flotilla into a scattered, broken mess.

"Maintain fire," I said.

On the screen, the enemy's return fire seemed to slow, their barrage dampening under *Arcadia*'s relentless assault.

My eyes never left the display. "Keep pushing, Valkyries."

"Captain," Vincent's voice came through with urgency. "The enemy is regrouping. I'm reading multiple hostiles on an intercept course."

My gaze snapped to Vincent, a frown creasing his brow. The enemy vessels bore down on us. Their forms grew larger on the interface.

In that moment, time slowed down, every single detail etched itself into my mind. Our defensive shield indicators flashed from green to yellow as we braced, the barely audible sound of controlled breathing from the crew around me.

"Deploy countermeasures," I said. The words echoed in the silent room like a ripple disturbing a quiet pond.

On the main screen, hundreds of tiny blips of light spread out from our ship, a cloud of metal and technology that swarmed toward the approaching Shaper fleet. As they collided with the enemy, brilliant flashes of light exploded across the display.

Despite the intensity of the scene unfolding before us, we remained silent. The usual conversation and quick exchanges were replaced by an eerie quiet, filled only by the occasional beep from the consoles.

"Intercept course adjusted, Captain," Vincent said. His voice snapped me back to the present and my gaze swiveled to the tactical display. The enemy vessels had veered off their initial course to avoid our countermeasures, giving us precious time.

"Valkyries, take advantage of the break in their lines." My gaze remained on the display. My words were met with a chorus of affirmatives, and the Valkyries plunged into the melee.

Each successful hit from our Valkyries was a brilliant display of destruction on the screen. One by one, enemy vessels succumbed to our relentless assault, their fiery demise lighting up the darkness of space.

I felt a rush of exhilaration as the Shaper fleet's numbers dwindled. It was a grim satisfaction, a feeling smothered by the harsh reality of our simulated situation. To me, this became as real as the real thing.

"We're not done yet," I said. "Continue the assault. Show them no quarter."

Klaxons shattered the silence. The holographic display painted the room a ghostly blue. More enemy loomed on the screen. The interface rippled as our plasma projectors fired.

"Enemy return fire detected," Chen said. "Impact in 3... 2..."

The ship shook. Alarms blared.

"Deploy countermeasures," I said.

Streaks of light burst forth from our ship. They reached the Shaper fleet. Each impact obliterated an enemy ship.

Soon, it ended.

We'd won.

Normality resumed in an instant. The whir of the simulation pods faded into silence. The pilots emerged as if waking from a dream, frazzled yet eager for another round. There were exchanges of triumphant glances, silent acknowledgments of a challenge well-met. Handshakes morphed into forearm bumps. The emergency illumination dimmed, giving way to the comforting glow of routine lighting. My heart raced. Adrenaline coursed through my veins. A single sweat droplet traced a path down my face. I had been engrossed, treating every simulated moment with the gravity of a real battle. I could only hope my team felt the same depth of engagement.

Coffee.

I needed a full pot of it.

Wildcat tossed me a look as her red locks trailed down her shoulders. "The Shapers will not be this easy."

"I can up the number of ships," Vincent said. "Make it a lot harder on your Valkyries."

She turned to Vincent. "I've managed to train a handful of pilots, five hundred and six to be specific. If we face the Shapers, our numbers won't be enough."

"How do you know that, Wildcat?" I asked.

"*Arcadia* is a prize, Captain. They want nothing more than to destroy it."

"Then we'll have to redouble our efforts. *Arcadia* can handle its own," I said. "We've fought them before."

"Sir, from what I've been told in passing, you engaged a reserve fleet meant to blockade Kahwin," Wildcat said. "If they discover *Arcadia*'s whereabouts, they'll come in force."

"We'll meet their force in kind," I replied.

There was one thing I didn't like about simulations. They weren't as real as we needed them to be. We'd learned our lesson early on with *Atlanta*. Still, everything had fallen into place. We might just be able to squeak out a win.

After training, I met up with the baron in a makeshift bar we'd set up to help speed up the normalization of our clashing cultures. If you've ever been in a Louisiana speakeasy, the ones with crates for chairs and pallets for tables, you wouldn't feel out of place here. Vincent gave it the name The Moonshine Club. Normally, it'd be filled with people, but not at this hour. It was completely empty.

"I hope you're enjoying the coffee, Baron," I said as I poured more rich dark brew into a pair of ceramic cups.

The baron was a teetotaler. Alcohol didn't sit well with him. Coffee it was. "It's quite pleasing."A faint smile crossed his lips. "Different from the spiced infusions back on Eos. You put creamer in yours."

"It's close. The fabricators haven't quite figured out how to make it. How are the repairs coming along?"

The baron's smile faded slightly. "Without the Numix Device, we are somewhat... hampered."

"In what way?"

"The device powered many critical systems. Without it, progress is much slower than anticipated."

"How long are we looking at for the full repair?"

The baron's eyes met mine. "To return *Arcadia* to peak condition? Decades."

His words hit me like a punch to the mouth. "Decades?" My voice choked with disbelief.

"I'm afraid there's no easy solution. We're doing the best we can. The problem isn't merely mechanical. There are power and software systems, artificial intelligence matrices, sensor arrays, and countless other subsystems that were fried, and those are just the ones we've been able to catalog thus far. My people are working triple shifts to get *Arcadia* back online as quickly as possible."

"So, we're stuck. I don't have decades."

"If *Arcadia* meets the Shapers without the proper repairs, you're likely to lose her."

"I have people back on Kahwin. I can't stay here that long." A convenient truth, but it wasn't the real reason. We needed to get home.

"I have a request, Captain. You have chief weapons officer, Lieutenant Jesus Luiz Gomez, in charge of *Arcadia*'s weapons, but no one knows them better than me. I'd like to replace him."

"Normally, I'd ask you about your qualifications. Gomez is a good man."

"I'm better. No one knows *Arcadia*'s weapons better than me," the baron repeated.

"That right? Well, I'll talk with him. I'll be honest with you, I want to trust you, but I've had issues before with personnel. I'd ask you how I know I can trust you, but that question always strikes me as stupid. Gomez is more than qualified to help in other parts of the ship. I'll let him know."

"Thank you, Captain. I won't let you down. If you wanted to know how you can trust me, I'll tell you this: I am more than ready to give my life on a moment's command. You do not understand our ways, but you will find us to be the most loyal people under your leadership." He reached into his vest and slowly withdrew a dagger and held it in the palm of his hand.

I simply stared at him.

"You have but to give the word, and I will take my own life, as will the rest of us."

"I'd rather not test that, Baron."

He stuffed it back in his vest. "All of us carry such a blade, Captain. Honor and duty are keys to the survival of our people. Without it, we fall upon each other. I am as devoted to you and *Arcadia* as I am to my heritage."

"We had several dark matter cannons last I checked and," I said, thinking back, "a gravity bell."

"They were tied in directly to the Numix Device. I'm sorry, Captain, but I cannot replace those."

I'd wanted to ask the ambassador for help locating Earth, but inside the system, it was impossible to gain a fix on any particular star, a side effect from the tech used to hide Eos in the first place.

How long would it take to find a grain of sand on a beach? We knew the general direction but with only two jumps, we had to be sure.

For a moment, the baron was silent, lost in his thoughts. "I've waited all my life to see this ship. I never thought I'd see it in person." His bloodshot eyes stared into the coffee mug. "If my family could see me, I wonder what they'd say."

"If your work is any judge of character, I'd say they'd be as proud of you as I am. Without your help, I don't know what we'd do."

"*Ramedis*. She's beautiful. It's an honor to be here."

"What's that?"

"*Ramedis*. The name of the ship."

"Wait a second. We renamed this ship *Arcadia*, but I thought this vessel was originally called the *Offer Vit*."

"Where did you hear that?" he asked.

"On Kahwin. We found clues about this ship there, and it took us years to find it."

He poured himself another cup. "No, *Offer Vit* is another ship. The *Offer Vit* no longer exists. It disappeared during the Heaven War."

"How can that be? Every clue we found pointed to this ship as the *Offer Vit*."

"I'm not sure, Captain. After a time, myths become so obscured, it's hard to make sense of them."

As his words echoed in the room, a soft chime cut through the silence. My gaze shifted to the holographic display behind the bar, which was now blinking with an incoming message.

I directed my attention to the display. "I have to take this."

"Of course." He stepped out to give me some privacy.

It was from Lieutenant Commander Chen. "Moore here."

Her face filled the display. "Captain, we've received an SOS."

An SOS. The words echoed in my mind, a chill of dread coursing down my spine. "From where?"

"Kahwin, sir," she said.

"Impossible. Communications can't penetrate the Eos System."

"That's what I thought also, Captain. The signal's clear. It's from Zoe."

For an instant, I went numb. "Zoe? Are you sure?"

"Yes, Captain. There's no doubt about it. The message is from her."

"Keep the channels open," I said. "Do everything you can to maintain contact."

"The signal hasn't been repeated, sir," Chen responded.

"Did she say anything else?"

"We did manage to decipher a fragment of the transmission. It cut off abruptly after a single word was sent."

"What was it?"

"'Help.'"

My pulse began to race. "I'm on my way to the bridge. Moore out."

I found Baron Ephadria waiting for me. "Something wrong?"

"Would it be possible to move your staff on the ship?"

"I don't understand."

"We're leaving for Kahwin immediately."

"But the repairs..."

"Can you or can't you?"

He hesitated. "Yes, Captain. It will take time to ferry everyone from our ships."

"You have 24 hours."

CHAPTER FIFTY-FOUR

Montana, USA
Scott Moore
December 25th
2178, 7 years prior to launch

We trudged through the fresh powder that blanketed the ground in a white sheath, our footprints marking a distinct path toward the old log cabin nestled amongst the Montana evergreens. Built over a century ago by our grandparents, the house was regularly a source of comfort to gaze upon for me. My gramps crafted the two-story home, my grandma gave it heart, and my parents raised me, my brother, and my sister here. It had always felt safe.

Except now.

A plume of smoke flowed from the chimney. The crisp scent of burning wood filled the air, and above the door, a basic Christmas wreath made from dried pine branches and red berries hung proudly, a touch of my sister's simple taste. It'd stopped snowing a few hours ago.

I knocked on the heavy oak door and closed my eyes for a second and swallowed the rising nausea. I'd killed a man. Pete said I didn't have a choice; it was either us or him. Behind me, Vincent's hand trembled, and not from the cold.

Pete held two grocery bags of MREs, Meal Ready-to-Eat rations: chili, beef stew, chicken with noodles, crackers, bread, fruit drinks, and instant coffee and tea. A small bag of rice and a can of beans were tucked inside as well.

We covered our tracks all the way from the cave to my truck. During the drive to my sister's house, Pete watched from my truck's rear window and made sure no one followed us.

Maybe someone did. The thought gnawed at me. If I led a dangerous person to my sister's home, I'd never forgive myself.

My sister Sarah opened the door, her body bathed in the soft glow of candlelight behind her. She smiled warmly, her hair tied back in a loose ponytail. Her son, Logan, a miniature version of her with an unruly mop of hair, peeked out from between her legs. The six-year-old clutched a teddy bear. His wide eyes sparkled when he saw me.

"Uncle!" Logan sprang at me, his arms raised.

I grabbed him in a hug. It was hard to grin with a death hanging over my head. I did anyway. "Well, hello!" I set him down and he jumped all over Vincent.

Sarah waved us in. "Don't stay out in the cold. Come in."

As we walked inside, she motioned to the coat rack. We hung our coats and Pete shut the door, Logan still in Vincent's arms.

Despite the lack of electricity, due to the government's rationing, Sarah managed to grace her house with the spirit of Christmas. In the living room stood a small, spindly tree, its branches heavy with handmade ornaments and popcorn strings. Delicate paper snowflakes hung from the ceiling.

Candles were lit on just about every shelf, table, and even on the fireplace's mantel above the roaring fire.

Sarah studied my eyes and worry crowded her face. "What's wrong?"

"What do you mean?" I asked.

"You look like someone died," she said.

Vincent shuffled back a step. "Logan, gonna set you down now, okay?"

Pete chuckled. "I'm always telling Scott he'd be a great extra in a horror flick."

Sarah shot him a confused look.

Pete hesitated. "You know, his ghostly face and... never mind." He gestured to his bags. "We've got a lot more food in the truck. I'll bring them in soon."

We brought enough provisions to last my sister and nephew for months.

"We forgot the..." From the expression on my face, Sarah figured it out quickly. Not that I killed a man, but that I didn't remember to bring Logan's presents. They were stolen out of Vincent's truck, but it wouldn't be wise to talk about the story. Clothes. Games. Toys. Gone. I also had new digs for Sarah. Those taken too.

Sarah's happy demeanor fell. "You're kidding, right?"

"What did he forget, Mom?" Logan tugged at her pants.

She huffed. "Nothing. Just adult stuff." She gave me an evil glare for a second.

Logan sat on his knees and played with a toy car. "What's adult stuff?"

Sarah eyed me. "Stuff that your uncle and I planned and talked about for a month now."

"Like what?" Logan pushed the vehicle across the wooden floor.

She ran her fingers through his hair. "Nothing. All that matters is our family is here."

Twenty minutes later, I used the propane stove in the kitchen to cook the food, and I had my little nephew to thank for helping me actually forget the most recent events. Or to at least ease the memory of a man dying under my weapon.

As I prepared the meal with my sister, Logan asked me a hundred questions a minute. All from what it's like flying a ship in outer space to if I've ever seen a bird land on someone's shoulder.

Shortly after, the rustic dining table groaned under the weight of a humble, hearty feast laid out in the candlelight. The flames cast shadows that competed with the sparse light on the rough-hewn cabin beams overhead.

Pete bowed his head and closed his eyes, his hands folded in prayer. "Dear Lord," he began, "we thank you for this meal, for the love that binds us, and for the roof over our heads. As we gather here today, we pray for strength, grace, and mercy. And most of all, forgiveness. Amen."

A silence lingered for an instant until Vincent spoke up. "Thanks for gracing us with your superstition, Pete." He winked, a joke they'd bantered about too many times for who knew how long.

"Well," Pete replied without missing a beat, "this here hocus pocus done saved my hide on more than a few times." He tapped his heart with his index and middle finger, kissed his fingertips, and pointed at the ceiling. "Thank you, Lord."

Sarah nursed a bowl of rice and beans, her dish distinctly separate from ours due to her dietary restrictions. Tulick's disease had ravaged her ever since I could remember.

I took a bite of chili before reaching into my pocket. I never planned on giving this away, but things change. I pulled out my pocket watch. The 18-karat gold case shined in the candlelight.

The perfect etching of the oak tree on the cover, the meticulous Roman numerals on the dial, the hypnotic movement of the inner workings visible through a small window—it was an expensive elegance of impeccable craftsmanship I purchased for top dollar in France.

I handed it to my nephew. "Merry Christmas."

Logan's eyes lit up as he held the watch, his hands dwarfed by the timepiece's substantial size. His excitement was so vivid, he almost dashed off to play with his new toy, but Sarah's voice reined him in.

"No, Logan. Stay and eat, and thank your uncle first," she said.

He kept his eyes on his present. "Thank you, Uncle Scott."

Sarah turned her gaze toward me and gave me a grateful smile. She mouthed a silent "thank you" and added, "For everything."

As I swallowed each morsel, I could barely keep any of it down. Pete said to forget about the incident. My mind wouldn't and my stomach and my nerves did their best to push out anything I ate.

Gladly, I kept it all down. Still, my appetite was gone and I consumed little.

After dinner, Pete brought out his guitar as we gathered around the fireplace. How could he be so calm after what happened?

"Any requests?" Pete asked.

Vincent lay on his back and interlaced his fingers over his belly. "Whatever helps me relax and forget things, then I'm good."

Sarah gave me a cup of hot cocoa and sat next to me, propping her shoulder against mine. "Frosty the Snow Man."

"Yeah!" Logan perched in my lap and I wrapped my arm around him, pulling him in tightly.

I nodded. "Play it, Pete."

Pete grinned. "Aye, aye, Captain."

As Pete gently sang the song, we swayed in rhythm with one another, joining him. Even my brother lent us his voice.

Outside, the snow began its gentle descent. I watched it through the window while we all nestled together by the warmth of the steady fire.

CHAPTER FIFTY-FIVE

Kahwin
The Scalding Ruins
Kol Washington

With a thought, I activated the jump jets on the Immortals. It was an indescribable sensation, feeling the roar of the jets, the sudden burst of speed, as I was being propelled forward. In a synchronized maneuver, we leapt into the sky and cleared the confines of the base.

The forest was a sea of green with trees towering high into the cloudy sky. The view from above was breathtaking. An unbroken carpet stretching as far as the eye could see, lush and vibrant. I felt the Immortals react to the terrain. Their sensors mapped out the landscape and identified potential threats.

It was good to be outside again.

We pushed on, soaring over the treetops, the wind whipping around us. As the forest passed beneath us, the surge of adrenaline burned hot in my veins. Despite the rush, I couldn't ignore the fear gnawing in my chest.

As the forest thinned out, the lights of Starport City winked in the distance. Its massive walls and force field surrounding the city would be difficult to breach. A sense of awe washed over me. Was this really happening to me? I smiled. What would my mother say to me now? I wanted to make Zoe proud.

I signaled for the Immortals to descend, guiding them toward a clearing on the outskirts of the city. As we touched down, I felt the vibrations through their feet, a strange sensation from the neural link. We stood there, on the edge of the city, an army ready to march on command. I steeled my nerves.

"Honor," Zoe had said, "was all there was. Without it, a man was nothing other than blood and bones." The Greeks on planet Earth valued honor. The Japanese had followed a strict warrior code.

I knew I'd lose a number of my Immortals that day.

Honor demanded it.

As we neared Starport City, my HUD registered a blip, then two, then several more, rapidly increasing. A sortie of General Vack's drones closed in on us. I stopped and focused on the lead drone.

Open a channel with General Vack, I ordered the drone.

Static.

An image of the general appeared on my HUD. He stood inside the Academy, surrounded by military personnel in what must have been a control room. Maps of the city glowed on screens in the background as his operators flashed into action. Officers barked orders. Non-commissioned officers responded like the professionals they were. I respected the Academy, and they knew we were coming.

I haven't talked about The Punishment Farm much, but I remember the killings. The firing squads. The obscenities I left out of my recanting. I remembered it all. What good was it to dwell on things in the past? I kept those experiences tucked away deep inside me during my time in Project 1.

When I saw General Vack's face, they all came bubbling to the forefront.

"General Vack," I said.

The general sneered. "I see Zoe trained you."

"A Shaper fleet numbering in the tens of thousands is descending upon Kahwin. Did you call them?"

General Vack's command room quieted, and several of his officers crowded around.

"What have you done, Kol?" the general asked.

"I will be marching the Immortals into the Academy. Stand down."

The general's jaw tightened as he squared his shoulders and locked eyes with me. "Kol Washington, now you listen to me carefully, boy. Now isn't the time for games. If you've found Project 1, you will surrender it to the Academy immediately, and *you* will stand down."

"General Vack, ten thousand Immortals stand with me. I do not want bloodshed."

"Now, you listen here!"

Lady Kullen leaned around him. There was a person I hadn't thought of in a while. "Mr. Washington, we've been trying to find you." She called herself First Among Equals. She would soon find how equal she was. Dark eyeshadow brought her blue-green eyes to life, and the white jumpsuit she wore fit snugly. Her collar reached up past her neck, where her hair cascaded down her shoulders. Clearly, I'd been away from women for far too long.

"Lady Kullen," I said, not sure what to say to her.

"We would like to meet with you. If the Shapers are inbound, you can help us with our city's defenses."

With a show of force, I focused on a single console inside the command center, but nothing happened. Zoe was right. The machines at the Academy were different.

"I wish to speak with the Senate," I said. "Who is in command?"

General Vack nodded to one of his subordinates. "Show him."

"No!" Lady Kullen yelled before the communication link died.

My heart skipped a beat about her offer to join forces to hold back the incoming Shapers. Wasn't Vack the one who signaled the Shapers like Zoe suggested?

"Zoe, do you copy?" I asked, using the lingo I'd learned from the Academy.

"I'm here," she said through my helm's comms.

"Are you sure General Vack called the Shapers?"

"Yes. There isn't much time. I'm currently jamming transmissions from the Academy, but if you don't capture the Academy in the next three hours, they'll find a way to send another signal to the Shapers. Don't believe their lies."

Sensor blips appeared on my HUD. "The Janissaries have arrived." There they were, on the other side of the clearing. They stood in front of the city, until as one, they headed in our direction.

"Destroy them."

"Are you sure?" I said.

"They will fight to the death to stop you. If you don't destroy them, General Vack will send his signal. Hurry, Kol. There isn't time."

What did it matter if he sent another signal since he already sent one in the first place? All I knew was Zoe was far smarter than me, so questioning her, especially right now, would only slow things down.

With a final glance at the city, I gave the order. Nothing would ever be the same. All of this, even the Janissaries, belonged to Captain Moore. What would I say to him? Did he even care about us? If he did, he would have stayed in the city.

"Prepare for engagement." My voice reverberated through the neural network.

The Immortals maneuvered into battle formations. With a mental command, they launched a salvo of Long Range Missiles. The sky lit up as the missiles streaked through the air, leaving trails of smoke and fire. They arced and descended upon the Janissaries in a shower of destruction.

Explosions blossomed across the battlefield. The ground trembled beneath our feet, the sound of the impacts deafening even within the insulated confines of my suit. The smoke did little to cloud my vision as my sensors picked up the enemy's movements.

The Janissaries were thrust into a state of disarray. They scattered, some seeking cover, others attempting to identify the source of the attack. Zoe must have been jamming them too. Communication lines died, but data streamed into my suit from Project 1.

My mind churned through various tactics I'd studied. A brilliant general had redefined tank warfare during a great conflict on Earth. It wasn't about overwhelming force. It was about flexibility, rapid movement, and concentration of forces at decisive points. I'd have to identify a weak point in the enemy's defensive line, focus a strong force at that point to break through, and push deep into the enemy's territory to divide their forces.

"Concentrate a team at the flank, using the cover of the forest to mask your approach. Once you've broken through the Janissaries' defensive line, press forward, exploiting the breach," I said. "Move into position and await my command to attack."

I organized my force and the Immortals repositioned themselves with ease. The trees provided cover, and although we numbered in the thousands, the Janissaries outnumbered us two to one. When you attack, the suggested ratio would be three to one in the attackers favor. I had an uphill battle ahead of me before I even reached the city.

New dots appeared. A screaming barrage of pain headed our way.

The Janissaries launched a salvo of incendiary Short Range missiles. Upon impact, fire erupted from the forest surrounding us. Orange flames gave rise to smoke.

Through the haze of the explosions, dozens of the Immortals crumpled under the force of retaliatory fire. Their signals faded from the network as their consciousness slipped away.

I clenched my fists. "Regroup."

CHAPTER FIFTY-SIX

Kahwin
Kol Washington

My gaze swept over the battlefield, the burning forest casting a fiery glow over the armored forms of the Janissaries. I took a deep breath and initiated my plan.

"Flank team," I ordered through the communication channel connecting me to the Immortals. "Move to position Bravo. Keep your profiles low, use the fire and smoke for cover."

Even as I gave the command, I felt my consciousness stretch out to the Immortals assigned to the flank team. Through their sensors, I saw the forest floor rushing beneath them, felt the heat of the fires, the whine of their engines as they accelerated.

As the flank team moved into position, I turned my attention to the rest of the Immortals. "Brace for assault."

The Immortals replied with a chorus of acknowledgments.

When the flank team was in position, I gave the order. "Charge!"

The response was immediate. The flank team surged forward and unloaded their weapons, their engines flaring brightly in the darkness. The Janissaries' defensive line grew closer and broke apart under the onslaught of the Immortals. It was a scene pulled from the training room, of these machines funneling a gap in the enemy line.

"All units, push forward!" I commanded.

The rest of the Immortals sprang into action as they followed the breach created by the flank team.

I engaged my jump pack and took to the sky, gaining a better understanding of the battlefield. The flank attack ripped into the Janissaries like an arrow, breaking their forces in half as the Janissaries fought back to slow our momentum. Explosions. Fire. Smoke blanketed the field.

The lead Janissary sported two shoulder-mounted rocket launchers and wielded a triple-barreled plasma rifle, the same kind many of the Immortals carried. I brought up my railgun, locked onto him, and fired.

The Janissary staggered back from the impact. Flames erupted from its chest seconds before it exploded in a ball of fire.

My jetpack meter, which told me how much time I could stay airborne, started to plummet into the red. I fired again, dropping another. Hundreds of Janissaries flooded into the breach, and on the horizon, I made out a thousand shapes heading our way. They'd called for reinforcements.

I brought my suit down in a burning crater right as an explosion took out a swathe of my forces.

Zoe's face appeared on my HUD. "General Vack has found a way past my jamming. He's powering up his transmitter." A timer started to click down. "In fifteen minutes, the Academy will contact the Shaper fleet."

"I can't possibly defeat all these Janissaries in fifteen minutes! Isn't there anything you can do?"

Zoe's voice turned serious. "I can buy you ten more minutes

by shutting myself down and focusing all my energy on the Academy's comm system. If I do, I'll be unable to advise you further. The choice is yours."

I knew full well I was way over my head. Losing her would mean losing the battle.

"I can't let you do that."

"There's no other way."

By the moons of Kahwin. "I'm scared of the Shapers."

"In war, there is no substitute for victory," Zoe said.

Where had I heard that before? "There's something you're not telling me."

"You must decide quickly, or I won't be able to stop him."

I winced. There was no good answer. "Do it. I'll see you soon."

"Good luck, my friend." Her signal vanished. Those were the last words I heard before I was plunged back into war.

Without warning, the Janissaries launched their counterattack.

We received a strong volley of enemy missiles. The air shook with a deafening roar. Metal met metal. The concussive blasts tore through my ranks. A dozen immortals erupted into a fiery mess, their bodies disintegrating into a thousand fragments. Amidst the storm, most of the Immortals stood their ground, weathering the onslaught.

I ordered a retreat to a protected spot south of the main battlefield. Janissary reinforcements attempted to cross the plains north of our location.

"Engage the Janissaries with Long Range Missiles!"

Our missiles landed in the Janissaries' assembly point. The canopy above the Janissaries, who had only just begun their crossing, exploded into a spectacle of shattered green and cracked brown as the projectiles sliced through with relentless accuracy. Once majestic trees were yanked from their roots, reduced to charred pieces. Countless Janissaries detonated into showers of sharp, deadly debris. And as soon as it had begun, it was over. The enemy gave up on their attempt to cross the field at that location.

A second wall of missiles screamed out from their lines toward our ranks. The Immortals responded by deploying swarms of anti-missile drones. The air above us ignited. Bursts of flame popped as most of the missiles were intercepted. The few penetrating our defenses exploded upon impact, churning the earth. Immortals were thrown into disarray, many burning wrecks.

The Janissary line surged forward. Hundreds bore down on us.

"Brace!" I ordered.

The Immortals tightened their formation, creating a barrier of armored bodies.

Plasma fire met with whirring railguns. The exchange lit up everything around me. The enemy sought to exploit any gaps. That was what I'd do. They lunged at us, their bodies clashing head-on with ours.

I formed two separate companies of Immortals, who remained in reserve and had them set up an ambush amongst the trees and dismembered robots from each side. When the incoming Janissaries came into full view, they'd be cut down.

Although I stood in the back, directing the battle, I felt every death, every parry, every blow.

"Counterattack!" I ordered.

The Immortals responded. Our lines advanced, each step taking us further into the heart of the Janissary ranks. Their numbers thinned rapidly.

Seizing the initiative, I gathered a group of 500 Immortals and made them form a shield wall in front of our lines. Their heavy armored bodies interlocked to create a barrier. With a mental command, they marched forward in unison.

I locked my rifle to my arm and drew my spear as I created a force field covering my other arm and most of my body.

While the shield wall held firm against the Janissaries' fire-power, I ordered a contingent of 2,000 Immortals to launch a high-altitude aerial strike, leveraging the jump jets to soar above the battlefield. Suspended against the scorched sky, they rained down a salvo of Long Range Missiles, destroying the enemy's middle ranks.

I was about to take a breath of relief, when a Janissary fired from the hilltop on the other side of our position. The missile hit an Immortal close to me and penetrated its frontal armor, and another missile tagged me. The hard blow sent me reeling inside the suit.

I'd never felt so alive being so close to death. How a strange a feeling it was.

Summoning up all of my strength, I crawled a few meters off to the side and moved through a tall field of debris back to my previous position. My comm system blinked and spat out error messages, and my suit's power supply whined uncontrollably. When I tried to stand, my left leg wouldn't respond, and I slipped back into the dirt.

Janissaries broke ranks and raced toward my location.

We had to continue the attack, even if I couldn't move.

The advancing enemy units stopped to launch their strike. Their missiles screamed over my head. I ducked in a depression and caught sight of the lead Janissary. I lined it up in my sights, and fired.

In seconds, the lead's torso was ripped from its base, slid along the ground, and crashed. A missile screamed past me in their direction and smashed into one of the middle Janissaries. It exploded in all directions.

My Immortals rushed to protect me, some providing covering fire. A few dove into the crater by my side.

With a whirring of servos and the crunch of hydraulics, an Immortal kneeled beside me, its armored knee hitting the ground with thud. A cloud of dust billowed around its lower half. One of its large, claw-like hands reached out and steadied my injured leg. The other hand moved to a compartment along its waist. It slid a panel open to reveal a tool kit. It picked through the selection of tools, finally deciding on a high-powered laser cutter. Cutting away my damaged circuitry, the Immortal replaced it with new parts.

Another Immortal used a cutter to remove my damaged armor plating. Twisted metal and shattered hydraulics lay underneath. Next, it selected a plasma welder and a chunk of spare metal from its kit. Its massive hands welded the metal piece over the damaged area, restoring the structural integrity of the leg.

I concentrated on the conflict. So many of us were dying. I couldn't think straight.

Once the repair was completed, the assisting Immortals powered down their tools and placed them back into their kits. They pushed itself upright. It was a routine repair, but not here on the battlefield. I hadn't ordered them to do it, not consciously.

Everything crystallized.

My forces had moved into position on instinct and gave ground when necessary. The Janissaries failed to notice they'd been sucked into a pincer attack.

I rose to my feet and stared down the remaining enemy. "All forces, engage!"

The Janissaries, caught off guard by the sudden counterattack from above, began to falter. This was the opening we needed.

Another force of 3,000 Immortals used the distraction to swing wide around the battlefield, executing a flanking maneuver utilizing the smoke as concealment, which blurred my optics.

With my remaining Immortals, I led a direct charge against the Janissaries. Jump jets filled the air, followed by the earth-shaking impact of Immortals landing behind the enemy lines.

The slaughter began.

I jumped toward the largest Janissary and rammed my spear through his face, exploding it.

The remaining Janissaries flew in behind us.

Right where I wanted them.

"Fire!"

Withering fire from our ambush blistered the air, and the enemy began to scatter. Detonations rumbled. Nothing sounds like two companies of Immortals unleashing railgun fire at close to point-blank range. The enemy never knew what hit them.

Our forces attacked from the front, the sides, and from behind until we surrounded the rest of the enemy. It was a classic encirclement maneuver; one I'd studied hundreds of times.

What followed was an all-out offensive that swept through the Janissaries like a devastating tide as both sides engaged in close-quarters fighting. Fists and swords replaced railgun and plasma fire, and the ground shook.

The tide of battle began to turn. The Janissaries couldn't withstand my coordinated attack.

It seemed to happen in an instant.

As the last of the Janissaries fell, the battlefield fell silent, save for the crackling of fires and the groan of cooling metal. Robotic limbs lay scattered across the field.

I'd lost half of my force. How could I possibly march on Starport City now?

"Zoe?" I asked. "Can you read me?"

Nothing.

Static.

"Kol...wrong. I can't... System failing."

In the distance, the force field surrounding Starport City faded in intensity like a candle ready to burn out.

"Zoe, can you read me?" I repeated.

An indigo pulse, like a tremor in reality itself, rippled across the surface of the energy shield. The dome flickered, growing erratic. It faltered and collapsed. The shimmer that had once painted the sky died.

With the force field gone, Starport City would be vulnerable and the walls more easily breached.

The districts below the towers followed suit. Residential spires dimmed. Markets turned silent. The bustling spaceport at the heart of the city was the last to fade. Its sprawling docking platforms and towering control towers gradually sank into darkness.

Almost out of view, I made out the only place still powered by electricity—the Academy.

Text ran across my HUD. "Shapers entering system in thirty-eight hours." It blinked off when a message from General Vack flashed on my display. I accepted the transmission.

"It's over," the general said. "Zoe is dead."

My heart sank. How did he know her name anyway? "That's impossible."

A new image appeared on screen. Thousands of Academy personnel swarmed inside Project 1. Zoe's lifeless body was surrounded by soldiers in camouflaged powered armor, their MAS-5s aimed at her. I glanced at their insignia.

Equinox? No. It was the one I saw during graduation.

"Project 1 belongs to me now," General Vack said.

I flung my consciousness to the base, but nothing happened. Where was the power? Zoe wouldn't answer me either. "What...what have you done? We're all going to die."

"I've established order. Meet me in the city. I have something to show you."

"I'm not walking into your trap, General. I'm going to kill you for what you've done. You're a traitor."

General Vack reached off screen for something. A woman yelped. He dragged her closer by the hair. Her face was so bruised up, I hardly recognized her.

"Kol?" my mother asked.

"Mom!"

The general pushed her to the side. "You have one hour to meet me at the Academy, or bruises will be *the least* of her worries. Come alone."

"I'm on my way."

CHAPTER FIFTY-SEVEN

Kahwin
Starport City
Kol Washington

The moment I stepped into the Academy, guards swarmed me and threw me in cuffs. I'd expected as much. I'd arrived without my suit for obvious reasons and told my Immortals to launch an attack when I gave the order or if I fell unconscious... or worse.

The same stale metallic smell clung to the Academy. Security searched me, and finding nothing, blindfolded me and escorted me to General Vack. It took forever to reach him as we marched down staircase after staircase and stepped into elevator after elevator that led us lower into the bowels of the place. I hated being back here with every fiber of my being. All I could think about was my mother.

"Remove his blindfold," General Vack said.

Finally, I could see, and I winced as my eyes adjusted to the light.

The grand room's vaulted ceilings held paintings depicting

old, bearded men hovering above voluminous clouds, their half naked torsos covered by white cloth.

Rows of banners hung from the walls, each one bearing the same symbols I'd seen at Project 1. One bore a cross, stark black against a white circle on a red background. There were others too. One held blue and white stripes intersected by a cross with white edges and a square blue center. Another hung silently beside it, showing an eagle in flight, its talons clutching thunderbolts.

The room, a coiling helix of circles, sloped toward the epicenter. On each level, glass-encased relics lay displayed, but the glass was too tinted to make out any details of what was inside.

I first noticed a geometric object about the size of a large flag. It looked like a stone carved with random angles. Faintly glowing circuits covered it. A symbol written above it radiated energy, and it crystallized into the words "Quantum Navigatrix Hyperspace Navigation Traverse Engine."

A floating metallic disc levitated beside it. Luminous nodes on its surface emitted a radiant purple glow, and it was bound together by metal tendrils, culminating in a crystalline apex. The symbol above it read "Hypercore Singularity Reactor."

To the right, a helmet-like object reflected the light. It had nodes and wires on its surface, indicating a blend of bio-tech. Alloy spines ended in softly glowing crystals. Maybe it was a neural enhancer, used to command armies like the one Zoe made me wear.

Behind Vack, small, spherical drones lay inactive. Their scale-covered exteriors gleamed like glass, suggesting each scale could act as a mini screen. Surveillance tools? Repair bots?

Underfoot, dark veined material mimicked polished marble and threw back a mirror image of the room. Faded glyphs and equations spiraled across the floor. Cushioned corners and low tables sat at the outskirts.

In the heart of the room, a dormant holographic projector stood like a crystal-metal tree, its surface etched with unreadable markings, like claw scratches you'd find in the forest.

Obviously, I was impressed, and obviously, I refused to show it.

"Now, Kol," General Vack said. His black uniform and polished jackboots made him seem taller than he actually was, but it was his holstered pistol around his hip that caught my eye immediately. He reminded me a lot of the warlords I'd studied with Melody. "It's time we have a little chat."

I rubbed my wrists, raw from the metal digging into my skin. "General, I need to know if my mother's safe. I'd like to speak with her."

"Paysha is safe." He held up a finger, and the metal tree flung a holographic projection of my mother inside a small room no larger than a storage closet. Her bed, if you could call it that, had a thin mattress laid over a metal frame, and a toilet stood across from it. As soon as I started to concentrate on the tree, the image vanished.

"You have me. Let her go."

"You were right to come here. In days, the Shapers will be upon us in force." He gestured around the room. "You can read these images, can't you?"

"You killed Zoe!"

The general gazed at one of the many display cases. "Zoe cannot be killed. She has been disabled. That is all. By the time she awakens, all of this will be over. What has Zoe told you about the Academy?"

I narrowed my eyes. "General Vack, release my mother and we can talk."

"I own Project 1. Your mother is under my protection. You are not in a position to demand *anything*, boy."

His tone made me purse my lips in anger. "If anything happens to me or my mother, my Immortals have instructions to march on Starport City, lay siege to the Academy, and remove it from the face of the planet. *You* are the one not in a position to negotiate."

"And what will you do once the Shapers arrive? Your Immortals will be swept aside without much effort."

"I'll stop them."

His face turned red. "You'll stop nothing."

I took a moment to gather myself before I said something I might have regretted. "Then what?"

"There is no way to stop the Shapers. We must evacuate Kahwin."

"But Lady Kullen said..."

"Lady Kullen does not understand what the Academy is, and neither do you, it seems."

I folded my arms. "How would we evacuate Kahwin? There's no place to go."

General Vack pointed at the ceiling. "Of course there is. Out there in the stars."

As I shook my head, I tried to piece his statements together. "We don't have a ship. I don't understand."

Right above him, I noticed a symbol I'd seen drawn by the linguistics doctor—a stylized mountain peak with a smooth, upward-sweeping curve. At the curve's pinnacle, there was a small hollow circle inside of it. You know when you see something or read something, and you could swear you've seen it before? The Earthers call it déjà vu.

The general walked over to a wall and pounded his fist against it. "You stand inside of one, Kol. The Academy *is* a ship, the same type of ship Captain Moore claimed for himself."

I glanced at my feet. "This place?"

"This is a replica of *Offor Vit*, Bringer of Life. The Regency built this. Within these halls lies over ten million citizens of the Regency. Now that I've gained control of Project 1, I will have the necessary fabricators and machines to launch it. With your army of Immortals, we can find a new place to live, far from the reaches of the Shapers."

Wait, what did he say? *Offor Vit*? This time, I could read it. "That's not what Offor Vit means, General."

"What did you say?"

"The term 'Offor Vit' comes from 'Astrolingua Antiquus.'"

"Did Zoe tell you how the Antediluvian language represents the multidimensional universe and its inherent principles?"

"No. She told me about the different dimensions."

"What does Offor Vit mean to you?"

My temples burned where I used to wear the neural headband. "The word 'Offor' carries two layered meanings. On a fundamental level, it signifies 'summit' or 'pinnacle.' It encapsulates the idea of the ultimate height or limit. In its deeper, metaphysical context, it also embodies 'divine dwelling,' reflecting a reverence toward entities residing in another existence."

"How do you know that?"

"I... see it."

"And Vit?"

"'Vit' translates directly to 'light bearer.' It's a term universally recognized for its association with celestial bodies radiating energy. However, in the philosophical depths of Astrolingua Antiquus, 'Vit' implies a beacon of wisdom and knowledge, illuminating the path for seekers. When combined, 'Offor Vit' means 'the divine dwelling of the light bearer.'"

"You're correct. My ancestors have given it the nickname of Bringer of Life before burying it into the ground. The ones from

Earth call it Mount Olympus." He waved a finger at the tree. "Let me show you."

A new hologram sprang to life, projected from one of the branches ten kilometers wide. It looked a lot like a colossal seed buried in the earth. Data started to stream next to the seed ship, along with Antediluvian writing.

"If this is a replica, this isn't *Offor Vit*," I said.

"You're right. She's *Offor Vit's* cousin. She does have a name; *Offor Nov*."

"That's bringer of death."

He gestured to the holo. "And if anyone gets in our way, that she will be."

Offor Nov's defense system was far beyond anything I'd seen before. The writing said it was armed with quantum disentangler beams that altered the quantum states of incoming hostile matter, rendering them harmless or redirecting them. For close range, it employed swarms of autonomous micro-drones, equipped with a miniature black hole generator, capable of swallowing any immediate threat and nullifying it instantly. The ship's shell itself was surrounded by an event-horizon shield, a field that warped space-time, causing any incoming matter or energy to simply curve around it.

The propulsion system utilized a hybrid, high-efficiency fusion drive, using the virtually inexhaustible hydrogen in the universe for fuel. The drive accelerated hydrogen atoms to near light speed, and their expulsion generated thrust. Additionally, it incorporated an Alcubierre jumpdrive, allowing it to manipulate space-time for interstellar travel. While in the earth, it employed a combination of gravitational manipulation and matter-phasing technology, allowing it to sink into the ground or rise without disturbing the crust significantly.

Something powered that, and it wasn't mentioned. The symbol for 'connection' clung to the side of the data.

"What do you think?" the general asked.

"I... I don't know what to say."

"*Offor Nov* lies far beneath Kahwin's multi-layered crust. The vessel's hull is composed of a structured quark-gluon plasma encased within stabilized monopoles, creating a super-fluid, ultra-hard shell that can withstand unfathomable pressures and temperatures. This configuration gives *Offor Nov*'s hull a nearly unbreachable resilience against the harshest conditions of Kahwin's interior and makes it impossible to detect. We've been hiding it under the Shaper's nose for eons."

The hologram showed new data.

Shielded by layers of metamaterials, the interior of the ship housed countless rows of cryogenic capsules. Each one sheltered a human, for a total of ten million Antediluvians. The capsules, designed for minimal thermal exchange, were held at a stable temperature of minus 196 degrees Celsius. A gaseous mixture of helium and neon permeated the interior, further lowering the risk of heat leakage.

"Who are they?"

"Those are who the Regency saved before we went into hiding." He gave a slight shake of his head and frowned. "We tried to save all we could. So many of us died back then."

Nanobots circulated within the cryo-fluid, maintaining cell integrity, repairing damage and ensuring homeostasis. The fluid itself was a crafted mix of cryoprotectants, designed to prevent ice crystal formation that might otherwise compromise cellular structure. These nanobots operated under the guidance of a highly efficient quantum computer, which constantly monitored and adjusted internal conditions for optimal preservation.

At the boundary of the hull and the interior lied a layer of meta-stable exotic matter. It formed a repulsive force-field, isolating the internal environment from external physical influences. It maintained the ship's structural integrity and the Antediluvians' cryogenic safety.

As complicated as it all was, it made sense to me.

A moment of clarity popped into my mind, crystal clear, like I could see through him, his thoughts, everything around me.

"You can't control this ship, can you?" I asked bluntly.

"Of course we can. We're going to evacuate. All I need you to do is give us some help."

"What happens when *Offor Nov* leaves? Won't it destroy Starport City? It's buried right below it."

"We will take everyone with us, but the city will cease to exist once we break through the crust."

Something wasn't sitting right with me. Maybe it was the concerned look on General Vack's face, or maybe it was the way he was so eager for me to agree with him. "What about the Senate? I wish to speak to them."

"There is no time. We were forced to disband the Senate and absorb them into the Academy."

"You killed them."

"Decisions were made."

I remembered what Zoe had said—*Sometimes, you have to make tough decisions in the face of uncertainty. Consider the benefits and risks.*

What if I attacked him, here, while he was alone? No doubt, he was armed, and he'd shoot me. I didn't like the idea of being shot. What would it accomplish?

Was Zoe really disabled? How'd he do that? She must've let them do that to her, or she was playing dead. What if I gave her a signal somehow? Why was she letting General Vack's forces occupy Project 1? There had to be more Immortals there. Could I command them at this distance, just by thinking about them?

This was a game without a good move to make. There was a phrase in English that didn't translate into my language very well, and we didn't even have a concept for it. It made the phrase hard to understand: Mutually Assured Destruction.

I pointed to the intersecting lines on the glowing symbol that lined a device to the ship's computer. "That symbol there means 'connection.' See it?"

"You have a keen eye, young man."

"What's missing?"

General Vack placed his hands behind his back. "*Offor Nov* can only be piloted by you."

I laughed. "I can't possibly pilot a ship."

"You defeated the Janissaries and have proven yourself invaluable to Zoe. You are capable of more than you know." He stepped toward a glass case and stared at his reflection. "The Shapers are incoming. We'll need to evacuate everyone we can into the ship."

"You want me to pilot this thing into space?"

"It's the only way we'll survive, Kol. Once the Shapers land this time, nothing will stop them."

My chest hurt. This couldn't be real. "I don't know what to say."

"Say yes."

"Release my mother first."

"As you wish." General Vack looked over his shoulder.

A door opened a few moments later, and when my mother came rushing in, I nearly lost it. I sprinted over to her and gave her the biggest hug I'd ever given her.

"Mom!"

Tears flowed down her bright brown eyes as she held the sides of my face and kissed my forehead. "Are you okay?"

"I'm great, Mom. Super great." I hugged her tightly. "I missed you."

"I missed you too." She'd been cleaned up. They'd put makeup over her bruises.

"Let me look at you." She bent down slightly and studied my face. "You look good. I'm so glad you're here." She pulled me in for another hug and kissed the top of my head repeatedly. "You don't know how worried I was."

"I've been fine. I was scared something bad happened to you."

She smiled. "As long as you're in one piece, that's all that matters."

When we finally separated, I stood straighter. "What about Zoe?"

The general said, "Zoe will come with us. However, she must remain inert for now."

"Why?" I asked.

"Zoe is not who she appears to be," my mother said. "She cannot be trusted."

"She's been great to me this entire time. She's taught me everything. I love Zoe."

My mother winced. "Don't say that. She's not..."

"Human?" I asked, interrupting her. "She's very human."

General Vack shook his head. "Zoe manipulated you, Kol. More than you will ever realize."

What did that mean? "She helped me when I needed help more than anything."

General Vack grimaced. "She's been using you to get to me."

"That's right," Zoe said, appearing behind him, seemingly out of thin air. "You won't be coming with us to Earth." She reached into his holster, pulled out his pistol, and blew his brains all over the floor.

CHAPTER FIFTY-EIGHT

**"Cowards die many times before their deaths; the valiant
never taste of death but once."**
—William Shakespeare, Julius Caesar, Act II, Scene II

Kahwin System
Captain Scott Moore

As we approached Kahwin, you could hear a pin drop. Erika sat at her console, trying to establish contact with the planet, while the rest of the crew monitored their respective systems.

We'd brought over a hundred thousand people aboard *Arcadia* in a day, a remarkable feat. *Arcadia* had enough food in her domes to feed ten times that number, easy, and enough space for each of our new personnel to have their own quarters. The baron seemed more than satisfied, and I ordered Chief to keep me abreast of anything that might present a security threat.

The jump to Kahwin came without incident, and it took us a

fraction of a second to appear. Once we departed Eos, all fell into place.

The system was silent, and our immediate passive scans showed nothing out of the ordinary.

"Still no response from the surface," Erika said. "It's like they're completely cut off."

Chief looked up from his station, concern etched on his face. "Any signs of interference or jamming?"

Erika shook her head. "Nothing. It's as if they've gone silent voluntarily."

"Maybe we should send a recon drone to get a closer look?" Chief asked. "We need to know what's happening down there."

I nodded. "Do it. In the meantime, let's run some advanced scans. I want to know if there's any unusual activity or power fluctuations on the surface."

Erika began to calibrate the ship's sensors, utilizing a combination of electromagnetic, gravitational, and subspace anomaly detection to gather as much information as possible. The rest of the crew watched the readings closely, waiting for any signs that could help explain the mysterious silence.

Where was Zoe?

As the data started to accumulate, Vincent pointed at one of the readouts. "Look at this. Starport City has gone dark. There's a massive power outage."

I examined the data. "What about the rest of the planet?"

Lieutenant Commander Chen studied the readouts. "It's not just Starport City. There are power fluctuations and infrastructure issues all over the place. It's like the entire plane's power grid went down. Sir, something's happened. The Janissaries are destroyed." She brought up a new feed. She was right. A war had taken place between my former forces and something else entirely.

I rubbed my nose to hide my dismay. My Janissaries? Gone?

It gnawed at me like none other and I took a few subtle breaths to calm myself. "Contact the Senate over the emergency channel."

Erika continued to send hails to the planet. "Priority message sent."

"Hopefully, someone will pick it up and respond," Vincent said.

I considered the possibilities. "We can't rule out anything. Erika, keep trying to establish contact. Vincent, prepare the recon drone for launch. We need eyes on the ground."

As the recon drone prepped for launch, I addressed the crew. "If Kahwin is under attack or experiencing a crisis, we need to be ready to help."

Vincent nodded as he remotely launched the drone. "Drone launched. I'll keep an eye on the drone's feed and relay any pertinent information."

"Feazer?" I asked. "Thoughts?"

"Sir, have we tried contacting Zoe?"

I glanced over to Erika.

"Not advised, sir," Chief said first.

"Explain."

Chief sent me a map of Starport City, which currently faced us, lit up by the distant star. "Any direct communication might be picked up by Starport City's passive sensors suite. If something happened there, we'd give away our position. Suggest we wait until the recon drove provides us with information."

"See to it," I said.

The crew continued to work in silence as the recon drone descended toward Kahwin's surface. All eyes were drawn to the live feed being transmitted back to the ship. As the drone entered the atmosphere, images began streaming in.

A fractured city lay beneath the rolling clouds as if a spike had pierced through it and cracked its spine. Towers were broken apart and collapsed. The earth rose like a volcano had erupted, and what few houses remained were charred and devastated. It was a landscape of destruction. What was left of the infrastructure was buried under the vast mountains of stone and iron. The evidence of the gargantuan upheaval of earth where the subterranean vessel had been was plain to see.

The massive Senate was indiscernible from the rubble.

Everyone I'd left behind had would have perished.

A silence fell over the bridge, the magnitude of the situation sinking in. Though she tried to hide it, Lieutenant Commander Chen's eyes betrayed her horror. "Chief, can we access any remaining city systems? Maybe there are survivors, or emergency services we can connect to."

"I'll try, but the signal's extremely weak," Chief said, his southern drawl heavier than usual. He started a series of encoded signals, attempting to reach any operational communication systems.

I turned to Erika. "Something destroyed the Janissaries, but we don't detect any Shapers. Nothing down there could have done this."

Erika scrutinized the sensor readouts. "No immediate signs of an invasion force, sir."

Meanwhile, the drone was closing in on a site some distance from the former Senate building, which now stood as a pile of smoldering ruins. Vincent zoomed in, revealing a device hidden in a forest, the potential origin of the distress signal.

"What is that?" I asked.

Vincent checked three different screens before responding. "It's a Space Force tablet. It's pinging us directly."

"Amongst all that?" Chief asked.

"The signal we received in Eos matches it," Vincent said.

Zoe left it for us to find. "Melody," I called to our ship's AI, "analyze this signal source. Is there any chance we can boost it or trace it back?"

Melody's soft voice echoed through the speakers. "The damage in the forest is extensive, but there may be some residual data I can extract. I'm picking up a structure beneath the ground."

"Another bomb shelter?" I asked.

"I don't think so, sir," Feazer said. "It's too large. A major military force marched through here."

I scratched my chin in thought. "What is it?"

"Unknown, sir." Vincent worked alongside Melody as they deciphered what scattered data they could harvest. "The tablet's signal is encrypted. Also picking up a lot of interference."

"It's definitely strange." Lieutenant Commander Chen echoed, an eyebrow raised. "There's something down there. They look like devices of some kind."

"We didn't see these before. Are they new?" I asked.

Chen gave her screen a second look. "Unknown, Captain."

We searched every forest within a thousand klicks of Starport City and never saw this place. Sure, we had limited personnel and time, but how did we miss this area? Although Feazer had been quiet, I could see gears working over his head. "Thoughts?"

"I don't want to speculate, Captain."

"I'm *asking* you to speculate."

He hesitated for a moment. "My people are down there."

"Were," Chief said.

"And still might be," Feazer replied.

"That's not much of a speculation, Mr. Feazer." I turned to Erika. "Any signs of life?"

"Negative, sir."

"Looks like the 2036 BTT," I said, referring to the "The Big

Tectonic Temblor," the name given to the major earthquake in California that killed over a hundred thousand people and split L.A. in half.

Vincent, who'd been observing our exchange with a growing focus, leaned closer to his screen, peering at the information being relayed. "Wait a minute. This isn't just any encryption." He brought up a side-by-side comparison of the unknown encryption and Melody's own secure protocols. He turned his screen toward us. "See that?" He pointed to the overlapping patterns of coding in the two samples. "This... it looks like it's another version of Melody's own encryption algorithm."

A ripple of surprise washed over the bridge.

"That's impossible," Chen said, her eyes locked onto the screen, studying the undeniably similar patterns.

"We have the only AI," I reminded them.

"Unless?" Chief said.

Vincent's face had grown pale. "Unless there's another one out there. And if there is, it's advanced. Possibly more so than ours."

The implications of Vincent's statement hung in the air.

Erika broke the silence. "Are we suggesting that there's an AI out there using the same base protocols as Melody?" She looked at Vincent. "Is that even possible?"

"I don't know." Vincent's gaze remained fixed on the screen.

"Could this be some sort of fluke?" I asked, trying to make sense of the situation.

Vincent's mouth gaped. "It's an encryption protocol based on multi-dimensional fractal matrices." His voice was barely a whisper.

I blinked. "Explain."

"Fractal matrices," Vincent said. "They're multi-dimensional structures with repeating patterns across various scales.

The idea has been floating around for a while in cryptographic circles as the next potential leap in encryption technology, but the sheer processing power required to generate and manage such keys was thought to be beyond even the most advanced quantum computers."

Erika nodded in understanding. "It's not just about processing power. Fractal matrices involve complex mathematical concepts like chaos theory, non-linear dynamics, and recursion. The encryption keys would not only be incredibly large but would also change unpredictably with every use."

"How long will it take to crack it?" I asked.

Vincent turned back to the console as he dug deeper into the encryption protocol. "The encryption is so tightly integrated with the data that the two can't be separated without the correct decryption key. Any attempt to brute force the encryption would result in the data being irretrievably lost."

"So, we're dealing with an encryption protocol that's theoretically uncrackable," Chen said. "It's showing up in a distress signal from a planet we thought was cut off from advanced technology."

If the technology we thought was unique to our AI had somehow made its way to Kahwin, the implications were disturbing.

"We'll need an away team to recover it," I said. "Another to search for survivors in Starport City. Chief, I'll need a list of volunteers."

"I'll go," Feazer replied.

"Negative. I need you here as the only Equinox..."

Feazer cut me off. "Sir, with all due respect, those are my people down there. If there's anyone alive, it's my job to find them."

I faced Chief, who nodded back to me. Feazer was right.

Ensign Clark Marston raised his hand. "I'll go, sir."

"I'd like to go with them as well, sir," Lieutenant Miller said.

Lieutenant Commander Chen turned to me with an expression of hope. "I'll lead the away team, sir."

I didn't like the idea of her going but could think of no one better to lead it. "Collect the tablet and search for survivors. You will take two shuttles. Fill the other with supplies. Chen, ask for volunteers amongst our security detail."

"Aye, sir. Semper Supra."

"Semper Supra," I said in a grim tone. "Out here, where the boundaries of morality blur, honor serves as our compass and keeps us firmly rooted in principles of justice, compassion, and respect. You guys better be careful down there." I turned to Ensign Marston. "Let's talk about your promotion when you return."

"Aye, sir," Marston said.

Chief stopped them at the lift and addressed Chen. "Godspeed."

"Don't worry, Chief," Chen said. "We're still going on that date."

During the time it took for the shuttles to depart, we spent time poring over incoming sensor data, and for the life of me, I couldn't understand how we missed a place in proximity of Starport City.

Offer Vit. I ran the conversation with the baron though my head again and again. No, there couldn't be two ships on Kahwin. It didn't make sense. Did the Antediluvians just bury all their ships? Couldn't the Shapers simply find them?

The shuttles descended into Kahwin's atmosphere, and new blips appeared on our sensors at a range slightly outside of Trion, Kahwin's moon. A red counter began registering them and counting them.

1,000.

5,000.

8,000.

15,000.

It continued to rise.

"My God," Chief said.

Vincent's jaw dropped. "The Shapers are here."

Erika watched her monitor. "They're heading straight at us, sir."

I punched the comm unit. "All hands to stations. This is not a drill."

CHAPTER FIFTY-NINE

Kahwin System
Captain Scott Moore

The darkness of space stretched out before me. I always envisioned my future would be somewhere out in the stars ever since I could remember, but never more than now. *Arcadia*'s sensors continued to reveal the approaching nightmare lurking in the depth of the void.

As the Shaper swarm blotted out the stars, my heart seized. The bridge, bathed in the ambient glow of monitors and holodisplays, constricted me.

Vincent and Erika sat at their stations, eyes glued to the sensor readouts as the first tendrils of the Shaper swarm slithered into our field of view. Their shapes mirrored those we'd encountered at the edge of the system when we left to Eos, but to compare the size and scope of that fleet versus this... cloud wouldn't be fair. The displays casted shadows across the faces of my crew. We stood at the precipice of a war unlike anything I thought possible.

The sensors painted a chilling picture of the swarm.

Twisted shapes writhed toward us, their grotesque silhouettes like a sea of snakes and squids. Their endless numbers created a threat I wasn't sure we could defeat.

The sheer scale of the enemy clawed its way toward Kahwin. Fear would be our greatest enemy. I took a deep breath.

In the center of the swarm, one vessel stood out amongst the others. It struck me as something straight out of a nightmare. It was immense. Its form was akin to a giant squid rendered on a scale that dwarfed the rest of the fleet. The ship was alive, pulsating with a vitality that seemed to ooze from its skin-like hull. Vast, bulbous appendages, reminiscent of the arms and tentacles of cephalopods, extended outward, reaching for anything and everything they could grasp.

Its propulsion system seemed to defy all known engineering principles. Instead of the conventional thrusters or nacelles, the beast moved with a slow, languid fluidity, as if it swam through the sea of stars. An alien rhythm coursed through its form, a visible ripple of motion that moved in tandem with the ship's own throbbing heartbeat.

My fingers tightened around the arms of my command chair, the cold metal biting into my skin. "Prepare all weapons and defenses. We'll skirt the swarm for as long as we can and then engage directly."

A new holoscreen popped up next to me. "Ready to deploy our Valkyries, Captain," Wildcat said.

"Standby, Wildcat," I replied. I liked her eagerness, but did she know what she was asking?

All at once, the Shapers halted in place in a wedge formation.

"Sir, I'm receiving a transmission from one of their ships," Erika said.

That made no sense at all. "Are you sure, Lieutenant? The Shapers don't communicate."

"Aye, sir." Erika and Vincent made several adjustments to her comm unit.

My brother gave me a nod. "It's coming from the middle of their fleet, sir."

"On screen."

The visual feed flickered to life, and an extraordinary sight materialized before us. At the heart of the Shaper fleet, a being of immense proportions rested, seemingly in control of the immense swarm. It was an entity of shifting form, as if water given consciousness, a living nebula contained within the confines of a Shaper's body.

Its body was mesmerizing. Luminescent blues and greens invoked images of an abyssal sea, rippling, surging, in a constant state of fluid motion. Its form morphed between abstract shapes, never settling for any defined shape or form.

At times, I perceived a visage eerily reminiscent of a wild beard of swirling aqua, eyes as deep and enigmatic as the fathomless depths, and a crown of cresting waves. However, the moment I tried to focus, the form dissipated, returning to the undulating, ever-changing water-like state.

Its voice, when it spoke, carried the weight of the ocean, the wisdom of the ages, and the wrath of the drowned. It was as though a being of myth had stepped out from the pages of ancient lore and now inhabited the heart of the Shaper fleet.

A voice resonated from the speakers. It carried with it an inherent, unspoken majesty defying description. "Captain Scott David Moore. I am Allo Quishar."

Gasps could be heard around the bridge.

"Return the Ekbotor, and I will spare you," the being said.

Zoe. Why did he want her?

I steeled my face. "She's not aboard this ship."

"Where is the Ekbotor?" Allo Quishar asked. "Have you let it escape?"

Vincent and Erika began working with the baron to maximize our attack. We'd have little time to react. As they worked, some of our screen flashed with static. Vincent threw up his hands and left the bridge. Something was wrong.

"I do not control her," I said. "You will leave this system immediately. You and your fleet are not welcome in this region of space."

Allo Quishar's voice filled the bridge, his tone cold and authoritative. "War is not a sin, Captain Moore. It is the most sublime of all spectacles, the ultimate nature of existence itself."

I shook my head. "I fail to see the glory in death and destruction."

"That's where your human perspective blinds you," Allo Quishar said. "You view war as a calamity, a last resort. In truth, it is the purest form of natural law. I will take great delight on crushing your species."

"Natural law?" I asked. "There is nothing natural about killing."

"Is that not what your species does to survive? Is that not what all species do?" Allo Quishar's face morphed into something indescribable then came back together a second later. "Your existence is predicated on the death of other life forms, from the food you consume to the microscopic organisms you crush underfoot."

"That's different," I said. "That's not the same as what you're doing."

"All beings strive to survive, to expand, to dominate. That is the universal law. The lion does not negotiate with the gazelle, the eagle does not parley with the rabbit. I will always be the lion, the eagle, and humanity's nightmare."

"Nature has a balance. It's rare that any lion or a similar species would eat itself out of existence by exterminating its prey from the natural world. What you're talking about is survival," I said. "I've heard what you have done to humanity. Those days are over."

"What is conquest but the hunger for survival taken to its ultimate extreme?" Allo Quishar's form seemed to blink out of reality for an instant before it pieced itself together like a puzzle. "Only the most ruthless, the most relentless, can hope to endure. That is the glory of war. It is the crucible in which we are all forged, the ultimate measure of our worth. It is time to add your essence to my horde. The stars will quake as I devour them whole."

The communication ended and for a moment, nothing happened. I was stunned, to tell you the truth. Now that I'd had a glimpse of Allo Quishar, he seemed almost mortal.

"Raise shields. We're going to pull the swarm away from Kahwin. All ahead full," I said.

As we commenced our maneuver, the first wave of the Shaper swarm swept our way, a tsunami of darkness and malice that sought to drown us in its chilling embrace. As I faced the oncoming storm, a spark of defiance flared within me.

As the swarm drew closer, the true scale of their numbers became horrifyingly apparent.

I detected Vincent on one of the lifts heading for Melody, so I contacted him. "Report."

"Captain," Vincent said, his voice tinged with terror, "Melody is no longer accepting commands."

I gripped the edge of my command chair, my knuckles turning white. "What's the problem?"

"Unknown. I tried everything up there. Something's wrong."

The baron turned to me. "It's *Arcadia*, sir. She's no longer responding to any of our controls."

The ship began to accelerate right into the heart of the swarm.

"What have you done?" I shouted at the baron.

All of our weapons powered up.

"It's not me, sir. It's *Arcadia*."

The main screen blinked with a message, and Michael's voice boomed inside the bridge. "I told you, Captain. I will have my revenge."

CHAPTER SIXTY

Kahwin System
Captain Scott Moore

On *Arcadia*'s bridge, Erika worked furiously to maintain our shields. The energy-absorbing crystals we had incorporated into our defenses glowed with the strain of the Shapers' relentless approach. At least we had control of our weapons.

The void around us illuminated with heat and power. *Arcadia* had run us right into the thick of it and nothing we did could prevent the ship from acting on its own accord.

"Still can't regain control of the ship's maneuver drives, Captain," Chief said from the engineering deck.

The ship trembled beneath me as we were drawn deeper into the Shaper fleet. My palms felt clammy against the cold metal of my command chair. The silence of the crew was broken only by the sporadic beep of the sensors. I stole a glance at the main monitor where the Shaper swarm, an ocean of metallic squid and snake-like entities, flew at us at an unstoppable pace. A knot of anxiety tightened in my stomach.

A small holoscreen sprang to life at my side. Vincent's face materialized. He was in the heart of the ship, the central server room where Melody resided. Neon light tubes radiated a blue hue and crisscrossed the chamber.

"I may have to reset Melody, but it's going to take time," Vincent said.

Reset Melody? Would this work? The mere thought of it was chilling. Without her, we were practically flying blind. But if it was necessary to regain control of *Arcadia*...

"I can't just flip a switch and restart her, Captain," Vincent continued. "I'll need to reroute power, disconnect her from non-essential systems, and restart her core without disrupting critical functions." His hands, wrapped in white gloves, entered the frame, moving with precision as they began to manipulate the labyrinth of cables.

"Start it, Vincent." I tried to keep my voice steady. "We don't have time. I trust you."

Seconds felt like hours as I watched him work, our survival resting in his capable hands.

I felt entirely helpless as our ship surged forward, her engines screaming as they thrust us into the sea of enemy vessels.

"Baron, keep those guns firing," I yelled. "Use pattern Sigma-Zeta. Time on target volleys, rapid succession. Keep them off balance."

"Aye, Captain." The baron's gruff voice thundered in the bridge, his focus narrowing to the tasks at hand. *Arcadia*'s primary cannons blazed, sending ferocious volleys of particle beams and torpedoes into the advancing swarm.

The outcome of this struggle would determine the fate of the *Arcadia*, and with it, our own.

Despite the intensity of our assault, it was like trying to hold back a tide with a broom. The swarm seemed endless, their numbers swallowing our attacks without diminishing their momentum. Each Shaper vessel destroyed was swiftly replaced by two more. It was a war of attrition we couldn't win.

I glanced at the holodisplay. *Arcadia* was threading us through the enemy armada, weaving a path toward the Shaper flagship. The ship's movements were aggressive, fearless. She took each evasive maneuver as though anticipating the swarm's attacks, juking and jarring to keep the enemy off balance.

"Chief. Status on our maneuver drives," I said.

"It's Melody, sir. She's not letting me gain access."

I balled my fist. "Vincent, reset Melody."

"Trying!"

Arcadia moved with a mind of her own, her course unpredictable as she zigzagged through the swarm. If she wasn't a hundred times the size of the biggest ships out here, we'd be dead by now. Still, her moves were daring, a blatant challenge to Allo Quishar's forces. We were outgunned and outnumbered, and her course was set, her target clear: the heart of the swarm.

"Shapers inbound, port and starboard," said Erika from her sensor station.

I clenched my jaw. "Diverge pattern Theta-Two, full power to aft shields." *Arcadia* swung wide on her own, engines flaring as she abruptly shifted course. The Shapers adapted, their flight paths adjusting like a school of metallic fish.

"Evasive maneuvers not effective, Captain. *Arcadia's* not responding to my commands. Shapers still on approach vector." Erika glared at her screen.

"Redirect to starboard, full salvo launch on Shaper swarm," I ordered.

Arcadia edged smoothly to starboard, her engines ablaze, her cannons aligning with lethal precision. The Shapers recalibrated their pursuit in a blink and shifted their paths with a synchronicity like a school of predatory fish.

"Starboard side, ready to unleash hell, Captain," Erika said.

From my holo, a flurry of light, our salvos plunged headfirst into the Shapers. Each brilliant streak bore our defiance, tearing through the space between us and the oncoming invaders. They evaded like seasoned pilots, and only a handful exploded in the dark void.

Erika faced me. "Not effective, Captain. Shapers still on approach vector."

"Baron, bring the CIWS online, full auto," I said.

"Roger, Captain. CIWS going hot," came the baron's swift response.

Close-In Weapon Systems, or CIWS, were our last line of defense, a storm of kinetic energy designed to cut down the enemy before they could latch onto our hull.

The tactical display lit up as the CIWS roared into life, shredding through the closest wave of Shapers. For every Shaper vessel we destroyed, another swooped in to fill the gap. They continued to throw themselves against our shields with a disregard for self-preservation.

"Brace for impact." I stiffened as a group of Shaper vessels crashed into our shields. They attempted to attach themselves.

The ship shuddered as our shields strained against the blitz. We had the power to hold them off, but the continuous attack was beginning to stress our systems.

"Power fluctuations in shield grid three." Erika's eyes scanned the energy readouts.

"Divert auxiliary power to compensate. Don't let them breach," I said.

Shapers continued their push, each impact a test of our ship's resilience. *Arcadia* shook while tremors echoed through her hull.

"Multiple breaches in the shield perimeter, Captain." Baron's report sent a chill through me.

I grimaced. "Baron, I need a firing solution. We need to cut them off at the source."

"Working on it, Captain," the baron replied.

Meanwhile, *Arcadia* held firm. We were the proverbial thorn amidst a storm of alien locusts.

"Shaper swarm massing at starboard," Erika said.

Without hesitation, I responded, "All countermeasures, deploy!"

As *Arcadia* plunged deeper into the swarm, a sense of surreal calm descended upon me. Here was where my fate would be decided, one way or another. The scene outside the bridge turned into a maelstrom of explosions and fire.

The vessel lurched as *Arcadia* obeyed, jettisoning chaff in an attempt to disrupt the Shapers, but the swarm was merciless. They struck like a tidal wave, their hulls gleaming as they crashed against our shields.

"Shields at forty percent," Erika said while klaxons blared.

I ground my teeth. "Divert power from non-essential systems. Maintain shield integrity at all costs."

The swarm converged on us from all sides. *Arcadia* veered and changed heading amidst the Shaper charge, her CIWS creating a storm of kinetic fury. The Shapers kept coming.

Erika turned in her chair. "Multiple Shaper signatures breaching the perimeter."

I flexed my fist. "Baron, target those signatures. Don't let them get a foothold!"

"Firing, but there's too many, Captain. We're being over-whelmed." Baron's tone was strained.

"Focus fire on the largest concentrations. We need to thin them out," I said.

The situation was quickly deteriorating. The once distant light of the shields became a dissonant wail as more Shapers rammed into our failing defenses. Their persistence took its toll.

A fresh wave of alarms filled the bridge.

"Shapers are attaching themselves to the hull. They're trying to breach," Erika said.

I clenched my jaw. "Divert all remaining power to hull integrity."

"Damage control teams, be ready for breaches," I ordered into the comms. *Arcadia* rocked from the continuous attack.

Was this the end?

"Scott." Vincent's voice broke through the turmoil. He filled the screen, bathed in the harsh light of Melody's server room. "Melody's not responding. I think Michael has infected her with some kind of virus."

"Can you purge it?" I asked, my stomach dropping at the implication.

"I'm attempting to. It's unlike anything I've seen before. It's..." He trailed off, his expression filled with dread.

"Just do it, Vincent. We need her."

Vincent nodded, his lips tight as he disappeared from the screen.

I raised my voice. "Erika, deploy all drones, defensive formation. Baron, arm the torpedoes."

"Aye, sir, arming torpedoes. It's a Hail Mary, Captain."

Even amidst the battle, I was momentarily surprised he knew that term. "Then let's pray." I glanced at the tactical display. The swarm's all-consuming darkness was a nightmare from which there was no escape.

"Shields at ten percent!"

Drones deployed from *Arcadia*'s hull to harass and distract the Shapers. Against such overwhelming numbers, it was like spitting into a hurricane.

As the first drones launched, the forward view was awash with blinding explosions. Shapers combusted under the hail of fire. However, their brethren continued undeterred, propelled by some unfathomable hive-minded determination.

Officers shouted commands, responded to status updates, and manipulated holographic displays. *Arcadia* pressed onward on her own, her determined drive permeating every meter of the ship.

Meanwhile, amidst the barrage of the Shaper fleet, the CIWS spat out a ceaseless stream of destructive energy. Drones zipped across the star-filled expanse, meeting the swarm head-on.

"It's done, Scott." Vincent's forehead dripped with sweat.

"I've regained partial control, Captain," Chief said.

At last! "Bow into the swarm. We're taking a direct approach."

The tactical display in front of me rippled as the starship made a hard turn, targeting the epicenter of the Shaper armada.

The swarm responded in kind, rallying on our position like a pack of wolves. They pressed as their advanced energy weapons charged and locked onto us. With each attempt they made to close in, *Arcadia* slipped through their grasp.

Every system on board buzzed with activity. Sensor arrays tracked the positions of Shaper ships. Defensive countermeasures flared to life, sending out pulses to confuse incoming projectiles.

A second holo materialized above my armrest with Wildcat's beautiful eyes staring into mine. "Valkyries are standing by, sir."

"Wildcat, there's too many of them," I said.

Wildcat gave me a serious look. "Captain, we swore an oath to protect you and the ship. Let us fulfill our destiny." In the background, all of her pilots were stationed at their consoles, prepped and ready; behind them, a holographic screen of the limitless expanse of the star-studded cosmos.

I checked the information on a separate display. The baron's crew had mounted several of the bombers and fighters with what appeared to be a new type of bomb. "XDM-44 Oblivions. Baron, explain."

"Captain, my crew took the liberty of siphoning the remaining dark matter energy into containment fields. Once these explosives erupt, they'll tear massive holes in the fleet."

"Your crew will die," I said.

The baron dipped his head. "And they'll save the ship, sir. One swift blow to the heart of the swarm, they'll scatter. We've got one chance to kill Allo Quishar."

I sat straighter in my captain's chair. "That's not him. He's possessed a Shaper to speak to us."

"That might be true, sir, but if you kill the brain, you kill the body."

I swallowed. Everything in me screamed no. As an American, I considered all life precious. These women were not Americans. If God existed, may He forgive me for the decision I was about to make. They'd tear a gap for *Arcadia*'s retreat.

"You're clear to launch, Wildcat." My words felt like knives in my throat. I hated every bit of the order I just gave.

Behind Wildcat, the Valkyries erupted in cheers.

Wildcat grinned. "As you say, Semper Supra, Captain."

CHAPTER SIXTY-ONE

Kahwin System
Captain Scott Moore

My heart pounded as I listened in to the Valkyries' comms.

"Vector six-two, Scimitar and Saber, you've got incoming on your six." Wildcat's tone echoed through the comm channel.

"Copy, Wildcat. Switching to Sigma-Echo-Niner," Scimitar responded. Her fighter veered hard starboard, venting lateral thrusters to reorient her attack angle.

"Thrust bearings on your three, Saber," Wildcat called out. The Valkyries navigated the space, dictated by the seething swarm of Shapers.

The baron had created a separate holo for us to watch the Valkyries on the main screen. This would be the deciding moment we'd all hoped for. Wildcat had stayed behind to direct her pilots, but the others had joined the new recruits. I admired each of them. Clothed in black jumpsuits with silver trim, they knew they were going to die. Several proudly wore their family crests around their necks. Not one of them seemed nervous or moved as they flung themselves headlong against the enemy. Orders were orders. Their sacrifice would be remembered.

Their goal would be to deliver the dark matter bombs right into the heart of the enemy armada and take out Allo Quishar. They'd also create a gap by which Arcadia could retreat. I'd always thought how sad it was for the Japanese kamikazes in the Second World War to blow themselves up for a lost cause. Now, how things had come full circle.

We were about to watch a horrible spectacle. Three hundred of our best would die. They'd redirected the Shapers, pulling them off us for a temporary reprieve. Maybe Allo Quishar knew what was coming and wanted to preserve himself.

If we survived, each of the women would be immortalized in statues, in our books, in our myths. Long live the Valkyries.

"Negative pitch coming up," Banshee said. A burst of exhaust from her ventral thrusters and her ship rolled, dodging the oncoming Shaper projectiles.

"Phoenix, retro-burn now," Wildcat commanded.

"Engaging retro-thrusters!" Phoenix's affirmation was drowned by the guttural moan of the her bomber's frame. Her signal blinked out moments after—a brave soul consumed by the Shapers, but not before she exploded her dark matter bomb. Thousands upon thousands of Shaper ships disintegrated in a matter of seconds.

I blinked twice to make sure I wasn't seeing things. I couldn't believe how many vessels it took out.

"Ace, you've got a breacher on your six. Accelerate, go evasive!" Wildcat's voice held a note of desperation as she watched the swarm close distance.

"Too close for comfort, Wildcat." Ace managed a laugh. "Executing Lambda-Six-Zulu. Wish me luck."

"Copy that, Ace. Sending you all the luck I can spare," Wildcat said, tracking her trajectory on the plotter.

One by one, the Valkyries succumbed to the Shapers, their noble sacrifice illuminating the battlefield in ephemeral bursts of violent light when their dark matter ordnance exploded. The enemy's fleet started to look like Swiss cheese. With each loss, the Swarm's numbers dwindled, buying us precious moments to mount our desperate counteroffensive. *Arcadia*'s crew watched, our hearts heavy as our comrades' lights went out. Their bravery fueled the will to fight on.

Feazer wiped his sweaty palms on a rag as he stared at Hammer. A man can fall for a woman faster than you can blink, and he was certainly in love with her. He said a quick prayer for her, and he wasn't the only one praying.

Hammer pushed the yoke, her fighter screaming in protest. Her targeting reticule swung wild, settling onto a pack of Shaper ships converging on her location.

"Delta-Tango-Three-Two," Hammer said, sending a salvo of missiles screaming into the heart of the Shaper formation. The space lit up as the Shapers met their fiery demise, the vacuum of space swallowing the incandescent shockwaves.

A stray Shaper projectile glanced off Hammer's shield, the energy sapping the ship's reserves. "Gamma-Charlie-Five," she said, adjusting her shields to compensate, trying to keep her critical systems protected.

Another glance at the radar showed more Shapers closing. "I'm out of Tau-Kappa," Warhawk said. She was out of counter-measures, defenseless against the Shaper onslaught.

Arcadia continued to deliver long-range death as we tried to pull away from the fleet. We covered the Valkyries as best we could during our retreat.

One pilot managed to thread her way through the swarm. Luna Valerius—Storm. "Initiating bombing run."

Wildcat narrowed her eyes. "Roger that, Storm. May the light hold you dear."

"Copy, Wildcat. Going evasive." Storm dodged several projectiles and enemy ships. The Shapers pursued, their numbers too great, and she could only maneuver around so many.

"Send them to Hapestrow, Storm," Wildcat said.

And, Storm did, to the very last moment, before she exploded into a cloud of lights that evaporated quickly in the vacuum of space.

Ace yanked her fighter into a sharp spiral, taking her through the heart of the Shaper cluster. She squeezed the trigger and sent a blistering torrent of plasma bolts into the fray. Shaper ships burst into radiant blooms of energy. For each that fell, it felt like two more took its place. Then Ace vanished.

"Echo-Two-Five is down." Wildcat's expression went grim.

A chill ran through me. Another one, slain.

"Omega-Thirty-Niner, engaging Sigma-Seven," Blackwing's voice burst through the comms. She arced around a mass of ships.

"Watch your six, Blackwing. You've got incoming."

Wildcat's warning came too late. A strafing run from a Shaper craft riddled Blackwings's port wing, sending her into a vicious spin.

Blackwing's breath came in ragged gasps as she fought to regain control. "I've been hit, Wildcat."

"Copy that, Blackwing. Damage report?" Wildcat asked.

"Port wing is gone, main thruster is at twenty percent. I'm not... I'm not gonna make it, Wildcat."

There was a pause on the other end. "I understand, Blackwing," Wildcat said, her voice thick. "I'll see you in Elysium."

With a grim smile, Blackwing aimed her dying ship at the nearest Shaper dreadnought and pushed the throttle to the max. Her final scream of defiance was swallowed by the roar of her bomber's death throes as she plowed into the dreadnought, taking it with her in a brilliant explosion of light and energy.

One by one, the remaining Valkyries fell, each taking as many Shapers with them as they could. Each death bought the *Arcadia* precious moments.

"They've opened a gap, sir," the baron said.

There it was. A way out of this mess.

"Where's Allo Quishar's ship?" I asked.

Feazer looked up at the holomap. "There, sir."

"Recall all remaining Valkyries," I said. "We're going to get the hell out of here."

The baron wiped sweat from his brow. "What about Allo Quishar?"

I nodded. "I have a plan."

CHAPTER SIXTY-TWO

Kahwin System
Captain Scott Moore

Erika's monotone pitch boomed. "Power fluctuations increasing, Captain. We're in the red."

I glanced at the power grid on the tactical display. The fluctuating lines, usually a steady green, flashed an angry red. The grid now looked alarmingly fragile, the signs of our faltering defenses all too apparent.

Arcadia trembled, lights flickering as our defenses strained to contain the attacking enemy.

"Damage control teams report multiple hull breaches. We're losing pressure in sectors three and seven," Erika said.

I steadied my voice. "Seal off those sectors. Order all personnel to evacuate."

"Valkyries reporting success, Captain," Wildcat's voice filtered through the din. "Significant reduction in Shaper numbers."

A flicker of hope sparked within me. It was short-lived.

Erika ran her fingers over her console. "Captain, the Shapers are changing tactics. They're targeting the Valkyries directly as the Valkyries retreat."

As the seconds turned into minutes, the dark reality of our situation began to seep in.

"Do what you can. Hold them off for as long as possible," I said.

We were fighting a losing battle. The Shapers kept coming.

"Saber down," Wildcat said. "Loner gone. Slider, dead." Her voice rang, calling out all those Valkyrie lost in the void, trying to get the last of her team back into *Arcadia*'s massive bay.

The Shaper fleet was a tide that we couldn't stem, and as the last of the Valkyries' signals disappeared from our tactical display, I realized the true cost of our desperate struggle. Months of training, eons of waiting, vanished into oblivion.

None of them had made it. War was cruel. They'd paid with their lives. Their sacrifice had bought us time, but not victory. As the hull groaned, the lights dimmed, and *Arcadia* plunged deeper into the swarm. I had to snap at Feazer to get his mind back in the game.

"Sir, a few of them have turned off their transponders," the baron said. "Hammer and Luna. They're still alive."

Feazer raised his fist in triumph. "Get some, you Shaper pricks!"

"They need to get their asses back here!" I shouted.

"They're heading right for Allo Quishar's ship."

"Well, I'll be damned," Chief whispered.

The Shapers formed a cohesive phalanx, a living shield wall, protecting their commander. We plunged onward, directly toward the shielded vessel.

"Captain, the Shapers are now breaching the hull," the baron said.

My eyes darted to the internal sensors, where red flashes

marked the intruders' positions. They were here, on *Arcadia*, about to feast on my crew.

The baron's crisp tone resonated across the bridge. "Captain, I'm deploying multiple units to the breached sectors. We're intercepting the Shapers at vector points Bravo, Delta, and Echo."

A window formed on the central display, showing a group of the baron's soldiers racing through a corridor. The rest of the bridge's large view screen displayed the expanse outside, pierced by the maelstrom of battle against the Shaper swarm. "Erika, adjust our course to 214 degrees. Keep our movements unpredictable."

"Aye, sir."

The holo flickered with the feed from the engagement zones inside *Arcadia*. My eyes darted between the fight with the Shaper armada and Baron's forces, who sprinted down another passageway.

As they rounded a corridor, a creature with a disturbing mix of flesh and metal, lunged forward. Its tentacles phased in and out of reality. Spinning cylinders tipped each tentacle, no doubt used for cutting. A Shaper on all fours moved behind this larger one, its back a mass of whirring machinery. It emitted mechanical whines and groans. Several smaller Shapers, black as shadows, raced at the baron's oncoming unit.

The baron issued the command to engage. The leading elements executed a tactical drop, initiating suppressive fire. In coordinated succession, the support units unleashed a concentrated barrage of rifle fire.

Blood and guts erupted, painting the screen with an azure mist. Through the sanguine fog, lethal projectiles found their mark in a soldier's neck, bringing him down in an instant. A moment later, a trooper suffered a direct impalement through the abdomen, collapsing to the floor.

The baron's unit advanced, the haze dissipating before their coordinated assault. The team moved in unison, pressing the advantage, driving forward. The Shapers, overwhelmed, retreated into one of *Arcadia*'s expansive domes.

From my tactical observation view on the screen, I observed additional soldier reinforcements navigate through multiple corridors. They engaged additional Shapers and also pushed them back into the dome. As they aggressively repelled the Shaper forces, they drove them deeper into a containment area. Indeed, the baron had committed several thousand troops to the operation, and it was working.

With determination, the soldiers activated the dome's gravity controls. It amplified a singular force upon the Shapers. Unbearable, the creatures writhed and twisted on the deck.

It was a tactic of pure genius and rendered the Shapers vulnerable. Easy pickings for the baron's men. I was impressed.

Without warning, the dome exploded in a ball of fire and debris. The screen momentarily went white from the intensity of the blast. When the image cleared, the scale of the devastation showed. Thousands of the baron's men were gone, along with the Shapers they had fought so hard to contain. The void where the dome once stood now revealed a harrowing vista of space. It was littered with the silent, drifting forms of fallen warriors and vanquished Shapers. An undeniable victory, but it was like watching the Valkyrie succumb to death's fate. The cost was immeasurable.

Silence fell over the bridge.

"Captain…" the baron started.

My heart sank deep into my chest. "I know."

"Initiating evasive maneuvers, Captain," Luna said. Her voice held a note of resignation, a knowing defeat as *Arcadia* buckled under the ceaseless assault.

I slammed a fist against my chair. "Damn it, Wildcat, I want them back here."

Erika punched up a new comm system as she tried to get through to them on an emergency channel. "They're not responding to our messages, Captain."

"Valkyries initiating final run," Wildcat's voice crackled through the bridge. The holographic displays lit up with the bright trails of the autonomous fighters, a last desperate arc into the midst of the Shaper swarm.

I rose and hurried to Erika's comm system. "Valkyrie Squadron, recall and dock."

No response.

"Detonation in five... four... three..." Luna's countdown was stark, the cold mathematics of sacrifice resonating in the empty space between each count.

When the Valkyries' dark matter weapons went critical, the resulting explosions weren't just detonations, they were miniature stars birthed amidst the darkness of the enemy. Each brilliant flash was a farewell etched in the fabric of space-time.

The Shaper fleet reeled, their coordinated assault fracturing under the explosions. The resulting shockwave rippled outward, rending the Shapers from their formation and creating a temporary breach. In a maneuver that would inspire countless pilots in the future, Luna had burst into the Shaper phalanx and launched her dark matter torpedoes. The result left Allo Quishar's ship open to attack. Hammer covered her like the wingman she was, and they both darted back to *Arcadia* at maximum thrust. I didn't know whether to laugh or cry. They'd done the impossible and were going to live to talk about it.

Erika leaned closer to her interface. "Sir, another Valkyrie has departed."

"Just me, Captain," Wildcat said. "I won't let my girls hang out there in the wind."

"Bring them back, Wildcat."

"Aye, Captain."

"Baron, what happens if we initiate an emergency jump in the middle of the swarm?" I asked.

"It's not recommended, sir."

I had a plan. "I didn't ask you if it was recommended. What will happen to the swarm?"

The baron did some quick calculations at the nav terminal. "Captain, if we initiated an emergency jump, we would essentially create a localized spatial anomaly. The immediate energy release would be equivalent to multiple fusion detonations. The real danger to the Shapers would be the spatial distortion. It would rip apart anything within a certain radius from our position."

"Meaning?"

"Meaning the Shapers in close proximity would be torn apart at a molecular level. Even those at a greater distance would be severely affected by the shockwave. In essence, Captain, we could potentially wipe out a significant portion of the Shaper fleet. However, the jump's precise effects are highly unpredictable."

Chief overheard us and faced us. "There's a significant risk of collateral damage to our own ship, Captain. Our own structural integrity could be compromised, and we could be torn apart just like the Shapers."

I looked off for a second. "I understand, but we don't have a lot of choices right now."

The baron gave a reluctant nod. "No, sir, we do not. We also need to consider the aftermath. We'll be effectively blind and helpless for several minutes after the jump. We won't be able to make another jump for some time."

I frowned. The thought of us being left defenseless was not a comforting one. The alternative was certain death.

I walked from Erika's station and sat in my captain's seat. "Initiate preparations for an emergency jump."

"Aye, sir," the baron said. "Diverting all available power to the drive core."

The ship vibrated as the power levels changed. On the monitors, the Shapers moved into formation after the sudden impact to their fleet. They seemed to sense that something was happening, and they were not going to let us go without a fight.

"The Shapers are increasing their attack," Wildcat reported. "They're about to throw everything they've got at us."

I looked at the viewscreen. The swarm became more aggressive, their numbers making up for their lack of sophistication. "All Valkyries, return to *Arcadia*, now."

The baron watched his screen. "Drive core at sixty percent and climbing. We should be ready to jump in approximately four minutes."

"Keep me updated. Erika, plot a course as close to Earth as you can."

"Aye, sir. I'll do my best."

The Shapers swarmed around *Arcadia* like a cloud of angry bees. We were doing our best to hold them off, but there were simply too many of them.

"Shields at critical," Erika said.

"Hold on." My heart pounding in my chest. "Just a little longer."

The ship groaned as another wave of Shapers slammed into us. The lights in the command center blinked off and on as the power fluctuations increased.

"Drive core at ninety percent," the baron said. "Almost there, Captain."

"Good." My voice sounded distant to my own ears. "Bring us around, vector one-niner-zero." I locked onto the wall of Shaper vessels on the viewscreen. "Ahead full."

A momentary disorientation swept over me as the inertial dampeners struggled to counteract the starship's abrupt course change. The deck plates shuddered beneath me, the ship's power plant stressing as we punched our acceleration to maximum.

"Captain," a helm officer said, voice tight, "we're now on an intercept course for the enemy command vessel. Estimated time to firing range, three minutes."

"Good. Tactical, what's our missile status?"

"Tubes one through eight are hot, sir. Torpedoes ready to launch on your command. PD grid at maximum readiness."

I scanned the readouts on my console. Every weapons system, every power conduit, every tactical variable was stretched to the breaking point. It had to hold. Failure was not an option.

"Comms, inform all hands to brace for impact. We're going to play chicken with a god." As the words left my mouth, a sense of grim resolve washed over me. This was it, the moment of truth. "Engineering, standby for emergency power transfer to the forward shields. We're going to need every bit of juice we can muster for this."

"On it, Captain," came the reply from the engineering deck. I could hear the tension in the voice, the horrible acceptance of what was about to happen.

In the silent void of space, the distance between us and the middle of the Shaper fleet rapidly dwindled. The enemy vessels grew larger on the viewscreen, their shifting forms glowing.

"Full power to forward shields," I said. "Helm, maintain course. We're going right down their throat."

"Aye, sir."

I couldn't believe how much *Arcadia* could take. Any other ship would have been nothing but stardust by now. As the Shapers continued their attacks, I turned to my crew. "Prepare for emergency jump. All hands, brace for spatial distortion. Open a channel to Allo Quishar's vessel."

"Aye, Captain," Erika said.

After a few tense moments, a static-filled image of Allo Quishar appeared on the screen. The alien entity was an imposing figure. His eyes glowed with a dark light, as if he fed on photons.

"Allo Quishar, we demand that you cease your attack and leave this system immediately. You've lost."

For a moment, the entity stared at the screen, his expression one of cold amusement. "Your resistance is admirable, human. Your ship, your people, they are nothing against the might of the Keepers. You are an insect facing a tempest. Your words are hollow, your threats meaningless."

Despite Allo Quishar's taunting words, I kept my gaze steady, not allowing any signs of fear or doubt to creep into my voice. "You're mistaken. We have faced countless threats, endured countless battles. Humanity will never back down. If we're going to die, we'll make sure to take as many of your kind with us."

Allo Quishar's eyes brightened at my words. "Very well, human. We accept your challenge. The Shapers will feast."

"It was a pleasure knowing you." My heart thumped hard and fast. "Full speed ahead. Prepare to engage."

The ship roared as the engines were pushed to their limit, the view outside the bridge shifting as we accelerated. It was us against them, and only one would emerge victorious.

"Arm all weapons. Target the lead ship," I ordered, clenching my fists. "Fire at will."

Blistering fire swept through the enemy, the void awash in plasma blazes.

A sudden message rippled across our communication band, digital interference clearing to reveal Allo Quishar's voice.

"Earthbound, Captain." Allo Quishar words hissed through the bridge speakers like a serpent's whisper. "The endless night will not swallow us. The Shapers will feast again and again, without let up, without care."

Chilling silence followed his cryptic message, leaving an uneasy feeling in my chest.

"Valkyries have docked, sir," Feazer said.

The countdown on the main display now hit double digits. As I braced myself in my chair, I glanced once more at the massive swarm of Shaper vessels on the holo.

"Jumpdrive at full charge, Captain," the baron said. "Structural integrity holding. We're as ready as we're going to be."

"Erika?" I asked.

"Course laid in, sir. It's a ballpark estimate."

"Well done, Lieutenant."

Allo Quishar's haunting words reverberated in my mind. "Earthbound, Captain... The endless night will not swallow us. The Shapers will feast again and again, without let up, without care."

Ten.

Nine.

Eight.

"Wait," I interrupted, "Make it a blind jump. We don't want them following us, especially to Earth."

"A blind jump, Captain? The variables—"

"Do it, Lieutenant!" The urgency in my voice gave her pause, but she nodded and immediately began inputting commands.

Erika's fingers flew over her console. "Aye, Captain. Setting coordinates for a deep space jump."

A holomap of a distant region of space bloomed before us. Our destination, an uncharted sector of the galaxy, flickered in the cold glow of the display.

"Emergency jump in 3... 2... 1..." Erika's voice sounded like a lifeline as I felt the deck drop out beneath me.

I gave the order. "Jump."

With a lurch, *Arcadia* catapulted into the star-studded abyss, leaving a mass of ruined Shaper vessels behind. Thousands of Shapers imploded, sending organic slime into the void. The world shifted around us as *Arcadia* made the emergency jump, the energy release causing a blinding flash of light. For a moment, everything was quiet. The ship shook violently as the spatial distortion wreaked havoc on our systems. Alarms blared, warning of critical system failures.

Then...

...time slowed into infinity.

THANK YOU FOR READING STARSHIP ARCADIA

We hope you enjoyed it as much as we enjoyed bringing it to you. We just wanted to take a moment to encourage you to review the book. Follow this link: Starship Arcadia to be directed to the book's Amazon product page to leave your review.

Every review helps further the author's reach and, ultimately, helps them continue writing fantastic books for us all to enjoy.

Also in series:
Farthest Reaches
Starship Arcadia

If you liked this book, check out the rest of our catalogue at www.aethonbooks.com. To sign up to receive a FREE collection from some of our best authors as well as updates regarding all new releases, visit www.aethonbooks.com/sign-up.

JOIN THE STREET TEAM! Get advanced copies of all our books, plus other free stuff and help us put out hit after hit.

SEARCH ON FACEBOOK:
AETHON STREET TEAM

Looking for more great sci-fi books?

Check out our new releases!

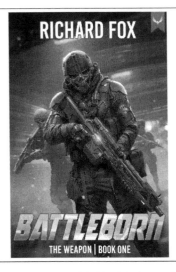

Order Now!

(Tap or Scan)

On the battlefields of the future, death is not the end for a soldier.
The Revenant Program collects badly wounded soldiers broken by war and
converts them into unthinking, unfeeling cyborg weapons. Their bodies are
immune to pain, their minds impervious to fear and doubt. All controlled
by a neural implant called the Imperative. But when one of the Revenants
awakens, he can only remember two things: that he must fight, and a code
name...Dead Man. Who was he before he became a Revenant? What are
the officers and scientists controlling the program to do with a soldier that
can question the horrific orders he's given? The more those controlling the
Dead Man learn of who he was, they realize they may have turned a
monster into something truly unstoppable. And with every memory
*recovered, the Imperative drives the Dead Man closer to insanity. **The***
Weapon: Battleborn is the first in a new series by best-selling
***military science fiction author Richard Fox, author of the** Ember*
***War Saga** and* Governor: Ascent to Empire.

Get Battleborn Now!

He thought impersonating a planetary Marshall would be easy...
Until he was needed. William Burton, wanted bounty hunter, has killed
Marshal Steelgrave, who tried arresting him. Desperate to escape, William
impersonates Steelgrave on the backwater where they fought: Pavo Dos, a
desert planet filled with bandits, cultists, and the oligarchs who pit them
against each other. But as 'Steelgrave' plays lawman while seeking passage
offworld, acting the part proves more than he bargained for. He finds
himself entangled in schemes within schemes while battling gangs,
gunfighters, androids, and drugged cultists. But it's the affections of Ori Jo,
a spunky deputy, that makes it hardest for Steelgrave to keep living the lie
—while everyone else wants him dead. **Don't miss the next action-**
packed space opera from Tony Peak. With everything you want in a
spacefaring adventure, including a western twist, it's perfect for
fans of The Mandalorian *and* Firefly!

Get Imposter's Gambit Now!

For all our Science Fiction books, visit our website.